More books by Earl Emerson

Thomas Black series:
- The Rainy City
- Poverty Bay
- Nervous Laughter
- Fat Tuesday
- Deviant Behavior
- Yellow Dog Party
- The Portland Laugher
- The Vanishing Smile
- The Million-Dollar Tattoo
- Deception Pass
- Catfish Café
- Cape Disappointment

Mac Fontana series:
- Black Hearts and Slow Dancing
- Help Wanted: Orphans Preferred
- Morons and Madmen
- Going Crazy in Public
- The Dead Horse Paint Company

Fire Department thrillers:
- Vertical Burn
- Into the Inferno
- Pyro
- The Smoke Room
- Firetrap
- Primal Threat

MONICA’S SISTER

MONICA'S SISTER

by

Earl Emerson

the 13th Thomas Black mystery

Monica's Sister is a work of fiction. Names, characters, places, and incidents are the products of the author's imagination or are used fictitiously. Any resemblance to actual events, locales, or persons, living or dead, is entirely coincidental.

MONICA'S SISTER
Earl Emerson

Published by Lost Dog Press

ISBN-13:
978-1493561544
ISBN-10:
1493561545

For Marlene, never to be forgotten.

A good friend can tell you what is wrong with you in a minute.
~Arthur Brisbane

1

OVER the years I've been hanged by clowns, knocked out by an Amazon with an alarm clock, chased by a twenty-nine-hundred-pound bull, sucker punched, slapped, kissed, dissed, ambushed and stapled, but the *coup de grâce* was delivered by Angela Bassman.

Angela made all the rest of it look like spit wads in study hall.

When I heard Angela's duck-squeak voice in the outer office and then a burst of her irritating machine-gun laughter, I stepped into the closet next to my desk and closed the door. It was a stupid thing to do and would haunt me for years to come.

I knew Kathy was busy with appointments, which made it a certainty I would end up entertaining her friend, who rarely had anything more important to do than pester me.

Angela was maybe five years older than me, not quite forty. It was hard to tell for sure, because her skin was so pale and baby-smooth. She was a woman most people thought of as unpretentious, unsophisticated, naive. She had a habit of hounding me with one question after another, her visits filled with relentlessly unwavering enthusiasm for my answers, which I purposely kept as vague as possible. Her interrogations drove me batty. It was as if she were trying to dissect my life and opinions in order to know how to live her life, to know what her own opinions should be, her queries running the gamut from my assignments as a licensed private investigator to whether the city should replace the viaduct two blocks away, to what I thought about colonizing the moon. Inspired by a misbegotten camaraderie she imagined existed between us, she even got her own private investigator's license.

Kathy and Angela had met each other as students in law school at the University of Washington several years back, though Angela stopped studying law for reasons unknown to Kathy, reasons she assumed were private, since Angela never offered an explanation. Kathy was too nice to pry, and the last thing I wanted to do was to give Angela an opportunity to regale me with one of her endless personal dramas. Thus her dropping out of law school remained a mystery.

From inside the confines of the tiny closet, I listened as they entered my office, which I rented from Kathy's legal practice to help out with her lease and to earn her a business deduction for the tax man. My hiding spot reeked of mothballs from a cashmere coat Kathy was storing for a gang member doing five-to-seven for manslaughter. The man had fired a gun through a wall at a party and killed one of his pals on the other side of the wall. "It's okay, it's not loaded," were his last words before putting a bullet through the head of his best friend.

Inside the closet I held my breath while their voices drew closer.

"He was here a few moments ago," Kathy said. "His computer is on. He wouldn't leave it on if he weren't close by."

"That's okay," Angela said. "I can wait."

"Is there something I can help you with?"

"Sorry, Kathy. This needs a man's touch."

I'd been hoping they would chat in Kathy's office so I could sneak out of the closet, which was beginning to feel like a coffin, but they remained only a few feet away from the closet door.

Before I could figure out a plan of action, the door popped open and Kathy squinted into the darkness, Angela hovering behind her shoulder. Kathy's liquid violet-blue eyes met mine, and I could see amusement as well as a familiar look of suspicion. "Thooommaaaas . . . ?"

"Oh, hey guys," I said, pleasantly.

"What are you doing in here?"

Angela chipped in, "Yeah. What are you doing?"

"Uh." We'd struck one of those junctures when only a coward would lie. "The eye doctor told me to do this."

"What?"

"The optometrist told me I needed total darkness for ten minutes every morning. It's an eye-health thing. Cornea health, really. Something to do with the corneal endothelium. It's a serious problem when it goes bad."

"Well, we don't want your endothelium to shrivel up, do we?" Kathy closed the door, and once again I was thrust into darkness, a sliver of light stabbing at my conscience from under the door. I could hear the two of them chatting, could hear the squeaking of my swivel chair, the burbling of the coffee machine in the other room. I knew Kathy thought this was hilarious, trapping her husband in a closet with his own lies.

I turned the knob and pushed at the door, but Kathy had jammed a chair against it. "What are you doing?" I asked, through the door.

"Trying to save your endothelium."

"I think ten minutes is up."

"Don't worry. I'll let you know when it's time to come out." It took two minutes to gently force the door open while they caught up on news of mutual friends. "All better now?" Kathy asked.

"I think so," I said, blinking at the unaccustomed brightness.

"Okay, then."

"The darkness helps." I couldn't stop lying.

"Thomas would live his whole life in the dark, if he could," said Kathy, grinning in amusement. "Wouldn't you, dear?"

"Sometimes I think I do."

"Well, I'll leave you two alone. I've got to get ready for a meeting up at the jail."

After Kathy left the room, Angela said, "Too bad about your eyes. I hope they'll be all right."

"It's more of a preventative measure."

"Do you think I should start doing that, too, just to be on the safe side?"

"I couldn't say, Angela. Did you have something you needed to talk to me about?"

"I've got a meeting set up in about an hour. I need you to come with me in case there's some heavy lifting. You and one other man. I'd feel better if I had someone there with me. Just an hour of your time?"

My afternoon was relatively free, and I couldn't recall her ever asking for anything before. Ordinarily, I might have gone for a bike ride with my free time, but we were suffering through the wettest, coldest Northwest spring on record, and I'd already slogged through enough puddles riding from the U District to the office that morning. Besides, I was curious to see what nonsense she had gotten herself into. "Okay," I said.

"Really? You'll help? I didn't think you would. Is there somebody else we could get? Because I might need two of you. I was thinking maybe someone slightly ferocious."

"Why ferocious?"

"I just thought there would be some guys like that hanging around the office."

"I thought *I* was ferocious. I thought that's why you chose me." Angela always thought I was serious, which allowed me to ride a bad joke into the ground without her knowing what I was doing. It was the only fun I had with her.

"A murderer would be perfect. Even a car prowler would do."

"A murderer? Hmmm. Kathy represented a panty-sniffer last year. But I think he's still inside."

"What's a panty-sniffer?"

"Guy breaks into women's apartments and sniffs their panties. Steals them right out of the drawer."

"Do people really do that?"

"This guy did."

"That's not what I had in mind."

"I think I have just the guy."

Like a puppy Angela followed me to the roof of our building. As usual, she was dressed in jeans and some sort of colorful sari-like affair in yellows and oranges, which did nothing to enhance her short, stout figure. Worn sandals revealed pale, stubby toes laden with silver rings and toenails painted turquoise. Her thick blond hair always looked like a wig to me, slightly askew over studious wire-rim glasses and a square face. She carried an enormous purse on a strap which crossed over her body, the strap dividing and highlighting her breasts, which looked larger than I remembered.

2

I'D thought of Angela Bassman as lacking all sex appeal until I saw Crane Manning's reaction when I introduced them. We were on the roof of the building, maybe eighty feet above street level, the three of us listening to the quiet sounds of traffic and people in the city below.

Crane was a blue-eyed boy who'd been a sniper in Iraq and had cashiered out of the Army six months earlier. Like a lot of returning vets, he was having a hell of a time finding the right career path. Standing well back from the roof ledge, he smoked a cigarette, drawing in deep breaths, staring out at the city and the portion of Puget Sound we could see from our aerie, the wind-chopped surface of the water laced with whitecaps like faces in a dark movie theater. He worked for a bonding company on the second floor of our building, tracking people who'd run out on their bail and hauling them back to jail. It was called skip tracing. He wasn't adept at it, and he and I both had a feeling he was going to get cut loose by his employer in the not-too-distant future.

Crane was six-three, two inches taller than me, and outweighed me by thirty pounds. He was still in good shape from the Army. His blue eyes were a match for Angela's pale blue. It was a little disconcerting to see them staring at each other, and to realize there were people who thought of Angela as attractive. "So what do you need?" Crane asked. He had been at the edge of the roof carefully *not* leaning on the balustrade.

"Only an hour of your time. I can pay you both."

"As far as I'm concerned, this one's a freebie," I said.

"How much?" Crane asked.

"Hundred dollars for two hours' work?"

"As long as I don't have to shoot anybody at farther than six hundred yards." He chuckled. Angela gave a snort, unsure whether or not he was joking.

"You're big," she said, slapping his shoulder. "And solid. That's good." She walked over to the low roof wall behind Crane, where she admired the view with her back to us.

"You need us to move some furniture, or what?" I asked.

"You guys will be just for looks. I want some people to think I've got a gang or something. You know, like you're a couple of leg breakers." It couldn't be much, I thought. She probably needed us to intimidate some schoolboys who were pestering her.

Behind her back, Crane and I began mugging at each other, practicing our intimidation skills, giving each other killer looks. We'd found a kinship early on, lots of dumb jokes and more nonsense than a pair of tomcats in a Dumpster.

Angela stepped up on tiptoes until she was riding the wall on her waist, teetering to and fro, her hands pinned under her. "Isn't Seattle magnificent?" she said. "Look at the snow on the Olympics. I once lived in Salt Lake City with my former husband. They have mountains, too, but in the summer they're just dry hills. And look down there. Some guy's robbing a parking meter."

"Better be careful," I said, stepping close in case she lost her balance.

"What? You're not afraid of heights, are you?" In one swift movement, she hoisted herself up onto the wall and began walking along it, not bothering to glance at her feet. Until then I might have grabbed her and pulled her to safety, but now all I could think was that if I touched her it would disturb her equilibrium and send her toppling to the sidewalk eighty feet below. I suddenly had a legion of angry butterflies in my stomach. "You don't think somebody who's climbed K2 would be intimidated by this, do you?" she asked.

"You were on K2?" asked Crane, who was as pale as I was. I'd heard the mountain-climbing stories from her before but didn't really believe them.

"The first trip we ran into a storm and had to turn back. On the second trip one of our Sherpas went to answer nature's call in the middle of the night and froze to death. And that Englishman. He died from altitude sickness. You probably read about it in *The Mountain of Death*."

"Christ on a crutch," said Crane, who couldn't take his eyes off Angela's gyrations. He was terrified of heights, could barely breathe on this rooftop at the best of times.

"Maybe you should get down," I said to Angela.

Angela made a hundred-eighty-degree pivot turn. "I'm afraid of a lot of things, but not heights. You should have seen some of the crevasses we had to pass over on the Godwin-Austen Glacier." I stepped closer to Angela. On the street below a man I recognized as one of the homeless habitués of the area was trying to jack a parking meter. I realized it was going to be hard to explain to Kathy how I'd let her friend fall off our roof.

Without warning, Angela leaped clumsily off the wall onto the roof. I'd never seen her do anything quite like it, either the wall-walking or the dismount. Angela coughed up tall tales like an old cat coughed up fur balls, but I hadn't believed a word of her K2 stories until now. Maybe she *had* been a mountaineer.

"Come on, guys," she said. "If we leave now, we'll be right on schedule. I'll drive. Neither of you is going to have to do anything except stand around and look tough."

If I knew Angela, neither one of us was going to have to do *anything.*

Crane and I made gorilla faces at each other after Angela headed for the stairs. She added, "If there's any fighting to be done, I'll do it. I'll use the Mandarin Duck Palm method. I was taught kung fu by the shifu in the Song Mountains in China. Fan was the world's master. In his eighties, I saw him defeat twelve twenty-year-old men at one time."

When we emerged from the stairwell on our floor we met Kathy, who was waiting to take the elevator to the lobby. When she heard we were going to help Angela, she gave me a warm look. I grinned stupidly.

"Okay. No. Really. You don't believe I know kung fu, do you?" Angela said.

"I believe you," I lied.

She turned to Crane. "Try to neutralize me." When Crane didn't move, she said, "Go on. You can't hurt me. Just try—" Before she could finish, Crane stepped forward and put her into a headlock a bull moose couldn't have escaped. It was a funny looking sight, because Crane was six-three and Angela was barely five feet. She was shaking every part of her body trying to get out of the hold.

She fought convulsively, but Crane did not relent. "That wasn't fair," she said, her words muffled by Crane's fleece shirt.

He held her tight while she flopped and spasmed and did everything but pinch him in an effort to free herself. Two people waiting for the elevator laughed uneasily at her predicament and stepped quickly into the car when it arrived. Kathy let it go down without her. Finally, Crane gave me a look and released Angela.

"I wasn't ready," Angela said. "And you're big. Even with the Mandarin Duck Palm, when there's a size variance as great as ours, you have to start with an even playing field."

The four of us stood looking at each other. Finally, Angela said, "You try it, Thomas. And no monkey business. Wait until I'm ready. I want to show you I can take care of myself. Kathy, you should watch. You could probably use some kung fu in your life."

"Angela, maybe if you—"

"No, no, no, Kathy. I know what I'm doing. Thomas, hurry up." She had gotten into a kung fu stance, one she might have copied from *The Matrix*. She certainly hadn't been taught by a master in China.

"I don't want to do this," I said.

"I'm not giving you any choice. Come on. You're making us late. I'll go easy on you. I'll probably have to throw you on the floor, but I won't hurt you."

Kathy gave me a look that was a mixture of curiosity and warning. Agreeing to help Angela probably would have gotten me out of the doghouse for hiding in the closet, but this was going to get me back in.

"Come on," said Angela, motioning to me with the fingertips of her forward hand à la Keanu Reeves.

I stepped toward her, then turned around and backed up, using my hips to shove her into the wall. Before she could get away from the wall I had her in the same headlock Crane had put her in. I heard her mutter, "Oh, no," under her breath, but other than that single exclamation, our struggle remained silent. Slapping, kicking, flailing, she tried to extricate herself, her long hair flopping against my arms. Angela had been lying to us ever since I met her, and now I had all of her hyperbole pinned under one arm. She wriggled and struggled and huffed and finally tapped out, saying, "Oh, crap! Crap, crap, crap! Jesus, Thomas. Let me go. We have to get there before I miss this appointment. Let me go."

Holding firm, I said, "Sure you don't want to use the Mandarin Quacker?"

"It's the Mandarin Duck Palm, and no, I don't want to use it. I have to get my car off the street before I get a ticket. Let me go."

"Thomas, let her go." Kathy gave me a look and pushed the elevator button. She and a disheveled Angela went down while I waited for Crane to get his jacket. So far, it had been a productive afternoon. I'd gotten on the wrong side of my wife, embarrassed myself in a closet, and managed to subdue a woman who weighed seventy pounds less than I did.

On the ride down in the elevator I said to Crane, "I should have warned you about her."

"What? The kung fu stuff?"

"The tall tales. She told us she was once married to a ninety-year-old billionaire. Told us she tried to adopt orphans from Africa. That she had dinner with Robert De Niro. You never know what's going to come out of her mouth."

"Hey, man. I think she's a delight."

"You do?"

"An absolute delight."

When Crane saw Kathy waiting for me in the building foyer, he said, "I'll be outside."

"Sure."

After we were alone, Kathy said, "Just try to be good."

"I'm not even sure I want to do this. She won't tell us what it is."

"Oh, Thomas. After all this, you have to. And try not to embarrass yourself."

"That's going to be tricky."

"It always is with you." She smiled and gave me a kiss on the cheek.

"You think she knew I was hiding from her?"

"She pretended she didn't because she's too much of a lady to put you on the spot, but she was hurt, Thomas. She was *really* hurt."

"I'll try to make it up to her."

"How? By putting her in another judo hold?"

"I didn't think it was safe for her to be walking around thinking she could take out twenty guys with the Mandarin Duck Quacker when she can't even take out a halfwit."

"It's the Mandarin Duck Palm."

"She needed a dose of reality."

"Just be nice. And you're not a halfwit. More like a three-quarters wit."

"Thanks. I love you, too."

"I know, sweetie. And be kind. She's had a rough go of it. I'm trying to be her friend. It would be nice if you could try, too."

"No problemo."

3

ANGELA Bassman hunkered over the wheel of an ancient Volkswagen bus that was so thoroughly plastered with bumper stickers people on the sidewalk stopped to stare: *Free Tibet. Who would Jesus torture? The Republican Party—Our bridge to the 11th Century. Don't pray in my school and I won't think in your church. Welcome to the USA: 5% of the world's population; 25% of the world's prisoners. Has anyone seen our Constitution?* There were countless others. I was looking for one that said, "I'm a nut job," but couldn't find it. Having run out of space on the painted surfaces, she'd blacked out the rear windows with stickers. To say it was embarrassment to sit in her car would have been like saying a guy going to the electric chair was going to get a tickle. I sat in the front next to Angela while Crane took the rear, though there was so much paper stacked in the vehicle—fliers and sections of newspapers—we both had a hard time finding a place to sit.

She took Yesler to Third and went south to the steep ramp onto I-90, which would take us east and out of the city across Lake Washington. Before we left town, her errant driving earned her the finger from two different drivers, but she didn't see either one. Crane and I tried to keep from laughing.

Seattle was built on a long piece of land wedged between two bodies of water, twenty-one miles of Lake Washington on the east and a hundred miles of the Puget Sound on the west. The lake was six hundred feet deep in places, and the two bodies of water turned the commute to and from Seattle into a slow ferry ride from the west or a crowded bridge crossing from the east. North/south travel was mostly constrained to I-5 and quickly choked up. Fleeing the city in the event of a nuclear attack was going to be a nightmare.

Late last year I watched a woman stop her car on the mile-long I-90 floating bridge, get out, and roll over the railing into the water, where she immediately sank out of sight, her coat pockets filled with weight plates from her teenaged son's body-building set. She'd recently lost her minimum-wage job cleaning hospital sheets in an industrial laundry and didn't know where to turn for help. It was a shitty job, a shitty turn of events, and an even shittier way to die. I thought about it every time I crossed the bridge.

Rain showers grayed out the southern part of the lake at Seward Park, but oddly, in the distance the snow on Mount Rainier glowed in a patch of rare spring sunshine.

Angela drove across Lake Washington, across Mercer Island, then went south on Interstate 405. After a mile or two, she headed up into the hills, once forested, now wall-to-wall housing developments, the various vintages of homes layered in cul-de-sacs like tree rings.

"In Australia when the missionaries first taught football to the Aboriginal children, the kids," Angela said out of the blue, "would play wildly until the score was tied, and then they would quit. It took the missionaries a long time to convince these children from another culture there were winners and losers in the world and that they needed to beat the other team into submission so they themselves would be winners. In the place where they came from, if one person in the tribe was hungry, they were all hungry. Until Christianity arrived, everybody took care of everybody else."

"What are you trying to say?" Crane asked.

"I'm trying to say half of the people in the world survive on less than two dollars a day."

"And?"

"And the guy we're about to see could use hundred-dollar bills for toilet paper. He thinks he's a winner. We're going to change that."

I'd helped Angela climb up onto her soapbox before and wasn't planning to do it again. The trouble with most of her tirades, besides a tendency toward fuzzy thinking, was that she could make you feel guilty about things you were realistically powerless to do anything about.

"You two are going to help me take down one of this town's billionaires," she said.

"Bill Gates?" I asked.

"No. But it's somebody you'll recognize. I want you to be careful when we get there. He has two factotums we have to watch out for."

"Fact what?" Crane asked.

"Their names are Goodnight Bonds and Marvin Gunderson. If Gunderson's there, we'll be in serious doo-doo. If it's Bonds, we'll use plan A."

"What's plan A?" I asked.

"Plan A means I handle him myself."

"And plan B?"

"You guys are plan B."

"I thought we were going to be moving furniture."

"Remember, there is an obscenely large amount of money in the balance. More than any of us will see in our lifetimes."

As usual, I figured she was full of baloney.

The VW was chugging up steep hills in a residential area called Eastgate, just south of Bellevue. Crane gave me a quizzical look and nodded at the spot where the car radio had once been, now nothing but loose wires. Angela refused to wear a wristwatch because the constant electrical interference from the battery impinged on her biological processes, subjecting her brain to possible catastrophic failure. She urged us to flip the main breakers in our house at night so the electrical fields from the wiring in the walls wouldn't disturb our sleep and give us cancer, or worse, drive us nuts. I'd come to accept her eccentricities in stride and assumed she'd removed the radio herself.

She coasted to a stop. "There he is," said Angela. "It's Bonds. I'll handle him."

She stopped a hundred feet behind a parked Mercedes, shut the motor off, jumped out of the vehicle, and approached a man who was idly poking around a haphazard pile of belongings near the sidewalk.

"Do you know what this is about?" Crane asked when we were alone.

"Don't have a clue. But this is plan A."

"That guy doesn't look dangerous."

"No. He doesn't."

I rolled my window down so I could hear her interact with a short man Angela told us was Goodnight Bonds. He had a close-cropped beard almost the same color as his brown suit, and he moved with fidgety, abrupt hesitations, as if he were an animated cartoon character. A blue tarp covered some of the pile of household goods he was poking through, but the rest, including what had once been a nice-looking sofa, a child's stuffed panda, and other sad items, were waterlogged from rain.

"What's all that?" Crane asked.

"Looks like somebody got evicted by the sheriff."

"Are you shitting me? They throw their stuff in a pile like that?"

"The tarp is a touch I haven't seen before. There must have been humans involved."

I didn't have a lot of confidence in Angela's ability to handle this man, although he looked perfectly innocuous. She had failed at the Mandarin duck business twice in a row. The last time I'd heard anything about her career as a private investigator she'd been following a neighbor she believed had murdered his ex-wife ten years earlier. Nothing came of that investigation, just as nothing had come of her law school efforts or most of her other passions. Angela chased life furiously, but rarely caught anything more than a handful of air.

"What are you doing here, Angie?" Bonds said, grinning through his beard. He had good teeth, white and solid and perfectly even like a television actor, and devilishly dark eyes that were so opaque they were almost black. Like buttons on a teddy bear. "You know you're not going inside."

"Don't get all paranoid on me, Goodnight. I just happened to be driving by. I thought I might get your opinion on something."

"What's that, honey-pie?"

"I recently got breast implants. How do you think they look?" She stood back and opened her sari-like affair, jutting her chest out. Bonds stared at her as if she were naked, even though she was wearing a t-shirt under the wrap. This was a side of Angela I had not seen before.

"Nice," he said, appreciatively, "but you should have made them bigger."

"I don't think he matched them up. What do you think?"

"They look like a matched set to me."

"I don't think they're equal. Maybe you could give them a squeeze."

Behind me, Crane said, "Hell, I would have given them a squeeze if she'd asked."

"She didn't have a boob job," I said. "This is a con."

Bonds was riding a wild horse of delight. They were standing on either side of a steel pole with a sign atop reading SLOW CHILDREN AT PLAY and when Bonds tried to step around to approach her, she stopped him, took one of his hands and placed it on her breast, then took his other hand on the other side of the pole and placed it on her other breast. "Close your eyes," she said.

"Why?"

"Why? You can't tell if they're equal with your eyes open, stupid. Feel them. Yes, that's right. There. Keep your eyes closed." Bonds was smirking like an idiot in a pillow fight.

Moments later, she was back at the VW and Bonds was handcuffed with his arms around the pole. "Come on, guys." She turned on her heel and headed toward a gargantuan sage green house two doors down. Crane and I followed.

Bonds jerked the cuffs against the steel pole, then tried to uproot the pole, which was sunk in concrete. "You bitch!" he shouted. "You stupid bitch!"

Angela opened the front door of the green house with a key, stepping inside. "Wait a minute," I said. "What's going on?"

"This is where I need protection," she whispered. "If Gunderson is here, there's going to be trouble."

"What sort of trouble?" Crane asked nervously.

"The kind you're not going to be happy with."

"Whose house is this?" I whispered. "This is breaking and entering."

Angela held up a silver house key. "Entering. I didn't break anything."

"I'm not going in."

"Thomas, you promised."

"I didn't promise to break the law."

"Everything I've been doing for months depends on what happens next. You can't let all this work slip through my fingers."

"It's called illegal entry, and I'm not doing it."

"Listen to me, Thomas. We have to."

"How do I know there isn't somebody in here with a gun?"

"Because I've been here before." Before I could stop her, Angela sprang up the interior stairs. She'd pulled a small video camera out of her purse and was recording each step. Crane and I looked at each other.

Against my better judgment, I followed her in. Crane trailed me.

We made our way up a set of lushly carpeted stairs to the second floor, where a balcony overlooked a quiet living room and an empty kitchen. In front of us Angela was proceeding down a long corridor with the video camera in front of her. She seemed to know where she was headed, bypassing several closed doors and stopping at the end of the hallway, where she used her foot to gently nudge open a door.

She stepped inside. I remained behind in the doorway.

A man in his sixties clad in nothing but socks sat cross-legged on an enormous bed, his rounded torso pushing out over his legs so that his crotch was hidden under his belly. He was hirsute to the point where he resembled somebody in a mangy ape suit. I had the urge to say, "Nice sweater," but kept my mouth shut. Remarkably, he didn't see Angela at first. A woman emerged from the connecting bathroom, naked, forty years younger than the man on the bed. I could feel Crane bump up behind me for a better look when the naked woman stepped into view. "Good God," he murmured.

His words alerted the woman, who gasped, which in turn alerted the man on the bed, who had been in the process of lighting a cigar with a wooden match. The room reeked of recent sex, the dampness of a hot shower, and the aroma of shampoo and bath oils. The young woman's hair was wet and tangled. She had been rubbing her head vigorously with a towel, which she now used to partially conceal herself.

The camera continued to run as Angela stepped into the room, panning from one occupant to the other. It took the man a few heartbeats to take in the situation and realize the implications. "Angela? What the hell are you doing here? Get out!"

"You explain to me and this camera what you're doing in Sophie's bedroom, and I'll think about it."

"Sophie? You know Sophie?"

The half-naked woman, who until now had been overwhelmed by

our invasion, noticed the camera for the first time. She said, "Angela? What are you doing here?"

"You are invading my privacy," said the man. "Give me that camera."

"Like hell."

"Give it!"

Oblivious to his own nudity, the man launched off the bed and strode toward her, his torso like a bowl of jiggling Jell-O. Approaching in quick steps, he reached for the camera, which she held away from him. He missed it, reached again, missed it again, then tried to slap it out of her hands. As nimble as a toreador in the bullring, Angela evaded him each time. By the time he planted himself to take a roundhouse swing at Angela's face I was getting ready to step in, but she stopped him herself, using some kung fu moves I had not seen before, at least not from her. She turned him around, shoving him onto the bed on his face.

He got up clumsily and tried to punch her again. She blocked each of his blows as if they'd rehearsed the moves together, turned him around, and again pushed him face-first onto the bed. It was clear she could keep pushing him onto the bed all day. I wondered why I'd been able to subdue her so easily. But then, she'd always been intimidated by me. This man didn't intimidate her at all. He glowered at her for a moment, then reached below the bed and came up with a revolver. It was a small weapon, stubby, about the size of his dick.

The gun was exactly what she promised would not happen. Why had I listened to Angela? I'd known all along she was a liar of mythical proportions. The man stood up and began moving toward her, confident he had the upper hand now that he was armed.

As he drew close, Angela made a series of Jackie Chan-style moves, slapping the gun out of his hands so that it disappeared in the discarded clothing on the floor, slapping his hands as he reached for her, slapping his face several times from both sides and then throwing him onto the carpet with a slick judo move. She was astonishingly fast and clever.

Like all men accustomed to success, he didn't seem to realize he'd been defeated. He got to his knees and said, "Give me that camera."

"I'm not giving you anything."

He climbed to his feet again, his breathing labored. It was hard to imagine him in the embrace of the slim, high-breasted woman in the bathroom doorway. "You know each other?" he asked the woman who was desperately clinging to her towel.

"She cleans my house. Angela, what do you think you're doing? And who are these men?"

"She cleans your house?"

By now Angela was backing out of the room, Crane and I moving with her. The man had every right to be outraged. We had invaded his privacy and, key or no key, we had done it illegally. I was furious. We'd come close to getting shot, all three of us, and what made it worse was that the law would be on his side. I promised myself this was the last time I would let Angela Bassman flimflam me.

Angela held up the video camera. "I'm going to tell you how it's going to be, Clark. You're going to give Monica a divorce. No more stalling. You're going to make sure she comes out of it protected financially. Is that understood?"

"You don't dictate to me, little lady."

"No? I just did."

Sophie said, "Angela. This is not what it seems. We love each other."

"If you could see yourself, you'd know how ridiculous that sounds. There's nothing more pathetic than a woman who claims she loves an old goat when everybody around her can see she's only after his money. Trust me. I've been there."

"We're just trying to do things so nobody gets hurt."

"Well, it's not working, is it?"

"Everything was fine until you barged in with these two clowns," said the man.

"Nobody was getting hurt," Sophie added.

"Shut up, Sophie," said the man. "Can't you see she's recording all this?" Sophie clasped the towel closer, her sides and backside bare. Crane had been edging up on me all along and now was pressed against my back. Crane was single and I had the feeling he didn't get to see a naked woman very often, probably not every day like I did at home.

We were outside before Angela turned to me and said, "That went even better than I thought it would."

"It went even worse than *I* thought it would."

"What are you talking about, Thomas?"

"The guy pulled a gun on us."

"Yes, but we've got incontrovertible proof he's cheating on his wife."

"This is a divorce case?"

"I thought I told you."

"You didn't tell me squat!"

"Thomas, that was Clark Lloyd Self."

"Isn't he a billionaire?" asked Crane.

"Bingo."

Outside, Bonds had bent the metal post halfway to the ground, was working on folding up the sheet metal sign at the top so he could set himself free. Of course, once free of the post, he would still be handcuffed.

"I'm serious about this," Angela said as she fired up the VW. "There may be billions involved. A lot of people are counting on me, so don't be so cranky."

"When you con me into breaking the law and nearly get me shot, I have a right to get cranky."

"Apology accepted."

"That wasn't a frigging apology, Angela."

"Clark Lloyd Self is one of the richest men in the country," Crane said.

"What he is is a man without a conscience," said Angela.

"He didn't shoot you," I said. "That's something."

"These people think they run the earth," Angela said. "Somebody has to step up and set them straight." I knew Angela was an inveterate reader of gossip rags as well as a chronic watcher of voyeuristic television shows that detailed the lives and habits of celebrities. It made sense she knew who Clark Lloyd Self was and thought she could insert herself into his life. Angela had always been a name dropper. She claimed she'd once talked with Mick Jagger at the airport. She and Anjelica Huston had rubbed shoulders in the lounge at the horse races. She claimed to have the personal phone numbers of two Presidents. She probably had Self's bio memorized and knew the names of his elementary school teachers.

"I know about cheating billionaires," Angela added. "I was married to one."

I turned around, knowing Crane would give me a quizzical look, which he did. I gave him a slight shake of my head, signifying her story wasn't true. I couldn't help myself. I was pissed. I'd been hoodwinked and wasn't going to countenance any more of Angela's lying. It was only the third time I'd heard Angela refer to her billionaire ex-husband, and I hadn't believed her the first two times, either. It made me wonder how much of this escapade had sprung from her loopy imagination.

We got on I-405, but when Angela bypassed the interchange to I-90, I said, "I thought we were going back to the office."

"I was hoping you two could hang around for another half hour. I have to see my sister."

"Now?" I whined.

"All right with me," said Crane from the back seat.

"Thomas? Please. I need to see her."

"Okay. Your sister. No more of this other business." We drove in silence for a minute or two. "Why bust up this marriage?" I asked. "Who's your client?"

"He just married her because she's beautiful, rich, and famous."

"That's a first." My sarcasm lingered in the air like bad breath. I could tell Angela hadn't taken offense. In fact, I wasn't sure she even heard me.

"I'm only trying to help her before she gets tangled in something she can't unravel."

"Don't they have a couple of kids together?" said Crane. "I think I read that. Self and his wife?"

Instead of answering, Angela made a call on her cell phone and, without introducing herself, said, "Can I come over? Ten minutes?" She listened for a moment and then said, "Where are you?" She shut the cell, powered it down, and stuffed it into her glove box so the electrical field wouldn't drive us all bat-shit crazy like she already was.

4

WE drove north on 405, past the high-rises of Bellevue, and then headed west on 520, back into Seattle over the second floating bridge on Lake Washington. It was raining at this end of the lake, and the roadway was shiny under the glare from the headlights used all day in the gloomy Northwest. The atmosphere in the vehicle was strained. I was pissed and Angela knew it.

As she drove, Angela began giving her take on the state of the universe and the moral failings of mankind. I'd heard it before, but Crane was drinking it in like a kid from the sticks auditing his first college philosophy class. He'd liked Angela from the beginning, found her a breath of fresh air in a way I never had. Crane had been in the Army eight years and fought in two wars as a sniper. I knew he didn't feel good about a lot of things he'd seen and done in uniform. He was a wounded dove, and Angela's preaching tended to speak to wounded doves, probably because she was one herself.

"How much do you think that house back there was worth?" Angela asked. "I'll tell you how much," she continued. She was talking a mile a minute, almost as if she were on speed. "Six hundred thousand. Seven hundred. There are countless similar neighborhoods within driving distance. Compare that to a person who survives on less than two dollars a day, which incidentally, accounts for about half the population of the world. If we could sell that house back there and put the money into an account, we could feed a thousand people for a year. Instead, Self buys the place and gives it to his mistress. Thomas?"

"Huh?"

"Are you listening?"

"Sure."

"I'm listening," said Crane eagerly from the back seat. He was having a good day. He'd brushed up against Kathy, whom he had a crush on, put a headlock on a woman he was instantly smitten with, watched a chauffeur feel up Angela, and saw a naked (or very nearly naked) woman. I knew how his thinking worked because mine worked the same way. It was a good day, all right.

"If you saw a neighbor child starving in front of your eyes," Angela continued, "what would you do?"

"Me?" Crane asked. "I'd feed him. Help out the parents. I'd do *something*."

"So how many children have you let starve to death today?"

"None that I know of."

Angela made a sound like a buzzer going off, indicating he'd given an incorrect answer. "Try twenty-nine thousand."

"What are you talking about?"

"Twenty-nine thousand children starve to death every day."

"Not in my neighborhood," said Crane.

"We've already agreed on what we should do," said Angela. "Now we're haggling over our definition of *neighborhood*."

It was quiet for a while as Crane thought through the implications of what she was telling him. A constant stream of cars continued to overtake us on the left. The water on the lake was choppy and I could see sailboarders in wetsuits near the shores of Kirkland. By the time we were past Union Bay and onto land again, the streets were dry. We diverted onto I-5 and headed into downtown Seattle from the north. I loved this view of the city. Too often, I was driving and couldn't look away from the roadway to appreciate it, but today I was a sightseer in the rainy city. Queen Anne Hill, crowned with its three radio towers, stood in the distance, overlooking the houseboats and marine activity on Lake Union, far below the elevated freeway. Behind it all, a line of snow-clad Olympic Mountains peeked out from the storm clouds to the west.

At one point, Crane caught my eye in the outside mirror and quickly looked away. I'd said some negative things about Angela, and I could tell that despite the way she'd gulled us in Eastgate, he'd decided Angela was the conscientious truth teller and I was either lying outright or badly mistaken about her. It was a shock to see all that in one quick look, but I knew him well enough to know what he was thinking. In the few months we'd known each other Crane and I had established a friendship, so it was disconcerting to see our bond disrupted so quickly and by such an obvious whack job.

She drove into a parking garage in Belltown under a high-rise with retail shops at street level and upscale condominiums above.

Angela parked a good distance from any other vehicle, as if afraid somebody would scratch her ratty old VW, or steal one of her stickers. "There he is," she said. "That's Marvin Gunderson. He's the one we have to be careful of."

"I thought we were visiting your sister," I said.

"Yeah, well, Gunderson comes with the package." Crane and I exchanged looks. The man waiting for us next to the elevator was the size of a small dinosaur.

"If Clark called ahead, we're in trouble," said Angela. "Be on your guard."

"Be on our guard for what?" Crane asked.

"A royal ass-kicking," I said, watching the giant by the elevator. We both laughed.

"Don't worry about it," Angela said. "Between the three of us, I think we can do some real damage."

"Between the three of us, I think we could get a royal ass-kicking," I said, and again Crane and I laughed. Angela didn't think it was funny. I knew right away if we got into a tiff with the man next to the elevator, I was going to run like a rabbit. We were never going to fight. Not me against this Gunderson fellow. Not me and an *army* against Gunderson. Less than half an hour after I vowed it would never happen again, Angela had gotten me into another situation. And how the hell was her sister mixed up in all this?

Angela meticulously placed The Club, which was probably worth more than the VW, on her steering wheel and locked up. "Don't worry, Thomas. I just have to set Monica straight and then we can leave."

I couldn't think of anybody less qualified to set somebody straight. Twice since I'd known her Angela had suffered some sort of nervous breakdown and gone back to live with her parents in their tiny trailer in Anacortes. She had dated more losers than anybody I'd ever known, each plucked from the margins of society, many of them a step away from financial catastrophe: dreamers, oddballs, tone-deaf musicians, perennial students, cultists, religious extremists—out-and-out misfits all. She was one of those people who read common social interactions erroneously. In relationships she was a color-blind drunk at a stoplight.

A year ago I'd done some work for the Seahawks when one of their linemen was having problems with vindictive relatives of an ex-girlfriend, so I'd been around some large men recently, yet I couldn't remember any as impressively huge as Marvin Gunderson. When we got into the keyed private elevator with him, he easily took up a third of the space. Crane gave me a jaundiced look. Neither of us was laughing now. Up close, there was nothing funny about this guy or our proximity to him.

I couldn't imagine what sort of car a man this size would drive or where he would buy clothing or how he would ever be able to get his fingers into a bowling ball. Normal socks wouldn't fit. When he got old enough for adult diapers they were going to have to use stacks of bed sheets.

Gunderson weighed somewhere between three and four hundred pounds. From what I could see, little of it was fat. I'd never seen feet as large as his, maybe size sixteen or seventeen. Everything including his head and ears was larger than normal. He had huge, sagging jowls, yet appeared to be between thirty and forty years old. You would have to drill the core and count the rings to be sure. I was six-one and Crane was two inches taller, but Gunderson towered above us both. If he wasn't seven feet, he was damn close to it. I hesitated to think about what sort of damage he could wreak in that elevator once he decided he didn't like us. As it was, he didn't move, didn't say a word, just endured Angela's prattling all the way up to the penthouse.

The messiness in the corridor on the thirty-third floor told us the building was still under construction: bare concrete floors, stacks of building materials, unpainted walls. We were taken through a pair of elegant oak doors into a foyer twice as big as my living room. A tall window overlooked the Sound and the Olympic Mountains to the west. We could hear workmen in another room, and wooden crates indicated somebody was moving in. Gunderson silently motioned for us to wait in the foyer, and when he returned a few moments later, he cocked a finger the size of a bratwurst at Angela, signaling her to follow him. Crane and I remained where we were.

After several minutes, we edged toward the first room and glimpsed Angela, still waiting at the far end of a large receiving area. I was guessing the condominium took up the entire top floor of the building. The two rooms I could see were immense. The furniture that was out was encased in plastic sheets. On one wall was a gargantuan photograph of a brunette woman running through the surf, her sheer clothing wet and sticking to her glistening, tanned thighs. The photo was nine feet tall. She was a beautiful woman, and the outfit left little to the imagination. I'd seen the photo before. Everybody on the planet had seen it. It was almost as famous as the woman it featured, although I couldn't remember her name.

A moment later the woman in the photo met Angela at the other end of the large room and said, "Oh, God. What now?" Angela said something I couldn't hear, to which the woman replied, "Haven't you caused enough trouble?" Then they both walked to another room beyond our view. Gunderson vanished. A minute later, a pair of Spanish-speaking workmen came into the room and began prying open crates beside us.

"Jesus," Crane said. "Do you know who that was? It was Monica Pennington. *The* Monica Pennington. She's that famous model. Hell, she even made a couple of TV movies. She looks great. I think she's got kids now. In fact, she's married to that guy . . ." He snapped his fingers trying to jog his memory.

"The guy we rousted in Eastgate," I said. "Clark Lloyd Self."

"Yeah. Aren't they married? Jesus. Is this the marriage she's trying to bust up?"

"It would seem so."

"Where does her sister come into it?"

"I'm guessing her sister works here."

"But why is she trying to break up the marriage of a billionaire?"

"Angela likes to think big."

"I don't know why she brought that video to the wife. It would have been worth more to him than her, don't you think?"

"That's not how Angela's brain works."

"You see her kung fu? I don't know how we got the jump on her before."

"Actually, neither do I."

The two workmen opened a crate containing a glass sculpture I was sure was worth more than either Crane or I had earned last year. I started thinking about how much money was involved here. Thinking aloud, I said, "Self isn't likely to let us get away with what we did today. We're going to end up in court. He's going to sue."

"More likely, he'll have us busted into little pieces. Guys like him don't keep apes like the guy in the elevator around for no reason."

"Him? He's probably an attorney or an accountant. A window washer."

"Did he look like a window washer?"

We looked at each other and laughed.

A private investigator in this state could lose his license for less than what we'd done to Self. Angela had endangered my livelihood. It was hard to tell how Monica Pennington would react when Angela showed her the video. There are times when you could tell a woman her husband was fooling around and she would thank you, other times when she would reach for a pitchfork.

"Jesus," Crane said. "Monica Pennington. She's gorgeous. Remember that *Playboy* spread? That was the best-selling issue of *Playboy* in years. They offered a million dollars for a second photo shoot and she wouldn't do it. Said she'd done the first one on a lark. Then she was married to that rock drummer for a while and was in those music videos. This has been one hell of a morning. One minute I'm smoking a cancer stick on the roof and the next I'm busting into a billionaire's love nest. And now this. Angela's a pip, don't you think?"

"She always has been."

"And Monica Pennington. I never thought I'd get this close to someone like her."

"You're having a great day, aren't you?"

"Aren't you?"

In fact, considering I might lose my livelihood, I was.

Ten minutes later, Angela and Monica Pennington reappeared and strode toward us, Pennington with the long slow stride of a fashion model, Angela walking beside her like a poodle tiptoeing through wet grass. Pennington had gained a few pounds since her modeling days, but the weight looked good. I knew from talking to him that Crane hadn't had a lot of luck with women, and I could tell from his ragged breathing beside me that being proximate to this much pulchritude was affecting his metabolism.

As they approached, Angela said, "Monica, I'd like you to meet my friends, Thomas and—"

"Just get out!"

"Okay, but you're making a mistake."

"You're the one who made the mistake, missy."

We went out the front door and stepped into the elevator unescorted. We were about halfway down when I said, "That seemed to go well."

Oblivious to my sarcasm, Angela replied, "It didn't. Not really."

"At least nobody pulled a gun on us."

"Gunderson wouldn't need a gun."

"No. He'd probably just pull our arms out of the sockets and make a wish."

Crane chuckled. Almost without thinking, Angela said, "In Montana I saw him kill a horse with one punch."

"You saw what?" Crane asked, incredulous.

"With his fist."

"He get mad very often?" I asked.

"No, but when he does, you don't want to be in the same county."

"You seem to know these people pretty well," I said.

"Yeah . . . well . . . Sophie . . . I kind of faked her out when I wangled a job cleaning her house. I had my suspicions, but after I snooped around, I was able to confirm she and Clark were having an affair."

"So you decided to intervene?"

"There's a lot more riding on this than you know, Thomas."

"You were housecleaning and snooping, and that's how you got into this?"

"Actually, I came at it from the other direction."

"What direction would that be?"

"She's my sister."

"Sophie's your sister?"

"Monica."

"Your sister is Monica Pennington?" Crane blurted.

"There. I've said it. Are you happy? You should see yourself," Angela said, turning to me. "You think I haven't seen that look a thousand times?" We walked to her Volkswagen and got in. "Everybody in this country is judged by how they look. By how much money they have. By how famous they are. It makes me sick."

It *might* have made her sick, but she was as hypnotized by it as anyone else, perhaps more so. "I'm sorry if I looked shocked," I said.

"It's just that I've known you quite a while, and it seems like if Monica Pennington were your sister you would have mentioned it before now."

"I might have, but I get so tired of people's reactions."

Despite her explanation, I had to wonder what other reasons she had for not mentioning Pennington. Angela had always been an unabashed namedropper, what with all the Presidents and celebrities she claimed as bosom buddies. But this wasn't another one of her whoppers. I'd watched Pennington treat her, and she Pennington, with the familial rudeness only a sibling might show.

5

THE next couple of weeks were less hectic than the afternoon I'd squandered with Angela Bassman. I trusted her less than ever, although I was impressed with how she'd managed to keep zipped about her sister.

As for Crane, I was sure he considered his encounter with Angela to be the best thing to happen to him since his Army days. Being a sniper had been the perfect niche for Crane Manning, the enemy four hundred yards away, everything in his own vicinity quiet and settled. Getting up close and in somebody's face, as was expected in his new job as a skip tracer, went against the grain of his natural demeanor, which was relatively shy and always non-confrontational. He told me of many sleepless nights both before and after apprehending bail jumpers. He got the jitters around women, too, and found hooking up almost impossible. When he was in the Army he had a chatterbox girlfriend, who, he said, had used him primarily as a passive listening post and who dumped him as soon as she found a better prospect. He found himself tongue-tied around Kathy and no better when interacting with Lakeesha, our receptionist. With Angela he'd been different, more relaxed. Maybe putting her in a headlock broke the ice.

Four or five days after our adventure together, I watched Angela drop him off in front of our building before driving off in a haze of exhaust. I asked Crane about it later that day. "Angela?" he said. "I just happened to run into her up town. She's a nice kid."

"Yeah," I said.

"Kind of sexy, don't you think?" I had no answer for that absurd statement, and when I looked at Crane to see if he was joking, he refused to meet my eyes. I hoped he wasn't dating her and afraid to tell me because I'd called her a wackadoodle. I *did* think she was a wackadoodle, but I didn't want it to get in the way of his love life. There was nothing worse than badmouthing somebody else's love interest, so that they resented you every time you crossed paths. More than one friendship had been shipwrecked on those shoals.

After the shock of learning Monica Pennington was Angela's sister, I was curious enough to do some minor research into Angela's past. As far as Angela having been married to a billionaire, I found records of her marrying a man named Bassman in Las Vegas eight years before, but I couldn't find information about a divorce, and no bank balances. He'd married Angela under the name "Hank Bassman" but I assumed "Hank" was a nickname. How he'd gotten away with that on a marriage certificate was beyond me, but it was a Las Vegas wedding, which hinted at haste, impropriety, scribbled paperwork, and perhaps alcohol.

"Why would she try to break up her sister's marriage when it was already on the rocks?" Kathy asked.

"What are you talking about?"

"Pennington moved out on Self weeks ago. It's been all over the news, as if it's something everyone needs to know. Anyway, that's why she's moving downtown. He still lives in Clyde Hill."

"So why was Angela . . . ?"

"That's what I'm asking you."

"I don't know."

"Maybe she was afraid her sister was going to get screwed in the settlement."

"If Pennington *is* her sister."

"Oh, come on, Thomas."

"Well, *maybe* they are sisters."

"I feel sorry for Angela. I've always felt she's been under a dark cloud. I remember when she bailed out of law school. There were rumors she was on drugs, but that doesn't seem like Angela, does it? At any rate, people said she'd been acting strangely. And then there was that time she threatened to kill herself. Remember?"

"I wish I could forget." It was the visit where she'd kissed me.

Over the next couple of weeks, my natural curiosity got the better of me and I began paying attention to the scandal channels on cable and the celebrity rags at the check-out stand, looking for Pennington on the covers. As the divorce progressed, there were flurries of frenzied accusations from both camps. From his: that she was a heavy user of cocaine all through their marriage, that she had strange and unnatural sexual appetites, that she'd been physically abusive to their children. From hers: that he was verbally abusive, had gotten her drunk and tied her to a chair, that he'd given a pair of dogs she owned to the animal shelter, that he believed in flying saucers and thought the planet had been covertly invaded by spacemen. That last accusation was particularly harmful, given the fact that Self ran an investment firm handling billions of dollars for upper crust investors. Oddly, there was no mention of Self's mistress, even though Pennington presumably was still in possession of Angela's tape.

And then one day Monica Pennington and Clark Lloyd Self called a press conference in L.A., where they appeared before cameras holding hands, exchanging kisses, and telling one and all the divorce had been cancelled, that they were getting back together, were more in love than ever. All was forgiven. Both husband and wife, as far as I could tell, looked agreeable to the reconciliation, even if their on-camera kisses were lifeless and staged. The last shot was of them holding hands as they walked back into the building, Gunderson lurking in the shadows.

"He *is* big," Kathy said, when I replayed it for her. She'd come home from the gym late. I had taken a two-hour bike ride with friends. The sun had shown itself, a rarity that spring, and temperatures soared to nearly sixty.

"I hope you never run into him again," Kathy said.

"Me, too. Unless I'm driving a truck."

Kathy put her purse on the table and riffled through the mail. "Angela once told me she knew a bodyguard who had been a Rhodes scholar. I wonder if he's the same guy. Or . . . you said there was a second bodyguard."

I thought about Goodnight Bonds handcuffed to the sign. "I'm pretty sure the other guy wasn't a Rhodes scholar."

The next evening, after heavy rains had cancelled plans for a late afternoon bike ride, we met at a restaurant on First Avenue outside the Pike Place Market, the Pan Africa Restaurant and Bar. The space was small and unpretentious, the food exotic. We were dining with another couple, an attorney Kathy knew from the courthouse and his wife, who also worked downtown.

We were still perusing our menus when Kathy took a phone call on her cell. "Who was that?" I asked, as she folded up her phone.

"Angela." Kathy looked at our friends. "I went to law school with her. She's an investigator now, like Thomas."

"Not like me," I said.

"Don't be an elitist. She's going to drop by in a moment. I hope you don't mind?" Kathy turned to me and whispered, "You be good when she gets here."

"Me?" I whined. The whole table laughed.

Ten minutes later she showed up, clearly distraught, her frizzy, sandy-blond hair a mess, a Rorschach of food splashes on the front of her blouse. She looked as if she'd been up all night, maybe two or three nights in a row. Her face was flushed. After introductions were made all around, Angela refused the chair I offered and glowered at me as if I'd done something wrong. "They're back together."

"Who's back together?"

"My sister and her husband."

"Don't look at me," I said. "I didn't do it."

"But they *can't* be together."

"Angela, I don't care any more about this than I did two weeks ago." In truth, I'd been following the divorce in the papers and on the Net, and I'd looked up everything I could find on Monica Pennington, who'd lived a fascinating, if somewhat depraved life until now, most of it in the limelight. Perhaps 'depraved' was too strong a word. She'd become a model at sixteen, world famous by eighteen. Over the years, she had several public affairs with famous men and three arrests for drug possession, although the last was fifteen years ago when she was in her mid-twenties. She'd made four TV movies. She had a child with a rock musician to whom she was briefly married and then had two more boys with Clark Lloyd Self, who abandoned a wife and five children in a very public scandal to be with Pennington.

"But he's taking her money," Angela persisted.

"He's a money manager. I'd be surprised if she let anybody else touch it. Besides, why would he need her money? He's a billionaire."

"You have to help me get her out of there."

"I don't want any part of this."

Kathy jumped in. "Angela, you can't go around messing in people's lives. In the long run, it's none of our business."

"Like all the people around the world living in poverty are none of our business?"

"What do you mean?" asked Glenn.

Angela turned on him, assured of at least one victory tonight. "When you see an injustice, it's your duty to do something, right?"

"I suppose."

"You suppose?"

"Okay, it's my duty."

"So now that we've got that straightened out, tell me what are you doing about the thousands of children who starved to death today?"

Glenn was used to making deals with prosecutors, getting chastised by judges and yelled at by clients, but until now I was pretty sure he had not been accused of letting children starve to death.

"That's ridiculous," I said. "There are injustices everywhere. If we all followed your advice, we'd do nothing but chase injustice."

"Bingo!"

"You think we should be doing nothing else?"

"That's exactly how we should be living our lives. It's a crime we're not, me included."

"People have their own lives to live."

"That's just another way of saying it's okay to be selfish. The cost of these meals alone would feed five Bangladeshi villagers for a week."

Once again, Angela had put her finger on the basic conundrum of life in America. We were living more comfortably and luxuriously than kings of yore, taking it all for granted, while a good portion of the world struggled in what could only be described as hell on earth. I'd heard Angela's lectures too many times and they always pricked my conscience, but so far, I'd yet to act other than to contribute what I could to aid organizations from time to time.

Kathy said, "So, if we invite you to sit down and eat with us, are you going to turn us down?"

Angela took a deep breath and sat heavily in the chair I'd offered earlier.

"It's not a sin to eat a nice dinner with friends," Kathy said, gently.

"But he's taken all her money."

"He does well with his investments. And like I said before, he's a billionaire. He doesn't need her money."

"He's a terrible person. He left his first wife alone with five kids. He screws over anybody he comes into contact with. He's got girlfriends. I've caught him lying so many times I can't even count."

I'd seen Angela agitated in the past, but never like this. The night she kissed me she'd been agitated. It started when she told a mutual friend over the phone she was considering suicide, and the friend, realizing Kathy was two hundred miles closer, called Kathy in a panic. Kathy drove to Angela's place—I was out interviewing witnesses to a fatality car accident—and invited her to spend a couple of days with us. That night I got up to get a glass of water and heard her weeping in the living room. When I went over to comfort her, she hugged me. She hugged me for a long time. I wasn't much of a hugging kind of guy, but when somebody is suicidal you don't take chances by withholding whatever feeble comfort they might ask for. Then, without warning or any encouragement on my part, she put her face up to mine and kissed me, a clinging, disgusting, slobbery kiss, which I cut off by pushing her away. She said, "I'm sorry. I'm so sorry. Please don't tell Kathy. I don't want to lose her as a friend. Please don't tell her what we just did."

"What *you* just did."

"Please?"

Early the next morning, assuring us both she wasn't going to hurt herself, Angela went home. When Kathy tried to contact her a day later, she learned Angela had suddenly moved to Maryland. Afraid it would compromise their friendship, I never told Kathy about the kamikaze kiss.

"It's imperative I separate the two of them financially and physically," said Angela. "I need your help, Thomas."

Facing into the restaurant as I was, my only view of the street-level windows behind me was in the reflections from framed photos on the wall. In the reflections I noticed a man step up to the window and then away, eyeballing the interior of the restaurant. Even in the tiny picture frame I knew who it was. He had a distinct and syncopated way of moving—like a cartoon character.

6

I caught him outside the front door of the restaurant trying to conceal himself alongside the storefront next door. He appeared to be wearing the same neatly pressed brown suit he'd worn the first time I saw him, his brown teddy bear eyes a perfect match for the buttons on the jacket. "What're you doin'?" I asked, casually.

"Who are *you*?"

"Friend of Angela's. You tailing her on your own or on orders?"

He was nervous, glancing up and down the street, away from me and back to me. I was significantly larger than he was, and while he looked wiry and plenty capable of handling himself, I was pretty sure he didn't want to get into a brawl. I crowded him on the sidewalk, standing too close, pushing him closer and closer to the building like a snarling sheepdog herding a postman. I surreptitiously snapped a photo of him with my cell phone while pretending to check for messages.

"Why are you tailing Angela?"

"You just stay the fuck away from Angie," he said. "Stay away from her."

"Is that why you're here? To keep me away from Angela?"

"That's part of it."

"You going to let us finish dinner first?"

He had to mull it over. "I don't think so."

As we sparred verbally, a man appeared behind me, moving as quietly as a shadow. He'd been coming toward us quickly, and even though I prided myself on situational awareness and peripheral vision, he'd sprung out of nowhere. On a city street, no less. It was Marvin Gunderson, the baby dinosaur. He began crowding my personal space in the same way I had been crowding Goodnight Bonds, standing too close, moving me back, doing his best to intimidate. I wondered if the two of them had worked this gig before: Bonds, the bait; Gunderson, the hammer.

"Hey, buddy," I said, looking up at him with feigned nonchalance.

"Goodnight gave you a message. Stay away from Angie."

"You guys are the ones who should stay away from her." My throat had gone dry. The man really was that immense.

"I don't think you understand," Gunderson said, in an unnaturally high voice you wouldn't expect from someone of his dimensions. "You are not to have further dealings with Angela."

"I don't take orders from you."

"You better."

"Is this coming from your employer or from you?"

"It's coming from us," said Bonds.

"Shut up, Goodnight."

"I was just trying—"

"Shut up!" Gunderson turned to me. "I hope we're not going to have this discussion a second time."

"I hope not, too."

"Our boss was none too happy with you guys," chimed in Bonds.

"What did I just tell you?" barked Gunderson.

"So you *were* sent by the boss," I said. "Complete with instructions on what to say and what not to say. You might as well tell me what else you weren't supposed to say. Goodnight is going to blurt it out anyway."

Before I realized what he was doing, Gunderson grasped my wrists. It felt as if someone was screwing a vise down on them. I tried to shake him off, but he was so strong I gave up, figuring he would relax in a moment and I would break his grip then. I could feel the blood pooling in my fingertips, his hands acting as massive tourniquets.

"You are going to leave the family alone," Gunderson said. "That means you and the bitch back off. No more snooping. No more panty raids." Gunderson drew me close and whispered, "No more meetings with Angie. You're done with the conspiracy. It's over. You can go back to tracking runaway dogs and getting escaped parrots out of trees."

"How'd you know about the parrot?"

Behind me I heard the door to the restaurant open. Angela said, "What are you doing, Marvin? Let him go."

"We're just scheduling our next book club meeting."

"You're hurting him. Let him go."

"Not until he understands what I'm telling him."

Gunderson was standing square with me, had each of my wrists enclosed in a fist that looked like a small engine block. He'd grabbed me in such a manner my hands were pointing at the sky, had done it so slyly nobody knew what he was doing except the four of us. Several lone pedestrians and a Japanese tour group had already passed, none of them realizing I was effectively being held prisoner. Gunderson didn't have any expression on his huge, jowly face. I tried on a smile myself, but gave it up when I realized it must look like a rictus mask of death.

I tried to get my hands close enough to each other so I could grab one of my own fists with the other and use leverage, but it was as if my arms had been cemented into a wall.

As I struggled, Gunderson's blank expression didn't alter. The strength of the man was unbelievable. I could bench press three hundred pounds during our rainy winters when I focused on weights instead of road riding, could punch a heavy bag hanging in my garage for forty-five minutes without a break, but I could not break his grip.

Gunderson tipped his head down so he could whisper in my ear and, as much as I tried to resist, I couldn't stop him. "This goes bad," he said, "—and by bad, I mean, you refuse to listen to what I'm telling you—there's going to be some misfortune in your circle of friends."

Moments later when Kathy came out of the restaurant, I found myself chagrined, if not completely humiliated to be caught trapped in a position of utter helplessness in front of her. Later, she would tell me it didn't matter, but it did.

Gunderson put his head next to mine, so close I was smothering on his aftershave. "Hey, Pencil Neck," he whispered. "That your wife?"

"She's not part of this."

"She is now."

I'd been pressuring Gunderson's grip, making him think I was exerting maximum effort, my face red with it. With a momentous jerking motion I redoubled my efforts, taking him by surprise, but to my astonishment I still couldn't free myself.

"What's going on?" Kathy asked.

"Oh my, that's a sweet voice," Gunderson whispered in my ear.

I was six-one, a hundred-eighty pounds, almost none of it fat, sturdy enough to take care of myself in most street confrontations, yet when I caught a glimpse of myself in the restaurant window beside Gunderson, I looked like a bread stick next to a fire hydrant.

Gunderson had lifted me up, was suspending my entire weight in the air. I was doing a partial pull-up, sagging my weight against him, holding myself high enough to get a clear shot at his face with my forehead, all the while hoping my body weight would tire him.

I head-butted him. It was a clean hit and actually did surprise him.

His nose began bleeding profusely, but he didn't release me. At that moment, he made a subtle motion that indicated he was going to head-butt me in return. I lunged to one side and he missed. He was quick, devilishly quick. Insanely quick. If I hadn't been anticipating it, he would have broken all my front teeth. I dodged another head butt. He wasn't going to keep missing.

Most people don't realize a blow to the testicles can be fatal, but I knew it. I kneed him as hard as I could and got a whiff of clove-spiced breath in my face when he dropped me and doubled over.

I rubbed my wrists and stepped away from the man while he pawed at me like a bear, his fist missing my jaw by half an inch. I could feel the wind from it, could feel the power and knew right away if he'd connected, he would have knocked me into the street, where I probably would have been struck by a passing Metro bus. "Get back, Kathy," I said, stepping around to his blind side. He was trying to huff away the pain now, both hands on his knees. I'd been smacked in the gonads a few times and knew the pain wasn't going to disappear anytime soon.

When he looked up to see where I'd gone, I clipped him in the side of the neck, striking him as hard as I could. It was like punching a sandbag. Had almost no effect. He dropped both hands off his knees and started to straighten himself up, and as he did so I came in close and threw a right hook at his Adam's apple, finding the soft spot.

He turned around in a crouch, his watery gray eyes focused on me, both meaty hands around his throat, gagging.

"Everything okay, folks?" The voice came from behind me. It was an SPD officer calling out from the driver's window of his blue and white cruiser.

I could tell from his voice he hadn't seen enough of our scrap to arrest anyone. He knew something was going on but wasn't sure what. He didn't look at me; he was busy registering Gunderson's immensity.

"Just fine," Angela said. I noticed for the first time that although it looked as if she and Bonds were holding hands, she had him in a thumb lock, was controlling him with it.

Gunderson stood straight, or almost straight, and began walking away, his eerie gray eyes damp from the pain. When Angela released Bonds, he followed. The police cruiser slowly trailed them up the street until they were a block away, then motored off.

I yelled after Gunderson, "Use some ice on your scrotum. If it's still hurting in the morning, see your doctor."

Angela laughed. It wasn't easy to make her laugh, but nearly getting killed in a head-butting contest with Marvin Gunderson had done the trick.

"What was that all about?" Kathy asked.

"I'm concerned about his scrotum. With an injury like that—"

Angela interrupted, "They know I'm going to throw a monkey wrench into Self's corporate life. That's what it's about. They're going to lose their jobs."

She was beginning to piss me off. "You damaging CLS would be like me taking down the Bank of America," I said, dripping sarcasm.

Oblivious to my insult, Angela continued. "If we can get them separated again, I'm sure she'll divorce him."

After we finished our dinners, Kathy and I walked Angela to her car. "Did you know they were following you?" I asked Angela.

"Don't get confused, Thomas. They were following you."

"They followed *you*."

"They weren't following me."

"Yes they were."

"I don't think so."

"Angela, they followed you here."

"Not possible. I keep an eye out. You know that, Thomas. And I'm sorry about what happened. Those two never would have been shadowing you if you hadn't done that favor for me two weeks ago."

"Angela, they were following *you*."

"Whatever."

"You have to be careful, Angela."

"Why? I can handle them. You know that."

"If you let him feel you up again, you might be able to handle Bonds. I don't think anybody on the planet can handle the other one."

"You just did."

"That was a streak of luck. It won't happen a second time."

"There's something I should tell you about Gunderson. He was a Ranger in the Army. They said he made a lot of kills. Also, I think he's been lifting weights."

"You think?"

"That trick he did grabbing you? I've seen it before. He works on his grip all day. When he doesn't have access to weights, he squeezes a hard rubber ball. He's strong."

"I already figured that out."

"I have to get Self and my sister separated," Angela said, as she keyed open her car door. "People's lives depend on it."

"Angela," Kathy said, gently, "nobody's life is depending on whether or not your sister's marriage breaks up. You're going to have to stop trying to save the world. The world is not your responsibility."

"Really? Whose responsibility is it?"

Neither Kathy nor I could think of a reply, not then and not later.

As Angela drove away, I scanned the multitude of stickers on her car for one that said, *I'm a wackadoodle* but didn't see it.

Later, as we walked back toward the office where we'd parked, I had a scary thought. There was going to be a rematch. That was how this would play out. People like Gunderson didn't slink away then not come back. There was *always* a rematch.

7

THE next afternoon I was on a training ride with some of my cycling friends when my cell rang. It was Angela. "Thomas? How soon can you get here?"

"What's going on?"

"I need help. Now."

"Where are you?"

"My apartment."

"Still at that same place, just off East John?"

"Same place."

"I can be there in an hour."

"I don't know if this is going to wait an hour."

"What is it?"

"I can't say over the phone. But I need you."

"Angela, I'm ten minutes from home. If I push it, I can be at your place in thirty-five minutes."

"Thanks. I wouldn't have inconvenienced you if it wasn't important."

It was typical of Angela that after I sped home, changed clothes, jumped into my car and raced to her apartment building, she didn't answer her buzzer. I'd parked down the street while faint echoes of thunder rumbled in the far-off foothills of the Cascades.

She lived in one of those older, brick apartment buildings near Seattle Central Community College: four stories, high ceilings, the flat roof maybe fifty or sixty feet above the sidewalk. It was a bustling neighborhood with lots of students and crowded on-street parking to serve half a dozen similar three- and four-story apartment buildings.

When Angela didn't answer the third time I rang the bell, I looked around for another way into the security building. I checked out the lock and figured I could slip it with a knife, but there was no cause for that. Angela's VW bus was parked smack in front of the front door, so I was pretty sure she hadn't gone anywhere.

Hers was a quiet street in the otherwise busy neighborhood, with chestnut trees directly in front of the building and blossoming cherry trees farther down the block. I stepped down onto the sidewalk and surveyed the building. If I remembered correctly, her unit was on the top floor and had at least one window facing the street, but I wasn't sure which it was. I walked around to the side and found a locked gate, but there was no reason to believe the back door would be any more accessible than the front or that Angela wouldn't show up in the next few moments. When I phoned her, I got her voice mail.

I was in front of the building again when, without knowing exactly why, I looked up. Maybe I heard something on the roof or in the treetops near the building. A branch snapping. Leaves rustling. I looked up in time to see somebody hurtling through the air. Falling straight toward me.

The body came flying off the roof as if jettisoned off a trampoline. Strange as it may seem, I thought I heard the human projectile say something on the way down that I couldn't quite make out. No screaming, but eerily calm and conversational.

It all happened quickly. The flight path was so close I actually ducked when the body thunked on the roof of Angela's VW next to me, landing like a huge sack of potatoes. After the heavy thud of the body making sodden contact with the roof of the Volkswagen, all was silent except for small pieces of glass tinkling onto the curb from the broken passenger window. It wasn't until I turned my head sideways to examine her face that I knew for sure it was Angela, her crushed body splayed out on the roof of her car, one broken arm outstretched. She'd caved in the roof of the VW, cracking two of the side windows. Otherwise the van appeared undamaged, as if somebody could drive it away with Angela still on the roof.

I glanced back up at the top of the apartment building. Other than a piece of drain pipe that was torn loose and hanging like a broken wing, I didn't see any evidence of her fall, no circling vultures, no broken branches in the trees, no one peering over the edge of the roof to see what had become of her. No witnesses except me.

I had my cell out and was dialing 911 when I realized she was still alive. She wasn't moving, but she was alive. Her eyes were open and she was staring at me. When I got close, she muttered something. Later we learned both her lungs had been collapsed and punctured, so she'd been using her last few breaths. Flail lung, they called it. She'd broken most of her ribs, but I didn't know any of that until later.

"A woman fell off a building, maybe sixty feet, and landed on the roof of a car," I said, when the 911 dispatcher asked how they could help me. "She's still alive but she isn't moving." I gave them the address, my name, and told them I would be there when units arrived. They, in turn, told me they were sending both police and fire.

By stepping close enough that I caught part of the rainbow of moist bloody spittle shooting out of her mouth, I could hear her whispers. "I screwed up. Didn't see this coming. You gotta finish it."

"Angela, the medics will be here in a few moments."

"Finish it. Promise."

"Okay," I said, not having a clue what she wanted me to finish. If I'd known how hard it was for her to speak and how precious her oxygen was at that moment, I wouldn't have let her say that much.

"It's up to you now."

"I promise." She didn't move and probably couldn't change her expression, but I swear she was relieved, even soothed by my promise. Whatever she'd been doing, she was handing the baton to me and was content to know I was vowing to carry on. As I watched her and waited for the emergency crews to arrive, I realized she wasn't relieved at all. She was dead. I'd mistaken death for an unnatural calm. I gave her my promise at the exact moment she decided to die.

Unexpectedly, I found myself in shock.

I'd seen people die before, but I'd never seen Angela die, and frankly it was the last thing in the world I expected when I came here.

On the drive over I had been running through the reasons she might have called. She sounded desperate, but she'd been sounding desperate a lot lately, and it was always the same theme: how to extricate her sister from her marriage. Or maybe Bonds and Gunderson had been hassling her. Had they taken her upstairs and thrown her off the roof? I'd seen no sign of anyone else up there. Was it possible she jumped?

It occurred to me Angela might have called me here because she wanted a witness to her death, because she wanted somebody to watch her commit suicide. It was a startling idea and, even for Angela, odd, but once the notion came to me, it became my number one hypothesis. She'd committed suicide in front of me like some sort of one-time, one-of-a-kind vaudeville act.

I knew she'd had a major crush on me since the day we met. Kathy had often commented on it. Mutual friends had, too. Knowing it would always be unrequited, Kathy and I thought her crush was cute. But Angela hadn't thought so. I humiliated her by hiding in the closet; humiliated her again with the headlock. I scoffed at her meddling in her sister's affairs. I mocked her for thinking Bonds and Gunderson were following me and not her. I knew it was strangely egotistical to blame myself for her suicide, because if it *was* a suicide, there were probably a lot of factors, but if this show was aimed at me, this desperate, pathetic, incalculably sad show, I was going to have to accept some responsibility. In the end, she'd meant almost nothing to my life while I'd meant far too much to hers.

I glanced back up at the roof of her building. It was then that I remembered she said something on the flight down. For these past few seconds it had been buzzing around in my head, a couple of words ejaculated on the fly. Just as the first sirens began keening in the distance, I put the sounds together and realized she had uttered, "It was the drain." I looked up and saw the dislodged drainpipe hanging from the edge of the roof where she'd launched. Had she been walking on the edge as I'd seen her do on the roof of my building two weeks before and tripped on some part of the drainpipe? Funny thing to say when you're flying from roof to terra firma, but who knew what their last words were going to be? Once when I was a cop I witnessed a young man die from bullet wounds. His last words were, "Tell Jason he owes me eighteen bucks."

The fire department moved so smoothly it might not even have been an emergency. They put a long board on her back, got three men up there and slowly rolled the board, and her, over as a single unit, then strapped her down to the board and passed her to men waiting below. I helped with the lifting because the full contingent hadn't yet arrived. They were performing CPR on her in the Medic unit when the first police cars pulled up.

I almost missed it when the front door of her apartment building opened and Crane Manning stepped out, looking as bewildered and surprised to see me as I was to see him, but my situational awareness had been on high alert since getting surprised by Gunderson the night before and I wasn't planning to miss anything here. Crane seemed only slightly less surprised to see me than he was to see all the rest of the commotion: two police cars, a couple of aid cars, a fire engine, and a long ladder truck, along with personnel from each of those vehicles. There were now dozens of pedestrians standing around hoping for a glimpse of whatever was at the center of the ruckus. When a news cameraman got there and set up for filming, I backed out of the frame.

Crane followed me to a spot behind the cameraman next to an idling police car. "You get a call, too?" he asked.

"Yeah. What happened up there?"

"Nothing. I went up to her apartment. The door to her unit was half open, so I went in but she wasn't there. I hollered for her, but she didn't answer. I was still waiting when I heard the sirens and looked out the window and saw all this. You remember her walking on the wall of our roof that day?"

"I remember."

"She called and said she had something important going on. Said I had to get here right away."

"That's basically what she told me. When was that?"

"Maybe forty-five minutes ago. An hour? I was taking a wife beater to the jail, so I couldn't break away just then."

I couldn't help thinking if I'd been closer to home when she called I might have arrived sooner, maybe in time to stop her from going to the roof. "How long did you wait in her apartment?" I asked.

"Not long."

"Didn't you hear me buzzing?"

"I figured it was Bonds and Gunderson. She told me on the phone she bumped into them last night."

"I know. I was there."

"After hearing about Gunderson last night, I wasn't going to let anybody in without her say so. Besides, she didn't tell me she called you. I thought I was here alone."

"She didn't tell me she called you, either. Was there a note?"

"You mean like a suicide note?"

"Yeah."

"Hell, I never thought of that. I looked out and assumed she fell.

A note? Not that I saw. Hell, I was waiting. I figured wherever she was, she'd be right back. I didn't know I was supposed to be searching the place."

"She must have gone to the roof just before you got there."

"You don't think she was walking on the edge like she did before? Maybe lost her balance and fell?"

"I didn't see her on the edge. But it could have happened that way."

Crane got a dark look in his pale blue eyes. Riding the ripples of second guesses was a common sport after something like this. "I really doubt she would kill herself," he said.

"She's tried before."

"She has?"

"Yes. And she was depressed over her sister's situation as well as her inability to affect it."

"She was a little eccentric, but she wouldn't kill herself, would she?"

"You see anybody else up there?"

"You thinking somebody might have pushed her?"

"I don't know what I'm thinking. You've seen her since we met Monica Pennington, haven't you? I saw you together. Were you two dating?"

"God, no. It was just stupid errands. She wanted me to hook up her television. She didn't know how to do it."

"New TV?"

"Hell, no. It's an old junker."

"How'd it get unhooked?"

"She wouldn't talk about it. I noticed just now when I was up there it was disconnected again."

"She had a thing about electronics. She tell you what she wanted today when you were on the phone with her?"

"No."

From where we were standing I could see into the open rear doors of the medic unit, where they were working on Angela. One of the first things medics do when there's substantial trauma involved, as in the case of somebody who fell sixty feet, is to cut off all their clothing. Her clothing now lay in a pile on the floor around the firefighters' feet. I couldn't see Angela through the mass of blue-clad bodies and gowns and smocks, but I could see her scissored clothes on the floor. I wanted to pick them up and fold the material neatly but realized it was a little like the desire to pat down the cowlick on a man who'd just been guillotined.

I gave the police her sister's name and told them what city her parents lived in. I recited the story of looking up in time to see her hurtling through the air. Told them what I heard her say about the drainpipe. A little later, Manning and I drove in my car to the hospital. We parked in the underground parking garage at Harborview, hiking up the concrete stairs until we were at street level and could see out over the city to the sound. We went to the emergency room waiting area but were told by one of the cops who recognized us from the scene that they'd stopped working on her, that she had officially been declared dead.

Not knowing what else to do, we went back outside and watched a thunderstorm blowing in over the sound, the black clouds highlighted by irregular lightning strikes. The lightning was bold and stark and so close it was almost scary. Angela would have loved it.

8

THE night of Angela's death I remained stalwart and silent while Kathy cried. As the days wore on, Kathy grew more resolute and accepting while I began to slowly crumble, until Saturday morning when I woke up so blue and moody I was afraid to attend the memorial service. Despite my moodiness, we drove downtown and found a parking spot near Virginia Mason Hospital.

Angela's will had stipulated any service held after her death should be secular and not be held in a place of worship. Angela, as I recalled, had referred to herself as a pantheist, regarding the entire universe as a manifestation of God.

Her funeral was being held at Town Hall on First Hill, an historic landmark and Seattle's community civic and culture center since 1998, when the former Christian Science church building was purchased for public use. It took deep pockets to rent the place.

After the service Angela would be cremated and her remains disposed of according to directions her will had laid out in detail. For someone who professed to not care whether or not there was a service after she died, she'd left a plethora of detailed, labyrinthine instructions, but that sort of contradiction was typical of Angela.

I sometimes speculated that there was a huge underground pool of grief in all our lives, a collection of everything bad we'd ever seen or heard or had happen to us, every dour thought, every tear shed, and that when an event like Angela's death bumped up against our lives, our subconsciousness drilled down to that aquifer of grief and tapped in, drawing up all the ancient oils of sadness.

Angela's death was officially declared a suicide. Angela had e-mailed a note to her sister before jumping, although her sister, in all the hubbub that followed, didn't discover it until the next day. The news was all over it. Monica Pennington's sister had committed suicide. Camera trucks and reporters camped outside Pennington's penthouse apartment in downtown Seattle, which she was now sharing with her husband. Of course, the stories were mostly about Pennington and how her celebrity friends were gathering around her. As had happened all through her life, even Angela's passing was overshadowed by her sister's fame.

A certain amount of gawker traffic was expected to show up at the service, which was apparently why Monica had chosen Town Hall. I assumed the service would be held in the smaller downstairs hall, but we were directed to the Great Hall, where an open casket was displayed amid elaborate flower arrangements in front of rows of curved wooden pews under a central dome.

I went in early and situated myself thirty feet from the highly polished casket. Kathy had run into some old college chums and remained outside talking quietly. I wasn't in a mood for chitchat.

On the way in I noticed Crane Manning passing out programs. In his dark suit, he looked dignified and somber and useful, and I wondered why I wasn't helping, too. It annoyed me that he seemed to have more social grace concerning Angela's death than I. He nodded a greeting.

The second thing I noticed was that most of the other people passing out programs and assisting with seating were beautiful young women in identical short, black dresses. There were young women at every entrance, at the head of every aisle. It took a few seconds to figure out they were models, Pennington's former co-workers.

The dearth of mourners in this magnificent old auditorium was going to be embarrassing. Angela had had enough embarrassments throughout her life without piling on more in death. As I sat pondering the approaching disaster, I continued to feel partly responsible for Angela's end. If I'd been more attentive, more thoughtful, if I hadn't brushed her off the night she came to me for help, if I hadn't been so bent on teasing her every time we crossed paths . . . . She'd looked up to me. She'd become a licensed private investigator because of me. I should have seen how much she needed my approval. I should have given just a little more of myself.

I couldn't help thinking about the day I hid in the closet. The prank was typical of my juvenile mind-set. At this late date, I couldn't even remember what I was thinking. If Angela had known me better she would have laughed at the way Kathy kept me in the closet while they conversed outside, but Angela had been genuinely hurt. I'd seen it in her face every time we met after that. And now it wasn't even something I could tell people. Anybody I related the story to would think I was an asshole, and enough people already had me berthed in that mental slip.

As the clock drew closer to the eleven AM start, people made their way individually up the main aisle to pay their respects in front of the open coffin. I'd taken a quick glance inside and realized it wasn't Angela, but rather some cosmetologist's version of her, probably inspired by her sister. Her sandy blond hair was arranged in a way I'd never seen it before, her makeup too heavy and artful. She more resembled, at least from my vantage, the squadron of models acting as ushers than the Angela I had known.

I knew one or two of the people coming up the aisle to pay their respects. Others I had never seen before. Ten minutes before the service was scheduled to start, when to my astonishment the building had filled to near maximum capacity, after I'd seen Pennington, her husband, and kids sit down in a roped-off section to the left of me, a man came forward and stood reverentially beside the coffin.

The man was vaguely familiar, but I was in no shape to figure out where I'd seen him. It was one of those situations where the person is out of context and your brain does a reverse back flip on itself. And then, as he touched two fingers to his lips and placed them on the side of the coffin, I realized I was looking at Robert De Niro. The actor.

De Niro had come to Angela's funeral!

I'd never believed Angela's claim to know Robert De Niro, to have been a dinner guest at his home. I told people the story and laughed at her because I was certain she was lying. Except she wasn't.

The service set me straight on a lot of things.

She *had* gone to MIT on a full scholarship just as she claimed. Despite the fact that she couldn't hurdle a six-foot fence at the police academy, she *had* high-jumped her own height in high school, no mean feat for anyone. She *had* married a wealthy elderly man and, after the divorce, had given almost all of the settlement money to charity. She *had* taught school for two years. She had climbed Kilimanjaro, McKinley, K2, Annapurna, and Rainier. It was during a storm on Annapurna when the group thought they were all going to die that Angela had an epiphany about her position in the universe.

I was embarrassed about how badly I was handling her death, so badly I didn't even realize Kathy had come to sit next to me, didn't realize she was holding my hand. I took it so badly I barely heard the service. When one of the sister's son's—they were eight and eleven—read a poem he'd written about her, there wasn't a dry eye in the house. I could hear sobbing from ten rows away. Beside me, Kathy was sniffling. At one point De Niro spoke, as did another Hollywood actor whose name meant nothing to me but whose presence elicited sighs of admiration from the crowd.

It ended with a slide show accompanied by music. Really sad music. Really, really sad music. Along with the photos of Angela mountain climbing, there were photos of her with Jimmy Carter and Bill Clinton, the same Presidents she claimed to have known personally. I'd called her a liar about that, too. There were pictures of her with top Hollywood stars and with public figures, as well as with a group of children in the dust of an African village, all of it verifying her version of her life, relegating my version to the dustbin. All of it proving she was humble and well-traveled and sophisticated, while I was a rube who called honest people liars behind their backs. They might as well have beaten me with sticks for an hour. I was that bruised.

As the mourners and assorted gawkers drifted out of the hall, Kathy ran into more friends she hadn't seen in a while, people with whom she wanted to chat. I told her we would meet up later and headed for the car. I couldn't take any more.

9

I was sliding into a pit of depression. Angela was dead and would shortly be trundled into a two-thousand degree furnace. As far as I could tell, it was partly my fault. Maybe mostly my fault. What the memorial service taught me was that she had far more friends than I thought, that she had accomplished far more than I ever gave her credit for, and was still, from what I could tell, one of the loneliest and neediest people I'd ever met. Nothing about her loneliness had been exposed during the service. Nothing about it had been expunged during her life. Little of what I had seen or heard explained it.

I'd seen two of her former boyfriends among the crowd, quiet men holding in their feelings, both as meek and unassuming as eunuchs.

Outside, I found Crane assisting an old woman into a waiting car. From the slide show presentation we'd seen minutes earlier, I recognized her and the driver as Angela's parents, older, more wrinkled, infinitely more weary and decrepit than they had been in the photos. Odd they weren't going to hang around for the reception. Perhaps they were like me and simply could not endure any more anguish.

While I stood and watched, a couple of men in suits approached. Their tans told me they'd come from some other part of the country. The one who did the talking wore a bright yellow tie which glowed like a putrescent sunflower against the widening azure sky to the north. We were finally going to have some nice weather.

"Are you Thomas Black?" he asked, flashing his credentials covertly so as not to frighten the wildlife. He was U.S. Secret Service. "Got a minute?"

"Did I accidentally pass a bad twenty?"

"It's about the woman who died. We're sorry to bring it up at a time like this, but we're traveling on a rather tight schedule."

"What's up?"

"We understand you worked with Ms. Pennington."

"She called herself Bassman, Angela Bassman."

"Maybe out here in Seattle she did, but she went by Pennington most places. What were you two working on?"

"I wasn't working with her."

"Our sources are giving us a different slant on that."

"Your sources are wrong."

Neither agent said anything, but the one who hadn't been talking glanced across the sidewalk toward Bonds and Gunderson. "Them?" I asked.

"We're not at liberty to disclose sources."

"They don't know anything about me, and they probably know less about Angela. Why is the Secret Service asking questions about her?"

"Just tying up loose ends. We've had a file on her for a while."

"She had her picture taken with two Presidents. If you were inside, you saw that."

"She did more than have her picture taken with them."

"What does that mean?"

"Let's just say, we've had our eye on her for years. If you would just tell us what you two were working on, we'll get out of your hair."

"She was trying to break up her sister's marriage. I helped her for about an hour a couple of weeks ago. She asked for more help the night before she died, but I more or less told her to take a flying leap. And then, that's what she did."

"What sort of help was she asking for?"

"She wasn't specific."

"But she wanted to break up Pennington's marriage?"

"That was the goal as far as I could tell. So now maybe you can tell me what the deal was with Angela and the Presidents?"

"We can't comment on an individual case, but sometimes our subjects think they're going to have some sort of romance with one of our principals. Kind of like groupies. Most go away on their own, but we have to keep tabs on them all the same. You'd be surprised how many people out there are nut jobs."

"Angela wasn't a nut job. She was an intelligent, caring woman who did everything she could to make the world a better place. Which is a hell of a lot more than most of us can say, me included." Considering how many times I'd said to Kathy I thought Angela was a wackadoodle, I was surprised to find myself defending her. But then, I'd recently viewed her baby pictures on the big screen; seen her in her high school prom dress; seen her wobbly junior-high-school thighs swimming at Lake Samish near Bellingham, where she'd grown up; seen her in braces; on her first bicycle; in a wedding photo with a man named Bassman, who was at least ninety, exactly as she had described him, exactly as I had refused to believe.

"We understand you were there when she died."

"Unfortunately, that's true."

"Can you tell us about it?"

I gave a brief synopsis of the events surrounding Angela's death and said, "You guys have reason to think this might be something other than an accident or a suicide?"

"The locals here seem locked into the suicide theory. There was a note e-mailed to her sister the day she died. Her sister said she'd tried this sort of thing before, written notes, made other attempts. We're only here to make sure she wasn't stalking one of our principals and to make sure nobody else was involved if she was."

"She played her cards pretty close to the vest, but as far as I know, she wasn't stalking any former or current Presidents."

"That's all we needed. Thanks for your cooperation. And again, we apologize for the intrusion."

As the agents wandered off, Crane Manning drifted toward me through the burgeoning crowd. When he got close I said, "You think Angela called us because she realized Gunderson and Bonds were on her tail?"

"If that was true, why didn't she say something on the phone? It would have been natural for her to mention it."

"Actually, for Angela, it would have been natural for her *not* to mention it. Plus, knowing her, she probably thought her phone was bugged. That they were listening in." Glancing in the direction of the retreating Secret Servicemen, I said, "Hell, maybe her phone *was* bugged."

"Are you saying Bonds and Gunderson were following her,

bugged her phone, and then threw her off the roof? The police called it suicide."

"All I'm saying is maybe they were there that day and we didn't see them."

"If they were on the roof with her, she would have fought like a wildcat."

I looked at Crane. "On the other hand, that Mandarin Duck Palm thing only goes so far." We looked at each other for a long moment and then both laughed, not at Angela, but somehow *with* her, as a tribute of sorts, a sick tribute that, ironically, Angela would not have understood or appreciated. I wasn't sure I understood it myself. When we finished laughing, there wasn't much else to say.

Crane opined, "It's too bad."

"Yeah."

"She was a nice kid."

"Yeah."

Angela had more than once hinted the federal government was watching her. I'd always written it off as paranoid grandiosity, but the feds *had* been watching her. The Secret Service had a file. They'd kept one for years.

I edged through the crowd toward Marvin Gunderson and Goodnight Bonds, who were talking to a tall, angular gentleman wearing wire-rimmed glasses, a nice suit, and expensive Italian shoes. Bonds and Gunderson appeared to be haranguing him, grinning mischievously as they spoke, while the man in the wire-rimmed glasses kept forking his fingers nervously through his lank blond hair. I'd been thinking a lot about Gunderson since the other night. I'd been unbelievably lucky during our punch up. I kept thinking through alternate scenarios in which I ended up dead. As I drew close, the two of them stopped talking.

Bonds looked at me with his vacant black eyes and puffed himself up to his full height, about a head and a half shorter than me. He brushed past me, playing it tough, bumping into me. Gunderson followed but made no pretense at physical contact. As he passed, he whispered, "We're not finished."

I smiled. "You might want to re-think that, pal. I might not go so easy on you next time."

He stopped and glowered at me and for just a moment I thought he was going to take a swing at me. "Keep talking like that, dick breath. See where it gets you."

I wanted to ask him if his balls had recovered, but he walked away too quickly. After he was gone, I realized if I shouted about his balls it would inform the entire crowd and would be embarrassing to him, and to me, too. I would sound like an insufferable jerk. Later when I mentioned it, Kathy confirmed that only a moron would do something in that vein.

"Hey," I yelled when he'd gotten a sufficient distance away, "your balls ever recover? I hope you iced 'em. The number one rule is, take care of the scrotum. Always take care of the scrotum."

Gunderson didn't turn back, but several people observed our interchange and stared at him—and me—as he walked away.

I turned to the man Bonds and Gunderson had been talking to and introduced myself. He told me his name was Henrik Federer. He looked ruffled, but I couldn't tell whether it was from my hollering about Gunderson's scrotal sack or something else. "You were having quite a conversation with those two," I said.

"It was nothing." But it wasn't nothing. He was rattled.

"My name is Thomas Black. You parked up here?" I asked.

"Up by the hospital."

"That's where I'm parked, too. Mind if I walk with you?" I figured he had something to say but didn't feel comfortable talking where Bonds and Gunderson could observe. "How did you know Angela?"

"She was interested in my work."

"And what is it you do?"

"I'm unemployed right now. I used to work for CLS Enterprises."

"CLS. That's the investment company owned by Clark Lloyd Self?"

"That's right."

When he didn't say anything else, I nattered on about some of the positive things I'd learned about Angela over the years, reflected on the things I hadn't known but had learned during the service. I made it all as matter-of-fact as I could, working hard to make him feel at ease. I could tell the service had affected him, just as he could tell it had affected me. I did not mention the Secret Service interview. I still hadn't had time to assess what they were about. I didn't know what to make of Angela stalking former Presidents, although I tended to believe the groupie theory. Everything about Angela spelled groupie. Hell, for years she'd been *my* groupie.

When we got to Federer's car, a brand new Lexus SUV, I said, "It was nice to meet you, Henrik."

He turned to me. "They were talking crap about her."

"Who was talking crap?"

"Marvin Gunderson was making insinuations about Angela's sex life, saying things I didn't want to hear. It was good you came along when you did and broke it up."

"What were they saying?"

"They said she slept with a lot of men. That she was wild."

"Angela was as prim as anybody I've ever known."

"That was my impression, too."

"They're liars."

"Why would they go to somebody's memorial service and tell lies like that?"

"Because they're pricks."

Judging from the impish smile that flashed across his thin lips, Federer had been thinking the same thing but was too much of a gentleman to say it. I didn't share that particular problem.

10

IT was close to ten-thirty that night when I got the call.

"Black? This is Monica Pennington. We need to talk."

"I'm sorry about your sister. We're going to miss her."

"Yes. We are."

"What can I do for you?"

"In person."

"Sure. How about first thing Monday?"

"Tonight." It wasn't a question. Pennington was used to getting things her way. Either that or today's events had ripped out some of the stitching on her social coat. "We're in Belltown. You know the place. Call up when you get here and I'll send somebody down. We're on the roof." She disconnected without waiting for a reply.

"Going someplace?" Kathy asked.

"I guess so."

On my way out the door, Kathy gave me a particularly heartfelt kiss. She'd been tiptoeing around my feelings since I got back from my group ride with the club after the memorial. We'd gone sixty miles, out and across the floating bridge, then around Mercer Island several times. She'd seen me cry twice today and knew Angela's death was bothering me more than anything had bothered me in quite some time. She attributed it to my having been there when Angela jumped, but watching Angela die hadn't disturbed me half as much as thinking about all the denigrating things I'd said about her and done to her. It's hell when somebody dies before you've gotten around to apologizing for being an ass.

It was Saturday night and there was a fair amount of foot and vehicular traffic in Belltown. I parked on the street and went through a security door behind three young men who knew somebody in the building. Two minutes after I called up on my cell phone, one of the elevators opened and Bonds stared out at me. I was relieved it wasn't Gunderson. I wasn't sure I could force myself into an elevator with him.

Bonds didn't say anything and neither did I. It was the same elevator Angela, Crane, and I had taken that first day and it ran non-stop from the lobby to the penthouse. At the top, Bonds stepped out and, without saying anything, walked down a long corridor before disappearing through a nondescript door.

At loose ends, I approached the double doors to Pennington's suite before I saw a lighted stairway off to one side. I heard music at the top of the stairs and went up, finding myself on the roof. The outdoor furniture was too expensive to come from any place I shopped, the rooftop landscaping probably required the services of a full-time gardener, and the covered bar was fully stocked with premium labels. Monica Pennington was looking out over Puget Sound and the city lights while her husband, Clark Lloyd Self, wearing an open linen shirt and black trousers, reclined in a lounge chair, a drink in his hand. Tony Bennett crooned in the background, but I couldn't tell where the music was coming from.

Judging from the look Self gave me, it hadn't been his idea to invite me here. I'd seen him at the service that morning, but he hadn't seen me. He did now, and his eyes were brimming with disgust. He could hardly have forgotten our brief stint together in Sophie Millwood's bedroom. He stared at me venomously, his look a reminder that we never should have barged into Millwood's house. I had to admit it was one of the low points of my year, an unfair and illegal imposition on Millwood, *and* on Self, and we were lucky he hadn't shot us. Even so, I couldn't help wondering if he was still screwing Millwood now that he was officially back with his wife.

Pennington was facing away, but as I approached she said, "Funny about sisters. I've always been afraid of heights. When we were children Angela loved to climb the tallest trees in the neighborhood. Later, she did her best to climb every major mountain peak in the world. She kept at it until she decided the expeditions were squandering world resources that could otherwise save lives. It's strange she would die in a fall, don't you think?"

"It *is* ironic."

Pennington turned around. In the half -light from the city she was more beautiful than ever. Although well past forty, she looked like an ingénue in her capri pants and bulky sweater. Her ankles were bare, her feet in slipper-like shoes. She clutched a drink in one hand. When she leaned against the hip-high wall separating her from a thirty-one-story drop and an ending even more dramatic than her sister's, it made me nervous in the same way Angela had made me nervous on the roof of our office building.

"Angela wasn't afraid of falling. Or of failure. I don't think she was even afraid of my husband."

"She was definitely not afraid of your husband," I said.

It might have been my pronouncement that spurred Self to stand up and stretch like a cat. He said, "Poor Angela. Poor, stupid, ineffective, laughable Angela. But you know, underneath it all, she *was* sweet. She just had a lot of problems." There was a current of forced sadness in his voice, as if he were trying to make himself feel particularly sorrowful about her death or as if he'd had too much to drink. "Do me a favor, Black. When you come down, bring Monica with you. I don't want her left up here alone in her condition."

Martini in hand, Self traipsed down the stairs.

After he was gone, Pennington said. "He told me not to call you. Told me to get somebody who knew what they were doing."

"For what?"

"I'd like you to look into Angela's death. Tell me everything there is to know about it."

"You have any reason to think it wasn't a suicide?"

"God, no. Of course it was suicide. Angela has been threatening to kill herself for years. Once when she was a teenager our mother came home unexpectedly and found her with her head in the oven. We all treated it as an everyday occurrence. As an adult, she was hospitalized for depression on at least three occasions. The last time was six months ago. I bet you didn't know about that one."

"I didn't know about any of them, although I knew she got depressed."

"Her suicide note was short and bitter. It was like the first page of a book. I want the rest of the book. Will you help me?"

"As far as I can tell, there were a lot of blank pages in Angela's life."

"And I want you to fill them in for me."

I knew what she was asking, because it was the same thing I might have asked, and for the same reason. She wanted to know why Angela had taken such a drastic step, and more than that, she wanted to know why *now*. Why this week and not last week? Why in Seattle and not when she'd been living in Atlanta? Why not on some distant mountain top? Had my unkindness contributed to it? Had Pennington's? I knew over the years that at one time or another just about everybody except Kathy had been dismissive or unkind toward Angela, who was one of those people who seemed to invite cruelty.

Pennington ambled over to the bar, where she awkwardly began making herself another drink, though she was already drunk. It didn't show up in her voice so much, but her physical coordination was a shambles. She might have been on drugs, too. Her dark eyes were luminescent, the pupils huge. No doubt about it, she was beautiful, even in a drunken state. Full, curved mouth; flawless, creamy skin; dark, chestnut-colored hair falling around her shoulders in waves. I was accustomed to being around a beautiful woman, was married to the most beautiful woman I've ever known. What I wasn't accustomed to was being around a creature who wore a halo of celebrity and seduction as if it were a crown she'd been born to, giving off an aura of feminine power that left no doubt about who was in charge. I couldn't help imagining she treated all mere mortals as her subjects.

"With Angela everything was always private," Monica said. "The secrecy deepened when she became a teenager. For a long time I thought she was just keeping things from *me*. But she was keeping things from everyone."

"That was my take on it, too."

Pennington began to weep. At first I thought it was an act, but it wasn't. After a while, she steeled herself, gulped down the drink she was making, poured two more, and offered one of them to me. "No, thank you," I said.

"Drink it. I don't drink alone."

"I don't drink at all."

She looked at me with a jaundiced eye, then downed her brandy and carried the one meant for me over to the wall, strolling in an erratic arc like a bumblebee. "Even though she was the youngest, Angela was always looking after me. I know it hurt her that she wasn't beautiful.

She told me so many times. Coming along after me in school and getting compared to me by everyone who mattered didn't help. I guess I never really valued her the way I should have."

"I wonder if anybody did."

"We'll double your going rates."

"If you want somebody to tell you this wasn't your fault, I can tell you right now. Ending your own life is not about other people, no matter how much it might feel like it is to those of us who are left." Maybe if I could convince Monica, I would be convinced myself.

She began crying again. The Space Needle wasn't far away and was lit up like a gigantic flying saucer. People sat five hundred feet in the air lingering over their quiet suppers or looking at the city through complimentary telescopes on the observation deck. Angela would have reminded us that each of those dinners cost enough to feed a third-world village for a month. Angela talked incessantly about the one thing I don't think I'd ever heard another American speak out on, our innate selfishness as human beings.

"Clark said 'don't hire the pipsqueak.' Told me to get a big agency."

Pipsqueak? "Big agencies are good."

"Clark doesn't like you."

"I don't imagine he does. So why are you hiring the pipsqueak?"

"Two things. Angela said you were good. I believed her. Also . . . did I say *two* things?"

"You did."

"Oh, yeah. You knew her."

"And?"

"You cared about her. I saw that at the service."

I hadn't been aware she'd noticed me at the service and was embarrassed my feelings had been so conspicuous. More than that, my distress at the memorial service was mostly for myself and my own failings as a human being, something she couldn't possibly have known. *Pipsqueak?* "Okay. I'll do it. I'll start tomorrow."

"Angela always said you liked her. She said sometimes you almost liked her too much." She let that hang between us, even though we both knew there was something wrong with it. Did Angela have an even more distorted take on our relationship than I thought? "Don't worry about the cost. Clark's paying for this. It's his penance."

"I'll need the key to her place. Also, a couple of pictures of her. Access to her banking and phone records. A copy of the note she sent you. The autopsy report, if there was one. Whatever else you can think of that might help."

"Already assembled. Bonds will give you the package on your way out. Look, Mr. Black. I know Clark had affairs. I had them myself. But Clark and I have something we're never going to find with anybody else, and we know it. He's the father of my children." Technically, two-thirds of her children. She had an older child from her first marriage to the rock drummer. The boys she had with Self were eight and eleven. I saw them at the memorial, somber, spindly lads in matching blazers, each with a thatch of hair the same thickness and color as their mother's. It occurred to me that she might be feeding me a line of bull, that she might be asking me to investigate Angela's life to pick up any stray evidence Angela had collected concerning her husband's peccadillos. Perhaps she was concerned stray videos of him having sex with some nymphet he wasn't married to would make their way into the public eye and cripple his business or once again land her on the front pages of the supermarket tabloids.

"Mr. Black? Tread carefully. Clark thinks you're going to take up where Angela left off and try to break up our marriage. He gets any hint of that, he's going to be very angry."

"Breaking up your marriage is the furthest thing from my mind."

"I just need to know why she did it."

"I'll find out."

"Since you were there, I have one question you can answer right now. Did she suffer?"

"She was dead maybe thirty seconds after she landed."

It occurred to me once again that Angela might have summoned me to witness her suicide. I shuddered to think she might even have tried to land on me, a two-for-one deal. Maybe on the way down she didn't say, "It was the drain." I wasn't a hundred percent sure those were her words. Instead, perhaps she said, "Feel this pain." After she landed, Angela asked me to finish things for her, although I couldn't be sure what she meant by that. For a brief moment I had thought she was asking me to finish her off, but quickly decided that was a result of watching too many B movies. Now that I was working for Pennington I hoped what Angela meant didn't have anything to do with breaking up her sister's marriage. It probably did, but I prayed it didn't. The truth was, working for Pennington would certainly give me better access to Angela's records than I ever could have gotten on my own.

"Black. Do what you think is right for her memory, but I want to know if her suicide had anything to do with me."

"Of course."

She downed her drink and let the tumbler slip through her fingers into the night. I peered over the edge to make sure it wasn't going to kill somebody on the sidewalk but quickly lost sight of it in the darkness. Moments later I heard it shatter on the distant pavement. It sounded like it was coming from a different world.

When I turned around, she was sliding toward the imported bluestone patio tiles. I caught her before she hit her head on the rim of a pot containing a tropical palm the servants probably had to haul inside each night. She was drunk, limp in my arms. "I need to get you downstairs," I said, scooping her up.

"No," she blurted, but her eyes were closed. I wasn't sure she knew what she was saying or even who she was talking to. Her head was hanging in such a way she was going to have a sore neck in the morning. I could feel her loose breasts under the sweater as one of them rolled against my fingertips. The sensation was not entirely unpleasant.

I walked to the top of the stairs and began descending carefully. I was almost to the first landing when she lifted her head, half-realized what was going on, and reached around my neck to hold on. "Can you walk on your own?" I asked. She burbled something that didn't make sense and laid her head against my shoulder, her hair brushing my cheek. Her eyes were closed when she said, "Will you kill my husband for me?"

"What did you say?"

She opened her eyes and looked into mine dreamily. "I was only joking." She continued looking at me in a way that didn't have anything to do with jokes. Before I began descending again, she grasped my face in both hands and planted a kiss on my mouth. There wasn't much I could do about it since I had both hands full. Tumbling down a flight of stairs with the wife of one of the wealthiest men in the country, a man who already detested me, wouldn't be the smartest move. But neither was kissing her. Except I wasn't kissing her. *She* was kissing *me.*

The same as Angela had done, only nicer. Angela had been a greedy, rapacious kisser. This was a long, mellow kiss I couldn't escape. I knew right away I was never going to tell anybody about it. How could I?

When she finished, she laid her head against my neck, and by the time we reached the bottom of the stairs she was conked out. The front door had been left open. I laid her on the sofa in the first room I came to, the same room I'd waited in weeks earlier with Crane. It was fully furnished now. A wall of windows revealed a view of Elliott Bay and the Olympic Mountains beyond. Across the dark waters of the bay a white and green ferry was gliding toward Bainbridge Island to the west. Set flush into the wall opposite the windows, an artfully rusted iron firebox was lit with a six-foot-wide ribbon of low flame flanked by beach stones. The wall behind the long sleek sofa where Monica now lay was dominated by a bright primitive-style painting of a woman working in a field. The spacious room was sparsely furnished, giving it a gallery-like appearance, designed to impress, not comfort.

"There you are," Clark Lloyd Self said, entering the room. He was followed by a woman in her thirties wearing a nondescript pantsuit.

"I brought her down."

He glanced at his sleeping wife. "Yes. I can see that. I see you and Monica have come to an understanding." I noticed for the first time that he was one of those people who look at your mouth as you speak instead of looking into your eyes.

"I'll need a phone number where I can reach your wife."

Self gave me a long, appraising look and said, "In the package." He then grasped one of his wife's hands and tugged her upright until she was standing. On the roof she'd moved like a drunk, and after that she hadn't moved at all, but now she was moving like a hundred-year-old woman. Meeting with me had been the last stressful chore in a stressful day. I didn't give any credence to the request to assassinate her husband. It had been the alcohol talking. A bad joke. The kiss had been a bad joke, too. Weird that I'd now been kissed by both sisters. I hadn't told Kathy about Angela's kiss, and there was no way in hell I was going to tell her about this one either.

"This is Carole Cooper from SPD," Self said, indicating the woman in the pantsuit. "She'll fill you in. When you're finished, Bonds will take you downstairs. He has the rest of your materials."

Carole Cooper was short and stout, with brush-cut hair and a businesslike manner. After we were alone, she showed me her detective's badge, although I already knew who she was, for she had interviewed me the day Angela died. "I don't know what to tell you," she said. "You were the only witness. We interviewed everybody we could find: friends, neighbors, family. We searched the apartment. We read the note. The toxicology report came back negative. The medical examiner could see no reason to nullify a finding of death by suicide. Neither could we. So that's how it stands. Death by suicide."

"You're convinced?"

"As convinced as I'll ever be."

"These people have the kind of clout to get you here on a Saturday night?"

"Seems they have an 'in' with the mayor. Might have something to do with money. I couldn't say for sure." She smirked, looking around at our surroundings. "I'm okay with it. I'm getting overtime. A friend's watching my dogs."

"Thanks for waiting around."

"Any questions?"

"One. You turn up anything you considered odd?"

"Just that she jumped from the roof of a fairly low building. Four stories. Sixty-seven feet. Most jumpers choose something higher, something with a cleaner fall line. The Aurora Bridge is a favorite. She could have gotten hung up in those trees outside the building. You saw it. You think she was aiming for the car?"

I thought she might have been aiming for me, but I didn't say it. "Hard to tell. I know people used to jump off the Space Needle before they put up the barriers. That was a sure thing."

"Before my time."

"I guess you had to grow up in this town to remember. Can I call you if something comes up?"

She gave me her card and we stepped out of the condo together.

Bonds was waiting in the corridor. He handed me an expensive briefcase, and then we all three stepped into the elevator and rode it to the ground floor."

11

THE three of us were at street level when I faced off with Goodnight Bonds. Remembering how he'd badmouthed Angela at the funeral, I said, "You ever think about using lifts?"

His eyes were as vacant as the windows in an old shack. "What?"

"Lifts. In your shoes. You know. To keep from looking like a midget."

He bristled. "I don't need no lifts."

"People as short as you should wear elevator shoes, lift you up so you can talk straight with regular people."

"Fuck you."

"No thanks."

"Also, you have lipstick on your face."

"Lifts would give you another couple of inches free. Like Tom Cruise. He wears lifts. Mickey Rooney used to wear them. So did Alan Ladd."

"Who's Mickey Rooney? Who are you talking about?"

"A lot of actors wear them. You saw Tom at the funeral today, didn't you? Tom Cruise?"

"Tom Cruise was there?"

"Oh, that's right. You were too busy slinging mud at the recently deceased to notice what was going on around you. Too bad. I heard he was looking for a new stand-in. You know. Somebody to hang out in front of the cameras so they can get the lighting right while he's in his dressing room rehearsing his lines. Somebody to pal around with, play poker with, go out on the town with. He said they needed a sawed-off guy about your build, brown on brown. You would have been perfect."

"I can play poker."

"Down there in Hollywood mixing with the stars. You might even have snagged a couple of bit parts in movies. Maybe get a love scene with Pamela Anderson. Course, you'd have to wear lifts like Tom does. You'd have to be the same height. You should think about getting lifted."

"Tom Cruise was there?"

"Gunderson saw him. I'm surprised he didn't tell you. Maybe he just didn't want you to get the job."

"You get his phone number?" Bonds asked. "You get Tom Cruise's phone number?"

"Matter of fact, I did."

I started to walk away. Cooper looked on with a bemused expression on her face.

"Hey, aren't you going to give it to me?"

"I would, but you told me to fuck myself."

He hesitated. "I didn't mean it."

"Uh, I think you did."

"Okay. Well, I meant it at the time, but I apologize. Just give me his phone number. It's no skin off your butt if I get to meet Pamela Anderson. And I know how to play poker."

"Tell me what you were saying about Angela today."

"It wasn't me. Marvin's always had a thing for Angie. But she's been a thorn in his side for months."

"Is that why she's dead?"

"Hey, man, talk to the cop here. Everybody knows she killed herself."

"But you're not sorry, are you?"

"Sorry about what?"

Cooper and I turned and walked away.

"Goodnight," I said to Cooper after we were outside and it was apparent we were heading in opposite directions.

"Night," she said. "By the way, there *is* lipstick on your face. Same color as Pennington's."

"What?"

"Just a little, but it's awfully bright."

The first thing I did in the car was check the mirror. Monica had left her brand on me, a color that might have been called *Fearless* or maybe *Ravishing Red.* No wonder Clark had been staring at my mouth. He must have thought I'd been up on the roof putting the moves to his incapacitated wife. Carole Cooper probably thought the same thing, which bothered me, since Cooper seemed like a nice person and I didn't want her thinking I was a dirtball. I made a mental note to check my face in the mirror the next time a client kissed me.

When I got home, Kathy was in bed reading. I did my ablutions in the bathroom and came out wearing pajama bottoms, then crawled stealthily onto the bed on top of the covers, on top of Kathy, moving as if she wouldn't notice, like a cat. She put her book carefully on the night stand and flicked the lamp off. "I thought you'd be asleep," I said, whispering into the darkness.

"Are you kidding? I want to hear all about this."

"Not much to tell."

"You talked to Pennington?"

"And her husband. And a cop. And Bonds."

"How is Pennington taking it?"

"Hard to tell. She was medicated."

"Tranquilizers?"

"Booze mostly."

"What's their place like?"

"Not as nice as ours."

"No. Really. What's it like?"

"Your normal thirtieth floor penthouse." I gave her a kiss.

"What is that perfume?"

"Huh?"

"That's Monica Pennington's perfume. I recognize it from the funeral. It's very expensive." I'd brushed my teeth—twice—and washed my face and even polished my entire head with a wet towel, but apparently that hadn't been enough. Mental note: After being kissed by another woman and before kissing your wife, look in mirror, take shower, scrub with a rough piece of lava, burn all clothing, drink a bottle of mouthwash. Visit lobotomist to have memory removed.

"It's a long story."

"That's okay because I have all the time in the world, sweetie."

"First of all, it's not what you think."

"You don't know what I think. You can't read my mind."

Sometimes I could, but this wasn't one of those times. "Monica Pennington hired me to look into her sister's death."

"I'm not asking about that. I'm asking why you smell like her."

"Oh, yeah, well . . . she kinda kissed me."

There was a long silence. Finally, Kathy said, "What's a kind of a kiss?"

"It's the type where one person is carrying the other person down the stairs because they're falling-down drunk and their hands are too full to push the other person away."

"She was carrying you down the stairs?"

"I was carrying her."

"Oh? How hard were you planning to push her away?"

"Really hard."

"Let me see your knuckles. Did you break a nail during the skirmish?"

"My knuckles are okay."

"Was she a good kisser?"

"Honey, it was disgusting."

"Yeah, right. How much did she weigh? More than me? Less? About the same?"

"When a body is that sloppy, I'm a poor judge of heft."

She laughed. "Good answer. Is any of this the truth?"

This was where personal integrity and strict honesty came into play, for they were the cornerstones holding a healthy marriage together. Kathy was more subdued than I expected when I confessed to the kiss, so I wasn't going to give any ground on the weight. I still hadn't mentioned Angela's similar advance over a year earlier and was becoming convinced this was not the time to bring it up. When I climbed into bed I'd had plans, but now I wasn't sure those plans were viable.

"She was heavy," I lied. "Monica Pennington, up close, is big and marshmallowy with no muscle tone and a little mustache that feels like hog's bristles. I think I got beard burn."

"Hmmm."

"Like a Hitler mustache."

"If she was so revolting, why is it the minute we started talking about that kiss, you started to get this?" She reached through my pajamas. I tried to move away, but she wasn't letting go.

"I get like that whenever I'm near you. You know that."

"You do quite frequently, but why did it show up when you started talking about the kiss?"

"It's in the genes."

"So it's your father's fault?"

A good husband, when kissed by another woman, goes straight home and tells his wife. A good husband might even confess about the secret thrill it gave him. He might confess to the daydreams that kiss had provoked on the drive home. While I never wanted anything other than to be a good husband, God knows I needed all the help I could get, especially now.

"Are you sure you're not maybe a little horny because you just got kissed by one of the top lingerie and fashion models of the last fifty years?"

"She modeled lingerie? I had no idea."

"Hah!"

"I'm horny because I'm with you and because I love you."

"I love you, too."

"Well, that settles it."

"Settles what?"

Kathy was a lot prettier than Monica Pennington ever thought of being, and I should have told her so in exactly those words. Instead, I said, "On her best day, she isn't fit to carry your jockstrap."

"What? What did you say?"

"Why? Are you wearing one?"

"Now you're really spoiling the mood."

"I didn't know we had a mood. Besides, it's not spoiled. Feel."

"Not for you, it isn't. I'm still trying to decide."

I said, "Did you know during any given night the average male gets ninety erections? It's a scientific fact. I read it someplace. *Scientific American*, I think. In our dentist's office."

"We've been over this before. It was in your barber shop and it was *Muscle* magazine. And it was one erection every ninety minutes, not ninety a night."

"I thought it was ninety a night."

"Maybe for you it is."

We kissed a little and then we kissed some more and then later I crawled under the covers with her and I took off her nightgown and she took off my pajama bottoms. We kissed some more and then did all the things I never believed I would ever really be doing back when I was fourteen years old and wanted them so much I thought I was going to die from it. There was always a little bit of wonder to it, wonder that I was really here, really doing it. There was even more wonder to being with Kathy. A little later, we fell asleep in each other's arms. A while after that, one of us half- woke and moved away, too hot from body contact to sleep soundly. I was almost asleep when I heard her murmur something which I found myself hoping wasn't *Will you kill my husband for me?*

"What did you say?" I whispered.

"Only eighty-nine to go till morning."

12

SUNDAY I woke up early and dug into the package Bonds gave me. On top of the pile was a retainer check for ten thousand dollars.

I found Angela's most recent bank statements, her rental agreement for the apartment where she lived and died, and a set of keys for her apartment as well as her Volkswagen. I had forgotten to ask whether the van had been impounded. I would want to look at it. There were color photos of Angela, including two of her atop some unnamed snowy distant Himalayan peak in full gear, her nose painted with sun block, pale circles around her eyes where the round climbing glasses had shielded her face from the sun's glare. At the bottom of the packet was the printout of Angela's suicide note. I set it aside. I didn't have the stomach to read it just yet.

There were contact phone numbers for Monica Pennington, her secretary, and for Goodnight Bonds, should I ever feel the need to gossip with him. There was a note stipulating I was authorized to talk to Angela's bank and could access her banking records. She had a small retirement account, and the valuations and stocks she owned were listed. All green companies. Surprisingly little money. There was a trust fund from her marriage, now completely drained, from which she had been taking pay-outs monthly. She had been, in fact, nearly broke. There was one large monthly expenditure I had no understanding of—to a place in Kent called McKay's.

So much of what I'd been thinking about her was just plain wrong. I'd avoided her whenever possible even though she'd been about as unavoidable as a muddy puppy, all wagging tail and eager anticipation and nothing I could ever do to stop it.

When Butch Cathcart called about a bike ride, I couldn't pass it up. All spring the Puget Sound area had been breaking records for cold and rain, and we were still waiting for the first day over seventy degrees; today it was sunny outside with the promise of a balmy day. Butch lived about a mile away. I usually got ready and sat at my kitchen table until I saw him in the alley leaning up against my fence on his bike, but today I was the one leaning against the fence waiting.

We rode downhill through the UW campus and across the Montlake Bridge, through the Arboretum and down to Lake Washington, where we met up with a group on Lakeside and cycled around the south end of the lake, then out to the Snoqualmie Valley and into farmland where traffic was sparse. We did a lot of jamming, so I was pretty mellow by the time we got back to my alley. I showered and shaved and read a note Kathy had left on the kitchen table: *Taking the dog to Hazel's. We're going to power-walk Discovery Park. Don't worry, I have my bear spray in case we spot the cougar everyone's been talking about. Love you.* I was a little worried about the cougar, but they were going to have their dogs with them and cougars were notoriously shy of dogs. Besides, it was Sunday and the park would have lots of people in it. Apparently Kathy didn't have a phobia about cougars the way she did about bears.

It was three o'clock in the afternoon by the time I reached Angela's apartment building on Capitol Hill. Except for the ugly dent in the roof of her Volkswagen, which was still parked in front of the building, you never would have known anything had happened here four days ago. I used her key on the front door and hiked up the stairs to the fourth floor, feeling every one of the seventy-five miles I'd put into my legs on the bike. I was fried. The place smelled of cooking rice and kids and vaguely of tapioca and cigarettes.

There was still crime-scene tape on her door, but I had no doubt the police were finished here and the place would be rented out to somebody who probably would never be told what happened.

I'd only been in the apartment once before, but it hadn't changed much, although it was untidy even for her. I could see the police had already gone through her things, but their goal was to determine if foul play was involved, not to find out why she'd killed herself. It was an efficiency apartment, slightly larger than a studio, with a tiny kitchen that adjoined the living room, a small bathroom, and a bedroom with barely enough space for a bed and dresser. True to her life philosophy, she was something of an ascetic.

There was a bookshelf, and just as one would suspect, it was stuffed with tomes on ancient and modern religion, political and philosophical books by Noam Chomsky, Thom Hartmann, and other progressive writers who'd influenced Angela. One wall sported a framed poster of a baby seal. There was a FREE TIBET banner adorned with prayer flags across the top of another wall. Taped to a bedroom wall were over a hundred snapshots of various people, some of whom I recognized, many of whom I didn't. There were several of Kathy and one of me I'd not seen before. In the midst of the collage, where one might be tempted to overlook it, I spotted a snapshot of Angela in glasses and a ponytail, sitting on a sofa, not the one in the other room, and staring directly at the camera with a brazenness I'd not seen from her in life. She wasn't wearing a top. Except for the night of the kiss, I never knew her to be overtly sexual; certainly never blouseless. I stared at the photo not because she was half naked, but because I couldn't figure out the context of the picture. Who had taken it? Why was it displayed here on her wall?

She hadn't owned anything expensive: a small TV, an even smaller microwave, a toaster. No radio. No bicycle. No sports equipment except for a racquetball racket and her climbing gear. A tiny closet full of clothing. Lots of bright colors and oddball outfits. The remains of her last lunch were on the kitchen counter. She'd eaten half an avocado with tortilla chips and a bowl of lentil soup. I found the other half of the avocado wrapped neatly in the refrigerator. It was going black so I put it in the garbage, cleaned out the rest of the fridge, washed the dishes, and, after digging through it for anything informative and finding nothing, took the garbage downstairs to the empty Dumpster behind the building.

When I got back upstairs a Latino boy of about eight or nine sporting a thick curtain of black bangs was standing at Angela's partially open door, two smaller children behind him. All three had the look of kittens who'd found a new room to explore but were afraid to enter. The two smaller children, a boy and a girl still in her Sunday dress and patent-leather Mary Janes, hid behind the older boy when I approached. "Hi, guys," I said. "I'm just cleaning up. Did you guys know Angela?"

They all nodded. I could tell from the look on his face the older boy knew she was dead. "Was she nice?" I asked.

"She gave us quarters. She told us things we should know, like about strangers and how not to get caught in the credit trap."

I couldn't help smiling. "The credit trap?"

"She made us watch a movie about it. Jesse and Maria left before it was over. I don't know why she jumped off the roof. Sometimes we used to go up with her, but now we can never go again. Jesse and Maria saw the ambulance take her away. I was at band practice. She wasn't moving, they said."

"What do you play in the band?"

"Trumpet. Angela rented it for me." The boy had on jeans, a red-striped T-shirt, and canvas sneakers, the same brand I used to wear when I was his age. I had no idea whether in today's world the shoes would be considered retro-chic or an indication of poverty.

One of Angela's concessions to modern technology was a laptop computer. I found it on the kitchen table, pushed back against the wall. It was broken in half, the casing shattered, the guts dangling out of it. There was no way for me to know if the destruction had taken place before Angela's death or after. She'd sent an e-mail to her sister prior to jumping, and I assumed she'd sent it on this computer. I made a mental note to ask Crane about it.

I looked out her kitchen window and saw the tops of the chestnut trees, below them her damaged Volkswagen.

She didn't have a land line, and I had no idea where her cell phone was. I would call Carole Cooper during business hours to ask about it. I would also ask if they removed anything from the apartment or her person and, if so, what. Also, I needed to know if the computer was broken before they saw it. I assumed it was, or else they would have confiscated it.

Self's people had given me a contact number at her cell phone company so I could pull her records, but I wasn't going to call until tomorrow, Monday. I knew her cell phone was a basic model that sent and received only phone calls. She was far too paranoid about electronic devices to have had a smart phone.

There was no notepad, electronic or otherwise, no diary, no journal. She didn't even scrawl notes on her calendar. There was nothing to find but a few family pictures she'd thrown into an inexpensive binder. I noted her sister had been the pretty one even when they were small children, found myself paying more attention to pictures of Monica than Angela, which apparently had been the story of Angela's life. I spotted a bundle of Christmas cards I guessed she'd failed to answer. It was May, but the bundle was out as if she intended to send her own cards any day now. There were magazines checked out from the library: *Vegetarian Times*, *Mother Jones*, and *Organic Gardening*, all of which featured articles on how to grow a rooftop vegetable garden, all overdue. I set the library materials aside so I could return them on my way home and pay the fines.

I remembered Crane telling me Angela had asked him to set up her television, but it was out of order again, turned to the wall, connecting wires loose, unplugged. In fact, everything electrical in the place was either unplugged or dismantled or hidden in a drawer.

I cleaned up the kitchen. There were newspapers scattered on the floor. One of the papers had a footprint on it. Judging by the tread and the size, it belonged to the boy I spoke to outside Angela's door, which meant he'd been in here after the police.

I checked all her drawers and found a horde of pre-1964 silver coins in a small flannel bag hidden under some sweaters, ninety-percent silver coins collected for their melt value. The back of her closet was filled with well-used climbing gear: boots, crampons, carabiners, descenders, two 150-foot nylon ropes, a pack, freeze-dried food in foil packets, goggles, an ice axe, and more. I went through the pack for anything she might have hidden, but all I found were some dried wildflowers that looked years old.

I went through all the pockets of her clothing, hoping to find a ticket stub, a journal, a cell phone, an earlier draft of the suicide note, the key to a safe deposit box, a packet of letters, anything that might point me in one direction or another, aware that I had two agendas. I was not only in the employ of Monica Pennington to discover all I could about her sister's motivations; I still didn't have any idea what my last promise to Angela entailed.

I couldn't locate the hard drive to the ruined laptop. There were no memory sticks or disks either. If she purposely destroyed the computer before killing herself, what had she done with the hard drive? I wondered if the police had taken it. Or if it was on the roof. Or somewhere between here and the roof. Or had she tossed it in the garbage out back? If so, it was gone, because the receptacles had been recently emptied.

Before I left the building with the sack of coins for her nephews and the magazines from the library, I stopped in the hallway, where two of the three children I'd seen earlier were playing a game involving marbles and a shoestring. The older boy looked at me, near tears. "She was showing us Kung Fu. She told us she could break bricks with her bare hands."

"I'm sure she could break anything."

"Why did she do it?"

"What's your name?"

"Alvarez."

"Well, Alvarez, I don't know why. But I'm looking into it. I have to ask you something. I saw a footprint in there. It looked like it could be yours. The door wasn't locked, was it? It was locked when I got here, but I'm guessing there was a time when it wasn't locked." He looked down, ashamed. This was probably his first experience with death, and it was bad enough without me showing up. "You were in there, weren't you?"

"Some men went in after the police. They left it unlocked. I locked it back up."

"But you went in first, didn't you?"

"Si."

"You take anything?" He didn't answer. "What did you take?"

"I wanted a memento. I wanted to remember Angela."

"Could you get it for me?"

Without a word, he jogged down the corridor and went through an apartment door, leaving me with his tiny brother. "What's your name?" I asked, but the little brother wasn't having any of me. Silently, he knelt back down and began playing with the marbles as if I weren't there. Alvarez came back carrying a small object with a wire dangling off one end. I'd expected him to bring me a coin purse or a photo, but he brought me the computer hard drive and a pair of women's fuzzy slippers.

"I just wanted something to remember her by," he said, tears in his eyes. I could see that Angela's slippers were probably the same size as his feet.

"It's okay. You keep the slippers. I think she would want you to have them. But I need this," I said, taking the hard drive. "You didn't break the computer, did you?"

"It was already broken when I went in there."

"You said some men were in there. What did they look like?"

"I don't know. My baby sister told me. Nobody else saw them but her."

"Thanks, Alvarez."

Stuffing the hard drive into my pocket, I trotted up a set of stairs at the end of the hallway that led to the roof. The roof door was locked and none of Angela's keys fit. My guess was the landlord had changed the lock after Angela's death. I slipped it with a knife. The roof was a simple affair, black torch-down cluttered with several ancient and obviously unused television antennae and a couple of mildewed plastic lawn chairs. Like everything else in her life, it was a startling contrast to her sister's roof. I walked around the edge looking for the exact point she leaped from. There were no scuff marks, no abrasions, and no signs of a struggle. The wall was higher than I thought it would be, high enough somebody of Angela's height wasn't likely to go over it by mistake. My original guess that she fell by accident was off base, unless she'd been walking on the ledge. The drain pipe, which was dislodged the day of her fall, was reattached now and was no longer positioned in a manner that would trip anybody.

13

MONDAY I was sitting at my computer thinking about Angela's suicide note when Brad Munch strolled into the office with a brand new external hard drive in his hands. I'd dropped off Angela's broken hard drive with Munch the day before, hoping he could salvage at least part of it. Brad was a slovenly, heavyset young man who'd been attending the University of Washington virtually his entire adult life, having gotten in on a special scholarship at sixteen. He was currently chipping away at a master's degree in business administration to go with his MS in chemistry, and various degrees in Russian and Slavic studies. He'd gone down the rabbit hole of computers while he was still in middle school and physically was about what you might expect, doughy and pale from lack of sunlight and exercise, no current girlfriend, a rigid but minimal social life.

"This was too easy," he said.

"What do you mean?"

"Somebody tried to destroy it, but most of these hard drives are pretty durable." He handed me a fresh hard drive loaded with data from the damaged original. "Most of it was still readable. You really have to take a blow torch to these things. Or you can overwrite the whole thing. I was able to retrieve most of the data." He handed me a drive.

"How much do I owe you?"

He named a paltry sum that probably wouldn't have paid his cab fare from where he lived near the zoo, though he'd ridden the bus. I named a much higher sum and, as always, we engaged in a session of reverse bargaining. I would raise the offer while he would lower it until we settled on an amount slightly lower than I was happy with. Munch didn't care about money and didn't want mine, even when I told him it was coming out of the client's pocket.

As he left with his check I said, "How much did you recover, percentage wise?"

"Eighty-five, ninety. You'll know better than me."

"Thanks, Brad."

"My pleasure."

"And Brad?"

"Yeah?"

"You sure somebody damaged this on purpose?"

"I think somebody stepped on it."

"Could it have been someone who weighed seventy or eighty pounds? A kid?"

"No way. An adult did this."

"Thanks."

I liked being in the office alone. I liked being able to get up and walk around while I was thinking. The phone rang, but it was Kathy's phone so I let her machine handle it. I called the bonding company Crane Manning worked for downstairs, hoping to talk with him about the day Angela died, but they told me he'd quit, had never really been suited to the hard-nosed job, that he'd found a new job. They didn't know where. They couldn't provide a follow-up phone number for him, nor did I have his personal number. In the past I'd never had occasion to call him. I looked him up and found a cell listing, but when I punched it in the line was out of service. The people at the bonding company told me he'd moved out of his apartment. Nobody seemed to know where he was. Angela's death had hit him harder than I'd thought.

The largest files on Angela's hard drive were a bundle of e-mails, both to and from. As far as I could tell, she wrote and/or received upwards of eighty to a hundred personal e-mails a day. Most were names I did not recognize, but then, Kathy and I had not spent a whole lot of time with Angela. An occasional dinner together. A ball game when we had an extra ticket; Angela had been an avid Mariner's fan. A chat on the phone. More often than not, she would drop into the office unexpectedly before vanishing for weeks at a time.

Among other places, Angela had lived and worked in Manhattan, Washington, D.C., and Atlanta. She received regular e-mails from a guy who called himself "Shaolin Temple Guard." I couldn't tell where he was writing from and e-mailed Brad Munch to see if he could. Munch told me the "Shaolin Temple Guard" was in China. Maybe she *had* learned her martial arts in Asia.

As one would have guessed, most of her friends were single women, and most were in other parts of the country, namely the three aforementioned metro areas. I assumed they were people she'd worked with. Angela had a Facebook page with a list of friends extending into the hundreds. I began reading her old posts.

What I learned was that Angela had taught school in Atlanta until she was terminated following a controversial Columbus Day speech she gave to her class. She had worked there close to two years. It was clear from the e-mails she was still smarting from the episode, and still had a dozen friends in the school district. She'd lost a job working for a large publisher in New York City, but the particulars weren't readily apparent. She might have quit, but it sounded like people were feeling sorry for her, asking how she was doing with a little too much concern for me to believe her leave-taking had been voluntary. In Washington, D.C., she worked in an insurance company and as a substitute teacher. She lived in each of those three areas between two and three years.

I e-mailed everyone in Angela's address book with a simple statement that Angela had died unexpectedly, that I was a private investigator hired to investigate the death, that I was seeking background information on Angela for the family, and that if anyone contacted me I would fill them in on the particulars. I did call her death a suicide. I left my phone number and encouraged responses. Within five minutes the calls started rolling in, and before I knew it I had fifty return numbers stacked up. I knew it was unlikely fifty people would respond to an e-mail about *my* death. The numbers made me realize how many lives Angela had touched.

My first conversation was with two former co-workers from Atlanta who got my message at work and called together on a speaker phone, both devastated at the news of Angela's death, both teachers in the elementary school Angela was fired from. "She was so talented." "Everybody here loved her." "She was like a godmother to my children." "She used to buy shoes for the homeless kids in her class."

"There were homeless children in her class?" I asked.

"Three. I've got two in my class this year."

Back when I was in school I didn't know any kids who were homeless, but then the world had revolved a few times since then.

They didn't know of any current boyfriends, said she hadn't been depressed or on medication when they worked with her, and remained astonished and admiring that she'd had the nerve to tell her students the unvarnished truth about Christopher Columbus, which was why she lost her job.

One of the least likely and perhaps most affecting tales came from a former co-worker in a large insurance company in Washington, D.C., Emma Jacobson. After we jettisoned the preliminaries she launched into what was almost a soliloquy.

"I remember Angela was saving money to visit a friend who was working at a church mission in Africa. Angela finally managed to get two weeks off, and after getting all her shots she flew to Uganda. In Africa she found a world she told us was an earthly version of hell. There was almost nobody left alive over fifty-five. In fact, most of the population was under seventeen. AIDS. There was little or no access to medication. There were orphanages everywhere. Angela's friend had gone over as a missionary but quickly gave that up so she could work fourteen hours a day in one of the largest orphanages. People lucky enough to be employed lived in huts or shanties on a dollar a week. She met people who had never owned a pair of shoes or worn an article of clothing that wasn't a castoff from the West.

"Angela arranged to buy sixty necklaces for a dollar each from a woman in the nearby village who'd made them. Her plan was to fly them back to the States, sell them for ten dollars apiece and mail the profits back to the village. When the woman brought the necklaces to make the deal, she was escorted by two large bodyguards to ensure she wouldn't get robbed and murdered on the way home. Sixty dollars was more than anyone in her village had ever seen at one time. There were starving children everywhere. Angela watched women walk four miles a day with forty pounds of yams on their heads trying to eke out a living at the markets. She signed up to adopt a Ugandan baby. And then found a five-year-old she fell in love with and signed up to adopt him, too. After it all fell apart she never mentioned the adoptions again."

"So she didn't adopt?"

"No. She was crushed. She made three trips to Uganda, and when she came back the third time she quit her job here in D.C. and moved to Manhattan. She had some sort of personal crisis. She wouldn't share the details, said her problems weren't of any importance. It took a long time before she contacted any of us. It's only been the past few months actually. But she was so sweet. She inspired a group of us here in the office. We've adopted a village in Uganda. Four of us have been over there so far. Angela changed our lives."

14

ANGELA had brooked multiple disappointments in her life. She washed out of law school, failed to complete training to become a police officer for the city of Seattle, and was cast out of teaching for telling the truth. She freewheeled through a short career on the bottom rungs of publishing and opted out of an even shorter career in the insurance industry. In her personal life she'd run through one aborted relationship after another, dating men she knew she would never want to share a life with while yearning for men she could never have.

Even with her mountain climbing and other attempts at greatness, each effort ended in some sort of bleak failure or heartbreak. Her childhood wasn't as easy to read, but it couldn't have been normal growing up in Monica Pennington's shadow.

As I took the phone calls and chatted with Angela's former friends and co-workers, her life and travels began to fall into a series of patterns. She would move to a new location, make friends, get a job, begin to climb the pyramid of success, then something devastating would occur, an event she would inevitably keep to herself. Leaving law school in Seattle was done clandestinely for reasons that were never revealed. While she was living in D.C. a catastrophe occurred during her travels in Africa, yet the details remained shrouded in mystery.

In Atlanta she managed to top the newscasts for a day or two when she got fired from the local school district for explaining to her fifth graders how Columbus and his cronies were rapists and slavers, detailing how they'd committed genocide on the Taino Indians and exported thousands of girls to Europe as sex slaves. Despite her hasty and sometimes secretive exit from each of these places, she was regarded fondly by everyone I spoke to. "Just a sweet, sweet girl," said her former principal, who remained in contact with her even after being forced by the school board to terminate her contract.

Angela was always an enigma to me, and it was comforting to know she'd been an enigma to others as well. Throughout her life she remained tight-lipped about even the most minute and inconsequential personal details.

One of my contacts in D.C. said, "She was a wonderful person. She lit up a room when she walked in. Then one day she started acting strangely. When we asked what was going on she told us she was working out some problems and had gone three days without sleep. Then, all of a sudden she was gone. She didn't even take her things. Later, she wrote and asked to have them shipped to New York, where she'd been in the hospital briefly but now had a new job. It was all very strange."

The story was similar in other places. When Kathy knew her in law school she was earning straight A's. Then, unaccountably, she left town in the middle of a semester without telling anybody where she was headed. Disappeared. Fourteen months later Kathy received a Christmas card from her with a return address in Atlanta. The one time Kathy asked about it, Angela gave one of her Mona Lisa smiles but no pertinent details.

When I began poring through her computer files, two things became readily apparent. The first: if she was investigating Clark Lloyd Self, she'd left no traces behind, at least none I could find. I expected to run across photos or videos of him sneaking around with illicit lovers, but didn't find any. Second: although it had been almost twelve years since she'd flunked out during her training for the SPD, Angela continued to maintain a voluminous file in which she tracked and recorded her choleric correspondence with the city. The most recent letters from the city attorneys were just four months old. At one point the city offered forty thousand dollars if she would just go away, but she claimed she still wanted the job; she still wanted to be a police officer.

She washed out of the state police academy at a point in the physical training which required the applicant to do as many pushups as possible, no time limit. She wasn't able to manage one. It seemed strange, given all her mountain climbing prowess, but she apparently didn't have a lot of upper-body strength, and it had posed an insurmountable problem. The failure stuck in her craw, prompting her to spend the next twelve years engaged in feverish correspondence with city attorneys. I'd been a Seattle police officer, and as far as I was concerned, if she didn't have the strength to do one pushup she had no business being an officer. I never said that to her, but a police officer's job was physically demanding and commissioning officers who could not handle the rigors was only asking for trouble.

Strangely, nobody I spoke to on the phone knew anything about a ninety-four-year-old husband.

Listening to her former friends and co-workers, I felt saddened for not having been a better friend. Our relationship had degenerated into a pattern in which she wore me down with endless questions on any topic that came to mind, and I, feeling battered by the unrelenting and often inane inquiries, eventually fell back on sarcasm as a defense. Even when I was being sincere, she never quite understood my answers to her questions and would frequently misquote me, usually in a manner that made me look like a dope. It didn't matter that I'd patiently and laboriously explained it only minutes earlier. It was almost as if there were a flaw in her central processing unit. Her constant misunderstandings, leaping to conclusions, and misquoting had been the toxin infusing our relationship. It got to the point that when I saw her coming I ducked and dodged and even dove into closets.

According to her friends, the constants in Angela's life were her travels, her slavish secrecy, her empathy for the downtrodden, her lovableness (the one quality I had never connected with), and her desire for constant change. Despite being determined to save the world, she managed, her friends told me, to squander vast amounts of money while living in Manhattan. Whether this money was blown on trifles or handed out to charity I could not tell, but it showed up as massive cash withdrawals from her savings accounts. Other than her climbing gear, her laptop computer, and her ancient Volkswagen, she had absolutely nothing left that I could find to show for her expenditures.

While poring over her computer files, I'd bypassed a file folder labeled "Poetry" several times. I finally opened it and found it was exactly what I'd been afraid of, her own slavishly amateurish poetry. Most of the poems were centered on a man named Rafael Gutierrez. I went back to the e-mails to see what contact she'd had with him, if any, and realized their correspondence came to an abrupt halt three months earlier.

I found out why on the Net. Three months ago on his way home from work, Gutierrez sustained a flat tire on one of the area's busiest freeways, I-405, which ran north and south on the east side of Lake Washington. Gutierrez stopped to change his flat in the dark. At some point a passing motorist clipped him and threw him into the slow lane, where a second motorist struck him. In all, he was hit by six cars. Some of the drivers later claimed they thought the body was a bundle of clothing in the roadway, others that they didn't see him. The State Patrol chalked his death up as a tragic accident. No one was charged with a crime, although the identity of the initial driver who hit him and fled the scene was still under investigation. According to newspaper reports Gutierrez had worked for Clark L Self Enterprises at the main office in Bellevue. There were any number of ways in which Angela might have known him.

The e-mails between Angela and Gutierrez were impersonal and primarily concerned with setting up meetings. None of the e-mails hinted at a personal relationship, although the poems, all written after Gutierrez's death, were romantic, histrionic, and often maudlin. It made me wonder if she'd had a secret infatuation with him or possibly a real romance. If so, his death might have contributed to her suicide. But Gutierrez didn't fit the profile of one of Angela's boyfriends, some of whom I had met over the years. I'd judged them all to be likeable enough, but they were also universally aimless, ineffectual, and withdrawn. Most looked like they were waiting to get sucked into a cult. Judging from the newspaper photo and articles, Rafael Gutierrez was too handsome, too successful, and too self-assured to have a romantic interest in Angela. But then, I'd misjudged Angela in just about everything else; why not this?

On the other hand, Angela had been just dopey enough to kill herself over a man she'd had an imaginary romance with.

To my great surprise, when I tapped into some online criminal databases, I found several misdemeanors and a felony attributed to Angela. I wasn't sure she'd spent any time in jail, other than the obligatory day or two before bail could be arranged or before a judge let her loose on her own recognizance. I wondered if Kathy knew this and hadn't told me in the same way I hadn't told her about Angela's kiss. I wondered how many people were keeping secrets on Angela's behalf.

In Manhattan, she'd been charged with trespassing and disturbing the peace, no further details available. At Jimmy Carter's farm in Georgia she was arrested for criminal trespass. In D.C. she was arrested for arson after setting fire to papers in the bathroom sink in her hotel room, but was released with the proviso she move out of D.C. and not return for ten years. It was the sort of illegal dictate cops used on kids or whack jobs. Angela's arrest record explained why she'd suddenly left D.C. but it didn't explain what she'd been up to.

I phoned Carole Cooper. "Thomas. I had a feeling I was going to hear from you again. I just got a lecture about cooperating with Self, which means cooperating with you. It must be nice to be tapped into all that power."

"I'm just a hired hand. I do have a couple of questions, though."

"Fire away."

"Three months ago a man named Rafael Gutierrez got hit by a car on 405 somewhere south of Bellevue. I'd like to talk to whoever worked on that."

"What's this got to do with Angela Bassman?"

"She had some sort of relationship with Gutierrez."

"It would be either the State Patrol or Bellevue. Probably the State Patrol."

"Could you hook me up?"

"You can't call the State Patrol yourself?"

"I was hoping to use the leverage from your office."

"I'll get back to you on it. Anything else?"

"I'm guessing you guys went up on the roof at Angela Bassman's place?"

"We didn't find anything that mattered."

"What about her apartment?"

"It was just an apartment. Her sister found the note the next day. It was e-mailed the same hour she jumped. The note and the absence of other witnesses as well as the absence of secondary wounds clinched it for us. That and her history. She had a history of suicide threats and attempts that went way back."

"When you were in her apartment did you see a laptop computer?"

"There was a laptop, but it was disassembled."

"If it was disassembled, how did she send the e-mail?"

"We figured she sent the note and then destroyed the laptop to prevent anyone from accessing her personal files after her death. The hard drive was there, but it was destroyed."

"How about memory sticks or disks or . . . ?"

"Nothing. We looked."

"So where did all that stuff go? Were there any strangers in the building around the time she went off the roof?"

"Just you and Crane."

"I wouldn't think jumpers usually invite people over to watch."

"Not unless they're former lovers and they're trying to teach them a lesson or send them on a guilt trip. Were either of you former lovers?"

"Not me. Crane only knew her for two weeks and told me he never dated her. But the thing is, every suicide I've had anything to do with was solitary in nature."

"It takes all kinds. She wrote a suicide note. She threw herself off. You said yourself you looked up and didn't see anyone else. What are the odds of somebody pushing her off and not taking a peek afterwards to see how it went?"

"I had that same thought. It is possible someone looked over the edge and I missed them. I was a little preoccupied right after she did it."

"You said it yourself. After *she* did it. She wrote the note and trashed the computer. I don't see anything that doesn't fit with suicide."

"One other thing. She had a cell phone. Do you know where it went?"

"We've turned it over to her attorney."

"Did you check for recent calls?"

"We got everything we needed off her phone records. That last day she called you, Crane, and REI. No one else."

"REI, the outdoor store?"

"She ordered a pair of hiking shorts."

"Doesn't it seem strange she'd order something and then kill herself."

"A little, but everything else adds up to suicide. Her sister said she'd been in an emotional whirlpool for weeks. Said she had a history of depression. Said the note sounded like her."

Carole Cooper called back a few minutes later with a number for the investigating detective from the State Patrol. When I reached him, he was brusque and maintained an official tone. After reviewing the basic facts of the Gutierrez traffic fatality, he announced, "A black Tahoe was the first vehicle to strike him. Our eyewitness says the Tahoe veered out of the lane and across the fog line, clipped him, slowed, then took off while the other vehicles were still striking him. We never found the driver of the Tahoe."

"No leads?"

"Not even a partial plate. No description of the occupants. Just a black Tahoe."

"Anybody get charged?"

"We ticketed four drivers for following too close."

"Was Gutierrez alone when it happened?"

"As far as we know."

15

ON my way back into the building from a late lunch, I got bushwhacked by Susan Djokovic, an attorney who worked for a law firm on the second floor of our building. Kathy had dealings with her from time to time, but I knew her only to say hello to in the elevator. She was short and stout and liked to stand close and look up into my face with her fists on her hips. She had blowzy blond hair with curls in unexpected places and a thingamajig on her chin that might have been a wart and which I tried not to look at. She was middle-aged and, in the same mold as some female politicians, wore pantsuits, the legs of which looked like smokestacks.

"Thomas. I was just going to come up and see you." She handed me a cell phone. "It belonged to Angela Bassman. I did her will a few months back. The police gave me her other effects, if you want to take them to her sister. I understand you're working for her sister."

"I am. What other effects?"

"A bracelet. A set of earrings she was wearing when she died. Some clothing."

"The phone work?" I asked, as I tried to figure out how to turn it on.

"I have no idea."

"Looks like the battery is dead."

"Her sister told me you were tidying things up for her."

"I'm looking into her death. She seem frightened or depressed when she was doing the will?"

"Not at all. She was a sweet person. She spoke very highly of you and Kathy. Especially you."

"Kathy was closer to her than I was."

"You wouldn't have thought so by the way she talked. I got the feeling she needed friends."

"I only wish I'd done a better job of it."

"You need to come into the office to sign a receipt for the phone and the clothing. Also, Angela was getting dunned by a place called McKay's. Do you know anything about that?"

"I don't. But I saw the bills."

"Apparently, it's an assisted living and dementia care center, mostly for Alzheimer's patients. They claim Angela owes tens of thousands of dollars."

"Tell you what. Give me the information and I'll drop by there this afternoon."

"I would appreciate it."

When I got to the office, Kathy was in the other room talking on the phone. I put the plastic bag with Angela's clothing in the bottom drawer of my desk and searched the office for a charger with a connection that fit Angela's phone.

I called Monica Pennington and caught her in the middle of a gym workout, music in the background, her breathing hurried and shallow. "Black? You find anything yet?"

"It's too early. I do have a couple of questions. Did you know someone named Rafael Gutierrez?"

"Never heard of him."

"Three months ago he was killed in an auto accident. He worked for your husband. Ring any bells?"

"It doesn't surprise me Angela was friends with one of my husband's employees. Angela was friends with everyone she met."

"One more question."

"What is it?"

While we were speaking, Kathy came into the office, strode across the small space and sat on the edge of the desk. I flipped the phone to speaker and continued. "Do you know any reason an assisted living institution would be dunning your sister?"

"I have absolutely no idea what you're talking about. By the way. Black?"

"Yes?"

Kathy was running her fingers through my hair. I was tilted back in my chair lapping it up like a dog with his head out the window of a moving car. "I want to apologize for what happened Saturday night. I'd had a lot to drink and my doctor had just put me on Valium."

"No problem."

"Thank you for not taking advantage of the situation."

When she didn't say anything else, I looked at Kathy and repeated, "No problem."

"To tell the truth, I probably wouldn't have minded." Kathy and I looked at each other. Her look was appraising, mine that of a moron who'd just been hit in the head with a baseball. "Recreational sex is something I have used from time to time to make myself feel better. It rarely works, but that doesn't keep me from trying it on occasion. All I'm saying is, thanks for being a gentleman. I think we should keep our relationship professional from now on."

"Right."

"So," Kathy said, after I closed the connection, "you were going to throw me over for the lingerie model?"

"Are you kidding? I wouldn't throw you over for two models, with or without lingerie."

"No?"

"I wouldn't even start bargaining until I was offered three, along with an unspecified draft choice."

"Very gallant. If she'd been fifty years old and morbidly obese, would you have let her kiss you?'

"I didn't *let* her kiss me. She just did it. And if she'd been morbidly obese, I wouldn't have been able to carry her down the stairs, so my hands would not have been full. I would have had to drag her down the stairs by her feet. Her face wouldn't have been close enough to kiss me. But I carried her. She weighs a ton. My back still aches."

"This is for your back." Kathy kissed me and we lingered on it for a while, enjoying the fact that we were alone in the office.

Ten minutes later as I was leaving, I grabbed my back and said, "I think I blew out a disk carrying that whale the other night." I could hear her laughing after I closed the door; whether with me or at me, I really had no idea.

16

BECAUSE of all the cycling over the weekend, when Monday morning came I needed rest badly and didn't mind the rain. The current regional joke was that it was good of summer to be on a weekend this year.

I used a portable GPS in my Ford for directions to McKay's Nursing Home in Kent. Each year more of the rich farming land in the Kent Valley was subsumed and turned into housing projects, all of it punctuated by long, flat roads lined with incongruous strip malls. I'd recently been to Tennessee on business and found strip malls indistinguishable from the ones I'd seen in Texas and Ohio and Tacoma. And Kent. At least here in Washington we could pick out Mount Rainier to the southeast—when it wasn't obscured by clouds—and know what state we were in.

McKay's was a large, two-story complex, cedar shake siding with a stone clad foundation. It was just off a six-lane arterial and next door to an apartment complex. In fact, it could have been an apartment complex itself except for the large gold sign and the black wrought-iron fence around it. Another clue was the dearth of cars in the lot since none of the occupants could drive. I found the guest entrance on the east side and parked two spaces away from a service truck.

Conversing in Spanish, eight workers in tall rubber boots pressure washed the roof and driveway while I remained in the Ford and reread the suicide note Angela e-mailed to her sister shortly before calling Crane and me. I'd read it earlier, but it kept drawing me back.

Dear Monica,

I've been thinking about this for a while and there just doesn't seem to be any point in going on. I find myself crying at all hours of the day and night. I know in the past you've told me depression can be treated but right now trying to go on seems like the most senseless thing of all. Tell mom and dad I wish I could have been a better daughter. Tell Ollie, Mason and Logan whatever you think best. I will miss them. I love them like my own and wish them all the best in their lives, you too.

Angela

While I'd been supplied a paper copy by Monica Pennington, I'd also located a copy of the note on the hard drive Munch restored. It was in a file she'd been saving titled "the end." The file had been sitting on her computer for two years. It seemed odd she would use a pre-written suicide note, but it was also odd anybody would *preserve* an unused suicide note. It was pure Angela.

Inside, McKay's had the look of a nicely appointed retirement home, fresh flowers, clean furniture, a gas fireplace with a tall mantel. The house dog, a grizzled lab, limped over and sniffed me, then hobbled back to her spot by the unlit fireplace. When the woman behind the counter looked up from her crossword puzzle and asked if she could help, I said, "I'm here about a bill past due. I'm representing Angela Bassman."

She went through the security doors into the facility and came back moments later with an attractive-looking blonde I guessed to be in her late fifties, a woman who looked and moved as if she were much younger. She had blue eyes and Nordic features and told me her name was Ms. Engebretson. She wore an aquamarine dress. She was pleasant and eager, probably because she assumed I was there to give her money. Angela's unpaid bills had mushroomed until she owed over ten grand.

When we got settled in her office Engebretson sat on one side of the desk while I took one of the green-backed leather chairs opposite. Before we could get started, a gray-haired woman who was obviously quite disoriented came to the door behind me and said, "You can't keep me here. I don't want to be here. I want my attorney. You can't keep me here."

Engebretson gave me the briefest of looks, then spoke kindly. "Ann? Go see Judy down the hall. Judy will help you."

"Judy?"

"Just down the hall."

The elderly woman tottered off, muttering to herself. "It's not fair. It's not fair. I have to tend my garden."

"New residents tend to be upset when they first arrive. Ann will settle in just fine," Engebretson said. "How may I help you?"

"My name is Thomas Black. I'm a private investigator working for the family of Angela Bassman. You may have known her as Angela Pennington. The family attorney tells me she owes a bill here."

"I was sorry to hear about Angela," Engebretson said, as if Angela had died ten years ago instead of last week. She reached across her tidy desk and opened a file. "Here I have a copy of her arrears."

It was an invoice for a patient named Hoshi Smith. The outstanding bill was for two months' lodging and care. "We would really like to get this settled. We love having Hoshi here. Everybody adores her. Would you like to meet Hoshi?"

"I would." Outside Engebretson's office was a large indoor courtyard with a fountain, park benches, an old-fashioned ice-cream parlor, and a gold-colored 1948 Dodge coupe, all of it designed to impress visitors, for the patients ignored it the way a dog ignored a jet overhead. Engebretson walked me to an elevator opposite the '48 Dodge. She was almost as tall as I was and moved gracefully, confident in her own skin.

"The way I understand it, Hoshi and Angela were childhood friends. I don't know all the details, but when they were schoolmates Hoshi nearly drowned and ended up with permanent brain damage. When her family couldn't care for her any longer, Angela stepped up to the plate. They're almost like sisters. Hoshi's going to miss her terribly. Does anybody know why Angela did it?"

"I can't answer that. Hoshi have any family left?"

"Her mother comes in about once a month. It's a long bus ride."

The carpeted halls were spotty with wandering figures, most everyone moving in slow motion. One woman was in an enclosed walker constructed of PVC tubing, her face molded into a perpetual silent scream. A couple of the patients looked me over eagerly as if I were someone they'd forgotten who was now coming to visit them.

Hoshi was alone in a small sitting room at the end of a long corridor. It was homey with overstuffed sofas and chairs, a fireplace, and a wealth of nostalgic decorative items. I couldn't help wondering how they managed to keep it all so clean and orderly, given the demented state of the residents.

Hoshi was a Japanese woman whose age was impossible to determine. She was quietly staring into space when we found her. I could see she was wearing an adult diaper under her sweat pants.

Angela once told Kathy and me a story that involved a near drowning, but as was the case with so many of her stories, it seemed too fantastical to be true, and to my shame I hadn't believed her. She'd talked of a sleep-over birthday party when her family had lived near Lake Samish south of Bellingham. It had been close to dusk and a flock of girls had walked down to the lake and out onto a long dock. They started to horse around, pretending to try to push each other into the water, even though they were all dressed in jeans and sweatshirts. One of the girls protested that she couldn't swim, which only escalated the horseplay. Angela and her sister, Monica, assuming the girl was joking or trying to be the center of attention, picked her up by her arms and legs and heaved her into the lake. They all laughed at her screams as she slapped at the surface. Some of them were still laughing when she went under.

A few minutes later a passing jogger heard the girls' panicked yelps and rescued the half-dead girl from nine feet of murky water. Fire department crews performed CPR on her and eventually restored her breathing, but they couldn't reverse the massive brain damage that had already taken place. The incident turned her into a lifelong moron.

Angela claimed it was one of the pivotal points in her life, changing her from a child to an adult, and bestowing on her an almost intolerable burden of guilt to lug around for the rest of her days. She told us the story the night she kissed me, but she told us a lot of patently screwy stuff that night.

Hoshi had blunt-cut bangs and a pudgy figure borne of institutional food and lack of exercise. She shook hands with me after Engebretson introduced us. "How do you do? How do you do?" she said.

We all stared at each other for an uncomfortable moment before Hoshi launched into a monologue of random words and gibberish, staring at me as if she were making perfect sense.

Hoshi was Angela's age, late thirties. She'd been institutionalized since age thirteen, her last twenty-odd years spent sponging up boredom, enduring lack of privacy, and wasting hours endlessly pacing the same corridors, wasting even more long hours trying to figure out where her room was, or sitting in her soiled diaper, or waiting for her next meal.

Before we could get organized as a trio, Hoshi forgot us and drifted down the hallway on her own to join the other zombies stalking the corridors.

"Angela would come at least once a week, sometimes twice," said Engebretson. "She used to take Hoshi on trips to the park or to Mariners games. Would you like to see Hoshi's room?"

I didn't need to see the room, but Engebretson was already opening the door, as if to show me what I would be paying for when I settled Angela's account.

It was a small room with an adjoining bathroom, two beds and night stands, two chairs, a closet with doors marked *Hoshi* and *Helen*. Aside from a large navy-blue trunk next to Hoshi's bed, there were pitifully few personal possessions belonging to either of the women who lived here.

Engebretson said, "Angela loved Hoshi so much. They would play school together for hours. Afterwards they would put everything back in the trunk until Angela's next visit."

I was at the window looking out at a mundane view of the parking lot. Without turning around, I said, "How long has Angela been paying the bills here?"

"Since before I got here. And I'm going on seven years."

"Five thousand dollars a month?"

"It's actually a little more than that now. The way I understand it, the father died several years back and the family ran out of money."

"So Angela took over?"

"All I know is she's been paying since before I got here."

No wonder Angela never had any money. Whatever she wasn't sending to orphans in Africa she was pumping into this place. At this rate, the remaining annuity she'd been drawing on would run out in a month. I wondered what she'd been planning to do after it ran dry. Commit suicide? Angela hadn't been working a regular job the past few months. A lot of people were out of work these days; she wouldn't be the first jobless person to off herself. She told me once about the 200,000 small farmers in India who committed suicide over the past few years, most often by drinking insecticide produced by the very companies that had driven them into bankruptcy. International chemical companies had patented the seed crops the farmers had relied on for generations, making it illegal to save seed from one year to the next and forcing them to buy patented, genetically modified seed each year at a prohibitive cost.

"Hoshi has a brother who visits occasionally. He has an anger management problem and my nursing supervisor had to ask him to leave the building several times."

Sitting in my car in the parking lot, I opened my laptop and searched newspaper archives on the Internet for any trace of the accident—or crime—that had crippled Hoshi Smith's mental capacity. I found an item in the *Bellingham Herald* from more than twenty years before:

Drowning Victim Revived

Hoshi Smith, 13, suffered a near-fatal swimming accident yesterday at Lake Samish near Bellingham when her companions noticed she failed to surface while swimming in the lake. A passing college student, Brent Worthyington, sized up the situation and plunged into the water, where he brought Smith to the surface and performed CPR until medical crews could take over. Smith was taken to St. Joseph Hospital in Bellingham, where she remains in critical but stable condition.

This version of the story had Hoshi swimming in the lake of her own volition. I wondered whether Hoshi's parents had any notion of how their non-swimming daughter had ended up in nine feet of murky lake water in her sweatshirt and jeans. Did they know Monica and Angela threw her in? I had to imagine Angela's version of the story was the true one and all the girls in attendance knew how it happened. Did they make a pact of silence? I wondered if they felt the same guilt Angela obviously felt?

17

AT the entrance to Costco in Issaquah a woman checking ID cards told me I could find Tiffany Gutierrez at one of the checkout counters. The greeter appeared to be in her late seventies and I wondered how demanding it was to be on her feet all day.

For a moment I found myself hypnotized by the thirty or so massive television screens just inside the Costco entrance, all playing the same soccer match, the colors magnificent. As I made my way past the cameras and computers, jewelry and watches, seasonal bedding plants and trees, I had an insane urge to buy as much as I could. Packed floor-to-ceiling with all manner of merchandise, the inner aisles of the warehouse beckoned me, though I managed to resist.

I found Tiffany Gutierrez, whom I'd called earlier, working register number seven with two other people. I waited and then, between customers, showed her my ID. She excused herself, and one of the other clerks took over the boxing and bagging she'd been doing. Several customers looked at me apprehensively as if I were a cop. I'd gotten that look before, and it recalled the years when I actually had been a Seattle police officer.

Gutierrez had delayed her lunch break for me and now took me outside to the food court, where there were four or five windows with hot food and cold drinks and about twenty-five customers waiting in line or eating at plastic picnic tables.

"We were getting divorced when he was run over and killed on 405," Tiffany announced. "I was angry with him. He gets a plush apartment. He keeps the same friends. Meanwhile, I'm forced to move out of the house I've been restoring for five years, and now I'm working here while my kids are in daycare. We're living in a cramped little apartment with neighbors who play music all night and smoke cigars we can smell through the walls. My car's been broken into twice. People peep in my windows. My life has been turned upside down. We're in hock up to our eyebrows. When it first started, I blamed Rafael, but it wasn't his fault. His problem was he'd been out of work so long he was beginning to lose faith in himself. And then he got killed."

She had a boy and a girl, seven and nine. She showed me their pictures and we talked about the negative effects of divorce on children. She blamed all their troubles on her husband losing his job at CLS Enterprises months before the accident that killed him. She told me he'd been on his way home from a temporary job when he got run down.

She was a big-boned woman in bullet-colored capri pants and a cadmium yellow top that showed off enough cleavage I had to watch where my eyes drifted. When we met I saw her sizing me up and quickly writing me off. I had an athletic look that put some women off. Or maybe it was the old jeans and the well-worn running shoes. Whatever, I was not for her. Not that she was my type either. They say we make up our minds about people in less than two seconds.

I was pretty sure her breasts had been augmented. She wore open-toed sandals and her toenails were the same brick red as her fingernails. There was a pendant that bobbed in the deep cleft between her breasts when she moved, a gewgaw clearly placed to attract the eye. As we talked, Tiffany Gutierrez ate from a small container of yogurt and sipped from a bottle of water she'd brought with her.

I said, "As I told you on the phone, I'm working for the estate of Angela Bassman. I've found correspondence between your ex-husband and Bassman that goes back months. I'm wondering if you knew her." I showed her a photograph of Angela I was keeping on my cell phone.

"I know Rafael was fooling around after we separated, but not with this woman."

"Are you sure?"

"Rafael liked women who could turn other men's heads. This woman wouldn't have cut the mustard. Don't you think it's weird how you can love someone so much and then not too long later, you think they're trash?"

"I've seen it happen enough times."

"Your turn will come."

I didn't think so but I wasn't going to argue the point. "What do you think the two of them were doing together?"

"Listen, Black, we were married eleven years. When we separated eight months ago, I still saw him twice a week to exchange the kids. I met most of his women. The ones I didn't see in person, my kids told me about. Now that you bring it up, they did mention someone. Some sort of business associate."

"What kind of business?"

"I have no idea."

"How did he lose his job with Self?"

"They accused him of talking out of turn to clients. Rafael said it was trumped up."

"What does 'talking out of turn to clients' mean?"

"I'm not sure I ever knew. I will say this: After Rafael died, even though he wasn't working for him anymore, Self put ten grand into a fund for each of the children for college. You can't say he's not generous. Couple of times a year he would throw a big party for his employees. Always some five-star restaurant. I saw the bill once. We could have bought a new car for that money."

Having finished her yogurt, Tiffany Gutierrez began scraping the bottom of the container with the plastic spoon she'd been using. "Tiffany, what did your husband do for CLS?"

"He was a numbers cruncher. And then, unaccountably, somebody accused him of malfeasance and he was out the door. Those two jackasses walked him out. You know. Lennie and George. Like in that Steinbeck movie. Except in this case, the big guy is the smart one and the little guy is the idiot. I call them Lenny and Squiggy."

"Bonds and Gunderson?"

"That's them."

"The papers said he died on his way home from working late at CLS Enterprises."

"The papers got his age wrong, too. He'd been gone from CLS for months. He was working as a temp in Bellevue. He'd only been there a week. Federal East Bank was going under, and they hired a team of accountants to help straighten everything out."

"Rafael never had anything to do with the investing part of the business at CLS?"

"Nobody from the west coast office did. All he did was talk to clients and take in money."

"What do you know about Bonds and Gunderson?"

"Not much. The little one, Bonds, hit on me at a party once. He got rude when I asked him to stop. When Rafael came over, he just disappeared."

"Your husband have any close friends at CLS?"

"There was a man named Federer, but he got canned before my husband."

"Henrik?"

"That's him."

The man I met at Angela's funeral. "You know why Federer got fired?"

"I think it was the same as Rafael. They called it disclosing proprietary secrets. Everything was hush-hush at CLS. They make all their money with secret computer algorithmic trading schemes. I'm not even supposed to know about it. Self likes to make sure none of his competitors know his business. He was a good boss, but you didn't talk about him and you didn't cross him."

"Rafael didn't think his termination was fair?"

"It wasn't!"

"Did Rafael have any suspicions about the company?"

"How do you mean?"

"That there might be something illegitimate going on?"

"Not that he ever told me. Oh, we speculated from time to time on how uncanny it was that Self could win even in down markets, but everybody speculated about that. It didn't mean anything."

"I suppose not."

"It was sad the way he died. Rafael always leased the best cars he could find. He didn't like dealing with repairs and he was always afraid of a breakdown on the freeway. His tires were new and the dealer did all the maintenance ahead of schedule. And then he goes and gets a flat and gets killed trying to change it in the dark."

"Pick up a chunk of metal at highway speeds and any tire will go."

"That's what the State Patrol told us. But it's still ironic that he would be so meticulous and then die changing a flat on the freeway."

"You think of anything else, here's my card."

In the parking lot I made some call-backs to the messages that were piling up on my cell phone service. More people expressed shock at the way Angela had died. More people told me what a splendid person she'd been. One woman told me she developed a social consciousness working around Angela. "I truly believe I'm a better person for having known her," said the caller.

"Maybe we all are," I replied, not quite feeling it. It didn't matter how many people praised Angela, or how badly I felt about the way I'd treated her, I was still having a hard time getting behind the feelings of approbation all these people were trying to shove down my throat. They loved her; always had. They all assumed I felt the same. But my feelings were conflicted, the primary overall emotion that of guilt.

18

ON Tuesday mornings our cycling club would gather at six-thirty in the parking lot at the east end of the Mercer Island floating bridge and do laps around the island counterclockwise, each lap eleven miles. Anybody who wanted to ride had best be warmed up and ready because nobody was going to wait, and each lap was done at terror pace, every rider taking a hard turn of maybe thirty or forty seconds at the front and then peeling off to find shelter at the end of the line, where it was fifteen to twenty percent easier, especially if there were a lot of riders. Usually there were around twenty of us. Anyone who got dropped, and a lot of people did, including me, could catch up before. the next lap started when we rode more easily across the north end of the island back to the start.

Despite some sporadic drizzle, as I rode to Mercer Island on my carbon fiber 20-speed Eddy Merckx road bike and met up with eighteen of my fellow club members, the roads were mostly dry under a low, gray cloud cover.

Traffic on the island was ninety percent local and usually courteous, commuters headed to work, parents driving their kids to school. Most of the island residents were thoroughly acclimated to hoards of cyclists. The banked S-curves on the east side of the island were famous in the cycling community in that a group of good cyclists could keep up with and even pass many cars.

We'd finished the first lap and lost about half our group. I was hanging on by my fingernails and timing it so I did not take a hard pull right before a hill. It helped to know the island roads. We all wore helmets and identical orange and black club jerseys with long sleeves to ward off the chill.

As we passed the parking area and began our second lap, I noticed a vehicle following us. Most people heading to work were driving the other direction, so it was rare to get tailed as we headed south on West Mercer Way.

The black SUV followed us for about a half mile, and then when some of the hotshots turned up the speed and broke the group apart the SUV began to drop back. Along with several other riders who weren't fit enough to keep up with the fastest racers in our club, I dropped off and watched as the abbreviated pace line powered away without us. We quickly hooked up so there were three of us working together in a slightly slower chasing pace line. The SUV lagged behind and I ceased paying it any attention.

Just before we headed into the tightest of the S-curves on our second lap, my front tire hit a small rock on the road and I suffered a pinch flat, or thought I did. I was wearing a heart monitor and my heart rate had been in the one-seventies for a while, which always made me feel like I was dying. Sometimes you got riding so hard you subconsciously wished for something to go wrong with your bike so you could slow down and accept a much needed rest. This must have been one of those times, because after I pulled into a random driveway I realized I didn't have a flat at all. Both tires still held a hundred ten pounds of pressure. I was standing in the driveway when the SUV that had been following us cruised past. For an instant I glimpsed the driver through the heavily tinted windows and thought I recognized him. But then I thought, no, not possible.

Now that I'd had a few moments to catch my breath, I was ready to ride again. I figured if I worked it right and the two teammates I'd been riding with eased off just a smidgeon, I might catch them.

I caught the SUV first, huge and lumbering as it tried to keep up with the two cyclists in the S-curves. Then the road turned back on itself until I was directly across from the cyclists. The two bikers were gaining on other riders dropped from the original group, overtaking them one by one. I turned up the speed, forgetting the pain in my legs amid the exhilaration of having someone to reel in. I was beginning to gain incrementally on all three, the two riders, as well as the SUV, a black Tahoe. I continued to work my way closer until I began to feel the draft effect from the vehicle. When I got two car lengths back I felt the full effect of the suction of his draft, my workload dropping precipitously.

And then the S-curves began to straighten out and we all sped up. There was a telephone pole near the entrance to the freeway, and it was our custom to sprint to that telephone pole, using it as an imaginary finish line at the conclusion of the hard portion of the ride. I thought it would be fun if I managed to catch the two riders I'd been with and pip them at the line, a shallow victory, since I'd been drafting the SUV and doing less work than them. Still, it would be fun. I followed the speeding Tahoe as it began to overtake the riders, who were now sprinting. According to my bike computer we were doing thirty-five miles an hour. My legs were on fire.

The Tahoe made a sudden and what appeared to be deliberate movement to the right, the passenger-side wheels running off the road and churning up bits of gravel, spitting them at me like machine-gun bullets. He was going to hit the riders in front of me. He was going to run them down. I couldn't believe my eyes.

It sounded like tree branches snapping. Before I knew it, the cyclist directly in front of me was under the Tahoe, tumbling, and getting spit out in front of me along with the gravel and dirt and a mass of broken bike parts, his tangled limbs so loose and raggedy they might have been on a dummy. The whole scene reminded me of one of those old videos of Evel Knievel biting the dust at the tail end of a high-speed miscalculation. It even seemed to be playing in slow motion.

Last week I watched a woman leap to her death, and now this.

As I skidded to a stop in front of the downed rider, I kept my eyes on the Tahoe. I thought it was going to run over the second rider, too, but the driver pulled wide and sped away. It was inconceivable that he hadn't heard the clatter of the bike and rider as they passed beneath his undercarriage. It was inconceivable that he hadn't stopped.

Incredibly, the crumpled, rag-doll of a man in front of me was still alive. He was breathing. I couldn't tell if the Tahoe's wheels had actually run over him, but I had the feeling at least the rear wheel had. The only reason he was still alive was the height of the vehicle. He'd rolled under most of it and to my relief was in one piece.

It seemed as if I was alone with the downed rider for a long while, but it was only seconds. He was normally a much stronger rider than I, but this year he hadn't had as much time to train. In a normal year he would have been a mile ahead with the first group, not back here with me and the other chasers. A nearby homeowner heard the accident and ran outside, calling 911 on his cell phone. The other rider came back to us wiping the tears from his eyes with the sleeve of his bright blue jersey.

I didn't move the injured man. Didn't touch him, other than to disentangle some of the fractured bike and twisted brake cables from his limbs. We were riding carbon fiber frames, and when carbon broke it tended to shatter, so his bike was in shards, most of it scattered along the road. Using my cell phone, I took photos that would become evidence.

The downed rider was alive. His face was bruised and bleeding, and his head was swollen. One of his legs was fractured in multiple places. I couldn't even look at it. One arm was underneath him at an odd angle, and the opposite hand was broken, still in the fingerless cycling glove.

The emergency medical personnel showed up, then the Mercer Island Police, some other witnesses who'd stopped, nearby homeowners, and at the end of a long line of cars delayed by the accident, a school bus full of gawking kids. The uninjured rider's name was Bill. I knew him only peripherally. He worked in computers. The rider who'd been run over was named Ron Prisham and was in his late twenties. He had a wife and two kids. They put splints on one leg and one arm after they placed him on a backboard, head taped down. They put a line into his arm, and before we knew it he was trundled into the back of a Medic wagon. A few minutes later they took off, siren keening. It was my second experience with a Medic unit in a week.

"Where are they taking him?" Bill asked no one in particular.

"Harborview," I said. "It's the only level-one trauma center in the Northwest. They all go to Harborview."

"I've heard bad things about that place."

"I don't know how their food is, but if you've got serious trauma, that's where you want to be."

We gave the officers our statements and contact information.

"You're sure this was done on purpose?" asked Zoepf, the first officer on scene. He was trim, with a military-style haircut, and you could tell he didn't think much of our cycling outfits.

"It looked deliberate," I said. "He swerved in and then swung out. Like he was doing it on purpose."

"Maybe he was changing the channel on the radio?" asked Zoepf. "Fumbling with his cell phone?"

"I'm just telling you what it looked like. I didn't see anything that looked like somebody drifting or losing control of their vehicle. It looked damned deliberate."

"And neither of you got a look at the driver?"

I'd already given him the license number, which I'd memorized. I said, "I thought I recognized the driver."

"You saw his face?"

"I saw *a* face. I think I know him. I wouldn't swear to it in court, but I think I know who it was."

"You got a name for me?"

"Goodnight Bonds."

"What?"

"His first name is Goodnight."

Zoepf gave me a skeptical look and wrote it down. "You know any reason this Bonds would want to harm your friend?"

"No."

He asked Bill to pen a statement, which he did, sitting in the back of the patrol car, then Zoepf drove me to the station, my bike in his trunk with the front wheel removed to make it fit. At the station, he had me write my own statement, including my thoughts on the identity of the driver. He read my paragraphs and then had me sign the page. He said, "The plates belong to a 2010 Tahoe that was reported stolen here on the island about an hour ago. Apparently somebody took it last night. We're going to get a team on it, look for fingerprints, witnesses."

"You have a lot of car thefts on the island?"

"A few last year but nothing lately. This driver? You said he was wearing a baseball cap and a hoodie, so most of his head was covered?"

"Most of it."

"Your friend, this Bonds character, doesn't wear glasses or have any distinguishing facial hair?"

"He's not my friend. No facial hair. I've never seen him in glasses."

"Except for today, how long since you've seen him?"

"Saturday night."

"But you really can't be sure it was him?"

"In a court of law, I would say I was seventy percent certain."

Zoepf stood in front of me holding my statement for a long minute. He was debating whether or not to tell me something else. I could smell it on him. Finally, he said, "We looked him up. He works for a man named Clark Lloyd Self."

"I told you that at the accident site."

"Yeah, well, we called anyway."

"And?"

"Bonds put us on with his attorney. The attorney was right there in the room with him."

"He was already lawyered up? Doesn't that tell you something?"

"Ever hear of Anthony Rona?"

"Who hasn't?"

Rona was a high-powered attorney who mostly handled corporate cases, but had, along with confederates who specialized in criminal law, defended some of Washington's upper crust when they were accused of criminal misconduct. I could think of only one reason Goodnight Bonds would be in the same room with him this morning. Bonds knew he was in trouble and, presumably, so did Self.

Pedaling into town across the Mercer Island floating bridge, I puzzled it out. Bonds could easily have mistaken Ron for me. We were about the same size and were wearing identical kits, including helmets. Add to that the dark sport glasses we all wore to keep bugs and wind out of our eyes and it would be easy to mistake one for another. The third rider in our group, Bill, was wearing a bright blue jersey, easily distinguishable from the orange and black club colors Prisham and I wore.

The way I figured it, Bonds had been after me. He was playing a game of which walnut shell was hiding the pea, except he'd lost the pea.

Ron Prisham lost almost everything else.

19

I rode up in the elevator with two businesswomen and my bike, took a shower before anybody else got to the office, then changed into street clothes from the same closet where I'd hidden from Angela. As a friend, I'd been a monumental failure. I had no illusions about making it up to her by keeping my promise. I *would* keep my promise. Yet I could *never* make it up to her. But then, I'd not chosen her as a friend, either. She was one of those inherited friends, came with the package when I got together with Kathy. I wondered if the distinction made any difference.

Last week a woman died in front of me. Today a man was mauled in front of me.

Because I believed I was the intended target, the hit and run spooked me like nothing had spooked me in a while; I'd watched what should have been my grisly future turn into somebody else's ghastly present. But for a slip of fate I would have been the pulpy mess of bandages in the Harborview ER and Ron Prisham would have been going about his business.

It was possible Bonds wanted me out of the way because he was afraid I was going to take up Angela's mysterious investigation, and that her investigation was going to find him culpable of a crime, perhaps the crime of running down Rafael Gutierrez on the freeway. If Bonds wanted me out of the way because I might be pursuing her investigation, he surely would have wanted Angela dead, too. It was beginning to look more and more to me as if her death might not have been suicide, even though the family and the police were convinced it was.

As was the problem with all fleeting witness identifications, the more time that passed, the less sure I was of my call. I had been going over and over the morning's events with such intensity my strobe-like glimpse of the driver was beginning to grow fuzzy in my memory, as sometimes occurred when too much thought was applied to such a small molecule of experience.

But even if I couldn't swear to it, I knew in my heart that Goodnight Bonds had been driving the stolen SUV. I knew it not because I was certain of my identification, but because it made sense.

The giant, Marvin Gunderson, maintained a page on Facebook and had lots of friends on it. I was stunned to learn he had a degree in physics from MIT as well as a degree in Russian studies. In college he'd been a power lifter and still held a national collegiate record for the dead lift. After college he joined the Marines and went off to fight in two different wars. Eventually he was recruited into a secret military unit, and there the public trail pretty much dead-ended except for his Facebook page, which he used primarily to keep in touch with his old Marine pals.

Lakeesha Washington was keying open the front door to the office when I got a phone call. "Black? Zoepf here. He's got an alibi. The man you fingered. It seems he and another man were running errands for their boss. They were together from six AM on."

"The other guy named Marvin Gunderson?"

"You know him, too?"

"They're a team. I wouldn't be surprised if Gunderson was in the vehicle with Bonds."

"So you think the alibi's bogus?"

"That's exactly what I think."

"Did you see Gunderson in the vehicle?"

"I told you. I'm not even sure I saw Bonds. The windows were tinted so dark that the driver was only visible through the reflections for maybe a tenth of a second."

"They found our stolen Tahoe in a parking lot in Eastgate. Looks like it was the one. It was wiped clean of prints, but we're going over it anyway. There was a piece of what appears to be a bicycle and some human hair stuck in the undercarriage."

I must have been looking unspeakably dejected by the time Lakeesha had the coffee going. Kathy had warned us she would be in court all morning. Kathy ran a one-woman business as an attorney, mostly criminal defense, and was garnering a reputation as a hardworking lawyer who was somewhat choosy about her clients, knew her way around the city courts, and who could be counted on to give good advice and get the best deal possible. It didn't hurt that she'd come back from the dead last fall after she turned out to be the only survivor of a plane crash that killed one of our state senators. For a few days she'd been the most famous attorney on the west coast, perhaps in the entire country. If she hadn't already become one of the go-to attorneys for anyone accused of a crime in King County, returning from the dead had clinched it.

Lakeesha glanced through the doorway and said, "What happened to you?"

"Nothing."

"It doesn't look like nothing."

"One of my friends got hit by a truck. I'm pretty sure it was supposed to be me."

"What?"

"I still don't know how he survived."

"Lord sweet Jesus."

Prisham was run down by a black Tahoe. Rafael Gutierrez was run down by a black Tahoe. No matter how hard I tried, I could not talk myself into believing it was a coincidence, even though Zoepf said the Tahoe this morning was stolen only the night before. Everybody, including car thieves and murderers, had their favorite models.

The pictures of Marvin Gunderson in uniform on his Facebook page showed him not nearly as gargantuan as he was now. My guess was that in the Marines he'd been pushing a lean two hundred and fifty or sixty pounds, that he was now around three-fifty, most of it honed muscle. He'd fought overseas for four tours and then gone back to the Mideast in the employ of a private security company whose claim to fame was guarding VIPs and launching special operations for the U.S. Government. There were Internet rumors of atrocities connected with the company.

One story held my attention. Five men in his unit had been accused of the torture, rape, and murder of eleven civilians. Originally, Gunderson had been implicated, but later he was unaccountably unimplicated. After that, the chief investigator, traveling in Afghanistan, was blown up by an IED. Following the story on the Net, I couldn't be sure how Gunderson had been eliminated as a suspect—nobody ever came right out and said he hadn't been involved—but after a while, his name simply dropped out of the coverage and, as far as I could tell, he was never charged.

A number of private security companies had sprouted up during the wars in the Mideast, and Gunderson worked for one of the largest, Brights.

Staffed primarily with discharged soldiers, ex-SEALS, Rangers, and former CIA operatives, Brights had a bulldog reputation, was known for abusing citizens' rights and the torture of civilian prisoners, and had once been linked to the theft of over a billion dollars in cash in Iraq, a crime that was never solved. I spent ten minutes reading one man's online account of his year working for Brights and the harassment he suffered after he resigned and began telling his story, harassment which included two separate, suspicious traffic accidents he barely survived. Hit and run was becoming a theme.

By ten-thirty, I was antsy. I went downstairs to find Kathy's Prius. When I didn't spot it right away, I walked up the hill to Harborview in the rain. Prisham was still in surgery when I got there. Melissa, his wife, was a short, buxom redhead with porcelain skin and, despite the circumstances, a kindly smile. She had recently lost her job and was afraid if Ron was off work for any length of time, he would be laid off, too. The morning's calamity threatened to dunk this family deep into poverty.

When Prisham came out of surgery at eleven-thirty, the surgical team assured Melissa his broken bones would heal. They weren't so optimistic about the injuries to his brain. Ron had been wearing a 250-gram helmet designed for a single impact, yet was repeatedly buffeted, pummeled and struck by the road and undercarriage of the Tahoe. After the first blow, the shattered helmet was about as effective as a chunk of cotton candy.

It was bad enough to be carrying the guilt about Angela's death, but I was certain Ron's tragedy was meant for me, that the only reason he'd been hit was because I'd pulled off the road unexpectedly, confusing the driver of the SUV. I asked Melissa where her husband worked and whether he had enemies. She said he worked for Chase Bank, where everybody loved him.

By the time I left Harborview, the rain had tapered down to intermittent drizzle. I walked back down the hill to have lunch with

Kathy in a small place across the street from the courthouse. On the walk, I couldn't help thinking about one of the poems Angela had written for Rafael Gutierrez:

> Like an eagle he soared
> like a dove he was gored
> the man was an icon
> preserved with my Nikon
> May Rafael rest in peace

As poetry it stunk big time, but along with dozens of similar finished and half-finished poems about Gutierrez, it showed how much Angela had been thinking about him. From what I'd heard from her former co-workers and buddies back east, and knew about her myself, Angela had been one of those people who was always desperately in love with someone who wasn't even faintly interested in her. It was a syndrome in which the more disinterest shown by the object of her affection, the more infatuated Angela became. There was probably even a psychological term for it, but I didn't know what it was. Gutierrez's ex-wife didn't think his relationship with Angela had been romantic, but some men will take advantage of a woman sexually, having no intention of pursuing the relationship beyond the nearest mattress. It could have happened that way. When it came to being slow to catch on, Angela was usually first in line.

Gutierrez had been canned from CLS Enterprises and harbored resentment about it according to his ex. If it wasn't a romance, it was possible he had been working with Angela to bring down Clark Lloyd Self.

In the tiny deli near the courthouse I bought a wrapped sandwich from the cooler, an apple, and a drink and met Kathy at a tall table she was holding for us. I knew she had to be back in the courthouse before one o'clock. In all the commotion, I'd forgotten to eat after my ride and was famished. She looked up at me and smiled. "Lakeesha tells me you've had a bad morning," she said.

I explained briefly what had happened. "Jesus, Thomas. Are you sure it was Bonds?"

"That's just it. It was hard to see through the reflections off the tinted windows."

"Is it possible you just *wanted* it to be Bonds?"

"I wish I knew."

"Have the police talked to him?"

"He has an alibi. Gunderson was with him."

"Not much of an alibi if it's that big creep who almost broke your arms."

"He didn't almost break my arms. He wasn't anywhere close to breaking anything. In fact, I was thinking about doing a reverse Hanson twist and breaking *his* arm. I would have, too, but I didn't want to embarrass the poor guy in front of his little buddy."

Kathy laughed indulgently. "Let's assume it was Bonds in the car. If it was, why would Gunderson risk a prison sentence by lying for him?"

"Because he was in on it?"

"Thomas, can you please stay off your bike until we find out for sure what's going on?"

"You know that's not going to happen."

"Any nut in a car can turn the wheel a couple of inches and you'll be in the hospital next to your friend. Or worse."

"Bad weather might put me on the rollers in the garage. This isn't going to."

"You realize you're obsessive, don't you?"

"I never said I wasn't."

"Please?"

"You might as well put me in a straightjacket."

"Sometimes I'd like to." She thought for a moment. "There must be something about Angela's life they don't want you to find out."

"Or about her death."

I didn't tell her Gunderson had been implicated in torture killings overseas. I didn't tell her he'd worked for a company staffed with former CIA operatives and might be one of the scariest people I'd run up against in a good long while.

20

I'D found a charger the day before and started charging Angela's phone but forgot about it until I came back from lunch and Lakeesha pointed at the cell phone on the corner of her desk as if it were a rat carcass. "Is *this* yours?"

"Thanks. I forgot."

Alone at my desk, I checked Angela's "recent calls" roster. My phone held four months' worth, but she apparently cleared hers daily, for the phone had only the calls from her last day, and I couldn't be sure it had all of those. It would be just like Angela to be constantly erasing her tracks. The police said she'd called me, REI, and Crane Manning, but the phone showed she'd also phoned a number with a Montana prefix. I couldn't find a name in a reverse directory, so I punched in the number using Angela's phone. A woman answered, "Yes?"

"Monica?"

"Black? Did I give you this number by mistake? I meant to give you the business number."

"I'm calling from your sister's phone."

"It freaked me out when I saw the incoming call. For a second, I thought she was contacting me from the dead."

"I'm seeing here that she called you the day she died. Can you tell me what you talked about?"

"She was just checking up on the kids—they were always first on her agenda. Also, she told me to leave Clark."

"You must have been getting tired of hearing that."

"I loved my sister."

"I know you did. What about the video she showed you a couple of weeks ago? What were your thoughts on that?"

"Are you trying to annoy me?"

"I'm looking for facts, that's all."

"Listen, Black. I'm not paying you to sneak around and poke into my personal life."

"Your sister's thinking was inextricably intertwined with *your* life, including your marriage. If I don't have at least some of the details, I'm going to be working in the dark. Nothing I find out here is going to be revealed to anybody else. I don't talk to the gossip rags."

"I'll tell you this much: Angela was wrong about Clark and me."

"She wasn't wrong about your husband cheating."

"We have an open marriage. She didn't understand that. Angela was such a prude. She thought I would care about Clark banging some secretary, but I don't. Our split was for other reasons."

"You mind telling me those reasons?"

"I do mind."

"Did money enter into it?"

"I'm not going to talk about it."

"Then tell me whether Angela asked if money came into your decision to get back with Self?"

"She did ask. She had some crazy notion Clark should be in jail, that the SEC was going to come after him."

"Did she tell you what that was based on?"

"I didn't ask."

"Who hired Bonds and Gunderson?"

"Clark picked up Marvin when he was having trouble with a large financial corporation trying to horn in on his business. They were actually having people follow Clark. Within a week Marvin put a stop to it. Bonds came on board later. Gunderson hired him for the driving jobs and what-have-you."

"You don't mind having two goombahs around?"

"I've had kidnap threats. And stalkers."

I wasn't sure having Bonds and Gunderson hanging around her

and her kids was preferable to the occasional stalker, but I kept the thought to myself. We signed off and I brought up the contacts list on Angela's cell phone.

There were three numbers for Gunderson. One for Bonds. My own name and number. Kathy's. I found an array of phone prefixes I wasn't familiar with until I looked them up: 212, 315, and 347 in New York; 202 in Washington, D.C.; and 229 in Atlanta.

I'd had my own phone turned off since the hospital and now found a number of messages in response to my blanket e-mails to Angela's friends. As I returned the calls and gave out the particulars of her death, listening to the shock and grief on the other end of the line, I began to see more facets of Angela's increasingly complex personality. Angela had met and mixed with people from all walks of life. She met one of her boyfriends when he delivered a UPS package to her door. One surprising nugget came from a woman in Las Vegas who'd been Angela's waitress when she stayed at the Venetian. "I've been corresponding with Angela for years. She was so lost when she was down here."

"When was that?"

"Ten years ago. Sat at the same table every morning for breakfast. She was trying to decide whether or not to get married. I thought it was strange, because at that point she'd been staying at the hotel for a week, maybe two, and I'd never seen her with anyone else. And here she was asking a complete stranger whether or not to get married. I don't think she had anybody else to confide in."

"What was she doing in Las Vegas?"

"All I know is she told this long story about meeting a gentleman and how he'd impressed her with his travels and how he'd fallen for her but she wasn't that keen on him and how he was pressuring her to marry him. We talked about it for an hour or so and then exchanged phone numbers. She called me that evening and we talked again. We've been friends ever since."

"Hank Bassman?"

"That's him. He was older than dirt. I was at the wedding. There were only about four other people in attendance, along with a couple of security guys. That was when I realized how wealthy and paranoid he was. I thought briefly about calling the police to see if I could stop it, because I thought the old man had drugged or brainwashed her. I mean, why else would a woman under thirty marry an old codger? Well, obviously there was the money aspect, but Angela didn't seem the type to give up her life for money. And she said the strangest thing. She said the government needed her to sacrifice herself, that in marrying Bassman she was somehow going to rescue the country. I can't tell you how close I came to calling the police."

"Sounds nuts."

"Just like always, I sat there on my hands and didn't do anything, and then they were married and we had a little celebration at the MGM Grand, where she seemed perfectly normal. I asked Angela at one point if she thought they were going to have sex, or if they already had, because I just did not see the relationship being viable, but she got all flustered and refused to answer. I actually got the impression she was a virgin. I was sorry I'd asked. And then they left town and the next time I saw her it was years later when she was flying through on some sort of layover on her way to South America to climb Aconcagua, I think it was. She was divorced by then. Over the years, I've sent pictures of my grandkids, and she kept me posted on her life. You must be the private detective she had an affair with."

Jesus! Angela was going around telling people we'd had an affair? "I *am* a private investigator. There was *no* affair. At least not with me."

"Well, she said it was an affair. Maybe it was affair of the mind. I hope you know she worshiped you."

"Did she say anything about her husband when you saw her those years later?"

"I asked if she was still married, and all she said was no. But he would have been over a hundred by then."

"You think of anything else, call back, will you?"

Angela had told her friends we'd had an affair? It wasn't the worst reconstruction of reality to come from her fertile brain, but it was close. I was never going to figure out how her mind worked.

Fielding more calls from Angela's friends and researching Goodnight Bonds took up the rest of the afternoon. Bonds had, as far as I could tell, been marginally employed as a roofer, a fisherman, a groundskeeper, and other menial jobs until he ran into Marvin Gunderson and basically became his factotum. Gunderson had been working for Self for three years. Three months after being hired, Gunderson talked Self into hiring Bonds. It was unclear where Bonds and Gunderson met, since Bonds had never been in the military, where Gunderson had spent most of his adult life.

Because Bonds was born and raised in Alaska, I had called a private investigator I knew who worked out of Anchorage, an elderly woman who was tenacious enough to chew off her own arm to get at the facts in a case. She was hard of hearing, so phone conversations tended to be almost comically repetitious, but in this instance, all I had to do was listen. She reported back to me in the middle of the afternoon.

Ruth Madison was her name, or Ruthie M. as her friends called her. She'd been a school teacher, a librarian, a wife, grandmother, divorcee, three-time widow, Bridge tournament champion, and for the past ten years, a private investigator. You'd be surprised what people will tell a doddering old woman.

"Thomas, I went out and talked to some of his old neighbors and came away with an earful. Goodnight Bonds was raised by his grandpop out there on a side road off Old Seward Highway. No grandma, no mother, no father. Best as anyone can piece together, grandpa was pretty hard on the family, which was the reason they ran away one by one. There's some speculation his mother was also his sister, that he'd been fathered by the old man, but nobody could verify it. The so-called mother is long gone. I'm not sure Goodnight ever knew her. Changed her name and died of a drug overdose. They were all on drugs before they left, although nobody ever accused Goodnight of anything worse than glue sniffing. For many years he and the old man were fundamentalist Christians. Or pretended to be. The old man had five kids by two different wives, and except for Goodnight, they all ran away before they were of age. The neighbors say the old man poached game and was always skinning something in the back yard behind the outhouse. They lived in a shack, slapped together with lumber and pieces of housing they'd stolen. They had a pack of dogs even the police were afraid of. Eventually the dogs were hauled off after they attacked a postman who was trying to do his job.

"Alaska tends to attract rough cobs. The kid was in and out of juvie more times than anybody could count, and each time he was returned home the old man would beat the tar out of him. The neighbors called the police on the old man more than once, but nothing came of it. They were selling brand spanking new television sets for a while, dirt cheap. Had to be stolen. The kid didn't graduate from high school. I couldn't find any records he'd even attended. From what I understand, he can barely read. And there's something wrong with him. Neighbors couldn't quite describe it, other than to tell me he was inbred. Maybe two generations of it, so that his mother was also his sister, and his grandmother . . . well, I get confused. Who knows if it's true?"

"Goodnight ever have a legitimate job?"

"Oh, he's worked on a crab boat. In a cannery. In town loading trucks. He did a little guide work. The old man would set him up with the jobs, then take his checks and cash them, give the kid a few dollars for spending money. Like I said, the kid did whatever the old man told him."

"You think that might include murder?"

"Well, it's interesting you should mention the darker arts. About eight years ago there was a high school girl came up dead. Goodnight was living here at the time, getting wild drunk and sniffing glue with his buddies. I said he didn't take drugs, but he huffed for a while. This girl got herself run over on the road out on Old Seward Highway, not far, actually, from the place where Bonds and his grandpa were living. At first people thought she was just out in her mom's car and it flatted and she was walking for help when somebody accidentally clipped her. Except the autopsy showed evidence of rape. The evening she died there were witnesses who saw Bonds talking to her at a convenience store. He was questioned, but his friends all said he'd been with them at the time of her death. There was no DNA and the police assumed the rapist used a condom. Right after that, Bonds left Alaska for good.

"About two years ago one of the friends who had alibied Bonds for the rape and the murder said the alibi was phony, that Goodnight had told them to lie or he'd sic his grandfather on them. Then the boy who recanted didn't show up for work one morning. They never did find him. They never connected the disappearance to either Goodnight or the old man. Six months later the old man got arrested for molesting the daughter of a member of the church he attended. He disappeared while he was out on bond. I talked to some of the neighbors, who think the family of the girl who was molested killed the old man, buried him up in Chugach Park. There were no official charges, so I have no way of verifying that."

Shortly after my conversation with Ruth about Goodnight Bonds, I received a phone call from a man who'd served in Marvin Gunderson's Ranger outfit. I'd located him through Gunderson's Facebook page. His name was Blackie Mazzetti. The first thing he said was, "You never heard any of this from me, right?"

"Confidential all the way. I just need to know about this guy."

"We were in Afghanistan together. We would get sent deep into an area of suspected insurgent activity. They'd send us up where nobody else had been for a while. I mean deep into the mountains, little villages looked as if they'd just come out of the Stone Age. I spent a lot of time with Marvin. One of his tricks was to line up a bunch of prisoners, ask them questions through an interpreter, and when they didn't answer to his satisfaction, he would reach out with both hands and break their neck. I saw him do five men in a row. You don't even want to know what he did to the women."

"Tell me anyway."

"Naw. I've said too much already."

"Blackie, if you're so scared, why tell me anything?"

"He needed to be stopped back then, and I never did anything. I've always felt bad about it. I guess I figured this is my chance to do *something*. Just be careful. Watching him go bug-ass crazy was the scariest thing I've ever seen in my life, and believe me, I've seen my share of scary."

"Thanks, Blackie."

"A piece of advice. He gets mad at you, run, change your name, don't ever come out of hiding."

Again, I had to wonder why a reputable financial wizard would keep thugs like Bonds and Gunderson on hand. True, they dressed in tailored suits and spoke politely when they weren't trying to wring your neck or run you down in a stolen vehicle, but why have them around at all? Were the upper classes so threatened they had to keep nincompoops like Bonds and Gunderson in the house just so their kids wouldn't get kidnaped and their wives wouldn't get preyed upon by the paparazzi?

Angela had once told me vast sums of money hinged on her investigation. If Self was engaged in fraudulent business practices, say, embezzling money from his own company, if he was playing fast and loose with client funds, and Angela had cottoned to it, it might make sense for him to send Bonds and Gunderson after her. It might even have made sense for them to harass her to the point where she could no longer withstand the stress.

As I became more familiar with Angela's phone, I was able to locate her stored photos. She had quite a collection of stills. I was shocked to find several of me I didn't know she had taken. A few of Kathy, including at least one I wanted to save, photos of Hoshi, some people I didn't know, people who appeared to be local merchants on Capitol Hill, a guy selling copies of *Real Change*, a local weekly peddled in the area by the homeless. There were photos of her three nephews, of Monica. There were, predictably, no photos of Clark Lloyd Self.

When I examined her computer hard drive again, I located the photo section, which had, incredibly, escaped me earlier. She stored her pictures in a folder with a code name, Lhotse, which I found among a raft of folders with code names based on the world's tallest mountains. I was searching for the video of Self and his mistress, the video we'd made together in Eastgate. It wasn't there.

What I found instead were photos taken of Angela on various mountain-climbing expeditions, as well as on local hikes in the Cascades and Olympics. Photos of her at airports with other climbers standing alongside huge stacks of gear. I'd been skimming the photos quickly and had to back up. In the middle of it all I came upon a series of pictures of naked men, no faces showing. Some of them were intertwined with a woman, also naked, a woman whose face wasn't revealed in the first few photos. It took a while to determine if they were commercial pictures or personal. I decided they were most likely captured with a cell phone or a video camera.

While I had never seen or heard Angela do anything that would lead me to believe she was anything but a virgin, I wasn't naive enough to think that at thirty-something, with one marriage and several boyfriends under her belt, she actually *was* a virgin. Angela never spoke of sex, never referred to it, and made it clear she didn't want anybody else to mention it in her presence.

About eighty photos in, I identified the female cavorting with a group of men.

It was Angela.

I was beyond stunned. There was a section of videos, too, but they wouldn't play properly, at least not on my computer. I called Brad

Munch. "Bradley? Thomas here. That hard drive you restored for me? Was there something else I should know about?"

"Why?"

"Just tell me what you're not telling me."

"It belonged to that woman who jumped off the building? I felt bad for her."

"You felt bad for her and then what?"

"There was some stuff I didn't turn over."

"Tell me about it."

"You found the videos?"

"I need to see what was on them."

"I'll send them in an e-mail. You should have them in a few minutes. Do you want a refund?"

"No. Just don't do it again."

"I didn't want her family to see them. They're awful darn explicit. I thought about erasing everything, but I corrupted them instead."

"I'm glad you didn't erase them. If I don't need them, I'll erase them myself."

While I was waiting for the videos to arrive via e-mail, I phoned a private-eye supply store in Washington, D.C., called Second Sight. I'd found the number highlighted in Angela's address book. Needless to say, they weren't going to give me a list of her purchases. I knew she did not believe in credit cards. She hated dealing with banks in general and did most of her commerce with cash or certified check. I spoke to a clerk who knew who I was talking about right off the bat. "Sure. I know her. She used to come in all the time. How is she doing?"

"She killed herself last week."

"Oh, God. I'm sorry to hear that."

"So were we. I'm trying to find out why. You think you could send me a list of the merchandise she bought in the past year or two?"

"She didn't buy anything in the past year. But I think she called about three weeks ago."

"Concerning what?"

"She thought her television was spying on her. Sounds nuts, but we get a lot of people in here who think that. Their television, VCR, cell phone, coffee maker. It doesn't help that the government really can listen in on your cell conversations, or that they can track you to within a couple of centimeters by triangulating on your phone. It doesn't help that we have all these Patriot Act provisions that allow the government to spy on us.

"She talk about anything else?"

"Not that I can recall. The only reason I remember her at all is she used to have a crush on Jeremy, a college kid worked here."

21

"YOU about ready to go home?" I asked. It was after five and Kathy and I were alone, Lakeesha long gone.

"Give me a few more minutes, could you?"

"I'll be downstairs. I want to see if Susan Djokovic has left for the day."

"Anything new on Angela?" Kathy asked as I walked out of the office.

"No," I lied.

I found myself harboring the same protective instincts concerning Angela's photos and videos as Brad Munch had. The videos Munch sent me were—astonishingly—movies of Angela having sex . . . with several men. All at once. Although having sex with two or three guys at a time was not a crime, you could be sure she had never intended for the videos to see the light of day. Why she saved them, or even allowed them to be made was a mystery. It was ironic that Angela had been producing and directing videos of Clark Lloyd Self with his mistress while these were tucked away on her home computer. Odd also that Angela had seemed almost asexual, especially in comparison to her sister, who was considered one of the sexiest women on the planet, and all the while she had been starring in her own secret porn trove.

Munch, who hadn't even known the woman, felt the urge to protect her. Munch was young and naive and had been raised in a strict religious home, so his instincts were understandable. The videos were extreme by Munch's standards—and by mine. They were obviously a home production, shot and performed by amateurs. Angela, the only woman in them, looked so . . . well, wholesome and just plain guileless. She must have been keeping them for a specific reason—surely not as trophies—and I needed to learn what that reason was.

It was probable these videos were the reason her computer had been destroyed. After making the decision to do herself in, she may have destroyed her laptop to ensure nobody would see these after she was dead. Or in the event it wasn't a suicide, her killer might have destroyed it for the same reason. Maybe she wasn't the one who wanted the videos concealed. Maybe it was one of the men. Maybe she'd been killed because of the films.

As I walked down the stairs to Djokovic's second floor office, I ticked through a list of possible scenarios for the videos. Perhaps she liked recreational sex. Her sister claimed *she* did. Angela might have belonged to a swingers club. Or she might have been pressured by a boyfriend, blackmailed, drugged, or otherwise coerced into making the videos. From the little I'd seen so far, she looked like a willing participant, but if she *was* drugged, it would have been rape.

Right now, I was working on the assumption somebody had blackmailed her with the videos. If so, that might be the reason enough for suicide. Jesus, how was I going to explain this to her sister?

On the second floor I caught Djokovic as she was heading for the elevator, wheeling a piece of travel luggage I knew contained all her homework and files. "Susan? You have a minute?"

"Thomas. Thanks for driving out to McKay's. It helps to know what that was about."

"Does her estate have some money I don't know about?"

"Not that I know of."

I wondered if Hoshi wasn't my responsibility now, if she hadn't been handed over to me with whatever else Angela had handed me; if I wasn't supposed to make sure Monica paid the freight from now on. Monica obviously had the money to do it, or her husband did. "What happens to her friend?" I asked.

"The state takes over. Of course, they're not going to put her up in a place as plush as McKay's. And there's something else."

"What's that?"

"At one time Angela was embroiled in a lawsuit against CLS Enterprises. She said they swindled her out of a small fortune she'd received in a divorce settlement. There were charges by her and countercharges from CLS claiming she kept withdrawing her funds, then putting them back in and that was the reason she lost money. Angela claimed it was outright fraud."

"She drop the suit?"

"Yes. I don't know why. I thought you might want to know about it."

"Thanks."

On the drive home Kathy and I listened to the day's news on the car radio. Kathy drove while I flopped in the passenger seat in a posture of defeat. The videos had shaken me. My bike was in the back, the front wheel on top of my bike frame. It was my first chance to decompress all day.

I checked my phone, dialing up the website that kept track of our home security system. We had cameras set up covertly around our house and were able to view our property in real time from any computer or from our cell phones. I saw our dog rolling on his back on something dead in the back yard. The FedEx lady left a package on our back porch and later the neighbor's cat came up and sprayed the package.

Our house sat two blocks north of the newly renovated Fire Station 17. The neighborhood was a hodgepodge of older houses, with retired pensioners, small apartment buildings filled with students and people on the margins, rental houses crammed with noisy students splitting the rent and sharing kitchen privileges. We lived in the small, single-story bungalow I'd owned since before I knew Kathy. She called it our cottage, which was a generous interpretation. I'd had a client once who referred to it as a hovel. It was here that Kathy had once rented the basement apartment from me, and it was here where we had become friends and fallen in love.

The payments were manageable, and we were comfortable in the way you're comfortable in an old pair of shoes. The house needed a coat of paint, but it would have to stop raining before we dragged out the drop cloths, which probably meant August. It was minutes from downtown by car, bus, or bike, and we liked living in the U District, where there were dozens of hole-in-the-wall restaurants and independently-owned shops within walking distance. The neighborhood had a diversity and a spark you could only get from the haloing effect of a large university. We liked the electricity in the air and the constant feel that life was jam-packed with possibilities.

Kathy pulled into the long driveway and parked in front of the garage. Though it was no longer raining, the streets were still wet and slick. I took my bike into the house and left it on the enclosed sun porch behind the kitchen. We fed the dog, checked the mail, looked at our phone messages, then Kathy changed and put on some walking shoes and we traipsed several blocks to Chaco Canyon, hoping to find an empty table among the lone diners hiding behind laptops. At the counter Kathy ordered the Thai Peanut Bowl and I chose my usual Mighty Mofo Reuben and stuffed some dollar bills into the tip jar on the counter.

While we ate, Kathy filled me in on a case she'd been handling. It was a mentally ill offender who'd set fire to his neighbor's garage while trying to burn scraps from a building project.

During the walk home, Kathy said, "Why do you think Angela called you a half hour before she killed herself?"

"I still don't know. I have some theories, but I need more information."

"Do you really think she set it up so you would be there to watch her die?"

"I don't like to believe it, but I haven't found anything to deflect that hypothesis."

"And you made a deathbed promise to her."

"I promised to finish up whatever it was she was working on. The trouble is, I can't find any records of what she was working on."

"Other than breaking up her sister's marriage."

"There was that."

"So you don't really know what you promised?"

"Not yet. But I'm only a couple of layers in."

After we got home, I called Munch and asked how long the videos had been on the hard drive. "I thought you were going to ask that. Two weeks, six months, and fourteen months."

"Three different dates?"

"Three videos. Three different dates."

"Thanks."

"You watch them yet?"

"Not all of them. Enough."

If she was being blackmailed, it made sense to keep the videos as evidence. On the other hand, if it was blackmail, why did she receive the materials on three separate dates? They most likely would have arrived at the same time.

Maybe she kept them because she wanted to be able to identify the malefactors, if those men were indeed malefactors and not partners. On the other hand, I'd run into swingers in my profession, and the one thing I'd learned was that they were never the kind of people you would expect. They were almost always ordinary-seeming folks whose only distinguishing trait was they thought it would be a good idea to have sex with a lot of people. Sometimes they were open about it, sometimes secretive. Angela could easily have been one.

I remembered having been at Angela's apartment with Kathy when Angela lived in Lynnwood, and noticing a note on her kitchen memo board. There were three phone numbers: her parents, the White House, and the local vice squad. I laughed and later told Kathy, who reprimanded me for snooping. I'd laughed at Angela plenty of other times. On the other hand, everybody needs their parents. And when you thought about it, having the phone number of the local vice squad handy didn't seem that outrageous. I wasn't so sure about the White House.

When we got home we kicked back in front of *High Noon*. It was my night to choose the movie. I thought about all the rumors that had circulated Hollywood about Grace Kelly, Gary Cooper's co-star in the film, the affairs she was supposed to have had, including one with Cooper. The stories didn't match the unapproachable ice queen you saw on the screen in the same way the videos didn't match what I thought I knew about Angela.

We weren't quite to the shootout in the movie when my phone began ringing. It was a club member who wanted to know the details of that morning's hit and run. Then Melissa Prisham called to tell me her husband was going to be in an induced coma for a few days, but his vital signs were stable and the doctors were hopeful he might return to a normal life. They said his fitness would contribute to rapid healing. I thanked Melissa for passing along the information and asked if there was anything I could do. She asked me to pray. I wasn't religious—but I lied and assured her I would.

Kathy watched the rest of the movie alone while I went to work on the home computer. The first thing I did was write a blanket e-mail to the club updating them on Ron Prisham's condition. Then I put the three videos Munch had sent into a file on my own computer and played the first one. It was filmed in what appeared to be a hotel room, one person wielding the camera while Angela and a man I'd never seen before undressed and frolicked in bed. Angela seemed nervous and a little giggly, not frightened, not intimidated. She didn't look drugged, either. After some time had passed, a second man entered the frame and the first man vanished, presumably to man the camera. The second man didn't waste a lot of time getting down to business. After trying out every conceivable position they concluded their business and the tape ended.

Later, I heard Kathy getting ready for bed. When I rolled my desk chair back to peek across the house into our bedroom, I saw her reading in bed. Just as well I wasn't in there, since my Reuben sandwich was beginning to kick in. I watched all of the earliest video, replaying portions to better distinguish what they were saying the few times anybody spoke. Angela was not overtly seductive or flirtatious and did not appear fearful. I'd seen anxiety in Angela, and I wasn't seeing it here. Instead, I found her demeanor workmanlike, steady, unruffled, sometimes encouraging, all of it conducive to getting the job done. She seemed content enough to be there, not necessarily eager, but accepting, all of it a far cry from the prim and virginal Angela I thought I'd known.

As I examined the videos and the people in them, two things stood out. The first was that I had spoken to one of the men on the phone recently. There was something familiar about his voice. The second was that the last video was dated the same day Angela asked me to escort her to Sophie Millwood's house, the day Crane and I had been introduced to Clark Lloyd Self and later to Monica Pennington's penthouse. She'd gone through all that righteous indignation with Self and a few hours later had taken part in her own little orgy—but she wasn't married to someone else, as Self was.

I tried hard to remember which of yesterday's phone calls had given me the snapshot of the voice I'd heard on the tapes. It was going to take a while to figure it out.

22

THE next morning Kathy took the Prius to work while I stayed home and took more phone calls from Angela's friends. Between calls I viewed the second and third tapes, scrutinizing each for clues that something was going on other than what I was seeing. There were several sections where she was lying on the bed alone talking to somebody off camera, naked and spent but seemingly relaxed. There were two men in the first tape, three in the second, then two again in the last, always the same two, joined by a third man in the second video. At least one of these men knew Angela was now dead because I recognized his voice from one of yesterday's phone calls. Unfortunately I'd spoken to so many of Angela's friends I couldn't put a name with the voice.

I drove my Ford to the International District and had a couple of hum baos and some hot tea at the Tai Tung restaurant while waiting for the town to wake up. The Tai Tung wasn't open officially but they were letting some regular customers sit at the counter.

The videos seemed less disturbing this morning. Perhaps I was getting used to the notion that Angela wasn't who I thought she was. Or maybe she seemed a more complete human being now that some sexuality had been thrown into the cauldron that had been her life.

I went through my phone logs from yesterday and the day before until I winnowed it down to one man who I remembered pronounced "asked" as "akxed," a colloquialism I'd heard on the videos. Once I obtained his name from my phone records, it wasn't hard to track him to his work place here in town. I wasn't sure they were the same man, but I would know when I saw him, even if he was wearing clothes.

The City of Seattle Weights and Measures Division was located just south of Chinatown on the south side of Dearborn Street, almost within spitting distance of the two corporate-sponsored stadiums that replaced the Kingdome several years ago. Across from the parking area sat the large police garage, where several Seattle blue and whites were parked outside waiting for servicing. I'd been to the yard many times in the past as an SPD officer.

The Weights and Measures building was two stories tall, with its backside along Dearborn and the main entrance facing a parking lot littered with dump trucks, various city and personal cars, and a row of motorcycles with wet seats from an early-morning shower. In the garage next door, I could hear an air compressor.

I went up a short flight of stairs and down a hallway to the left and came to a sliding glass window. A woman with dyed red hair sat at a desk behind the window brushing dog hair off her black slacks. When she glanced at me, I said, "I'm looking for Charles Washington."

"Down at the end of the hall on the right. By the window. He expecting you?"

"Oh, yeah," I lied as I walked toward the offices at the end of the corridor.

Four or five people sat at nearby desks. A meeting was taking place in a glass-walled conference room beyond them. It was a typical office: desks piled with papers, photos of loved ones, crayoned drawings done by children or grandchildren, a bowling trophy, and, tacked to the walls, pithy sayings. *"The trouble with quotes on the internet is that it's difficult to determine whether or not they are genuine." --Abraham Lincoln.*

Charles Washington was returning to his desk as I walked in. He was dressed neatly in pressed khaki slacks, burnished dress shoes, and a pleated, button-down shirt that had been done at a laundry. His hair was short. He had a wide nose and dark brown eyes. He was maybe five-eight and spindly. Late forties. African-American. He looked like somebody who took his job to heart. Less than an hour ago I'd watched him on a tape having sex with a woman who was now dead.

"Hey, Charles," I said.

"I know you?"

"We spoke on the phone yesterday regarding Angela Bassman. My name is Thomas Black."

He held his coppery hand out to shake. "What can I do you out of?" He smiled, showing flawless white teeth.

"What can you tell me about this?" I showed him my cell phone, which displayed a photo of him from the waist up, naked.

"Hey, what the hell?" he whispered, making calming motions with his palms, as if I were a skittish horse somebody had let into the office. "Damn. I knew we shouldn't be shooting no movie." He sat heavily in his chair.

"There's more where this came from."

"I'm not going to say anything till I get me a lawyer. You want money? Well, you came to the wrong person, 'cause I got four kids to feed and two ex-wives banging on my door every month for rent money. I got a daughter who's about to start college. I'm paying cable TV bills for three households. And now you come in here with this bullshit?"

"Give me a couple of answers and I'll go away."

"I answered your questions on the phone."

"You didn't tell me everything, did you?"

"This is where I *work*, man."

"Tell me what this was about."

"You know what it was about. I need me an attorney." His voice had gone up an octave. Even the people in the glass-walled meeting room were watching us now.

"You can waste money paying an attorney to listen to all your secrets, or you can tell me now. But one way or another, you're going to talk."

He took a deep breath and let out a long sigh of exasperation. "Let's go outside."

The sky was gray, clouds scudding in out of the southwest, from where Seattle got most of its inclement weather. Once in the parking lot, Washington kept walking until he was far enough from the building nobody could eavesdrop through an open window. "You know I'm married?" he said angrily. "I can't let this reach my home."

"Don't take an attitude with me. I'm the one with the leverage."

"Okay, but you can't come back to my place of work again. Man, I don't need these people to see this shit."

"Why don't you explain what happened?"

"Nothing to explain. She was a freak."

"How long have you known her?"

"Couple years. I swear I never thought she would kill herself. Man,

I haven't seen her since the last time we fucked. God damn. She said she was going to erase them as soon as she watched 'em. She said she liked to watch but afterwards she would erase it. She lied to us."

"Start from the beginning. How you met her. Names of the other guys."

"All I know is she liked to do two at once. I was kind of embarrassed the first time, but Nate was good with it, she was good with it, so I figured what the hell."

"Who's Nate?"

"My friend. He likes to borrow his buddy's Corvette and cruise the high-end bars. One night he rings me up and says he's got this freak down at the Alexis and she's expecting two guys and do I want part of it. I told the family there was an emergency at work and went on up."

"At the Alexis? Wouldn't a flea-bag motel be a more suitable setting for this sort of activity than a luxury hotel like the Alexis? Her room? Your friend's room? How did this happen?"

"Don't akx me. I wasn't footing the bill. I just know Nate gave me a room number and when I walked in, they were sitting there on the sofa sipping Bourbon. He introduced me. She says something like, 'Well, should we get started?' and she walks over to the bed and starts undressing, then undresses Nate and starts working on him. Pretty soon she's working on me, too. I guess you seen the rest."

"You think she was on drugs?"

"I'm telling you, the woman was a freak."

"Then what?"

"What do you mean, then what? We did her until we couldn't do her no more. I showered and went home."

"You left her in the room alone?"

"I wasn't going to take her home with me."

"And that first time was filmed?"

"All three of them was filmed."

"Who did the filming?"

"First one we did ourselves. After that she brought a guy. White dude. A couple of different ones. I never knew who they were. First time I thought it was her husband or something. But the second time it was a different guy. They never did nothing till the last one. Just watched and filmed."

"What happened with the last one?"

"The last one got on her after we finished."

"She was good with that?"

"I didn't hear her complaining."

"You hear any names?"

"She never introduced us."

"It was just you and Nate and these chaperones?"

"And Portman."

"Who's Portman?"

"Nate's brother. He came once but never came back."

"Were there any other women?"

"Nope."

"When was the last time you met with her?"

He looked in his phone calendar. It was the night of the day Crane and I escorted Angela to Sophie Millwood's house, same date as had been stamped on the last video.

"You recognize any of these guys as the chaperone?" I had photos in my phone and began showing them to him. Federer. Bonds. Gunderson. Guys from the memorial service. Even Clark Lloyd Self. He didn't recognize any of them.

"I need to talk to Nate. Where can I find him?"

"Hell, Nate got hisself laid off six months ago. Part of the city budget problems. Lives with his sister."

"He worked here?"

"Over in the tire shop. We been friends goin' on twenty years."

"You got an address for his sister?"

He gave it to me, then said, "I guess I should tell you about his brother."

"Portman?"

"Portman got into trouble when he was younger."

"Tell me about it."

"You're not going to like it."

"Spit it out."

"He was a banger. They had this girl in the club. Some sort of initiation rites she was supposed to go through before she became a full-fledged member. Had to prove she wasn't scared. Portman was running it. They were up over the Mount Baker tunnel lid, fooling around. He forced her up on some fence and ended up more or less pushing her off the hill onto the roadway. She fell about sixty feet. Got hit by a couple of cars. They said the fall killed her before the cars even touched her. He spent some time in the penitentiary over it."

"What was Portman's relationship with Angela?"

"Same as ours. He came in, had a few words with her, fucked her, and left."

"You say he never came back?"

"Not when I was there."

"Did Nate meet her other times? Times when you might not have been around?"

"Not so's I heard. I think I would have heard. Nate likes to brag."

"What about Portman? Did he meet her again?"

"Couldn't say."

"Where is Portman?"

"You'll have to akx Nate."

"I'm not sure I understand how Nate's brother became part of this."

"We were there doin' our thing and she said something to Nate and he went and made the call. I guess she wanted another partner. Portman showed up half an hour later, saw what was going on, jumped in the shower, and became part of it. God, this sounds awful, doesn't it?"

"Yeah, it does. You remember any of the conversation between Portman and Angela?"

"I had my mind on other things."

As I walked toward my car, Washington shouted after me. "Hey, you ain't comin' back, are you?"

"Depends."

"Sheeeeit."

"One last thing." I turned around and walked back to Washington, who was already headed into the building. We both stopped as a dump truck came into the yard and sat idling fifty yards away. The air brakes hissed loudly. Nobody was going to hear us over the rhythmic thumping of the diesel motor. "Was it something she *wanted* to do?"

"She did it, didn't she?"

"I know she did it, but was she doing it because she wanted to, or was there some other reason?"

"You saw the videos. You know as much as I do."

"Ever talk with her?"

Charles Washington had to think for a few moments. "We talked national security a few times. She thought maybe the President was in trouble. That he needed to be protected. Yeah. She talked about protecting the President a couple of times."

"Didn't it seem strange that would be on her mind when you guys were doing what you were doing?"

"It *all* seemed strange, but I wasn't going to pass it up. One thing. Was she important? Is that why you're doing this?"

"What do you meant important?"

"Like some politician's wife or daughter or something?"

"She wasn't important."

"So who was she?"

"Just an ordinary woman trying to get through life the best way she knew how."

"But she *was* a freak?"

"I don't think so."

"Then why was she . . . ?"

"I wish I knew," I said. "Why were you?"

23

NOT quite close enough for a view of the water, the pleasant residential neighborhood above Lake Washington was predominantly white and largely Jewish before World War II, and in the fifties and sixties black families slowly relocated to the area. There were a lot of large houses, often two or three stories. As property prices in the city climbed during the eighties and nineties, many black families were no longer able to afford the large places, which were bought up by remodelers and speculators, and the controversial gentrification of the area set in.

The address Washington gave me was a white colonial with two columns framing the front porch. A woman with a baby in a stroller and a toddler on a small bicycle made their way down the sidewalk while I knocked at the green and white door. The boy on the bike was about as proud of himself as a boy could be and kept watching me to make sure I knew he could ride. I told him he was doing an excellent job and watched him beam. An African-American woman answered the door in slippers and a silk bathrobe. Her makeup and hair were done, so I had the feeling she was dressing for work.

"I'm looking for Nate Marshall."

"I don't know where he is."

"But he does stay here sometimes?"

"Sometimes."

"Are you his sister?"

"Who told you I was his sister?"

"Charles Washington."

"Charlie? Charlie with you?" She stepped out and glanced up and down the street.

"No, ma'am. He's at work. He told me Nate stayed here."

"We let him bunk in the sewing room. Who are you?"

I gave her one of my cards, one without a machine gun on it. "Thomas Black. I'm investigating a death."

"Then you're looking for Portman. I don't know where Portman is. Haven't seen him in two years. Last time he was here he stole all my jewelry. He shows up on my doorstep, I'm gonna kick his big nigger butt down the street till my shoe get stuck in it. You can tell him that when you see him."

"I'd be happy to, but right now I'm looking for Nate."

"He might be down at the lake. Says fishing calms his nerves. Sometimes he'll take his old yellow truck, but that's only so he can tote malt liquor down there in a cooler."

I started at tiny Denny Blaine Park, the lesbian/clothing-optional beach of choice affectionately known as Dykiki. It was just a few doors away from the house where Kurt Cobain blew his head off with a shotgun years ago. Near the park I spotted two Japanese youths, dressed as if they just got off the plane, cameras, guidebooks, and wallets suspended on chains around their necks. The neighborhood suffered a sporadic stream of tourists from all over the world. I might have told them where Cobain's house was, but I was getting a little touchy about suicides, and the thought of people traveling five thousand miles to pay tribute to one was more than a little disconcerting.

After coming up empty at Denny Blaine, I drove south on Lake Washington Boulevard, checking out each fishing spot and dock. Old men sat in lawn chairs with poles, buckets next to them. Using my binoculars, I didn't recognize any of them from the videos and I didn't see any yellow pickups. Lake Washington Boulevard was a road I'd ridden a thousand times on my Eddy Merckx. I knew every pothole, every crack in the pavement. I drove south past Daniel's Broiler, past the boat moorages and the fancy condominiums and houses on the lake. I cruised the Stan Sayres Pits, where hydroplanes docked every August for the Seafair races, and made my way a mile farther along to Seward Park, which jutted out into the lake on a wooded peninsula. Bicycle races were held here every Thursday evening, some of which I'd participated in. If Nate Marshall was fishing along the lake I didn't see him.

As I drove downtown I called Zoepf at the Mercer Island Police Department and asked if they'd made any headway on the hit and run.

"We processed the stolen SUV. We got no usable prints."

"How did our boy get on the island?"

"We canvassed the neighbors, but if somebody dropped him off, they most likely didn't do it in front of the house."

"If it was Bonds he would be mid-thirties, Caucasian, short, brown on brown. Yesterday morning he had on a baseball cap with a hoodie over it."

"Remember, Bonds has an alibi."

"I think his alibi was probably in on it."

"Hey, by the way? Are you the guy was involved in all that stuff last year with the Senator's plane crash?"

"Which part of it?"

"Your wife the one who got kidnaped?"

"I'm afraid so."

"And you got blown all to hell in that gymnasium bombing?"

"I'm all healed up."

"Yeah, well, that was a messed up deal. I'm surprised either of you lived through it."

"So were we."

Forty minutes later I was at Harborview. Ron Prisham had been transferred out of intensive care and onto a floor that specialized in neurological disorders. His wife and mother were there, along with a bevy of nurses. He was still unconscious and would be for at least a few days. I waited with them for half an hour and then said my good-byes. I was outside our building by the toy store when my cell rang. The first raindrops were splattering windshields and pelting pedestrians like tiny wet insults. "Black? What have you got for me?"

"Monica. I was going to call today. Where are you?"

"We flew out to the ranch last night. We decided to spend a few days in the mountains. You should come out. You're an outdoorsy kind of guy."

"Where's the ranch?"

"South of Flathead Lake."

"Montana? I'm not—"

"The jet's back at Boeing Field right now. I could make a call and you could be here in a couple of hours. Spend the night and be back in town tomorrow morning. The jet has to come back out here anyway. You'll love this place."

The private jet was tempting, if only because I hated modern commercial airports with all their intrusive anti-terrorism precautions. My friend Elmer claimed the regulations at airports were designed to acclimatize the populace to a fascist state. Whether that was the intent or not, it certainly worked towards that end. "Call your people," I said.

Five minutes later a secretary called back and gave me an address on Perimeter Road at Boeing Field just off I-5. I was to report within the hour. Upstairs in the office I waited for Kathy to finish a phone call and told her where I was headed. "Are Bonds and Gunderson going to be there?" she asked.

"I don't know."

"I don't want you to go."

"Why not?"

"Because you're going to disappear and they're going to claim you fell off a mountain or a bear ate you or you went for a hike and got swallowed up by an old mine shaft. Thomas, this trip is just a setup for a disappearance. Don't play into their hands."

"Monica wouldn't set me up. You're being paranoid."

"Somebody already tried to kill you once this week." She sat on the edge of her desk in front of me, sizing me up, trying to read my mind, which she was pretty good at. "You're going anyway, aren't you?"

"Yes."

"Why?"

"We don't even know if Bonds and Gunderson are in Montana. If they are, I doubt they'll try anything."

"You think you can handle just about anything they throw at you, don't you?"

"Yes."

"That's just the sort of Errol Flynn attitude that will get you killed."

"Errol Flynn died in bed. It wasn't *his* bed, but he died in bed."

"Errol Flynn had stuntmen."

"Not for the bedroom stuff. Neither do I." I grinned but she didn't find me amusing. "If something happens, get hold of Snake. Have him contact his brother. The two of them will sort it out." I hadn't been scared of anybody in the way I was scared of Marvin Gunderson since I was in seventh grade and the Haglund brothers were after me, so it was hard to know why I was flying into the mouth of the volcano.

"First you tell me nothing is going to happen and then you give me instructions for after you're dead."

"Nothing's going to happen."

"Now you're repeating yourself."

Before I left we kissed, and later on I realized it had the sweet, lingering feel of a man being sent off to his execution. I was convinced this was going to be a non-eventful twenty-four-hour jaunt and that I would be back in one piece by tomorrow afternoon, but in the kiss I could feel all of Kathy's tension and some of mine. She'd wanted to make love last night but I'd turned her down. I hadn't been able to stand the thought of making love to her with all of those images of Angela and her friends roiling through my brain. I wished now I'd been more accommodating.

24

AFTER months of mostly gray skies, it was a kick in the head to ascend above the clouds into the sunshine, to gawp at a snowy Mount Rainier and the other volcanoes along the Cascade Range: Mount St. Helens with its top blown off by the 1980 eruption, and Adams, which I'd climbed once with a group of amateurs. It had been just enough excitement to put all of Angela's mountaineering into perspective.

I was the only passenger. It was a Falcon 10, the interior outfitted as if it were a limo, with a couch affair at the back that looked as if it might also serve as a bed. We were headed for Montana, but the pilot advised me there would be a stopover in Portland.

I was thankful for a chance to relax and gather my thoughts concerning the events of the past week. Without the airport hassles and the U.S. government peeking down my underwear, flying was more like the old days. I'd parked just off Perimeter Road on Boeing Field, was greeted by the pilot while the co-pilot attended to business inside the cockpit. I had a small bag with a toothbrush and shampoo, some cash I'd withdrawn from an ATM, and a fair idea of who I wanted to talk to and what I wanted to ask when I got to Montana. I wasn't planning to reveal the videos to Pennington just yet. It seemed the more sullied it became, the more prepared I was to shield Angela's reputation.

As we passed over the deformed peak of Mount St. Helens, the young pilot came back and sat across from me. He was a tall man with blond hair and a Scandinavian accent, who, in the course of our conversation, told me he had three kids. "You going to see Mr. Self on business?" he asked at one point.

"His wife, actually."

"I'm trying to get a little nest egg together so he can invest it for me. His policy is a million to start, but with employees, he will accept a hundred grand. Their main fund earned eighteen percent last year. The guy's never had a losing year. It's incredible."

"Yes, I guess it is." I'd read articles about Clark Lloyd Self in *Fortune*, *Business Week*, and the *Financial Times*. Inside the industry he was regarded with almost universal awe and approbation. When Angela spoke out against him, she'd been spitting into a hurricane of approval from admirers, disciples, and sycophants.

"You're not investing with him?" the pilot asked.

"If I had something to invest, I might."

"You have any questions about the flight or you need something, feel free to come up front and ask one of us. Sophie will be doing the flying, getting in more hours for her rating."

"Sure."

When he went back to the controls and pulled the curtains aside, I leaned out into the narrow aisle to get a gander into the cockpit. The last time I'd seen the co-pilot she'd been naked. Sophie Millwood. I wondered if the co-pilot and Clark Lloyd Self were still sleeping together now that Self and Pennington were back together. Odd that Sophie Millwood would be ferrying Monica Pennington around. But jobs were scarce and the ways of the über-wealthy were beyond my commoner sensibilities.

We made a quick stop in Portland, descending through cloud cover onto a small, private field. After taxiing toward a series of hangars, a man in a dark suit trotted out to the plane with a suitcase in one hand and a case in the other which might have contained a rifle. He climbed into the plane, stooping under the low interior as the pilot secured the door. I guess I was about the last person he expected to bump into. "Hey, Thomas. Long time no see. You working for CLS Enterprises, too?"

"Doing a job for the wife."

"They hired me right after the funeral. I just went through a seminar in body-guarding skills. People are targeting the wealthy. A fourteen-year-old kid in Florida got kidnaped and had one of his nuts mailed to his parents by a gang of Cubans."

"Sorry to hear that. Speaking of which, how are Gunderson's nuts?"

"I didn't know there was anything wrong with them. Something happen?"

"Somebody used them as door knockers. By the way, you changed your number."

"They gave me a company cell. It's a security thing. It's not like I left a bunch of girlfriends in Seattle who are going to be calling my old number." He laughed.

Crane stowed his luggage in an empty seat and sat heavily in the plush, leather-covered seat opposite mine. It was good to see him. I didn't have enough friends that I could afford to lose track of one. We taxied for takeoff and then felt the sudden drag-strip acceleration as we lifted off.

We were silent as the jet rose steeply into the sky. I could feel the G-force pulling at me in the same way this case was pulling at me.

Out the window I saw another private jet landing on the same strip we'd just used. Then we were higher and I could see Mount Hood and the Columbia River before everything went gray as we were buried in the clouds. Minutes later, after we were back in the sunshine, I turned to Crane.

"You wouldn't believe how much they're paying," he said. "These people crap money. And all that experience as a sniper in the Army I thought was wasted? It was what made me attractive to CLS."

"How so?"

"They've got all this land in Montana and in South America. One of the things they're afraid of is snipers sneaking onto the property. They need somebody like me to tell them where a sniper might set up, how far they can shoot, how they could use night vision, all that shit. Right now I'm the cat's meow. I've already spent two hundred grand of their money on equipment."

"Gunderson hired you?"

"Pennington did. After the funeral she spoke to her husband and they found a spot for me. You want the truth, I think she might have hired me as a gesture of goodwill towards her sister. Because we'd been friends."

"You only knew her two weeks."

"I don't think Pennington realizes that."

"And you aren't going to tell her?"

"Hell, this is a good job."

I wondered if Pennington wasn't playing a game of paying off Angela's former friends with pissy little jobs, writing checks and feeling better because of it. I wondered if investigating Angela's suicide wasn't a make-work job spurred by charity or guilt. Surely, from Monica Pennington's point of view, Crane Manning and I must look like paupers.

"I feel like I've gone over to the enemy," Crane said. "I mean . . . except for her sister, these people all rubbed Angela the wrong way. I can't even imagine what she would think if she saw me wearing a CLS blazer. But I need the job, and Self treats his people well. Among other perks, we all get a one-week vacation at their estate in the Antilles every September. Self is not a bad guy to my way of thinking. He was just sowing wild oats the day we saw him."

"Crane, people sow wild oats in their late teens and early twenties. Self is sixty-three and married."

"No, you don't understand. He likes women. What's wrong with that? Thomas, I'm telling you, body-guarding the top one tenth of one percent is the next big thing. People like you and me can make a lot of money. Half the country's lost their jobs, and these people need to be protected from the rabble."

"From their point of view, we *are* the rabble."

"I know that. But you should get in on this body-guarding gig. Ex-cop. Private eye. You'd find a job in a heartbeat." Crane was drunk on his own good fortune. In some ways I was glad for him. On the other hand, Self now had both Crane and me on his payroll, the two people who'd been assisting Angela in her attempted take-down of his marriage. Angela had been working night and day to gather evidence on Self, but oddly all she did in the end was destroy herself. I once saw a dog break its neck running into a parked car while chasing a bus. Angela had been chasing a bus.

"Crane, can I ask you something?"

"Sure."

"Did you sleep with Angela?"

"What? Hell, no." I'd asked because they'd been flirting the day they met. And because I'd discovered she was a sexual creature after all. He seemed embarrassed. I wasn't sure if his discomfiture came because he thought of Angela in a brotherly way or if she was somebody he *never* would have dated, in the same way I never would have dated anyone who was that cuckoo.

"The afternoon she died, how early did you arrive at her place?"

"Ten minutes before you got there, maybe fifteen."

"You see anybody else in the hallway or downstairs?"

"No."

"See any signs anybody else had been there? Anything broken or disturbed?"

"No."

"Nothing strange at all?"

"When I was waiting I heard somebody going down the stairs. Sounded like two guys. Or a couple of fat chicks. I didn't actually see them. But I already told you this."

"No, you didn't."

"I know I told the police. I thought I told you."

"No."

"It was probably just some kids who lived in the building running down the stairs, making a racket. It didn't have anything to do with her. Jesus, I wish one of us could have been up there to talk sense to her. Being so close when it happened still bothers me. It bother you? I guess it would. You were a lot closer than I was."

"Yeah."

"By the way, what are you doing here?"

"Pennington hired me to look into Angela's death."

"I thought it was a suicide."

"She wants to know why."

"You would have thought they would want to bury the whole thing as quickly as possible. I keep thinking I could have done something to stop her. If she hadn't been so intractable."

"She was always like that."

"She was a good kid."

The word 'kid' said it all. He hadn't thought of her as a full-fledged woman. I wasn't sure anybody except the men in the video had. Maybe that was why she kept the videos, as proof that somebody thought of her as a grown up.

"You work with Bonds or Gunderson yet?" I asked.

"I don't know if you'd call it working. I've seen them around."

"What do they do, exactly?"

"They're Self's private bodyguards. Bonds is more of the driver. Gunderson is kind of a second-in-command-slash-valet. I heard he killed a horse with his fist."

"That story's going around. Does Self have more bodyguards than just those two?"

"Well, he's got me now."

"What else do you know about them?"

Uncomfortable with my prying, Crane hesitated. "They've been good to me, Thomas. Bonds isn't too bright, but Gunderson does the crossword puzzle in the paper almost as fast as he can write. Then he does the Sudoku and the other puzzles at the same speed. Bonds doesn't believe it and double checks him just about every day. The guy's a genius."

"They do strong-arm stuff for Self?"

"As far as I know, it's all straight bodyguard work."

"Would you be willing to call me if my name pops up?"

"Thomas, I have to be loyal to my employer. This is a good job. I don't want to screw it up. Besides, for all I know, Self hired you to test my loyalty."

"He didn't. You think there's a chance those two were following Angela the day she died?"

"If they were, I didn't see them."

"They were following her the night before. Why not the next day?"

"I can't answer that, but honestly, I didn't see them."

Hours later Flathead Lake appeared out the window. It was enormous and very blue and had tiny dots I identified as water craft scratching white arcs across it. We descended over the lake but kept heading south. The Self property was off in the boonies, mountains on two sides, lots of snow even though it was May. We landed on a private air strip cut down the center of a small valley. Crane said, "They own a couple thousand acres. Maybe more. They keep twelve people out here working year round. I'd love to live in a place like this year round. Wouldn't that be great?"

"Terrific."

Clark Lloyd Self met us at the airstrip in an open Jeep. He was wearing a sheepskin jacket and looked hardy, his face flushed from driving in the cool air. "Crane, my man," he said. "How was the class?"

"Terrific, sir. Thanks for sending me."

"It was Gunderson's idea. Thank him. And Black?" He had the self confidence, ease of command, and simple, honest persuasiveness that could overwhelm any sort of miscasting society might try to impress on his life. You had the feeling nothing would ever go wrong for this man. He gave off the aura of somebody who knew what he was doing at all times, a man in perfect control of all the natural and artificial forces surrounding him. It was easy to see why people trusted him with their money.

Self's eye control was amazing; he only once glanced toward the cockpit and Sophie Millwood before motioning for us to get into the Jeep. If he still had a relationship with Millwood, he was determined not to reveal it to me or Crane. I wondered if his wife even knew who the co-pilot was. I wondered if it was my job to tell her.

We drove almost a mile down a dirt road until we reached a cluster of buildings constructed of logs, precisely what one would expect in Montana. The air was nippy enough we could see our breath, and although I was dressed in jeans and a thick fleece zip-up, the drive in the open Jeep chilled me to the bone. One of the buildings had a date of 1910 on it, so I gathered there was an original homestead here, all the later architecture designed to blend with it. Farther back from the main house I spotted a cluster of small cottages tucked away in the gully almost like a small factory town. There was a scull cap of snow on the mountain behind the main house.

As we arrived in front of a cottage to drop off Crane, Self glanced back at me. "I guess Monica called you here?"

"We're having a meeting."

"Anything important?"

"Just an accounting of what I've got so far."

"Making headway?"

"There are still a lot of blanks to fill in."

"Monica's out horseback riding with some friends. They're usually gone a couple of hours."

"I can wait."

I got the feeling he hadn't known I was coming until he saw me at the air strip.

After we dropped Crane off, Self wheeled the Jeep around in a tight circle, taking far too much pride in his ability to handle the machine.

"Give you the Cook's tour," he said when we got to the front of the large log house. He parked, leaving the keys in the Jeep, and walked up the broad, wooden steps to the main entrance in a sprightly manner that belied his sixty-three years and hinted at a personal trainer.

"I'd like a chance to talk to you," I said, when we reached the enormous maple double doors.

"We can chat while I show you around." His eyes were grey and piercing. He was an ugly man, and I didn't think so simply because Angela hadn't liked him and he detested me. He'd been an ugly boy and he'd probably been an ugly baby. It was just one of those things. He'd overcome his looks with the sheer force of his personality. He had a box of rifle bullets in one of the chest pockets of his jacket. I wondered if he was expecting a horde of renegade prairie dogs and was thinking he might run out of ammo.

"I'm trying to figure out Angela's reasoning during her last few days. As you well know, her thoughts were pretty much centered on this family."

"She spent too much time worrying about other people's business and not enough tending her own."

"She invested with you, didn't she?"

"I never handled any of that personally."

"She wasn't happy with the results. Surely you heard that much?"

"She came unglued over it. For months there were suits and counter suits. But that's what lawyers are for. From what my people tell me, she lost money but not because we had invested it poorly. It was because she kept yanking it out at the wrong time. It's all about timing, and she was second-guessing us, spoiling every transaction. That's all I can tell you about it."

He knew more. I sensed it in his reticence.

The interior of the mammoth main house sported varnished log walls and looked like the lobby of a luxury resort. Self nodded at a stuffed grizzly off in a corner next to a massive river rock fireplace that rose forty feet to the ceiling. "They say that old boy was shot back in the 1870s by Jeremiah Johnson. Ever see the movie? Had Bob Redford up here to the house a couple of times. He wanted to buy that old bear, but I couldn't part with it. Jeremiah Johnson. What a story. The Crow murdered his wife, so he went on a vendetta. He killed more Crow than smallpox did. Used to eat their livers. The Crow were scared out of their wits by him. Hell of a man. I got his skull in my office. I'll show it to you sometime."

"Robert Redford's?"

"Jeremiah Johnson," he said, in a tone that told me he was not amused by my caustic remarks. We were heading through the library on our way to the dining room when Self stopped abruptly. In the distance, I could see an open door to a huge kitchen stocked with copper pots suspended over stainless-steel counters and more than one huge Viking range, squads of people in white bustling about.

I said, "The two goons you have working for you scared the hell out of Angela."

"You talking about Marvin and Goodnight?"

"Surely you had somebody investigate Bonds before you let him mix with your family. And Gunderson was a killer in the Army."

"We were all killers in the Army. That's what the Army's about. I believe Crane was a killer in the Army, as well. And he's *your* friend, isn't he?"

"He was a sniper, yes. Is that why you hired him?"

"People hire thieves to stop theft. In the past, I've hired reformed computer hackers to keep hackers out of our computers. It's the way of the world. Take Marvin. He has a sterling service record. Won all kinds of awards. As far as the runt goes, I believe in giving people a second chance. After all, that's what my life has been about. When I flunked out of college I had an advisor who said I was going to end up homeless. I started a car business and made it work. I raised a good, solid, God-fearing family. I started an investment business. And then, just when you would have thought my life was settled, I had the good fortune to run into Monica. I'm an expert at re-creating myself. I've had too many second chances not to offer one to somebody else. I don't like being questioned about my business practices, but I will tell you this. I hire people for their skills. I pay them well and I expect unquestioning allegiance. Any other personnel decisions you want to help me with?"

"Not if you can tell me why Bonds and Gunderson were following Angela the week she died."

"As far as I know, they were doing no such thing."

"I saw them."

"Marvin Gunderson has a great deal of latitude in how he protects me. If he was following Angela, which I don't think he was, he had good reason. You might ask him yourself." Self seemed a little smug about my ability, or inability, to get anything out of Gunderson. Certainly he knew how intimidating Gunderson could be. I found it not credible that he didn't know they'd been tailing her. Angela had abhorred this man, had plotted against him. He had every reason to have her followed. While I certainly didn't trust him, I found myself slowly beginning to admire what he'd done with his life. Maybe it was the absurd wealth. Even if we think we're not, we're all impressed by fortunes, especially hard-earned fortunes. And Self had come up from nothing.

Twenty-five years ago, he had an anorexic spouse, a passel of kids, and was selling broken-down Toyotas fifteen hours a day. Now he had a famous wife, a fortune, and a mistress who could fly a jet.

25

WE were on the second floor when Goodnight Bonds came trotting up the wide, wooden staircase. The eager look on Bonds' face vanished when he realized who I was. Until thirty seconds ago I believe he thought I was dead, or close enough. I must have looked like a ghost to him.

When Self addressed him, they stepped away from me and whispered together for a moment before Bonds went down the stairs. He had a pair of expensive ear protectors around his neck, as if he'd been at a gun range, or was headed to one.

"Black? We've got a few hours of light left. Would you like to do some shooting?"

"I was hoping we could talk."

"We can talk on the range."

I was assigned a comfortable room, where I stashed my kit and washed my hands and face in the adjoining bathroom. I met Self on the front porch five minutes later.

There were two Jeeps out front now, both topless despite the chilly mountain air, one carrying Marvin Gunderson and Clark Lloyd Self, along with gun cases and boxes of shooting paraphernalia in the back seat. Goodnight Bonds was driving the second Jeep. I was to ride with him, which meant I wouldn't be asking Self or Gunderson any questions on the drive. I was to ride with the man I believed had tried to murder me yesterday morning. By the time I got in, Gunderson and

Self had taken off in a flurry of exhaust. Bonds accelerated while I still had one foot on the ground, but I managed to save myself and get belted in without comment. We drove in silence for a few minutes. I'd fallen into the exact scenario Kathy had warned me about.

"It's about two miles," Bonds said. "You're not afraid of guns, are you?"

I didn't answer. I was wondering how many abandoned mine shafts were in these mountains.

"Because I heard you were afraid of guns."

"Where'd you hear that?"

"Marvin ran a background check on you. You afraid of guns?"

"Guns hurt people. Of course I'm afraid of them. I'm wearing a diaper in case I wet my pants."

Bonds laughed moronically. I had to look over at him to see if he was serious, but that was apparently the way he laughed. After a few moments, I realized he wasn't laughing at my joke. He actually thought I was wearing a diaper. He said it again and again. "Diaper. Diaper." I began to wonder if he didn't have Asperger's syndrome. After a while he settled down and said, "Last time I saw him my grandpa was wearing a diaper."

"Did you laugh at him?"

"Are you kidding? You don't say anything to my grandpa unless you want to get knocked into next Tuesday. He's a tough old bird."

Against my better judgment, I began to feel sorry for Bonds. Life was difficult enough without innate stupidity dulling every decision you ever made. He wasn't to the point of needing to live in a home like Hoshi Smith, but he wasn't too far behind either. Most people did stupid things, but the great majority of us were not inherent morons. Bonds seemed to be just that. He'd been raised by a sociopathic grandfather, without a mother, without a father, and didn't have the brains, skills, or gumption to make it in any part of the world I'd ever seen. How he landed here, working for one of the richest men in the country, was beyond me. Actually, to be fair, I had to admit he was doing pretty well for himself.

"You were a cop?" He said it in the way people who are sworn enemies of the police said it, the way people who'd had trouble with the police their whole lives said it. As if it defined me. I guess, for him, it did.

"Used to be."

"How does a cop get to be afraid of guns?"

"Good question."

"Do me a favor, will you? Don't get panicked out here. It's just target shooting. We're not going to be shooting *at* anybody."

"I'll try not to soil my diaper."

He laughed again.

I wondered whether to confront him with the hit and run from yesterday but decided to do it when we weren't standing around with weapons in our hands. Instead, I said, "Why were you and Gunderson following Angela?"

"We weren't."

"Yes, you were."

"When?"

"The week she died I found you lurking outside Pan Africa on First Avenue. You guys followed her there."

"We were delivering an invitation to her apartment."

"You weren't *at* her apartment. You were on First Avenue."

"We got there just as she was leaving. We drove behind her downtown and saw her park. We were waiting to give her an invitation."

"An invitation to what?"

"I don't know. I didn't open it."

"You didn't give it to her, either."

"Got distracted."

"Who was the invitation from?"

"Not my business to ask."

It was a small gun range with covered benches to accommodate ten or twelve shooters, target placements for pistols at one end, rifles farther down. There were earthen bunkers in the field behind the targets to absorb the lead, which at most ranges would later be dug out of the ground and recycled. The long, dormant grass between the shooting stands and the targets was tamped down, as if it had been laden with snow pack until recently. There were twenty-five- and fifty-yard targets at the pistol range. The rifle range next to it was sectioned into one hundred- and two hundred-yard stretches. The targets were already set up, some with fresh bullet holes in them.

Bonds jumped out of our Jeep and began helping Gunderson unload the first vehicle.

In a party of four, it was hard not to notice when one of the group didn't acknowledge your existence, and Gunderson was making a point of ignoring me. Even though I thought he had been part of a plot to kill me, I was strangely offended. But then, I already knew Gunderson was the enemy.

While Bonds and Gunderson went about laying out rifles and pistols at the various shooting stands, Self handed me a box with a set of ear protectors in it, the kind that screened out gunshots while allowing one to hear sounds at a conversational level, battery operated and complex enough to require a manual.

"Couple more questions," I said, stepping close to Clark Lloyd Self, who had pulled a pistol out of a holster on the back of his belt and was inspecting it. He'd been carrying it fully loaded, an expensive Kimber, a custom-made 1911 replica with gold-plated handles. Though some quarreled with the fact that they were based on a hundred-year-old design, the Kimber was a solid gun, accurate and pricey. It packed a punch, too.

I said, "Clark, do you have any reason to think Angela might have been looking into something other than your love life?"

He gave me a look more raw than anything I'd seen from him, more like the stare-down a fighter might give upon stepping into the ring with a particularly troublesome rival. I wondered if he was angry because I'd had the audacity to call him 'Clark.' Whatever the cause, it was as if I had opened a window into his soul, as if he'd forgotten himself, had lifted the lid on the furnace and, for just that one moment, allowed me to feel the full heat. It only lasted a moment before he reverted to the avuncular and commanding presence he cultivated for the rest of mankind.

I continued to probe. "You had an employee named Rafael Gutierrez. Sometime after you canned him he was killed in a traffic accident. Angela was in contact with him until his death. Were you aware they knew each other?"

"News to me. What is the relevance?"

"I was hoping you could tell me."

"It seems it never rains in a man's life but it pours. Rafael was a good man until some of my people caught him smuggling restricted materials out of the building. It was too bad."

"His death affected Angela deeply."

"Angela could get very emotional, but I doubt his death was related to anything you're dealing with. It was just one of those unhappy accidents."

"Do you have any idea what the nature of their relationship was?"

"Like I said, I didn't know they had a relationship."

I wanted to ask about Henrik Federer, too. Along with Rafael Gutierrez, he had spent time with Angela. But I hadn't talked to Federer yet and didn't need Self's men visiting and intimidating him before I got there. The orbit of Angela's life already had two dead people in it, Angela herself and Rafael Gutierrez. It might have been three if yesterday's hit and run had been executed more cleanly. I couldn't help thinking CLS Enterprises was tied to those two deaths and to the hit and run. I'd convinced myself yesterday's driver was Bonds, yet the fact was, I wasn't certain enough to testify to it in a court of law. I wasn't even certain enough to punch him out. I didn't have any more proof than the one incredibly brief glimpse.

For twenty minutes, we shot the expensive Kimbers, the four of us lined up alongside each other, first Self, then Gunderson, then Bonds, with me on the far end. I noticed Bonds was keeping track of everything I did. I thought at first it was because he'd never shot with me and was worried I might exhibit unsafe range practices, but it was more than that. He'd grown up with guns in the house, had hunted and poached with his grandfather from an early age, and displayed the arrogance and show-off panache of some long-time gun-handlers when they're around someone they imagine is a neophyte. He was waiting for me to screw up, shoot myself in the foot or accidentally point a pistol at one of the others. My first round with the .45 went dead center into the black of the target at twenty-five yards. Thinking I'd missed the paper altogether because he couldn't see a bullet hole in the broader white of the target where he was expecting it, he snickered. I decided to have some fun with him and began missing deliberately. As each of my shots went farther afield, Bonds found it harder to contain his laughter. I shot into the dirt berm around the targets and even hit the post supporting *his* target. "I think you're flinching," he said over the sound of shots from the other two shooters. "You're flinching. You're scared of the gun."

"Guns are dangerous."

We'd gone through a box of ammo each, were feeding the heavy

.45 slugs into the Kimber magazines for another cycle, when Self received a phone call and announced he had to go back to the lodge for better phone reception. He took the same Jeep he'd come out in, which left me alone with Bonds and Gunderson. For a moment, I wondered if this wasn't the set-up Kathy had warned me about. If so, it would be a surprise all the way around. I would be surprised when they came after me and they would be surprised when I turned the Kimber on them. If they killed me, Kathy would call Snake and they would be even more surprised when Snake and his brother unleashed their own brand of hell. Snake didn't need evidence. He only needed to be pointed in a direction, and if his brother was along I was pretty sure he would kill anybody who got in their way.

"Hey, Black," Bonds said, after a consultation with Gunderson, who still hadn't looked at me. "Wanna step out there and straighten out that target for us?"

A hundred yards away, the corner of one of the rifle targets had come loose and was curling down against itself. Bonds was asking me to jog across the shooting field while he and Gunderson remained in place with loaded weapons, including some tricked-out military rifles with attached scopes, flashlights, lasers, and gizmos I didn't even know the uses of. The rifles also had suppressors, known commonly as silencers. I said, "You go."

"Me?"

"Yeah, you."

"Why don't you?"

"It's too uncomfortable to walk that far in a wet diaper."

Bonds began laughing, then jogged across the field toward the targets. Yesterday he'd wanted to kill me. Today he thought I was hilarious.

Gunderson still hadn't looked at me. It would have been creepy in a purely social context, but knowing we'd had a physical altercation in the past and believing the two of them had tried to murder me yesterday, knowing he could swat me into next week with the back of his hand, that there were loaded guns on the hand-carved plank in front of him, it was downright threatening. I kept the loaded .45 semi-automatic pistol close.

"You know a man named Rafael Gutierrez?" I asked, but he ignored me. "You don't want to talk, that's fine. We'll do it on Self's dime. It'll irritate the hell out of him, but it makes no difference to me."

"What does Gutierrez have to do with anything?" Gunderson asked, still without looking my way.

"You knew Gutierrez?"

"When they let him go I escorted him out of the building. Bastard was crying like a baby. Said he needed the job. Said he was going to lose his marriage."

"He *did* lose his marriage. What did you tell him?"

"Told him if he needed the job so bad, he shouldn't have been stealing from us."

"What was he stealing?"

"I can't reveal that."

"Where were you the day Angela committed suicide?"

"I'd have to check my scheduler. What's this about?"

"I'm eliminating suspects."

"Suspects to what? It was a suicide. I, for one, was sorry she did it. And . . . I wish I'd behaved more appropriately at the funeral. If you heard anything I said, I want to apologize. I had a few drinks beforehand. I knew she'd talked about killing herself in the past, but I never thought she would go through with it."

"She talked about suicide around you?"

"A couple of times. I thought she was joking. Once again, I'm sorry if I offended you. Angela was a good woman, and despite all the aggravation she caused, I admired her." He turned and looked at me with clear blue eyes like marbles, the first time he'd looked at me since I arrived in Montana. "She deserved more than she got."

"Most of us do. What sort of aggravation did she cause you?"

"You were there. You saw some of it."

"Why were you guys following her?"

"You mean that night on First Avenue? We were going out to dinner when we saw her getting out of her Volkswagen. We thought we'd stop and see what was going on."

"You weren't following her?"

"Of course not."

"Funny how your story and the one Bonds just told don't match up."

"Fuck Bonds. Somebody should sew his mouth shut."

"Why didn't you want me to have contact with her? Was that on orders?"

"I didn't want her to get hurt."

"Hurt how?"

"I just didn't want her hanging out with you."

"So it was personal?"

"Yeah."

There was an intercom between all of our hearing protectors that I didn't know about until Gunderson pushed a button on his headset and I heard him talking in my earpiece. Gunderson picked up one of the scoped AR-15s, jacked a loaded magazine into it and threw the bolt, which slid a live cartridge into the chamber. To my astonishment, he pointed it down range and flicked off the safety with his thumb. "Goodnight. Just stay out there for a minute. I want to see if these are still sighted for two hundred yards."

"Don't be shooting when I'm out here," Goodnight said, alarm etching his voice.

From a hundred yards away, Bonds looked back and saw Gunderson aiming at him. He dove behind the dirt berm. I could hear him clearly in the earpiece cursing like a longshoreman.

Gunderson let loose a couple of shots, each muffled by the silencer. With his ear protectors still on, I didn't believe Bonds could hear them downrange. He would, however, hear the slap of the bullets as they dug into the earthen berm next to his head. "How'm I doing?" Gunderson asked.

Without showing himself, Bonds said, "Nine ring and nine ring. Both to the right. Can I come out now?"

"Yeah. Sure. Come on out." After Bonds was several feet from the sanctuary of the berm, Gunderson shouldered the rifle and fired three more quick rounds.

"What the fuck?" Bonds shouted into our earpieces.

Gunderson laughed and fired twice more. By now Bonds was scrambling around in front of the targets, unsure whether to run across the range or to leap back behind the berm where he'd been hiding earlier. He looked more like a cartoon character than ever. Gunderson was firing on all sides of him now, kicking up dirt to his right and his left. Bonds let loose a string of profanities while dodging this way and that, like a nervous squirrel trying to cross the road in front of a car. He finally ran to the right, hurdled a berm in front of an empty target and disappeared from sight.

Gunderson was laughing so hard he was having trouble keeping the AR-15 level.

"Cut it out," I said.

In my headphones, I could hear Bonds say, "Marvin? Are you crazy? Let me out."

"Okay. You can come out now." Bonds raised his head and Gunderson fired another round, kicking up dirt three feet to Bonds' left. At a hundred yards it was incredibly risky, criminal really. I didn't know what sort of lethal games these two were in the habit of indulging when I wasn't around, but I couldn't let them continue this one while I had the ability to stop it.

"Cease and desist!" I said, pushing the button on the side of my head phones so Bonds could hear me as well.

"Mind your own business," Gunderson snapped.

"You shoot him, it *is* my business."

"I'm not going to shoot him."

"You done now, Marvin?" Bonds shouted.

"All done." But Gunderson wasn't finished. He was still aiming at the berm where Bonds had concealed himself. I saw Bonds wave his hand over the berm with a white hanky, saw Gunderson tighten his finger on the trigger.

I reached out and pulled the hot barrel of the AR-15 downwards, or tried to. Gunderson had his own ham-hock of a fist wrapped around the hand guard, so all I had left was the heated barrel. It burned my hand, but I didn't let go. The rifle moved at first, but only because Gunderson hadn't been expecting me to grab it. I'd never touched another man's gun while he was shooting and wasn't happy about being forced to do so now, but I didn't know how else to stop him. He probably wasn't planning to shoot Bonds, but then again, if he *did* shoot him and I didn't do anything, I would be an accomplice. It was ironic to be championing a man I believed had tried to kill me. I wondered if Gunderson hadn't thought about the irony before he began shooting.

Because I'd jarred him, Gunderson fired a round into the turf in front of us. I expected him to put the rifle down and turn on me, but he was bent on keeping Bonds in his merry little trap, so he lifted the rifle once again and aimed at the berm. I was pulling on the hot barrel as hard as I could, but I couldn't stop him. I'd never felt such massive animal strength.

"What's going on?" Bonds asked in my headphone. Gunderson was holding his aim on the berm a hundred yards away while I was gripping the hot barrel and trying to move it off target. Except I wasn't moving it anywhere. Gunderson was holding steady, and no matter what I tried, no matter how much weight I applied to the rifle, it didn't budge. I knew Gunderson was strong, but I couldn't believe *how* strong. I had almost my full weight on his rifle.

There were Olympic athletes and circus strong men, and then there were freaks of nature. What we had here was a freak of nature. I'd known Gunderson possessed extraordinary physical abilities, but never dreamed he or anybody else on the planet was this strong. I'd known men with a fitness level that was one in ten thousand, known a weightlifter who was probably one in a million, but the odds of ever running into anyone as powerful as Gunderson were well above anything I could quantify. I stood back, my Kimber at the ready. I wasn't able to stop him from intimidating Bonds, but then again, I wasn't going to give him a chance to draw down on me. If he pointed the rifle in my direction, I would blast away with the Kimber.

Finally, as if sensing his game had slipped into something else, Gunderson lowered his rifle, released the magazine, cleared the chamber, and slipped a yellow rubber safety block where a bullet would normally go. It was as if it hadn't happened.

I spoke into my headphones. "You can come out now, Goodnight."

Five minutes later Bonds and I were picking up the weapons while Gunderson rooted around inside a small, windowless shed off to one side. We were just about finished when I picked up the Kimber I'd been using and held it in both hands. Sighting on a metal target on the one hundred-yard range, I squeezed off a shot, waited, and heard the satisfying ping as the heavy .45 slug plinked the steel.

"What was that?" Bonds asked.

"I just fired off my last round."

"I thought I heard something clink."

"It was Gunderson with the tools."

"It sounded like it was on the range."

"In the shed."

26

I was served a light supper at a small table in the cavernous white-tiled kitchen while the three-person kitchen staff bustled around me. They told me they had all graduated from the Pennsylvania Culinary Institute at the same time and were shuttled around to Self's various estates as required. They'd been flown here two days ago and had been working madly ever since. Tonight they were serving dinner for eighteen visitors, plus the help, including me. In the main dining room, I could hear Self entertaining his raucous, laughing guests.

I'd already waited two hours for Monica Pennington to show up, only to be told she'd come in from horseback riding and was taking a nap, apparently having forgotten our appointment.

Not wishing to intrude on the festivities in the other room, I finished dinner and sat with my chair against the wall, reading off my phone, which was plugged in to the Wi-Fi in the building. At one point Marvin Gunderson retrieved a snack out of the fridge—half a turkey—and left without speaking to me. I'm not sure he even realized I was there. I scanned the Internet for more gossipy articles on the Pennington/Self marriage. It seemed they'd run through the cycle several times, the penultimate reconciliation three years ago when she accused him of mental cruelty and drugging her dog, while he accused her of trying to seduce a waiter at the wedding of one of his daughters from his first marriage. I don't know about 'trying' to seduce. It seemed like all Pennington would have to do was crook her little finger and any waiter in the country would crumple. One rumor had it Pennington needed to resurrect their relationship because she was deep in debt and had signed a prenup severely limiting the amount of money she might walk away with.

Self was said to be worth upwards of twenty billion dollars—hell, he owned a major league baseball team on the East Coast, a NASCAR racing team, and a symphony orchestra he once transported across the continent to play for his wife's birthday party—yet reports asserted that if he and Pennington divorced she would get limited living expenses for ten years, child support, and little else. After ten years, she would be on her own. The living expense money, according to one reporter, was limited to a hundred fifty thousand a month, which Pennington's lawyers claimed would barely cover housing. I took it with a grain of salt. Stories had been written about me in the press, and they'd never been completely accurate.

I made a few calls, managing to contact a psychologist in Portland whose services Kathy had used in a trial last year. I had a theory about Angela and fed him the details as I understood them. I told him about Angela's bouts of depression, her reckless behavior on our building roof the day we all went to Eastgate and caught Self in bed with his mistress, her series of lost jobs, her mixed history with the opposite sex, the porn tapes, the long stretches without sleep, and her paranoia concerning electrical appliances. We spoke for half an hour. According to him, Angela fit a mental health pattern I'd tentatively identified myself but hadn't felt qualified to diagnose on my own.

I was still mulling it over ten minutes later when Monica Pennington burst into the kitchen for a clean wine glass. For a moment, she couldn't quite establish who I was or why I was in her kitchen. Finally, she said, "Oh, there you are. Did you get dinner? We're having a wonderful time out there. Brad and Angelina are here. You should join us. No need to be a stick-in-the-mud. Gosh. You're taller than I remember." She laughed. It sounded like a chicken clucking and was almost as irritating as her sister's whinnying.

"If you can find the time, we should talk," I said, hoping it was going to happen before she got completely soused and forgot who I was.

"Sure, honey. Let me go back out and excuse myself. Would you like to meet everyone?"

"Thanks, but I'll wait here."

"Okay, sweetie." Forty minutes later I found myself wishing I hadn't told her I would wait. The chair was uncomfortable, and I was beginning to feel like an insurance salesman parked in somebody's living room while they finished dinner.

To keep myself occupied, I texted Kathy, who wrote back and said she was having supper with friends. I checked the cameras around our house for signs of intruders in the past few hours and spotted our retired neighbor, Horace, peering through the window into our sun porch. I caught him snooping on our place three or four times a week.

"Oh, you're here?" Pennington said, bursting through the swinging doors to the kitchen. "I've been looking all over for you. Let's go someplace where we can get comfortable." Carrying a cup of coffee, she led me out another door and toward the back of the cavernous house to the library, its shelves lined mostly with popular fiction, one wall reserved for business and political tomes. Judging by the political titles, whoever selected them was vying for an apprenticeship with Attila the Hun. I could hear men's voices and women's laughter in another part of the house.

Monica wore riding boots and jodhpurs along with an off the shoulder white sweater. We sat on opposite ends of a leather sofa, she tucking her legs up, leaning toward me, sipping from her gold-rimmed coffee cup. Even though she'd been ignoring me all afternoon she now managed to make me feel like the most important person in the world. I said, "First, a few questions, if you don't mind."

"However you want to do this. I'm in your hands."

Brushing aside the double entendre, I said, "We know your sister was investigating your husband. Do you think she might have been investigating something other than his personal affairs?"

"For instance?"

"I was hoping you could tell me. She didn't say anything to you in the last few weeks to indicate where she was poking around? I'm guessing you've had some time to think about this by now."

"She told me to leave Clark, but she's been telling me to leave him since she lost money with him. She also told me he came on to her in the early years of our marriage when I was pregnant with Oliver. She reminded me of it the other day."

"You sound like you didn't believe her."

"With Angela, an accusation like that could be a matter of interpretation. She often got oddball notions that had no basis in fact. It was almost as if she would get the wiring in her brain crossed."

I agreed with that but didn't want to say it out loud. "You ever ask your husband about it?"

"About his coming on to her? No reason to. It never happened. And the money? That was her fault and everybody told her so."

"I don't have any proof yet, but I believe she was looking into your husband's business practices. Which brings me to another question. Did you realize Bonds and Gunderson were following her before she died?"

"I have no idea what those two do on a day-to-day basis."

"Also, I haven't been able to locate any really close friends. Lots of casual friends, in fact, far more than I expected, but none who were close enough to know her secrets. I was wondering if you could give me a name I haven't already run across. Someone who was close."

"I doubt she ever had a close friend. She loved my boys though, and they knew it. They were devastated when she died. Once she got this bee in her bonnet about Clark, I just felt I couldn't spend as much time with her. You realize, don't you, that Angela was a star fucker. Excuse my French, but you know what I mean. She took a little too much interest in famous people."

"You came close to divorcing this last time," I said, changing the subject.

"People change their minds. I'm sure you've had a change of mind once or twice. And while she may have been looking into my husband's finances, I don't want you doing it."

"I need to follow whatever trail she left."

"You're not listening. Certain areas of our lives are off limits."

I stood up, took the retainer check out of my wallet and tossed it onto the coffee table.

"What's this?" she asked.

"You want to start putting rules on this, get somebody else. I think she was looking into you both, and I need to follow the trail."

She thought about it, sipped her coffee, and tucked her legs tighter against herself.

"I'm going to find out why she killed herself," I said. "I think she was more than somebody who got depressed one day and decided to jump off a roof. It's got something to do with this family or your husband's business or both." We stared at each other for a few beats. I could see she had some of her husband's steel, for it soon became a contest of who could stare the longest, the iciest.

"Okay," she said. "Keep the check."

"And?"

"Angela thought my husband had stolen her money and was going to steal the rest of mine."

"That's what she told you?"

"Several times. I know it's absurd, but there it is."

"And you told your husband about her allegations?"

"How could I not?"

"And he told his goons to follow her?"

"I have no idea what he told them."

"But he hit the roof?"

"No. Of course not. He thought she was bat-shit crazy. Nothing new there."

I could see what an untenable position Angela must have placed her sister in. It couldn't have been easy to have a sibling urging you to dissolve your marriage. Even if she didn't talk about it incessantly, which Angela did, it would have been there between them every time they had any contact. Considering the pressure her sister had put on her, Pennington's reconciliation with her husband seemed almost a miracle.

I placed the check back in my wallet.

"Why would your husband be stealing from you? He's one of the wealthiest men on the planet. He is also, apparently, one of the most magnanimous employers around."

"My point exactly. I'm always telling him he gives too much to his people. If he has a weakness, it's the way he wants everyone to love him."

"So why would Angela think he was stealing from you?"

"He lost some of my money early on. She thought he wanted me broke so he would have more control over me. I blamed him for a while, but then I realized it was just business. Angela heard me blame him and never got over it. You know how she was. Once she got an idea in her noggin it quickly became hardwired."

"So he *did* lose some of your money?"

"Some of it. Most of it. Yes."

"But it wasn't done under the rubric of CLS Enterprises?"

"No."

"And Angela knew this? That it wasn't with CLS?"

"I told her everything. If you were around Angela, you realize she didn't always listen closely, or if she did, she had a tendency to misinterpret."

"How much money are we talking about?"

"A little under eleven million dollars."

"When did this happen?"

"Soon after we were married."

Angela had seen it as a control issue. Marry a beautiful, younger woman with her own money and everybody knows she can walk away any time she wants. Without funds, she might not feel so free to flee, especially if she's locked into an ironclad prenup agreement.

"Did your sister tell your husband she didn't think everything was on the up and up with CLS?"

"I doubt she ever said it in so many words. She had so damn many secrets."

I knew what some of them were, but I wasn't sure how much I wanted to reveal tonight. I was afraid if I told her about Angela's sex life, she might go into lock-down mode, fire me and tell her husband's people to stop talking to me. Whatever else happened and despite my threat to walk out, this investigation was going to continue and it would be a hell of a lot easier with her cooperation.

"Will your husband talk to me about this?"

"Please. Don't even mention we had this conversation. He is extremely touchy about any accusation against him. So are the people around him. You start poking around asking about his business, you're going to get doors slammed in your face. I'm not trying to stifle your investigation. I'm just telling you how it is."

"Angela told me a story once about two sisters celebrating a birthday party at a lake. When one of the young women announced she couldn't swim, the two sisters thought she was kidding and threw her in. She sank to the bottom and drowned. A passing jogger jumped in and brought her up, resuscitated her. She ended up brain damaged. That story ring any bells?"

"I don't think so."

"Hoshi Smith?"

"Hoshi? Gosh, I haven't given her a thought in years. Oh, yes. The lake. But that was just one of those things that happen when you're kids. Nobody's fault, really."

"You know what became of Hoshi?"

"I don't have the foggiest. She never kept in touch."

"You wouldn't be likely to hear from her, since she can't write her name or operate a telephone. She can barely open a door to get out of a room."

"You've seen her?"

"She's in a home in Kent. Your sister has been paying the rent for years."

"Tell me you're kidding."

"For at least seven years."

"That accounts for some of her money. I wonder what she did with the rest."

"You mean the portion she didn't lose with your husband?"

"I told you Angela lost that, not my husband. She lost it by withdrawing all of her funds and then putting them back in. She kept withdrawing when the market was down. Going back in when the market was high."

"You didn't have any contact with Hoshi after the incident?"

"I don't know what your preoccupation with Hoshi is. A few days after it happened, her parents took her out of the hospital and we never heard from her again. You say she's disabled?"

"I can't believe you didn't know that. Angela must have felt guilty over what you two had done."

"Guilty? Whatever for? It was just one of those things."

"Monica, people have gone to prison for less."

"Don't be absurd. We were kids."

Her tone was even more dismissive than her words. Odd that an event which had so obviously dominated Angela's life and had destroyed Hoshi's had barely registered in Monica's. In the face of her indifference, I was beginning to feel angry on Hoshi's behalf. I had the feeling that Angela had brought up the topic of Hoshi with her sister over the years and that the ignorance Pennington now professed was an act.

I changed directions again. "Did your sister have a regular doctor? If she did, I can't find any bills."

"Angela hated doctors. You couldn't drag her to one."

"So you don't know if she was ever diagnosed as bipolar?"

"What? No. Not as far as I know. What are you talking about?"

"I think your sister had manic-depression—bipolar disorder."

"Are you serious?"

"I've been suspecting this for a long time, but the more I learn about her the more sense it makes. I talked to a professional about it just tonight and outlined some of her behaviors for him. He agreed she may have been bipolar. That she probably was."

I could tell by the way she was shaking her head she'd never entertained the thought.

"I knew Angela could sometimes get depressed for long periods. But what makes you think she was bipolar?"

"She could also get very excited about things, obsessed with various notions, go on what you might call a manic tear, stay up several nights in a row, sometimes for almost a week. She apparently had fantasies, or maybe delusions, about saving the world, rescuing the President from . . . I don't know what exactly."

"I knew she'd met several ex-Presidents."

"And was working very hard to meet the current one. The delusion of saving the whole world is a common component of the manic phase. It frequently involves the head of state. She could also get very depressed, as you know from her suicide threats. About a year and a half ago, she stayed at our place for a couple of nights because we were afraid she might hurt herself."

"I didn't know that."

"At times, she also showed signs of delusions and hypersexuality."

"How do you know that?"

"I just know. There were other indicators. She seemed to think her electrical appliances were spying on her. All of these traits are common with bipolar patients."

"Angela was always sunny and happy around here. I knew she'd thought about suicide, but . . ."

"It takes a great deal of effort to project joyfulness when you're feeling the opposite. She once told me going to your Christmas party every year was the hardest thing she ever did, that it took hours to shake herself out of her funk and put on a smile. She would cry for hours before one of them."

"Is that true?"

"That's what she told me."

"I guess that explains why she was always late."

"Also, I think she might have been having psychotic episodes, believing things that weren't true, maybe even seeing things that weren't there. In their manic state bipolar patients can get so hyper they can't sleep, and the lack of sleep becomes accumulative. Ultimately anybody who's losing that much sleep can have a psychotic break. I think she had some of those. She tore the guts out of her TV and the radio in her car because she thought the Feds were using them to spy on her. Oddly enough, that's a common delusion in people who are bipolar, thinking their TVs, computers, and other electronic equipment have been set up to spy on them. It doesn't help that the technology is there to do it. Also, they tend to invent conspiracy theories and think they alone can save the world or the President. It's always something huge. The Secret Service talked to me at her funeral. They kept a file on her because of her obsession with more than one President. People who are bipolar frequently have trouble holding down a job, too. Obviously, if you're up all night dealing with conspiracies, you're not going to be too sharp at work, if you even make it in. Sound familiar?"

Pennington stared at me while she mentally went over everything she ever thought she knew about her sister. Finally she said, "Now that you're telling me this, it seems to fit some things I could never figure out. In college our father was called to the U one night after campus security found her wandering the campus. She'd been walking through the dorms all wide-eyed and speaking gibberish. At the hospital they pumped her stomach, thinking she'd taken drugs, but they didn't find anything in her system. We never figured out what that was about. Then there was the time she ran off to Las Vegas. Some sort of big secret she wouldn't tell us anything about. I've put this all out of my mind until now. When we finally found her again, she was married to some old goat. She told me once after what we thought was a head injury—she was in the hospital but they never did really diagnose anything—that Hank Bassman, the old guy she married, was really John Kennedy in disguise, that the Secret Service had faked Kennedy's assassination in order to save his life. I thought a head injury was causing delusions. But she never had a head injury, did she?"

"Probably not."

"She suffered with this her whole life and never told anybody?"

"She may not have known what she had. Even after it's diagnosed, it's the least medicated of all mental illnesses. People who are manic depressive don't want to take medication. They say the medication tends to take away the lows, but it also levels out the highs, and people tend to like their highs. A lot of artists have done their best work under the highs."

"I see you've researched this."

"Yes."

After we'd both thought about it a few moments, Monica said, "Are you saying she got depressed and killed herself and that's all there was to it?"

"I think it's vastly more complicated. To begin with, I don't believe she was in a depressed state when she died. I've seen her depressed, and I saw her the night before she died. She was closer to manic than depressed. From what I've seen, she didn't cycle through her states quickly enough to have been depressed less than twenty-four hours later."

Before I went up to my room for the evening, I asked for and received the autopsy report from the King County Medical Examiner's office. Angela hadn't had foreign chemicals in her bloodstream, had no hidden infirmities, no structural abnormalities, and no injuries inconsistent with a fall. There was one thing I hadn't been expecting, even though I'd heard it from her own mouth. She had breast implants.

27

THE next morning we lifted off at nine. There were five of us: two other guests from the estate, the pilot, and Sophie Millwood, the co-pilot.

As we lifted off and banked, we had a glorious aerial view of the valley floor. I picked out the main house, the stables, and finally the shooting range. There were men at the range. They were tiny dots, but I identified Bonds and then Gunderson, and there was another man I couldn't recognize but who may have been Crane Manning. Rifle in hand, Goodnight Bonds looked up at the jet and astonishingly, shouldered his weapon. He aimed it at us. He appeared to be firing. The odds of hitting a jet at our altitude and speed were minimal, but what sort of moron would shoot at his employer's Falcon 10? When I told the pilot about it he said he would keep an eye on his instruments and survey the exterior for damage when we arrived in Seattle.

I re-read the autopsy, paged through some financial magazines I found in the plane, and snoozed through the rest of the flight. I hadn't actually thought Marvin Gunderson was going to sneak into my room the previous night and smother me with a pillow, but once the thought entered my head, sleep hadn't come easily, so I was drowsy.

When we arrived at Boeing Field, a limo was waiting for the other two passengers. I climbed into my Ford, and even though the sky was gray, the interior was oddly warm from the greenhouse effect. I drove downtown to the office at First and Yesler, where I was greeted by Lakeesha, who said, "Hey, I heard you were talking to my cousin."

"Who's your cousin?"

"Charlie Washington. But he wouldn't tell me what it was about. I'm dying to find out."

"Don't hold your breath."

"He's not in trouble, is he?"

"I don't think so."

"You mean he might be?"

"We all might be."

"Thomas. I've been thinking about this. You thought you might have recognized the driver of that SUV the other day."

"*Might* is once again the operative word."

"I was wondering if you've considered hypnosis?"

"No, Lakeesha, as a matter of fact, I haven't."

"I could hypnotize you."

"No, you couldn't."

"Sure I could. I've hypnotized all my friends. People recall things under hypnosis they wouldn't otherwise be able to remember. I could get you to identify the driver. While we're at it, we can get rid of some of your bad habits. I could get you to dress a little better and maybe even put a stopper to your flatulence and—"

"You're not going to hypnotize me!"

"I could keep you from telling bad jokes."

"I like my jokes."

"You're the only one who does."

"No, he isn't," said Kathy, now in the entranceway. "I like them."

Kathy gave me a heartfelt kiss. I couldn't be sure if she was just glad to see me or surprised I was still alive.

I told her about Bonds taking potshots at the plane as we were taking off. "Are you sure?"

"He was shooting at us."

"I hate the thought of you dealing with anybody that crazy." She thought for a long minute, then walked me into her office and closed the door. "I have a confession."

"I was afraid of this. You've found a better-looking, funnier man who makes more money than I do and never farts. You're going to move out of the house, but you still need me for sex."

"Right—except for that last part."

"You found a guy better hung than me?"

"No. This is serious. My computer's power source was acting up last night, so I borrowed your computer. I was looking for something on the electronic desktop when I saw the file you named 'Angela's indiscretion.' I couldn't help myself. I took a peek. I'm sorry."

"How much did you see?"

"I couldn't look away. It was like a slow motion train wreck."

"Geez."

"I feel so bad for snooping, but once I saw them I couldn't stop."

"Actually, I felt funny not telling you about them. It was a breach of *her* trust to tell you and a breach of *yours* not to."

"No. You were right to keep it to yourself, and I was wrong to be snooping. I'm sorry I found out. What do you think was driving her?"

"Maybe she was just living out some strange sexual fantasies. If so, she wouldn't be the first. I'll have to talk to more of the participants before I know for sure."

"Do you think it has anything to do with her suicide?"

"*If* it was a suicide."

"What do you mean?"

"She asked me to take care of things for her, but I can't find any record of what she was working on. I think somebody got there before me and removed evidence. The kids in the building said some men had been in her apartment."

I gave Kathy a brief description of Angela's various jobs, her marriage, and her other problems. Then I told her I thought Angela was bipolar.

"Now that you bring it up, it makes sense."

"Plenty of people are bipolar and get along fine. There are mild forms and more aggressive forms. They say Teddy Roosevelt was bipolar. Ernest Hemingway. Lots of very successful people."

"Do you think maybe somebody was blackmailing her? I mean, if she thought those tapes were going to get out . . . maybe that was why she killed herself."

"That's theory number two."

"What's number one?"

"Somebody murdered her."

"But you spoke to her as she was dying. If somebody threw her off the roof, don't you think she would have said something?"

"She only had enough air in her lungs for a few words. I'm thinking she'd been planning to say more but died before she could. Bonds and Gunderson wanted her to keep away from Self. That would be motive enough for the likes of them."

Late in the day I thought to open the drawer with Angela's clothing in it, the items she wore as she lay dying. I pulled the blouse and pants out of the thick plastic bag the police had stored them in and laid them out on my desk. The trousers had been scissored off by the medics. The blouse was cut right down the center and then scissored into smaller pieces. I fitted it all together like a jigsaw puzzle, matching the pieces as closely as I could. Using Scotch tape, I pieced her outfit together, including shoes and socks. Lakeesha came in while I had it all laid out on the floor, said, "Oh, God, it's Angela," and left.

There was only a little blood on the blouse around the neckline. There was something else—marks where sections of the material was stretched out of shape. The two most noteworthy were at the back of the neck and on the back of the pants—as if somebody had grabbed her in those places and suspended her by her own body weight long enough to distort the material. Long enough to throw her off the roof. It gave me something to think about. I packed everything back up in the plastic bag and locked it in our office safe.

On the way out of the office that afternoon I spotted a grocery store tabloid on Lakeesha's desk. It was splayed open to a full-length color photograph of Monica Pennington and Clark Lloyd Self in a full-on kiss, as if in the movies, as if they were Clark Gable and Vivien Leigh instead of Clark Lloyd Self and Monica Pennington. Actually, Pennington was the rough equivalent of Vivien Leigh, but Self was certainly no Clark Gable, even though he might have been named after him. What struck me about the photo was the incongruity between the two of them. He was an old man whose heavy black stubble made him look like a thug, while she still looked like the model she had once been.

On the way home we drove along Lake Washington Boulevard to do another search for Nate Marshall. Kathy told me that while I was gone Lakeesha received a phone call from a private investigator in Los Angeles who offered her five thousand dollars for a copy of the suicide note—I hadn't thought to lock it up—but instead of making a deal with him, an outraged and loyal Lakeesha told Kathy. The PI was obviously working for one of the tabloids and was hoping the note would perhaps implicate Monica and provoke juicy headlines.

He was on a single dock and had a rod and a reel and a small creel next to him, a soda can sitting on the edge of the dock, a yellow pickup parked across the street.

I parked next to the pickup and walked across Lake Washington Boulevard, dodging a pair of cyclists I recognized from the Thursday night races. Kathy stayed in the car.

28

"THEY biting today?" I asked.

"I got two earlier."

"You're Nate, aren't you?"

"You must be that detective fella."

"Thomas Black. I want to talk about Angela Bassman."

"Sure."

"You realize she's dead?"

"Me and Charlie talked about it after you called him a few days ago."

It was a simple dock jutting straight into the lake from the shore. At this part of the lake the west side of the road rose steeply and was covered in deciduous trees. To the distant south I could see a section of Stan Sayres Park, to the north a string of moving traffic on the Mercer Island floating bridge. The water was getting beaten into a chop by a stiff breeze out of the south. I liked southerly breezes. I could ride my bike south against the wind, then have it at my back all the way home to the University District.

Nate Marshal looked the same as in the videos except he wasn't naked. Today he wore floppy old pants with tattered hems and a jacket with so many holes in it he might have been wearing it as a joke. Under that, he wore a frayed dress shirt that hadn't been ironed. His shoes were worn at the heels.

"Can you tell me about the first time you met her?"

"It was two years ago. The Vice President was in town. Remember?"

"Vaguely."

"She called it a parade, but it was more like a traffic jam. I had one of those Bluetooth phones in my ear. I guess it made her think I was

Secret Service. I was wearing a suit, too. She came up to me and akxed if I was with the Vice President. I told her I wasn't. Then she told me she knew I was. I told her I knew I wasn't. I guess we were flirting. She was really jazzed about seeing the Vice President in person. He came by in a car with a bunch of motorcycle cops all around. We saw him for about ten seconds. He waved at her. After he left, she asked if I was going back to the hotel with the Vice President or was moving on to work with the President. She really thought I was Secret Service even though I kept telling her I wasn't."

"Charlie said you two met at the Alexis Hotel."

"That's where we ended up, but we met on the street. She came up to *me*."

"And?"

"I told her I wasn't with the Secret Service, but then I started denying it like I really *was* with them, you catch my drift? It seemed to be what she wanted to hear. She asked what it would take to get her into a private consultation with the President. I told her that was a tall order but pretended I could do it under the right circumstances. She wanted to know what it would cost her. I told her she would have to sleep with me—just as a joke, ya know? But she took me serious. We made the appointment to go down to the Alexis. She was very direct about it, like it was a business arrangement. I tried to talk her out of the Alexis, 'cause it's expensive, but she insisted 'cause that's where the Vice President was staying. Tell you the truth, I never thought she would do it. But she showed up and I got us a room and took her upstairs."

"Just like that?"

"Just like that."

"She had sex with you so you could get her in to see the President?"

"We both knew it was a joke."

"Are you sure *she* knew?"

"That's an interesting question, because later on I began to have doubts. But by that time we'd already slept with her and I wasn't going to give up on that."

"Where did the other guys come in?"

"After I found out she was a freak, I called Charlie. You know, doing a favor for a friend."

"What do you mean by freak?"

"She kept asking if she was going to have to sleep with other people, or just me. She asked so many times I got the idea that's what she wanted."

"This was which time?"

"First time."

"How many people were there?"

"Me, Charlie, and one time, my brother."

"Portman?"

"Charlie warned me he told you about Portman. We met with her three or four times over the next two years. She would call, always in a rush, like she had to have it right now. We would get it on and when I was leaving I would tell her I was going to call her later about the President. 'Course, I never followed up. One other thing I should have mentioned. We were only alone with her that first time. After that, she brought along a white guy. Different guy each time. A chaperone."

"What did he do?"

"Filmed it."

"Each time you had a meeting, she told you she had to see the President?"

"And each time she said it was an emergency. But she was really talking about the sex. *That* was the emergency. See, the President was code for sex."

"Think hard, Nate. Did she actually think you guys were Secret Service?"

"I don't know."

"Charlie and Portman? Would they have gone along with it if they thought she was mentally ill?"

"Mentally ill? What are you talking about?"

"You just said yourself she might have been having delusions."

"I didn't say that. I don't know what she was having. Hell, Portman only showed the one time. He really seemed to like her. It was like he fell in love or something. All goo-goo eyes, ya know? My theory is he wanted her all to himself. There was a lot of hinky stuff with that woman. Every time we met, she asked me to unplug the television, radio, clock, you name it. Made us turn off our cell phones. But then she wants to take all these pictures with her video camera. Right from the start she wants to document everything."

"And you didn't mind?"

"Hell, I'm not shy. Not when they're giving it away."

"She say anything else that sounded off?"

"Hell, everything about that woman was off. She was a freak."

"You and your friends were taking advantage of a woman who was clearly delusional and *she* was the freak?" I was surprised at my own anger.

"Hey, man. I know she's dead and all, but don't get all up on your high horse. I'm just telling you what happened. I got no reason to lie."

"Just don't call her a freak."

"You know, I ran into her at a ball game once. She was with some retarded Asian gal. She didn't seem crazy then. Seemed perfectly normal. We talked a few minutes, said we'd call and then neither of us did."

"When was the last time you saw her?"

"Couple weeks ago."

"Same deal as the others?"

"To a Tee."

I'd been surreptitiously collecting photos on my cell phone of each of the people I'd interviewed. I'd gotten into the habit on another case and found it handy to have photos. As I was preparing to leave, I showed him pictures of Gunderson and Bonds, and then Rafael Gutierrez, Self, and others from the memorial service, asking if any of these were the males she'd brought along as chaperones. "There's one I recognized," he said. "Go back a couple."

He stopped at a photo I'd taken on the flight from Portland to Montana. "That's him. That was the last chaperone. Couple of weeks ago."

"*This* guy was a chaperone?"

"Right. That guy there."

"You're sure?"

"'Course, I'm sure. He's the only chaperone who actually screwed her. When we left, he was banging away like a steam engine."

We were looking at a photo of Crane Manning. How the hell did he get involved in this nonsense? "And then what?" I asked.

"Then nothing. We left."

"You ever see him again?"

"Not till now."

I knew that Angela and Crane hit it off as soon as I introduced them, but I never would have guessed at this. Crane had obviously been embarrassed to admit his involvement when I asked him about his relationship with Angela. No wonder.

"Getting back to Portman. He was only there once, but you said you thought he was smitten with Angela and wanted her to himself?"

"That's how it seemed to me. Couldn't figure it out, myself."

"Where can I find Portman?"

"I wish I knew. I'm thinking he got hisself in trouble and is laying low."

"You mean legal trouble, like another murder maybe?"

"That was a long time ago. He was a kid."

"And the woman he killed would probably have kids of her own by now if he hadn't killed her."

"All I'm trying to say is . . . he's a different person. He found Jesus."

"I didn't realize Jesus was lost."

"Listen to me, fella. The job market around here sucks. Portman's been out of work two years. Lord Jesus will make sure he finds something. Me, too. No matter what you say or think, Lord Jesus lookin' out for us. And you're going to hell for talking like that."

"I may be going to hell, but it won't be for talking like that."

I thought about Portman Marshal as I walked back up to the road to my car, where Kathy was waiting. I had already dug up his criminal record. After serving nine years for his involvement in throwing Katreena Ann Murphy off the hillside and onto the I-90 roadway where she died, he went through a rough patch—as if serving nine years wasn't rough enough—where he was arrested several more times for public drunkenness, assault, reckless endangerment, and twice for violating restraining orders against former girlfriends. He didn't serve any appreciable time after that first nine-year stretch: thirty days here, sixty days there, and hadn't been in trouble officially for over a year.

If Nate was correct about Portman taking a proprietary interest in Angela, he might have tried to hook up with her on his own. If Angela had rejected him, might he not have pursued her anyway? Stalked her? He had a history of stalking women who'd spurned him.

When I got in the truck, Kathy was staring at Nate Marshal on the dock. "Is he one of them?"

"The ringleader."

"He looks so normal. Why were they doing it? Why the videos?"

"The videos were her idea. I don't know why."

It occurred to me suddenly that she'd been recording her sex sessions so she would have the goods on the men she thought were Secret Service, that she wanted to use the videos as leverage against the government, that Angela hadn't thought of herself as a victim at all but instead had been or was planning to become a blackmailer. If the "Secret Service" people she was having sex with didn't voluntarily take her to see the President, she would force them. I wondered if the threat of releasing one of those videos would be enough to spur one of the participants to murder? Charles Washington had been massively upset when I showed up at his work place.

We stopped off for an early dinner at Chaco Canyon. While Kathy was in the restroom, I checked our house surveillance tapes for the day. More crows. No deliveries. I'd been planning to take a quick ride down through the campus and out toward Seward Park, but it began raining just as we got home, so I rode the rollers in the garage in front of a small television, catching up on the local news.

After my workout, I called Ron Prisham's wife. Not much had changed there. He had not yet regained consciousness.

Later, I got out my Glock 27 in a small, well-oiled holster, and prepped it to carry on my next bike ride. I had a concealed-carry permit and threw that into the package as well. Inside the holster, the outline of the gun would not be visible through my jersey pocket. The Glock 27 was a .40 caliber pistol and held nine rounds. It was small enough and light enough to be easily carried, but deadly enough to be reassuring.

Not that Ron Prisham would have had time to whip out a gun.

29

THE next morning I got in a quick bike ride to Seward Park and back, a little less than twenty miles round trip. I did not pack the Glock, common sense having overtaken paranoia. After my shower, I made some phone calls and took a hasty trip up the hill from the office to Harborview Hospital. Melissa was sitting with her unconscious husband in a room filled with flowers and cards. *The Seattle Times* had carried an article about him, a short profile with details of the accident. Prisham had been all-state in basketball in high school, an Eagle Scout, and later a Rhodes Scholar, oddly, the same as Gunderson. It was the proverbial it-couldn't-have-happened-to-a-nicer-guy scenario. I spoke with Melissa for a few minutes, handed her the coffee and a bagel I'd brought for her, and told her I would be back the following day.

I'd been thinking about the reactions I was getting as I talked to people about Angela, their voices, the pitch of their emotions as we discussed Angela's life and suicide. At the memorial there were people who hadn't realized it was a suicide, but since then the tabloid television had picked up the details. God help the family if the tabloids ever got hold of her sex videos.

I'd gotten unusual vibes from several people, including Bonds and Gunderson. Their open mockery of Angela at the memorial continued to niggle at me, Gunderson's apology notwithstanding. And, largely because of their unexpected reactions, there were at least two people I'd spoken to on the phone from the East Coast who I would have liked to interview face to face. One had laughed nervously and the other had been literally stuttering with shock. On this side of the continent, aside from Charles Washington, whom I'd already interviewed, the person I most wanted to visit was Henrik Federer, the man I'd met outside the memorial service.

Federer lived in a small house on Second Avenue N.E. near the Northgate Mall and within sight of I-5 to the west. Despite the freeway buzz, it was a quiet neighborhood and looked pleasant enough. His was tiny box of a house alongside other tiny, boxy houses, not what I would have expected to accompany the brand new Lexus SUV he'd been driving the day of the memorial and which was now parked out front. Federer's place was on a small embankment, as were most of the houses on the block. Two doors farther down I saw a bank repossession notice on a front door.

"From the funeral," he said when he opened the door.

"Right. Thomas Black." He'd seen me on the walkway and opened the door before I could knock. He wore slacks and a neatly pressed shirt. His hair was blonder than I remembered and longer. He had a narrow, wan face framed by wire-rimmed spectacles. He wore expensive shoes that looked handmade, which was only one of the features about him that didn't seem to be in sync with the modest house.

"Won't you come in? What can I do for you?"

"You used to work for CLS Enterprises?"

"I did."

The house was only half furnished, had the look of a home in which at least one of the occupants had moved out. There were blank spots in the tiny front room, where furniture was missing; circles in the faint dust on a window ledge, where plants had been removed. "Excuse the mess," Federer said. "We're losing this place to the bank. It's been a tough month. First my wife decided we were going to break up. There was Angela's death. Then we got the notice on the house. I guess I'm going to live here until the banksters show up and sell it out from under me. I've been out of work almost two years. Kirsten got some part-time work. But for me there's nothing out there."

I noticed children's artwork clinging to the refrigerator with magnets, toys for a missing puppy, an assortment of bright yellow and blue and red plastic blocks designed for the youngest engineers.

"Have a beer?" he asked.

"No thanks."

"I guess it *is* a little early. Without a real schedule, you lose track of things. Have a seat."

I sat on the edge of a sofa under the front window. He chose the loveseat across the room, the only other piece of furniture not made for tots, and looked at me as if he was glad to have the company. "What can I do for you?"

"I saw Gunderson yesterday. I thought I should tell you he apologized for his statements at the funeral."

"I still think he's a buffoon."

"I only passed it along because I thought it might make you feel better about things."

"Somebody make him apologize?"

"I don't think anybody makes Gunderson do anything. For what it's worth, I believe he actually feels remorse over how he acted."

"The day I got canned, he escorted me out of the building. You could see he got a hell of a kick out of it."

"How'd you lose your job?"

"They told me I didn't flaunt the company product properly, that I needed to stick to a strict discipline of telling people . . . basically . . . what a genius Self was and leave it at that. I recommended diversity in investments, not too much in any one sector. I didn't think people selling their houses so they could invest with us was a great idea, and I told them so. I should have stuck to the script. Now my friends back at the company are making out like bandits while I'm losing my house and my kids. Keep your head buried in the sand if you want all the dumb luck."

"Have you been in touch with any of your co-workers?"

"Only at the memorial. You know how it is when somebody's been terminated."

"How about Rafael Gutierrez? Did you know him?"

"I knew him. We never worked together."

"What can you tell me about him?"

"I know he's dead. Traffic accident."

"Did you know Angela Bassman was seeing him?"

"No."

"His ex-wife swears it was all business."

"Ex-wife. I don't like that sound, but I guess that's what I have now, too. An ex." He looked around the house. "Losing my job contributed to it. I mean, we were fighting all the time. We traded down to this house and now we can't even hold onto this. In the end, Kirsten ran off with one of my best friends. He was in the Navy Reserves. Iraq. It's a strange story. Maybe that's why I have to tell everybody. I told the meter man yesterday. My friend got his legs blown off over there. His wife couldn't handle it and left him. Kirsten started spending more and more time over there. I thought she was just helping out. Finally, she told me three months ago she was leaving me and they were going to get married. I'm still trying to figure it out. But enough of my problems. You wanted to talk about Angela?"

"She was seeing a lot of Rafael Gutierrez. Some business I haven't been able to get a handle on. Angela was extremely upset over Gutierrez's death."

"Now that you mention it, it was right around when he died she stopped coming here."

"What were you doing together?"

"Can I ask why you're asking?"

I'd already given him my card. A lie would be harmless enough and would probably allow the interview to continue unimpeded, while the truth might squelch our conversation. But I wasn't comfortable lying to this man, who was only beginning to experience the musty underside of the American dream. "I'm working for the family, investigating her last days and weeks."

"By the family, do you mean her parents?"

"Her sister."

"And what about my old boss?"

"I can keep your name out of it, and anyway, I don't answer to him."

He thought about it for a few moments. Maybe he'd been one of the chaperones behind the camera while she was with Charles Washington and his confederates. The cameraman possibility had not occurred to me until that moment.

"Angela was convinced her brother-in-law was some sort of a crook," Federer said. "I was helping her with it."

"Because he'd lost her money?"

"Nothing to do with that. It was CLS. She thought Self was running a Ponzi scheme."

"You worked there. Do you think it's a Ponzi scheme?"

"It's possible. Self has never revealed where the money is being invested. It's what he calls a proprietary secret."

"So you were helping her?"

"I knew how things worked at CLS, who did what. I knew names and had phone numbers of people who still worked there."

"And one of her other contacts was Rafael Gutierrez."

"I would assume so."

According to what I'd seen in her few scattered notes, Gutierrez might well have been her key informant. She certainly spent enough time with him. I thought again about the black Tahoe that struck and killed him. It was never located and could have been stolen, as was the black Tahoe that almost killed Ron Prisham. Car thieves tended to go for the same models over and over.

"People were placing their entire life savings in the CLS Fund," Federer continued. "If she was right it was a horrible thing that was happening. It's one thing for some movie star to throw away ten million they can raise again with next summer's blockbuster. It's another to see mom and pop putting their entire retirement and then all the rest of their nest egg on the table. Seventeen, eighteen percent gain per year, day in and day out . . . It does seem a little farfetched when you think about it. All Angela was trying to say was, 'why doesn't somebody look into it?' She called the SEC umpteen times, but nobody would listen."

"Wouldn't it be easy to know if he was running a Ponzi scheme while you were working for him?"

"There are two distinct divisions in the company, the investment side and the client handling side. Ours is the client side. The money managers are all in New York. We never saw them or had contact with them."

"If it is a Ponzi scheme, he wouldn't need a whole lot of people moving money around, would he? Because there wouldn't be any investments."

"That's right."

"So there might not be too many people in the New York office."

"That was what Angela and I were beginning to suspect."

"Henrik, I haven't been able to find any of her paperwork. Tell me she wasn't keeping it all in her head."

"Heck, no. She had documents out the kazoo. She got them from Gutierrez. She brought over all sorts of papers for me to look at. She wanted to know if they were authentic."

"And were they?"

"As far as I could tell."

"Do you have any now?"

"She kept them all. She was going to turn them over to the State Attorney General."

"Did she ever say anything to indicate where she might be keeping these materials?"

"I assumed they were at her apartment."

"I searched her apartment."

"Then I have no idea where they might be."

"What about the Feds?"

"She sent some of it to the Feds, but you'll never see that again. As far as I can tell, the SEC is a black hole."

30

THE further I dug into Angela's life the more unanswered questions I came up with.

Was Clark Lloyd Self running a Ponzi scheme? If so, Self would have been terrified of Angela's poking around, and he and his minions would have plenty of motives for harassing her, maybe even killing her. *If* he was running a Ponzi scheme, her investigation would have jeopardized his wealth, celebrity, his marriage, social standing, even his freedom. Thousands of cheated investors would be shouting for his head. There *would* be a prison term. After his Ponzi scheme was uncovered, Bernie Madoff was sentenced to a hundred fifty years in prison, an outcome that could hardly have escaped Self's notice. Angela had already proved her ability to catch him in bed with another woman. There was no reason for him to believe she wasn't capable of catching him swindling investors. There were regulatory agencies that should have been on his back, but Madoff had gone years without being investigated.

Was Rafael Gutierrez's death part of a plot to get rid of anybody who might be snooping around CLS Enterprises? Were there deaths I didn't know about?

Were Charles Washington and Nate Marshal telling the truth about their trysts with Angela? I didn't like their story, but so far they'd both agreed on the details, and I'd found no other witnesses or real reason to dispute their yarn. The most astounding piece of information about these trysts was Crane Manning's participation in the last one, alleged or otherwise. I introduced him to Angela only two weeks before her death, and apparently, that same day he engaged in group sex with her. He'd been lying to me about his relationship with Angela. Kathy would have said he wasn't the man I knew, but I'd been around long enough to know men lied about sex without believing they'd betrayed you. With a lot of men, maybe most men, there was your life, and then there was your sex life. I didn't know if it was a gene thing, a cultural artifact, or an extreme ability to compartmentalize, but I'd seen it too many times to discount it.

When I called Crane's new cell phone, he sounded as if I'd woken him up. "Crane here."

"You lied to me."

"Who is this?"

"Who do you think?"

"Thomas? How'd you get this number?"

"You gave it to me."

"Fuck, I'm still in bed. We were up half the night working with the new night vision stuff we bought. What are you on about?"

"You slept with Angela." My statement was met with a long silence. "And don't hang up on me. You hang up on me, I'll track you down. I'll be there before you can get your slippers on."

"Jesus. Okay. I slept with her. Are you happy?"

"Why lie about it?"

"I didn't lie. I just didn't mention it."

"You lied. Tell me about it."

Another long silence. "It was that first day. She was high on something. Drugs, life, I don't know what. I know you thought she was a ditz, but I liked her. She took me to some sort of private party and told me to just be quiet and photograph everything. It turned out to be a sex thing."

"Why didn't you tell me about it?"

"Tell you Angela took me to a party where she was the focus of an orgy? Are you kidding? I was embarrassed. I thought she liked me. I thought . . . I don't know what I thought. When I figured out she was using me I couldn't tell anybody. It's the story of my life. Women using me."

"What else have you lied about?"

"Nothing. Man, we are friends. And trust me, I don't have that many friends. God. I feel worse about her death than anybody."

"Did you see somebody that day at her apartment?"

"I swear, the only thing I held back was screwing her. When I brought it up the next day, she pretended she didn't remember it, like she was all confused. It was weird. I just wanted to forget the whole thing."

"Swear to God you're telling me everything?"

"Swear to God."

"Okay, then. I'll be in touch."

"You find out anything else about why she did it, call, would you? I think about her every day."

"So do I."

If Angela was bipolar, as I strongly suspected, perhaps the group sex and the videos were really nothing more for her than the result of some delusional fantasy about Presidents and Secret Service agents. One of the key traits of bipolar personalities was an alternating manic and depressed phase. The spectrum ranged from those who cycled through manic to depressed every twenty-four hours, to those who took a year to work through a cycle. There were those for whom the disease made ordinary life a challenge and those for whom it seemed to provide tools for success. There were all levels of depression and mania, depending on the severity of disease. In severe cases, people could become caught up in grandiose delusions, losing control of spending habits and sometimes becoming hyper-sexual and sleep deprived, losing enough sleep that they underwent psychotic breaks. They saw things that weren't there, believed things that weren't true, and made improbable or impossible connections between events. I wouldn't be surprised if random sexual trysts had always been a regular part of Angela's manic phase.

Angela had a history of suicidal threats and attempts, but how many suicides left a note penned two years earlier? A quick phone call to a psychologist Kathy knew at the University of Washington who had made extensive studies of suicides uncovered the fact that she'd never heard of anybody leaving a suicide note that was penned years earlier. On the other hand, if anybody was going to break the mold, it would be Angela.

When I got back to the office, Kathy was out and Lakeesha was taking a personal day off. The tabloid with the picture of Monica Pennington kissing Clark Lloyd Self was still on Lakeesha's desk, where I'd left it the day before. I sat on Lakeesha's pillowed chair and thumbed through the rest of the tabloid while I called Zoepf, the cop on Mercer Island.

"There's a new angle on this, Black. A lady who lives in the neighborhood where the Tahoe was stolen said she saw two African-

American males in the neighborhood on foot. She didn't call us until she read about the hit and run in the paper. Other neighbors confirmed there were two black men, thirties, possibly early forties, in the area selling magazine subscriptions the day before. I'm going back out with a tech to check the Tahoe for fingerprints one more time. This could change the whole ball game."

"You'll let me know if anything comes of it?"

"Of course."

Was it possible Charles Washington and Nate Marshal were the men in the black Tahoe, that they'd run down Ron Prisham while trying to run me down? Getting rid of me wouldn't get rid of the videos, but maybe they were planning to come looking for the videos later. The road accident happened before I saw Charles Washington in person, but after I'd spoken with him on the phone. Maybe the incident with the Tahoe explained why Washington was so nervous when he saw me in his office.

I phoned Brad Munch. "Bradley."

"Thomas. I'm sorry I held back on you. I was just shocked at those videos. They were so personal and so . . . damned indecent. I knew—"

"Listen, Brad. Is it possible there are hidden files on the hard drive? Something we haven't seen yet? There's a bunch of missing material, and I can't figure out where it might be."

"I looked, but I'll look again."

"Thanks for all your help."

The next few days passed quickly. Ron Prisham was brought out of his coma, and it was beginning to look as if he might make a complete, if prolonged, recovery. It was going to take months and would undoubtedly drain the family's finances, since his meager insurance wasn't covering everything. Zoepf didn't call me back. I didn't hear from Bonds or Gunderson, which made me nervous. *Keep your friends close and your enemies closer* was a motto I tried to live by. I talked to more people who'd known Angela, including many of her former climbing buddies, who all said she had been quite the mountaineer, making up in enthusiasm what she'd lacked in strength.

I went back to the apartment building where she lived and checked out her storage space in the basement. I'd forgotten it the first time. It was empty, and judging by the dust on the floor, had been for quite a while. I went to the roof again and didn't see anything I hadn't seen before. The apartment had already been cleaned out and was awaiting a new tenant. One of the neighbors told me a cleaning service had come and thrown everything away, which I thought showed callousness on Pennington's part. Last fall after Kathy returned from the dead, she found all her things untouched, right down to the toothpaste tube on the edge of the sink. I'm not sure I ever would have moved them.

I spoke to every kid I could find in the building. When I showed photos of Bonds and Gunderson, two kids said they recognized Bonds. They couldn't say whether it was before her death or after, but they'd seen him. I flashed Gunderson's photo around, but unfortunately a photo didn't convey the immensity he projected in person. Nobody remembered seeing him. I knocked on doors and talked to everybody I could find.

Bonds had definitely been in the building, perhaps more than once, but nobody could pin down a time. Parking in this area was so congested it was probable that if Bonds and Gunderson were together one would have stayed in the car circling the block, while the other went inside. If they were trying for stealth, it would make more sense to send the unobtrusive Bonds inside. On the other hand, I didn't think he was capable of throwing her off the roof by himself. Not unless he surprised her.

I rode my bike on successive days, keeping my eyes peeled for suspicious cars and oddball traffic interactions. I knew if they tried again, it wouldn't necessarily come in the form of a hit and run. In Montana they'd been playing with guns and silencers.

We basked in two days of sunshine, and then the clouds rolled back in.

At least once a day Lakeesha offered to hypnotize me.

Thinking a respite might spur new ideas, I took time out to work on a case I'd been handling before Angela's suicide. A young woman had come up HIV positive and wanted me to trace which of her recent sexual partners might have given it to her. She'd already spoken to the ones she could find and they all denied it. I finally found him, a man who'd been sent to prison at eighteen for burglary and arson. He worked for a trucking firm now and had met my client on-line. She'd thought him fairly mature because he had an ex-wife and daughter and was making child support payments, at least that was what he told her. When I contacted his ex she didn't know his whereabouts, though he was living less than a mile away, and she had never received any support payments. He'd given her HIV, too.

It made me wonder if Angela might not have found herself HIV positive. But if she'd been HIV positive, it should have shown up in the autopsy.

On Friday of that week I located Nate Marshal's brother, Portman, in the King County lockup in Kent. After his attorney found out who I was, she decided she didn't want me visiting alone and we made an appointment for a joint visit. I drove out the West Valley Highway and parked at the Regional Justice Center, where I met his attorney, Sandra James Bumiller. She walked me to a visitors' room. We chatted. It turned out she knew Kathy.

Portman didn't look anything like his brother, Nate. He had a large face, exceedingly dark skin, and longer hair than most black males wore these days. The sleeves of his long underwear were rolled up, revealing a thick scar, like a weld mark on metal, running the length of his left arm. Portman was stocky, muscular, and moved aggressively. I said, "I spoke to your brother."

"You want a prize for that?"

He glanced at his attorney, a squat woman with horn-rimmed glasses and a nose like a tiny toadstool. Her eyes were gray and she wore no makeup. She was clad in a gray business suit that hung on her loosely.

I said, "I came here to talk about a dead woman. Maybe I should go to the police and let you sit and wonder what I was going to ask."

He took a breath and sat back. "How's my brother doin'?"

"Fishing."

"If I had a nickel for every worm he's thrown into that lake I'd have me a new Lexus."

"What can you tell me about Angela Bassman?"

"Don't know no Bassman."

I held up my phone with a photo of Angela on it.

"Her? Talk to my brother. She's his bitch."

"*You* slept with her."

He glanced at his attorney. "I'm tellin' ya, she was my brother's bitch."

"How many times did you see her?"

He shot a look at his attorney. "Up to you," she said. I knew Portman was in jail because he couldn't make a minimal bail on a charge of stealing steaks from the Red Apple store at 23rd and Jackson. The steaks would have been sold to friends or neighbors at a pittance of the actual cost, producing easy cash for Portman. He'd sewn pockets into a large coat and filled them with meat. When he tried to walk out of the store the third or fourth time he worked the scam, he was spotted by security personnel who'd been watching him through ceiling cameras and who tackled him in the parking lot. He was also charged with assault on one of the store managers.

"I understand you liked Angela," I said.

"She was okay."

"Did you know she was dead?"

It took him a few moments to digest the information. "How? How did it happen?"

"You don't already know about this?"

"I don't know shit. I been in here."

"She went off a roof a week ago."

Portman leaned across the table and gave me a look. He didn't like talking to me and now he didn't like what I was telling him. "What's this got to do with me?"

"I saw you in a video with her."

"I don't believe she's dead."

Scrolling through the pictures on my phone, I found one I'd taken at the memorial. It revealed her coffin and her name on a curtain on the stage.

"How'd it happen?"

"I told you. She went off a roof. The cops are saying she killed herself."

"What roof?"

"Tell me about your relationship with her."

"If you saw the video, you saw my relationship with her."

"You didn't see her before or after that video was taken?"

"Why would I?"

"Your brother seems to think maybe you liked her too much to participate a second time."

"What they were doing wasn't right."

"Then why did *you* do it?"

"It was before I knew her."

"How'd you know she was such a nice person if you only saw her once, to have sex?"

"I could tell."

"Who did the filming when you were there?"

"Some white sissy."

"You get a name?"

"Wilbur. Hell, I don't know. I didn't pay no attention. He could have been the Hunchback of Notre Dame for all I remember."

"Did anybody give an explanation for why they were filming it?"

"I assumed it was the same reason we were doing it."

"Which was?"

"Layin' pipe, man. You get a chance, you lay pipe."

For half a minute or so, none of us spoke. I thumbed through a small notepad I kept but rarely used, as if looking for more questions, or checking my facts against his. I waited. I knew he wanted to say something more. I flipped through the notebook again. Finally, he coughed and said, "What roof?"

"The roof of her building."

"Wasn't that tall—two, three stories."

"You said you saw her only the once. How do you know where she lived?"

He didn't reply. When it was clear we'd reached a stalemate, his attorney told me to leave.

I waited outside. Five minutes later, when Sandra Bumiller emerged, I said, "He mention Angela Bassman?"

"We talked about *his* case."

"He did time for murdering a woman. You know that, don't you?"

"If you've seen his sheet you know it was manslaughter, not murder."

"Angela Bassman committed suicide. I wonder if *that* was manslaughter, too."

Sandra James Bumiller gave me a piercing look. "If the police charge him, I'll worry about it. Otherwise, my caseload is too heavy to sweat things that *might* happen."

"Listen, Sandra. Along with two other men, your client had sex with a woman who's dead now. A group deal. The other men said it was consensual. It may have been. The others told me Portman took a strong interest in her. He says he never saw her again, but now I find out he can describe where she was living. I know he saw her again, or tried to. Was he in jail last Thursday, a week?"

"He's been in three days."

"Then he was free the day she died."

"A lot of people were free that day."

"Not a lot of people who've already done time for throwing a woman from a high place and who were stalking my girl."

I was driving back to our office on First and Yesler when I got a call from Pennington. "Black? What can you tell me?"

"I was preparing to call with a report this afternoon," I said.

"Why not now? I'm back in town. I'd like to visit Hoshi. You can take me out to see her. Come by and pick me up."

"I'll be there in half an hour."

"I'll be in the lobby."

31

AS I might have predicted, she wasn't there when I arrived.

While I waited for the elevator, I saw Goodnight Bonds bustling through the lobby and out to the sidewalk as if fleeing the scene of an execution. He didn't show even a flicker of recognition. When the elevator opened on the penthouse floor, the front door to the condo was wide open.

I caught sight of Crane Manning, his back toward me. Moments later, Monica Pennington came through the living room past Crane, waving him off without a word as he tried to follow. When he saw me, he stopped in his tracks. Pennington and I stepped into the elevator together.

"That your bodyguard?" I asked.

"Clark hired him, but I didn't have anything to do with it. I *do* need somebody when I go out, but I've got you today. You *are* a competent bodyguard, aren't you?"

"I've been guarding my own body for a long time."

She looked at me as if I were an idiot. I recalled Crane telling me Pennington hired him, but today she claimed her husband had. Given a choice between Pennington and some hairy old billionaire, I might be telling people Monica Pennington hired me, too. It wasn't important, but it surprised me in the way that white lies from friends sometimes do. It was the second lie I'd caught him in. But then, a half hour ago I'd lied to Pennington when I told her I'd been planning to give her a report today.

"I've been thinking about Angela taking care of Hoshi," Monica said. "I wonder what else Angela was doing that I didn't know about."

There was plenty she didn't know about, but I didn't say anything. "Have you seen Hoshi?"

"I have seen her."

"How is she?"

"She needs to be where she is."

"Where is this place?"

"Kent." Oddly, I'd just come back from Kent, where Portman Marshal was incarcerated.

By the time we got to McKay's Assisted Living and Dementia Care, the skies were black and rain was barreling down in sheets. I drove past the sliding wrought-iron gate and found a parking spot close to the front entrance. It was a high-class facility, clean and neat, the perfect place to stash your senile grandmother if you were lucky enough to have the dough. We got out of the car and ran through the puddles and slanting rain like lovers making a dash for a motel room.

"We're here to see Hoshi Smith," I announced to the attendant, who was playing solitaire on the computer.

"Hoshi's been transferred."

"Transferred where?"

Scooting on her rolling chair, she opened a book on the low counter. "Mueller's, in Seattle."

"On Martin Luther King Way?"

"That's the one."

"Why was she transferred?"

"You'll have to talk to Ms. Engebretson, but she is in a meeting. I could have her call you. Or you could wait."

"Thanks. We'll go to Mueller's."

Once again we crossed the narrow parking lot in the rain, and as we opened our opposite doors, I noticed the attendant in the window watching us. My guess was she recognized Pennington.

"Is it far?" Pennington asked.

"Yes, but we have to go that way to get you home, so it's not really out of our way."

"You know I don't have all day."

"Like I said, it's on the way."

Years ago one of my elderly neighbors had been forced to send his ailing wife to Mueller's, though the facility had a different name then. I had visited weekly until she died and knew the place well.

"Why do you think they moved her?" Pennington asked.

"I have to assume it was for nonpayment. Angela was behind."

"I don't understand why Angela was paying in the first place. Even if the family couldn't afford it."

"Maybe she felt guilty."

"Why would she feel guilty?"

Twenty years ago two young women had picked up a friend and tossed her into a lake where she drowned and was subsequently resuscitated by a stranger, living the rest of her life as a functional moron, destined to sit out her days in a nursing home in a damp diaper. God only knew how somebody could be part of that and then ask why anybody would feel guilty. I realized people could rationalize anything, and I had seen worse, had probably done worse, but still it always amazed me to run up against this convenient human foible. I said, "She felt guilty because Hoshi would have lived an active, healthy life if you two hadn't drowned her."

"Drowned her? What are you talking about?"

"She told you she couldn't swim right before you threw her into the lake. Some people would consider that a criminal act."

"Criminal? Don't be ridiculous. We were horsing around. It could have been any one of us at the bottom of the lake."

"Angela told us Hoshi said she couldn't swim."

"I don't remember it that way. And we never would have been charged with a crime. You're ridiculous."

I might have let it go, but my temporary moral superiority had me by the scruff of the neck. I said, "If the right people had seen it, or somebody had videotaped it, it would have been decided in a prosecutor's office, or in front of a judge. Your life would have been almost as different as Hoshi's."

"You have quite an imagination."

I did. It was the difference between us. She completely lacked the ability to see what could have been and she used that inability to her advantage wherever she could. Her comments and snide attitude pissed me off, just as my accusation pissed her off. I couldn't tell which of us was angrier. She wasn't going to accept even a grain of responsibility for Hoshi and resented me for thinking she should.

"I don't know why you would listen to Angela. She used to get mixed up about everything." Two weeks ago I would have agreed with her, but now I wondered whether Angela's version of the near-drowning wasn't more accurate than Pennington's vapid, self-serving recollection.

Mueller's was a three-story building fronting Martin Luther King Way, only a few blocks from the Red Apple store where Portman Marshal had been arrested for shoplifting and assault. I parked in the long, narrow parking lot on the west side of the nursing home. The interior smelled of urine and disinfectant. The floors were linoleum, the brick walls painted institutional green. Compared to the homey atmosphere and friendly staff at McKay's, this was a major downgrade for Hoshi.

We found her sitting on her bed in a room that looked a lot like a hospital room, minus the monitoring devices and medical paraphernalia. A television mounted high on a wall was tuned to *Divorce Court*, but neither Hoshi nor her one-legged roommate in the next bed were watching. Hoshi looked like an orphan who'd just gotten off a plane. She still had her traveling clothes on, and there was a bag next to her bed which hadn't been unpacked, though the receptionist said she'd been admitted twenty-four hours earlier.

I could see Pennington was doing her best, but she ended up being patronizing to an extent even Hoshi recognized, in much the same way small animals could instinctively sniff out friend or foe. Once as a teenager I'd watched a drunken farmhand attempt to entice a pig to the slaughter, and it had been worse than this, but just barely.

"Hoshi? Hoshi? How nice to see you. I guess you must remember me. You look different. Of course, we all look different. Do you like your hair short? It might be more attractive if you grew it out. Can't they find you a younger roommate? I would think—"

"I heard that." It was the roommate, her voice croaking behind the drawn curtain dividing the two beds, through which Hoshi could glimpse only a slice of the TV that must have belonged to the other woman. Hoshi seemed to remember me and stared pleadingly, as if I could rescue her from this ungainly new life. Or from Pennington.

They sat rigidly side by side on the bed for a few moments saying nothing. Finally I said, "Hi, Hoshi. I'm Thomas. We met last week. I was a friend of Angela's."

"Angela?" She glanced behind me as if Angela might appear in the doorway. "Angela?"

"This is Angela's sister, Monica." When Hoshi didn't respond, I added, "You played school with Angela, didn't you?"

"Yes," she said, quietly. "I'm the caretaker."

"No, honey," Pennington said. "You're the patient. Those people out in the hallway are the caretakers."

"*Me*! I'm the caretaker."

"No. They are."

"*Me*!"

"No. They are."

Pennington was perfectly willing to argue with a halfwit all day. I wasn't sure what that made her. Closer to home, I could have said it made her my wife, but that would have been a bad joke. As I watched them squabble, I realized something was missing. "Excuse me, Hoshi?" I interrupted. "Where's your trunk?" She scrutinized me with dull eyes as I knelt in front of her. "Where's all your stuff?"

"What's going on?" Pennington asked.

"I just got a brainstorm."

"I was talking to her."

"This could be important."

Pennington left the room in a huff without saying goodbye, as if Hoshi wouldn't realize she'd left, as if I would follow her because that's what her people did.

"Goodbye, Hoshi," I said. "I'll come back. I'll see you again soon."

"Angela?"

"Angela won't be back. Angela died. I'm very sorry."

"Black? Are you coming or not?" Pennington was in the corridor.

"Angela?" Hoshi asked.

"Angela won't be coming back."

"Black?"

I wasn't sure if Hoshi could conceive of death the way the rest of us did. Hell, I wasn't sure *I* could conceive of it the way the rest of us did. If not, maybe it was for the best, to not realize she was going to die, to not know how many loved ones and friends were going to be taken away from her before her own final reckoning. On the way out, I stopped at reception and waited while the receptionist paged the plant manager for me. Pennington wasn't happy about the delay and borrowed the key fob to the Prius so she could wait in the car. The plant manager was short and wiry and reeked of cigarettes. I gave him one of my cards with the machine gun on it because I thought he would get a kick out of it, but he grew wary, as if he'd had a bad experience with a private eye, or with a machine gun.

"What can I do for you?" he asked.

"You've got a new patient. Hoshi Smith down the hall on the first floor."

"Yeah?"

"She should have more bags."

"The transferring party is responsible for her belongings."

"You don't have someplace where you keep a patient's extraneous gear?"

"Everything she came with should be in the room with her."

"Were you here when she checked in?"

"Listen, Mr. Black. I don't know anything about her stuff."

I went back down the corridor and performed another search of Hoshi's room, including the roommate's side. "What are you looking for?" asked the roommate when I stooped to peer under her bed.

"The truth."

"You're not going to find it under there."

"I might not find it at all."

I spotted Hoshi at the far end of the corridor, still in her coat, peering into another patient's room. It was like watching a stray mutt checking out an open door. This was a locked ward, so unless she could read and comprehend the fine print next to the keypad that released the door locks, she wasn't getting out anytime soon.

Outside, I performed a thorough inspection of the contents of all three Dumpsters, letting the metal lids slam shut when I finished. I couldn't tell if I was slamming the lids to irritate Pennington or because I liked the noise. I *did* like the noise. And I *did* want to irritate Pennington. When she glanced through the car's windshield and realized I was going through the garbage, Pennington gave me a look of sheer revulsion. She didn't get off the phone or acknowledge me when I drove her to her condo. In fact, she was still on the phone when I parked and went around to help her out. Without any acknowledgment, she went into the building and stepped into the private elevator, still on the phone.

My return trip to McKay's Assisted Living in Kent took over an hour. A logging truck had dumped its load on 167 and traffic was backed up four miles.

When I got there, the receptionist in McKay's was buttoning up for the night. "Ms. Engebretson is just about to go home. Would you like to speak to her?"

Engebretson was the same efficient, attractive woman I'd met on my first visit. "Yes, of course. Angela's friend. Can I help you?"

"I understand you had to move Hoshi Smith. There was a trunk in her room. Do you know what became of it?"

"I wasn't here during the move. I find sometimes it's better if I'm not part of it. Hoshi's brother took her to her new facility."

"You think the trunk might be in her old room?"

Engebretson walked me to the elevator and took me upstairs. In the hallway we walked among the zombies and the droolers and the people wearing only one slipper. Engebretson addressed them all by name and spoke kindly to each. She keyed open the door of the room Hoshi had been in. "You have any idea what became of that trunk?" I asked, looking around.

"We keep a list of all valuables belonging to each resident, but there wasn't anything in the trunk except crayons and butcher paper. Even so, it would have been transferred with Hoshi when she left."

I asked the aides, but they didn't know anything. Outside the building I climbed inside two Dumpsters, kicking aside bags of loaded adult diapers and food slops in order to ascertain the object of my search wasn't engulfed in the detritus. I went to the office and asked Engebretson if I could see the head of maintenance. He was no longer in the building, but she managed to get him on the phone. He told me he didn't know anything about a trunk. I was thinking maybe her brother had taken it somewhere after he moved Hoshi. If so, I would have to track down the brother.

I went back outside and circumnavigated the building. On the far side I found another set of garbage cans, cardboard boxes stacked next to them. I began pulling the boxes away. Underneath I found a navy-blue trunk, still padlocked. I could hear the contents sliding around inside when I shouldered it and lugged it around the building, stuffing it into the hatchback of the Prius.

In town, I picked up Kathy and we drove home together. I dragged the trunk into the garage, then went into the house, took a long, scalding shower, and threw my clothes into the washer and had dinner with Kathy.

"What did you do?" Kathy asked. "To get like that."

"I always smell like garbage. I thought that was what first attracted you."

She laughed. "What attracted me was when I caught you measuring your skull with a tape measure and you told me you were checking to see if you'd gotten any smarter."

"I was checking my hat size."

"I've seen you measuring your biceps, too."

"I do that weekly. Other body parts as required."

"You've always needed a keeper."

"And now I've got you. It's perfect."

"It is rather, isn't it?"

After dinner I went out to the garage.

In the movies people shot locks off strong boxes, but the truth was a lead bullet would never break a case-hardened steel lock. You break a padlock open from the inside out. It's weakest from inside the radius of the shackle and the body. I inserted a small wooden dowel inside the hasp of the lock and tapped it with a hammer. The lock came apart with the third whack. When Hoshi Smith said she was the caretaker, my guess was she was parroting something Angela had told her.

The trunk contained stacks of butcher paper with crayoned pictures and words crudely drawn as if by a child. 'Hoshi' was spelled repeatedly. So was 'mom' and 'cat'. Hoping for gold, I dug under the butcher paper and found crayons. Then an old purse. Inside the purse, where I hoped to find a memory stick or a hard drive, I found two pounds of pennies. Under the purse and the pennies were several of the boxes typing paper came in. The document in the first box said, "Confidential: CLS Enterprises memo re customer complaints."

There were other memos about jacking up the rate at which investors poured money into the company. There were tables and graphs I didn't understand. Affidavits signed by Rafael Gutierrez and four or five others requesting the SEC to launch a probe of CLS Enterprises. I didn't recognize the other names, but one affidavit was sworn out by Gutierrez and was notarized shortly before his death. There was a receipt showing some sort of package had been mailed to the SEC a week after his death.

Having sent her package to the SEC, Angela had then focused her efforts on breaking up her sister's marriage. It was as if she'd started an avalanche and wanted to get her loved ones out of its path before tons of ice crushed them. Except the avalanche never came, because it had been months now, and as far as I could tell, the SEC still hadn't moved on the complaint.

I spent twenty minutes sorting through the contents of the trunk, separating the crayoned papers from the documents Angela had gathered. High finance was not my forte, nor was I an expert on Ponzi schemes. I couldn't understand the figures or even some of the terms. There were multiple written interviews with various financial experts and a few CLS insiders who were disgruntled enough to talk to Angela. It all added up to: *CLS needs to be investigated.*

I phoned Henrik Federer and asked if he would come over. "I know this is short notice, Henrik, but I found something of Angela's and I need somebody to explain it to me."

Federer was generous with his time, staying with me in the garage until midnight, both of us listening to the sporadic spring showers pattering on the roof while we worked. Unable to shake the suspicion armed goons were going to barge in and demand the materials, I wore my Glock under a loose sweater. I felt stupid and paranoid for wearing the gun. I checked the security cameras on my cell phone every fifteen minutes. The garage where we were working was at the end of a long driveway alongside the house. It was dark and there were at least two ways to sneak onto my property that were not covered by cameras. Also, they could go through the house and use Kathy or the downstairs renter as a hostage. I was becoming as paranoid as Angela, but according to Federer, the trunk contained the seeds of destruction for a billion-dollar empire, and there were already two dead people linked to it.

In the end, Federer said, "It doesn't prove there's a fire, but there's an awful lot of smoke."

"Is it enough to get the SEC to dig into it?"

"If I were working there, it would be, but you never know with the SEC. Everything in Washington is political. For years they ignored complaints about Bernie Madoff. What we have here are a lot of complaints from people who are suspicious, all of it ignored by the SEC. Of course, if there's any truth to even half of this, CLS will collapse when it turns up on the evening news. Ponzi schemes fall apart as soon as they see the light of day."

"But what we have here doesn't prove it's a Ponzi scheme?"

"It proves a lot of people who should know something about where all this money is invested don't have a clue. That alone makes me suspicious. It also proves he's keeping a hell of a lot of the company funds in raw cash. Far too much, I would say. This trunk is worth around a billion dollars."

"Meaning?'

"Meaning we could take it to Self and sell it for that."

"That's five hundred million each." He looked at me and laughed. I laughed, too. Neither of us was inclined toward extortion and we both knew it.

"They figure Madoff bilked people out of sixty-five billion. I'm guessing Self took at least that much from his investors, maybe more."

"So CLS Enterprises is an enormous house of cards?"

"We're not going to prove it. Not with what we have here. But from what I'm seeing, I think it is a Ponzi. Bear in mind Bernie Madoff carried it off for almost twenty years. There are people who think it was closer to forty. Self is sixty-three. Maybe he figures he'll be dead before anybody finds out."

32

KATHY and I were in the elevator riding up to the Columbia Tower Club, one of those private clubs with a prohibitive annual membership fee and a ritzy clientele. We'd been invited to dinner with Clark Lloyd Self and Monica Pennington, during which Pennington expected a report on her sister over our meal. I had a feeling this was the end of my assignment as far as Pennington was concerned. She'd gotten fed up with me on our visit with Hoshi Smith.

Self was bent on getting his hands on anything Angela had dug up against him and was undoubtedly hoping I would hand it over tonight. He should have used some other investigating agency, because I wasn't going to roll over and let him scratch my tummy like a grizzled old dog. Henrik Federer and I were convinced he was running a Ponzi scheme, and he couldn't pay me enough to keep quiet about it.

Tonight I was going to tell Pennington her sister had been murdered. My hope was she would keep me on the payroll after I told her, if only so I would have access to her husband and his flunkies. Once they offloaded me, I would become, I was sure, public enemy number one, and Self would bar any CLS Enterprises employees or associates from speaking to me. I hadn't told her about the hit and run. I had the feeling if I did, she would think I'd gone mad; all I had were suspicions and coincidences and a flighty identification of one of her husband's employees. As far as Angela's death was concerned, I was bogged down with suspects, including Pennington's husband, who, as far as I could tell, could not account for his whereabouts on the afternoon in question. However, like Bonds, I felt Angela could have handled him if he'd been alone. If there'd been two of them . . . I wasn't so sure.

Even though I warned her it might not be exactly what she would call a 'date night', Kathy was delighted by the invitation to the Columbia Tower. She'd slipped into a black cocktail dress and now looked like an ad for diamonds or cigars or whatever it was fabulously beautiful models posed for. Whiskey. Condoms. Well, maybe not condoms.

Kathy had located my one pair of dress pants in the back of my closet, which I wore with a dress shirt and sport coat. I drew the line at the tie, making me the most underdressed man in the building.

Instead of a cozy dinner with Self and Pennington, we walked in on a mob scene; just about every individual from Self's company must have been in attendance. In the middle of the room on a table stood an eight-foot ice sculpture of Self and Monica, probably in celebration of their reconciliation. I should have known. Somewhere along the line I'd been told he never went out to dinner with less than twelve people. There were more like six dozen guests here. We'd stumbled into one of Self's famous quarterly dinners, everything top drawer, spouses and partners invited, every penny paid for out of Self's pocket. It was a tried and true technique of robber barons everywhere—buy off the serfs. When I stepped close to the ice sculpture I could feel the coolness radiating from it, just as I could feel the coolness from Monica as she glowered at me from across the room. She was never going to forget my insinuation that she had been complicit in Hoshi Smith's drowning.

Self had commandeered the entire top floor of the Columbia Tower, the tallest building in Seattle, so we had an expansive view over the rest of the city and Puget Sound, watching airliners as they descended toward Sea-Tac airport to the south of the city, lighted container ships anchored in the Duwamish waterway, a ferry gliding away from the city docks headed toward Bremerton. "I love the panorama," Kathy said. "This is going to be so much fun."

"Right."

"Why? You don't think it's going to be fun?"

"It's going to be fun, all right."

All of the cozy tables had name placards on them. Kathy and I were assigned a table by ourselves next to a window. After we were seated, I said, "My report's not going to make Pennington happy."

"What's she going to do? Throw a tantrum?"

"She might throw us out on our ears."

"We've been thrown out of nicer places."

"Not recently."

"But we have."

"I like your attitude, sister."

"It always pays to have an attitude when I'm out with you."

"Check that out. They did an ice sculpture of you standing next to Self. Look. They made your breasts too small."

The breasts on the sculpture were ridiculously humongous. Kathy smiled at me as if I were an inmate in a rubber room. "Perhaps, but I believe that's supposed to be Pennington and Self."

"Really? Is that why they're too small?"

"Don't you wish."

There were five separate courses to the meal, and as each course was served, Self and Pennington moved to another table, at first in tandem, and then individually, a young man in a tuxedo hauling their chairs for them as if neither was capable of moving a chair. The plan was to share at least part of the meal with every table in the room. I had to admire their social grace. I would have choked if I'd been forced to swallow that many doses of small talk. Finally, as the desserts were being brought out, Monica Pennington's chair got dragged to our table.

"Having a good time?" Pennington asked.

"Scrumptious," I said.

"It was nice of you to invite us," Kathy said.

"Our pleasure," Pennington said dismissively. She scooted her chair up to the table. "I'm sorry this had to be done here. It was either this, or we could talk on the flight tomorrow on our way to the Antilles. I'm assuming you didn't want to be in another hemisphere tomorrow night?"

"This is fine." Pennington sat back, waiting for me to say more. I shocked her when I added, "Your sister's death wasn't suicide."

Pennington had read the suicide note, had viewed the body,

grieved, gotten drunk, and hired me to absolve her of blame. Now, she spent some moments mulling over what I was telling her. "You're saying it was an accident?"

"Angela was too comfortable with heights for it to have been an accident. I doubt she fell off the roof."

"But that's what you thought that first day."

"I was wrong."

"If it wasn't suicide and it wasn't an accident, what was it?"

"Somebody threw her off."

"No. She killed herself. I'm not happy with it, but that's what happened."

"Is it? The only real evidence we have is the note you got in your e-mail. But anybody can send an e-mail. If somebody was there to throw her off the roof they were also there to send the note. I think they were with her when Crane arrived, that they took her up to the roof before Crane reached the apartment. Crane said her door was ajar. Would she have left it ajar if she'd been planning to go to the roof and jump?"

"Maybe she left it open for Crane or you."

"I very much doubt it."

"But that doesn't mean she was murdered."

"It means somebody left her door open, and I doubt she would do that. When we reconstructed the hard drive, we found the suicide note in a file that was two years old. She hadn't amended a word. Somebody destroyed that computer and wrecked the hard drive either before she died or right after. There are reasons she might have destroyed the computer herself, but there are even more compelling reasons somebody else might have. Also, when Crane was waiting in her apartment for her to show up, he heard somebody barreling down the stairs, possibly from the roof access. Unfortunately, he didn't look to see who it was. I think it was her killer. Or killers."

"But you said you spoke to her after she fell. If somebody threw her off the roof, she would have told you."

"She made me promise to keep her work going. That was the most important thing to her. Because that was about helping other people, and other people always came first with Angela. Before she could say more, she died."

"Was there anything else on her computer?"

"Names, e-mail addresses, and some videos of a personal nature."

"What do you mean by that?"

"I'm not sure anybody should see them, not even you."

"But you've viewed them?"

"And my technician. They're not going anywhere. One of the tapes involved a man I later learned did time in prison for murdering a woman. Oddly enough, he threw that woman off a highway overpass. He was interested in Angela, but I don't think she was interested in him."

"So how did he come to make a tape with her?"

"That's a story for some other time."

"I gather he's your chief suspect?"

"He is *a* suspect. There are others."

"But he must be the main one?"

"I'm looking into it."

"You thought she was bipolar?"

"I believe that now more than ever."

"I've been doing some reading. People who are manic-depressive sometimes kill themselves."

"A manic-depressive also cycles back and forth at predictable intervals. I don't know what her time frame was, but I believe she was still in a manic phase, or close to it. I'm just going by her voice on the phone and the talk I had with her the night before she died. Neither time did she sound depressed. In fact, she was pretty revved up. She was going full guns on a project. It was the first thing she talked about after she fell. I can't see her giving up on it to kill herself."

"You just said 'fell'. That implies an accident."

"A poor choice of words. She was thrown or pushed."

"But the police said she killed herself."

"The police have been wrong before."

"You've been wrong before, too. What makes you think you're right this time? And what was this project she talked about?"

"She was trying to prove fraud at CLS Enterprises. I found some of her materials." I was well aware that by telling Pennington I was also telling Self, and in turn, alerting Bonds and Gunderson. The dogs would soon be loose.

"Good grief. I thought she'd given all that up. Black, Angela killed herself. I hired you to find out why, and you come back with this theory about how somebody who nobody ever saw pushed her? Are you sure you're not hatching this out of thin air so you can squeeze more money out of me? I assume you want me to pay you to find her killer?"

"I'm going to the police with this. My hope is *they* will find her killer."

"This man you were talking about? The ex-con? What about him?"

"Maybe. I can't say."

"Or are you thinking it's somebody from my husband's company who wanted to stop all her nonsense? You realize if Angela had spread certain rumors about CLS it would have had catastrophic consequences?"

"All of this would be something for the police to look into."

"So now you want the police to investigate us? For this wonderful outcome, how much do we owe you?"

"You hired me to uncover the truth about your sister's death."

"Of course I want the truth. But not at the expense of having you sic the police on my husband and possibly ruin his business. Besides, if I'm reading between the lines correctly, I believe you're implying my husband might have had something to do with killing her."

"I'll be honest. I'm not ruling it out. You knew your sister was investigating your husband's business. He knew it, too. Also, I find it more credible that she called Crane and me that afternoon because she was afraid of someone, as opposed to calling us so we could watch her jump off the roof. If she was going to kill herself, it would have been a secret, like everything else."

"That's the first thing you've said that makes sense." Across the room her husband was working his way toward us, glad-handing and schmoozing people at nearby tables. Pennington hadn't been happy with me when she got to the table and was even less happy now. She turned to me, laid her hand on my knee, and said, "Don't say anything to Clark. I need to think this over. I still want to know what happened to my sister."

"So do I."

Self approached the table and quipped, "Why the long faces?" After some small talk, his manservant brought his chair so he could sit.

"Mr. Black has been telling me he's come up with an alternate theory of how Angela died," Monica said, touching her husband's arm as if to warn him.

"Oh?"

We weren't supposed to mention this, yet the first thing out of her mouth was an invitation for me to give out details. "Just a few questions first," I said, nonplused by her betrayal of her own conditions.

"Always with the questions." Self sat back, amused, and sipped from a Chardonnay his personal waiter had carried from the last table.

"I'd like to know everything you can tell me about Rafael Gutierrez."

"Who?"

"Rafael Gutierrez. He worked for you at one time."

As Self looked around the table, the genial smile evaporated. "What's this about?"

"Angela knew Rafael Gutierrez."

"If she did I imagine the two of them were colluding to dish out dirt on me. Gutierrez was an ex-employee with an axe to grind."

"You don't have any idea what that dirt might have been?"

"Listen, Buford . . ."

"It's Black. Thomas Black."

"Right. Listen. I've had too much to drink tonight to be dealing with this bullshit. I'd rather talk about this when I have a clear head. Comprende?"

"I understand perfectly."

"I'm guessing you've had a lot to drink yourself. Probably going to say something you'll regret later."

"I don't drink."

"Is that it, then?"

I glanced at Monica. Federer and I had an appointment at the State Attorney General's office on Monday I hadn't told her about. "Black," Monica said. "Tell my husband about the man you said was bothering my sister."

I told him she'd been in contact with a felon, that he'd been interested in her, that he'd done time for killing a woman he had pushed from a high place.

"Well, there you go," Self said. "Tell the police. We're through, you and I. Send my people a bill."

After a moment of silence, Monica said, "Honey, I'm not sure he's finished."

"I think Buford *is* finished," said Self.

I looked at Pennington, who clearly was ambivalent about canning me. I knew she'd been considering it herself, but now that it was actually taking place, she wasn't so sure. Staring into her eyes, I said, "I'll send you a bill. If I find out any more of the personal details, I'll provide those without charge."

"Well, well," Kathy said as we headed for the elevators. "I guess that's over."

"Not by half," I said. "I'm more certain than ever she was murdered."

"Then you should keep working on it."

"I have no intention of quitting."

"Buford?"

"What is it?"

"That guy's been staring at you for a while now." Goodnight Bonds was following us toward the elevator. He wore the same suit he always wore, dark, a little too large, the sleeves too long, the same periwinkle tie. When our paths intersected in the doorway, he glanced past me into the room where the party was still going on and then back to me. The last time I'd seen him he'd been on the ground in Montana shooting a rifle at Self's private jet. No. The last time I'd seen him was at Monica's when I'd picked her up to visit Hoshi. He'd been racing out of her condo building.

"Looks like you're history," he said.

"Looks that way."

"My grandfather never liked cyclists like you, and neither do I. He always ran them off the road. Even if they didn't give him the finger."

"How do you know I'm a cyclist?"

"Your Facebook page."

"I'm not on Facebook."

"Whatever."

"I heard your grandfather wore diapers."

He snickered uneasily. I could tell he'd forgotten he told me about his grandfather and was now wondering what else I might know. My statement put him on edge, which was what he'd been trying to do to me. And had done to me. His words had sent me into the stratosphere.

He winked. "Keep your eyes open next time you're hogging the road on your sissy bike. Never know what might happen if you keep getting in the way of those of us who actually belong on the road."

For just a moment, I saw a flicker of recognition in his dead, flat-paint, cinnamon-colored eyes. Facing him now, witnessing the self-righteousness in his face and knowing he'd tried to run me down and had crippled Ron Prisham instead, I did what any reasonable man would do. I lost my mind. I guess you could say it was ten years of road rage and car/bike entanglements coalescing in the one encounter. Kathy was beside me, Bonds directly in front, nobody else anywhere close. I hadn't seen Gunderson all night and quickly discarded the notion this was a setup, though it seemed like one. Even if it was, I was too blinded with rage to be wary.

At the last second Bonds saw the insanity in my eyes and turned to run. Before he got two steps, I had his necktie. I pulled him around in a circle and slammed him bodily into the wall. The blow came close to knocking him out. I pulled the knot in his tie as tight as it would cinch, strangling him until his neck veins were bulging and his eyes were beginning to cross, then swung him into the wall again.

33

WHEN his head bounced off the wall a second time a photo of one of Washington's former governors fell to the floor. Sounds of laughter in the adjoining room began to diminish. I was only vaguely aware I was probably going to spend the night down the street in jail. People were pulling at me, blood was flying, and all sounds in the other room ceased.

It was Kathy who finally pulled me off him. All I could think about was Ron Prisham's body rolling under the Tahoe, his wife slumped silently next to his bedside, their kids tended by babysitters and family members. I must have looked like a maniac. In the end, the only reason I stopped was because one of my flying elbows slammed Kathy hard enough to make her grunt with pain.

"Thomas! Thomas! Stop it! Stop it!"

As I stepped away, several of the men from the dinner party began taking my measure, as if planning to jump me, presumably to hold me for the police. Clark Lloyd Self pushed his way through the assemblage and surveyed the situation. Bonds was on his knees, face dripping blood, one eye swollen shut. He gave out a weak grin. Two women rushed over and helped him stand up. It took them a while to realize he was strangling on his knotted tie.

Self turned to me and said, "You can forget the bill. We're not paying any bill."

"Your man pretty much admitted to a hit and run," I said.

"If you're waiting for the police to come and get you, forget it. I'm not going to allow the police to interrupt our celebration any more than you've already done. Now get out."

Kathy and I waited for the elevator while about fifty well-dressed people stared at us. None of the men were willing to step back into the dining room until I was safely in the elevator. I kept my eye on the reflections in the granite wall in front of us in case somebody decided to jump me from behind. When we stepped into the elevator and turned around to face the crowd, I could see I'd gotten the attention of Monica Pennington, who was looking at me in a way she never had before, her glacial cool replaced by something I couldn't quite identify. And then it came to me. She liked it. She liked the fact that I'd attacked her man. She liked the violence, was attracted to it. All of a sudden I was fascinating.

We rode down to the street level wordlessly. Finally, as the elevator doors opened, I said, "I didn't hurt you, did I?"

"I'm going to have a bruise."

"Sorry."

"That's okay, Buford."

"I suppose I'm going to have live with that for a while."

"You should have new business cards printed up."

I felt bad about injuring her and even worse because she'd seen me lose my mind. I'd only had a couple of incidents like that in my life, and one of them had to be tonight. The intolerable gall displayed by Bonds had been magnified by the fact that Ron Prisham, who had been so horribly mauled, was a complete innocent. It was the second time I'd done damage to Bonds or Gunderson, and I had a feeling they were too smart and too mean to let me get away with it a third time.

As we exited the building into a light mist, I said, "Want to walk up to the hospital? I'd like to see Ron right now."

"Is that what that was about? Bonds is the man you think ran over your friend?"

"I *know* he ran over him."

"Do you know how lucky you are you're not sitting in a cell?"

"I'm lucky to be alive. I should at least be in Ron's place."

"That's one way of looking at it. You think you could identify him as the driver now?"

"No, but you heard him. He as much as admitted it."

"Thomas, you screwed the pooch here. You get up there on the stand and say you saw him run over your friend—"

"I *think* I saw him run over my friend."

"Or if they ask what he said tonight, the defense attorney is going to ask if there's any bad blood between you two. They'll introduce photos of Bonds' face from tonight. Suddenly you're no longer an impartial witness. You're his worst enemy. Beating him up made you worthless on the stand. Why did you do that? It's so unlike you."

I didn't have an answer for her.

"You always were a bad boy, Buford."

"Not this bad."

"Pretty bad, though."

Before we could say anything else, Marvin Gunderson jumped into our path. Once again he stepped out of nowhere. He folded his cell phone, closed it, and put it into his coat pocket, blocking the sidewalk, his thick arms dangling at his sides like tree limbs. He grinned genially. "I heard you spoke to my little buddy upstairs." When I said nothing, he added, "I've been wanting to do that myself."

"I'll bet."

It occurred to me the reason Self didn't want to call the police was because he was planning to send Gunderson after me. I made a slight motion as if I had a gun on my hip and was checking to make sure it was still there.

Whether he bought it or not, he stepped aside and said, "Probably what you should do now is buzz off. The kids will be with them starting tomorrow."

"Thanks for the advice."

"It wasn't free. You show up again, you'll see how much it costs."

We walked past him slowly. I knew I was giving him an opportunity to reach out and knock me to the ground, but there didn't seem to be any way to avoid it. Walking past him was as scary as walking close to a moving freight train. When I checked on him in the polished marble on the building next to us, in the windows of parked cars, he wasn't getting ready to pounce on me at all; he was staring at Kathy's legs.

On the walk up the hill toward Harborview Hospital, Kathy broke our silence. "He gives me the creeps."

"He's not such a bad guy. I was thinking of having him over for dinner." We both laughed.

I could feel the residual adrenaline coursing through my bloodstream like poison, not from my scrap with Bonds, but from walking past Gunderson. I'd been incredibly lucky during our first two encounters, and part of me, the dumbest part, believed I was going to be lucky if we ever got into it a third time. I hadn't seen a lot of people die, but of those I had seen, I found it noteworthy that several had been really, *really* surprised by it. I had no doubt I was going to be surprised, too. I just hoped Gunderson wasn't the surprise.

After we'd visited Melissa Prisham at her husband's bedside and found ourselves disoriented in the hospital's labyrinthine nighttime corridors, Kathy said, "Did you even know you were going to beat him up?"

"About a tenth of a second before it happened."

"Doesn't that scare you?"

"I'm okay with it," I lied.

34

In life, Angela Bassman was deadly serious every minute of every day. She'd never been a comedian, never wanted to be one, and in the beginning was not impressed with my incessant wisecracks and opportunistic mugging. Somehow, over the first weeks I knew her, she grew to countenance me and even seemed to look forward to our meetings. Kathy said the reason Angela liked me was because I was incorrigible, that I could, and often would, make fun of everything I came across, including myself. Kathy said my dumb jokes helped dull the razor edge of the angst Angela felt toward the world, that when she met me she was introduced to an entirely new way of relating to the universe.

The first time we saw each other was at Bellevue Square Mall during a harried Christmas season. I said a few stupid things about the professional elves in the mall actually being an organized gang of pickpockets, Kathy showing gracious amusement by laughing, and after some time had passed and my stream of jokes hadn't slowed, Angela finally stopped staring and joined the laughter. Along with her innumerable questions about everything under the sun and her faulty reports to our mutual friends on what I'd said, her on-again off-again reluctance to laugh at my dim-witted humor was part of what made her a pest, that and the god awful squalling cackles when she finally did laugh. Then there were the legends she'd built up in her mind about me. To Angela, *everything* about me was impressive. She even kept tabs on my resting heart rate, though she frequently quoted it wrong. Some years I would get two birthday cards from her, on two different dates. She did it from memory, she boasted.

Angela had almost no sense of irony, so when Susan Djokovic, the attorney who'd written her will and was administering the estate, approached me in the foyer of our building and told me Angela had expressed the wish for her cremated remains to be scattered on top of Granite Mountain by all her friends, I couldn't help grinning. "What's so funny?" Djokovic asked.

Granite Mountain was a popular hike on the I-90 corridor about twenty-five miles east of Seattle, a trek attempted only by the fit or the foolhardy. The top of the mountain was diabolically gorgeous, but it was an eight-mile round trip with almost four thousand feet of elevation gain, close to a mile straight up, a lot of it in the open, which made it something of a death march on hot summer days. While it was a maintained trail and didn't require any special skills, sections of the path rose at a pitch verging on twenty-five percent grade. The payoffs were tarn- and huckleberry-laced meadows and enormous granite slabs and boulders near the top, where one found a panoramic 360 degree view which included a snapshot of Snoqualmie Pass and the ski areas from high above them, and in the distance, a snow-covered Mount Rainier, the fifth highest point in the contiguous United States. To the north one could, hypothetically, see all the way to Canada.

"Should I wear hiking boots?" Djokovic asked.

We were going home for the day, and Kathy had just caught up. "What is it?" Kathy asked. I was still grinning like an imbecile with a lollipop. Djokovic told her what we were talking about.

"Honey," Kathy said, touching Djokovic's shoulder. "That trail is heart attack city. A lot of people who hike it are getting ready for ascents on Mount Rainier or McKinley."

"You're kidding, right?"

"Your call," I said. "If you're not in condition it will be slow going."

Later, in the car, Kathy said, "When is the hike scheduled?"

"Sunday."

"Two days from now? I don't have time to get in shape."

I reached over and patted Kathy's thigh through her dress. "I like your shape. And you don't have to come."

"Of course I'm coming. Angela was my friend."

I started laughing. Then Kathy laughed. We thought it a splendid joke and entirely unexpected, so unexpected I finally decided Angela had probably done it by accident. Angela had played one joke in her life and it was an accident.

* * *

After getting fired by Self, I had several conversations with Carole Cooper, the Seattle P.D. detective who'd handled Angela's case. She listened politely while I explained the new evidence, including the fact that the suicide note sent from Angela's computer was two years old. "You've done a lot of work on this," Cooper said.

"I think it deserves another look."

She sighed. "I'll look at it, but don't hold out any hope things will change. You told me yourself she had a history of suicidal thoughts. Now you're saying she was bipolar. Her being bipolar doesn't help your case. Bipolars get depressed, and depressed people *can* commit suicide."

Four days later when I contacted her again, she said, "You get fired by Self for beating up one of his people?"

"More or less."

"You're on a wild goose chase, Black. I can't reopen the investigation on what you've given me."

"Fine. I'll find her killer myself."

"Don't do anything crazy."

"Me?"

"We know all about what happened at the Columbia Club."

"Bonds as much as admitted being the driver on that hit and run on Mercer Island."

"If he admitted a crime, you should have called us."

"Yes, ma'am."

* * *

Portman Marshal refused to see me a second time. It was possible all the dust and smoke and mirrors I'd been dealing with were merely peripheral effects, that it had been a simple case of unrequited love. Portman had sex with her, got sappy and fell in love, followed her. But Portman had a history of throwing women from high places. I began to wonder about his relationship with the girl he'd been convicted of murdering. Had she spurned his attentions? It was possible the story about a gang initiation had been tripe. I called the King County Prosecutor's office and asked if they could give me the name of the assistant prosecutor who sent him up. I could tell they weren't going to get back to me. I called Crane, who was on Grand Cayman with Self and his family. I wired him a photo of Portman through our cell phones, asking if he'd ever seen the man, possibly on the day of Angela's death. He texted back and said the man in the photo looked familiar, though he couldn't figure out exactly where he might have seen him. They hadn't met at the Alexis with Angela, because Portman hadn't been there on the same night as Crane.

Carrying a selection of photographs, I went door-to-door in Angela's building, then scoured her neighborhood. One of the photos was of Portman Marshal. At one point a middle-aged woman in a run-down house across the street, who told me her mother had worked as a slave laborer for Hitler in WWII, scrutinized the photos for a long time, as if trying to hold me there for my company. I got the feeling she was trying to glean hints from my body language as to which of the four pictures I wanted her to select. Finally, she pointed to Portman. "I seen that one before."

"Where?"

"Hangin' around the neighborhood. I thought he was casing the houses, going to break in somewhere."

"When was this?"

"Three months ago. *And* last week." I knew she hadn't seen him three months ago, because he hadn't known Angela three months ago, but she might have seen him last week. In any event, she wasn't much of a witness.

On my third visit to Angela's apartment building I found a young couple I hadn't met before. After I showed them pictures, they told me they'd seen Portman Marshal lurking outside the building the day Angela died. "You're sure it was the day she died?"

"Absolutely," they both agreed. "We'll never forget that day."

Counting the woman who lived across the street, that made four people who could place Portman in the neighborhood, including Portman himself, who'd confessed to knowing the approximate height of Angela's apartment building. Putting him on the roof with Angela was an entirely different critter.

I spoke to Portman's attorney again, and surprisingly she told me I was now free to visit him in lockup in Kent if we didn't discuss his pending charges. We met in the same room we'd used previously, this time without his attorney. I pushed my four photos across the table. He spent a lot of time examining his own photograph as if he'd never seen it before. It was an old arrest photo. When he was finished studying the photos, I let him stew for a while, then said, "I've got witnesses who put you near the building where she died, on the *day* she died. I'm going to put you in her apartment destroying her computer, too. Eventually, I'm going to put you on the roof with her."

"What do you want from me?"

"The same thing I want from everyone. The truth."

His face had the sort of deadpan affect people perfected in lockup. "It was wrong what they were doin' to her."

"You did it, too."

"Before I knew how she was."

"Tell me about it."

"Nate said she was a freak. He told me the rules were you pay your share of the hotel room, do her, and that's it. But I liked her. I followed her after. I had to. There was something wrong with the setup."

"But you thought it was okay to follow her?"

"Listen, she told me about starvation in Sudan. She told me they only have twenty-five miles of paved roads in the whole country. And we thought *we* were poor. She made me look at the world in a whole new way."

"So you followed her and talked about Sudan?"

"We talked first time I met her. In the hotel room. There was a news report on the TV about Sudan. They liked to keep the TV running when they were laying pipe. She wanted it unplugged, but they kept it running. She told me then."

"But you followed her?"

"I had to know why she was doin' it."

"What did you find out?"

"She pretended she didn't know who I was. I guess she was embarrassed to see me in the daylight."

"What did she say?"

"When I akxed about the sex, she said she didn't know what I was talkin' about. She wasn't going to give up. Said she was going to call the cops if I didn't go away. I went back and fronted Nate. He said she was supposed to be on some medication. Dep-something. Except she wouldn't take it."

"Depakote?"

"Yeah, maybe that was it. She didn't like the side effects. He'll tell you different, but he knew she wasn't right in the head. He knew what we were doing was wrong. He said she thought the United States was in danger of being taken over and she had to warn the President. She believed Nate and Charles were Secret Service and could get her in to see the President. Nate went along with it but kept putting her off about meeting the Prez, telling her they had to have sex one more time before the President would see her. I only wanted to help her. And now I'm in here for stealing rib eye."

"How many times did you talk to Angela after that?"

"None. I was afraid she would call the police."

"But you spied on her?"

"I wanted to see her again."

"You feel as if she'd spurned you?"

"I don't know what spurned is. All I know is I didn't kill her."

"You were there the day she died."

"You going to have a hell of a time proving that."

We went around and around for a while, and then I said, "Just out of curiosity, why'd you steal the meat?"

"Why you think? I didn't have no money. Sheeeeit."

I couldn't decide if I believed Portman's story. He might have been an accomplished jailhouse liar who thought he could gull me, or he might have been telling the truth. What he said had a certain ring of truth to it, but hanging around outside her apartment was definitely not normal behavior.

* * *

After almost two weeks of daily and persistent attempts and over a hundred phone calls, I got hold of a gentleman at the SEC who had information concerning the package Angela mailed them. He told me they'd decided her allegations were not worth pursuing. "There are a lot of reputable people on her list who were as suspicious of CLS as she was," I said. "Have you talked to them?"

"All I can say is, it was decided we had more pressing business."

"What do you mean? If she was right, there are billions of dollars being stolen."

"We had our analysts go over her complaint. That's all I can tell you."

"So you're not going to pursue it?"

"You're not listening, sir. We *did* pursue it."

35

SUNDAY morning at the Granite Mountain trailhead parking area, we found balloons and signs welcoming "Angela's Friends."

The I-90 freeway was close enough to the trailhead one could hear the fast-flowing river of rubber and steel. It was a large paved parking area with a single rustic privy and a well-traveled dirt path leading north into the woods. To my chagrin a young man in a green REI vest stood behind a small concession table piled full of freebies: small rucksacks, bottled water, Band-Aids, maps, sun hats, energy bars. Another example of Self's generosity. The trail entrance was marked with balloons, making it everything Angela would have despised. Beside the entrance stood a large easel with a photo of a snowy Denali high camp near the top of Mount McKinley, a smiling, tanned Angela in her wire-rimmed glasses in the foreground. The picture was so lifelike and just plain overpowering it almost brought me to tears.

Pennington and the rest of her crowd had been chauffeured from Seattle in a stretch limo. The limo and the liveried driver looked strangely incongruous in this wooded parking area, which otherwise was infested with four-wheel-drive SUVs and Subarus. The boys were outfitted in new gear and boots, Pennington in hiking shorts, boots, and thick wool socks almost identical to Kathy's outfit. Most people carried small day packs. I was in shorts, trail-running shoes, and carried a small hip pack. Kathy, who had only one real fear in this world, carried a canister of bear spray and her own hip pack with a bell that jangled every time she took a step. Hiking with Kathy was always a magnificent escapade in bear avoidance.

Grizzlies had been spotted in the state in the past few years, though none nearby, and it was all Kathy could talk about on the drive up. "We see a bear," I said, "I'm going to run."

"I know that joke."

"What joke?"

"Two guys see a bear. One stoops to tie his shoes. The other says, 'why are you tying your shoes; you can't outrun a bear.' He says, 'I don't have to outrun the bear. I only have to outrun you.' You tell that joke every time we hike."

"You thought that was a joke?"

"You wouldn't run. I know you. You'd grab my bear spray out of my frozen fist and fight for me."

"Over fifteen pounds, I run. Bears, raccoons, obese squirrels. If it's over fifteen pounds, don't count on me because I'm going to be gone."

Somebody had attached a newspaper clipping to the corner of the huge color Denali photograph. It warned of target shooters taking potshots in the I-90 corridor area. According to the clipping, last weekend a man had narrowly missed getting hit by a stray bullet. The clipping included a photo of a bullet hole in his backpack. As I finished reading, I saw Goodnight Bonds exit the restroom and traipse up the trail, where he was joined by Marvin Gunderson, who once again appeared out of nowhere. When I caught Gunderson's eye, he did a slight double take, then nudged Bonds and pointed me out.

Before I could think through the ramifications of Bonds and Gunderson being here, Crane Manning appeared in front of the large photograph of Angela. He was entranced. Just about everybody who'd seen it had been. Pennington and family, meanwhile, were gathering in front of the large wooden sign that pointed out the different hikes and distances available from the parking lot. Pennington's younger boy was lugging Angela's urn in a backpack, trying to belie the seriousness of his charge with a casual air I saw through right away.

I sidled through the gathering and picked up a couple of free health bars from the REI table and then peered into the woods where Bonds and Gunderson had disappeared. Bonds had a black case on his back. It looked as though it could contain a musical instrument or perhaps photographic equipment. Or an AR-15 with a collapsible stock. I hadn't seen the word "photographer" anywhere on his résumé and I doubted he was musically inclined. A mouse under one eye and stitches in his upper lip were all that remained of our confrontation in the Columbia Tower Club.

"The family's not too happy about you being here," Crane murmured.

"I'm not here for the family. I'm here for Angela."

"That picture makes me sad. I feel worse about her death now than I did at the memorial, or even the day she died."

I picked up another free health bar from the REI table. "How's the job going?"

"It's okay." I noticed his former rabid enthusiasm had waned. It was easy to see Crane was demoralized to be here remembering Angela.

I glanced around the parking lot. There were, as near as I could tell, fifty people here for Angela, including Susan Djokovic, who was going to be sorry tomorrow morning when she tried to get out of bed. Others had arrived early and were already on the trail along with Bonds and Gunderson. "You know which car they came in?" I asked.

"Who?"

"The ape and his little pal."

"Over there. The white Land Rover." Crane followed me to the vehicle. On the way, I grabbed another free bar from the REI table. Without talking about it, it was assumed by both of us that Crane and I would do this hike together, that we would take the opportunity to renew our acquaintance. I was glad of that.

The Land Rover was locked, but when I cupped my hands to the tinted windows I saw various pieces of equipment inside, including several empty magazines for an AR-15 rifle, a gun that was accurate out to four hundred yards. If they used a suppressor like the ones I'd seen in Montana, bullets could rain down the mountain without anybody hearing the reports or even knowing where they came from. I turned to Crane, who was still staring dolefully at the Angela Bassman photo across the parking lot. "Did they bring guns?" I asked.

"What makes you think so?"

"Goodnight had a case on his back. It could have been a rifle."

"I don't think they have guns," Crane said. "Why would they?"

I'd seen Henrik Federer and others start up the trail when we arrived, which put him twenty minutes ahead of us. I called him on his cell to warn him Bonds and Gunderson were coming up fast behind him, but he either didn't have his cell turned on, or was getting limited service because of our remote location. I called again a few minutes later with the same result.

Federer had been working with me to convince the authorities to open an investigation into CLS Enterprises. Over the past few weeks we'd both become convinced CLS was a Ponzi scheme. Self's company was as crooked as a Ukrainian election, and it would be revealed the first time a legitimate examiner looked into the books. Ponzi schemes were based on paying off early investors with the money from later suckers rather than from actual profits, and they continued only so long as the operators continued to draw in new money. The minute an official entity started asking where the money was invested, the fraud would unravel. The sad thing about most Ponzi schemes was that somewhere a banker knew it was a fraud. Nobody kept billions of dollars under the mattress. Bankers were always in on it.

If there was any justice in this world, Clark Lloyd Self was going to spend the rest of his life eating powdered mashed potatoes and reconstituted egg product and pacing an eight-by-twelve cell wondering why he hadn't been nicer to Angela. Though she claimed no knowledge of his business dealings, Monica Pennington might also be implicated. Angela had been trying to protect her sister from ignominy and a possible prison sentence.

I was certain Bonds and Gunderson had run over Ron Prisham and was nearly as certain they were responsible for murdering Rafael Gutierrez in a similar hit and run months earlier.

What was more, in the past few days I figured out who threw Angela off the roof.

The woods were cool and dark, though there was sun in the open spaces of the parking area. There were patches of fog and clouds on the top of the mountain, so nobody quite knew how to dress. Even in the summer, underdressed people could succumb to hypothermia in these mountains. I dressed light but carried a hat and gloves just in case.

Most people were starting the trek more or less in a group, but that was going to blow apart as soon as we hit the steep stuff.

I approached Kathy, who'd been chatting with Susan Djokovic. "I think you two should stay here. Take the car home. I'll get a ride with somebody."

"Not on your life."

"I think Bonds is carrying a gun up the mountain."

"He wouldn't dare."

"Federer might be the target. Or even Monica."

Kathy said, "Why Monica?"

"They're talking about divorce again."

"Yes, I heard that. But if anybody's a target, it's you. He hates you with a passion."

"Bonds didn't know we were coming. If he's brought a gun, it wasn't meant for me."

"I'm not going home. Besides, how are they going to get away with it?"

"You saw the note on the easel over there. People have been shooting indiscriminately in this area. Somebody gets beaned today, it could easily be chalked up to an accident."

"Well, I'm not going home." There was no point in arguing with her. She had a stronger will than I did.

Kathy and I left shortly behind a group that included Monica Pennington, Clark Lloyd Self, their two kids, Monica's older boy, and a smattering of sycophants who worked for Self. Crane hiked alongside me while I said hello to one of the chefs I'd met in the kitchen in Montana. From time to time, we met other hikers coming down the trail, most returning from Pratt Lake, an easier destination on a gentler trail. When I picked up the pace, it was apparent that Crane, despite being an occasional smoker, was going to stick with me for as long as he could.

I caught up to Monica and said, "I think Bonds is carrying a gun."

"Even if he is, so what?"

"A couple of weeks ago he tried to run me down in a stolen car. He sent another cyclist to the Neuro ward at Harborview. Now he's carrying a gun up the mountain. They're going to shoot somebody, and they're going to try to make it look like an accident."

"I'm glad we fired you. You're as batty as Angela was."

"Mom," chastised her middle son, who was close enough to eavesdrop. "Aunt A wasn't batty."

"Give me a reason for him to be carrying a semi-automatic rifle up this mountain," I said.

Her husband, twenty yards behind us and already in a sweat, was hustling to catch up so he could listen in. "I'm not going to cancel this just because you've come up with another hare-brained theory, Black. And furthermore, my husband knows you're planning to talk to the State Attorney General. Somebody from the State called him. He's getting ready to sue your pants off."

"That's okay. I'm wearing boxers underneath."

"He's going to destroy you."

"Not before we destroy him. Monica. You have kids with you. If there's even a chance I'm right, you need to call this off."

"The final goodbye to my sister? I'm not calling anything off." I was hoping in another mile or two Pennington would reconsider and turn her family around. The mountain had a hundred ambush spots on the upper slopes. If Bonds was using a rifle equipped with a suppressor nobody would even know where the bullet came from. With officials warning the public about errant shooters in the area, it might end up being the perfect crime. In the same way I couldn't testify I'd seen Bonds run down Ron Prisham, I couldn't testify I'd seen him with a gun either, only that I'd seen him with a suspicious looking case and that I'd seen gun paraphernalia in his vehicle.

I dropped back and spoke to Clark Lloyd Self, who was huffing loudly. Shaded by thick firs, the trail hadn't gotten steep yet. "One of your guys is carrying a gun," I said. "Call him off."

"One of *my* guys?"

"Bonds."

"If he has a gun, it's to protect me and my family."

"He's got an assault rifle, and it's not to protect you."

"Black, I'm not going to let you ruin this the way you ruined our dinner the other night."

"You put him up to it? Is that it?"

"Get out of my face."

I walked away from him, joining Kathy and Crane up ahead. The three of us quickly began overtaking those who'd left earlier, and after a while we saw only sporadic returning hikers unconnected to our party, people who'd started at seven or eight in the morning and were now returning to their cars. I figured Bonds and Gunderson would keep well ahead of us until we were on the upper slopes. I wasn't sure how fast Marvin Gunderson could propel his bulk up a grade as steep as this was going to get. He was brutally strong and unbelievably quick, but he was also huge, and his girth and weight would be a profound handicap in these mountains.

The trail started off in heavy forest with deep loam on the ground from years of dead plant life and fallen fir and hemlock needles. Every once in a while a small stream cut through our path. For a mile or so it was a shared trail, and then the spur for Granite Mountain peeled off on a switchback which jogged right and headed up at a dizzying angle.

Kathy kept with us until the trail grew absurdly steep. I'd already warned her I wanted to speak to Crane alone and would try to engineer a separation, so when it happened, she realized what I was doing. I said, "I think I hear a bear behind us. I'm going to speed up. You stay back here and guard the rear."

We were on a twenty-five percent pitch trail. Kathy was nearing her upper physical limits or she would have answered me in kind. A wheezing Crane was managing to stay with me through sheer dint of will. "What? What bear?" Kathy gasped as we separated.

Even though I was pulling her leg, I knew Kathy carried a small spray canister that shot a stream of Capsaicin, a potent irritant derived from hot peppers. As a police officer, I'd taken the pepper spray class and, like everyone else in the tutorial, was given a dose so I would know its effects firsthand. In order to recuperate, most people kept their head in a bucket of cold water off and on for most of twenty minutes, and even then it stung like hell.

We were heading through patches of fog now, and although the sun shone through like a dull orange, it was cooler than it might have been for June.

I took the lead, Crane straining to match my pace.

If somebody got killed today, it would be credited to bad luck and errant target shooters. I was not signed up for this hike, so it wasn't likely I was the primary target. Henrik Federer *was* signed up.

On the other hand, there were reports of renewed discord in the Self/Pennington relationship. They were no longer living under the same roof. Word was Pennington's attorneys had figured out a way to break the prenup agreement, and it was highly likely Self didn't want a court poking into his finances, personal or otherwise. Had he targeted his wife to be gunned down in front of her boys? As ghastly as that sounded, I couldn't discount it. A man who would steal fifty or sixty billion dollars from people he called friends would do anything, especially if he felt an impending divorce settlement might pull the rug out from under his shenanigans.

If he knew about or had ordered the hit and run on Gutierrez, or the one meant for me, he was already involved in conspiracy killings. So why would a wife who wanted to divorce him and perhaps expose his business practices be immune? People who get away with murder tend to return to it. If Self killed her and tried to make it look like an accident, he certainly wouldn't be the first rejected husband to take such a tack.

At the rate we were moving it would take close to two hours to get to the top. I did it faster on my own, but it was important I keep Crane with me.

After we'd been alone on the switchbacks for a while, after the trees thinned and the trail began to get more open and rockier, Crane said, "I just feel so bad about her. I think about it all the time."

"Of course you do."

"She didn't deserve to die."

"She didn't deserve to be murdered, that's for sure."

"What makes you think that's what happened?"

"First, there's the fact that people who are intensely involved in a project the way she was are not the kind of people who kill themselves. Then there were physical details of the actual scene that didn't feel right after I thought about them."

"What details?"

"The back of her blouse had a stretched-out spot near the neck, as if somebody had grabbed it and slung her around by it. Her pants had a similar pucker. And she called us beforehand. She wasn't the type to drag in witnesses to her suicide."

"That's it. That's what you've got?"

"There was an ex-con who was briefly involved with her. He was seen hanging around her building."

"So he did it?"

"I wouldn't say that, no."

"Why would she be hanging out with a black guy?"

"Did I say he was black?"

"Well . . ."

"How did you know he was African American?"

"Uh . . ." He hesitated. "You already know I was there. At the party. The other two guys were black. I figured it had to be one of them."

"And?"

"There's something I didn't tell you."

"I think there's a lot you didn't tell me."

"After she killed herself I destroyed her computer. To protect her. There were some tapes. Don't worry. You'll never see them. They're gone now. I destroyed them. After I looked out the window and saw what she'd done, I decided it would be better if nobody else saw the videos. I did it for her."

"It's a natural instinct, protecting a woman's reputation," I said. "But I *have* seen them."

"All of them?"

"Every last pixel."

36

"MY man reconstructed the hard drive."

"What good would it do for anybody to see those videos? It was private stuff. Like dirty underwear, or something."

"You realize if her death was in any way connected to the videos, or to anything else on the computer, you were destroying evidence."

"I didn't think about that. I just thought about people seeing her with those men."

"Of course you thought about it. You were trying to make it as hard as possible to find her killer."

"I wasn't. Why would I do that?"

I stopped, turned and faced him. "Because you killed her."

"What?"

"You killed her."

"That's bullshit."

"You did, though."

"I thought we were friends, Thomas."

"This has got nothing to do with being friends. You threw her off the roof, Crane. You killed Angela." When he didn't respond, I continued. "You must have been surprised when she invited you to the party and you saw what was going on."

"I didn't even want to go. Angela portrayed it as this party with some friends. Said she needed me along because she got nervous by herself. We get there and she tells me they're Secret Service and it was all going to be confidential and I was just to ignore whatever I saw. Hell, I would have beat the shit out of those fuckers if she hadn't convinced me they were Feds. One of them was even carrying. I didn't know what to make of it."

"But you filmed them like she told you to, didn't you?"

"I didn't know what else to do. They were acting like it was normal. One minute we were all sitting there talking and the next she was undressing one of them. It was . . . so casual and so far away from anything I ever would have dreamed she would do. But then, you know the old saying, don't you?"

"What old saying is that?"

"A stiff prick has no conscience."

"I've heard it."

"I liked her, man. I liked her a lot. I don't know why she had to pull that shit. I saw her afterwards, but after that every time I looked at her all I could see was that bed and what she did on it."

She had the last sex party the same day she took Crane and me to Eastgate, the day she met Crane for the first time. She'd been on a high that day, euphoric, wanting to fight us in the hallway, walking on the wall on our roof in a mild state of mania. Then the party. I stopped walking one more time and turned to look at Crane Manning, who seemed near to tears. It was hard not to believe his remorse was genuine.

I said, "The day she died she told me who killed her."

"Bullshit."

"She told me, but I didn't understand. She told me while she was flying through the air. I misheard what she said. She was alive for half a minute on the roof of her car, and she didn't say anything else about you because she'd already said it. Thinking she'd already called you out, she used her last few seconds to make me promise to keep on with her work."

"I don't understand."

"Sure you do. On the way down I thought she yelled, 'It was the drain.' It seemed strange, but people do strange things when they know they're going to die. Then, a few days ago, I realized she hadn't said, 'It was the drain.' I should have known it the minute you came out that front door with that look on your face. The problem is, most people don't want to think of their friends as murderers, me included. She said, 'It was Crane.'"

"I thought I was a dead man when I stepped into the street. I thought you were going to hand me over to the cops right there."

"What I can't figure out is why you would do it. Lover's spat? What?"

"I'm not going to admit anything."

"The cat's out of the bag here. You don't gain anything by stonewalling now."

"Jesus, Thomas. I can't tell you how sorry I am."

"We're all sorry."

"I've killed before, Thomas. In the war. Lots of people. But never like that day. I dream about it. It's with me every minute. I'm so ashamed of myself some days I can't even look in the mirror. Have you ever been to that point? Where you can't look at your face in the mirror?"

"Tell me about it. Maybe I won't hate you if I can understand."

"Hate? Jesus. You and I are friends. Don't hate me. That day I got a call from her, same as you. I got there and she said she was going to take a shower and change clothes. While I was waiting, I snooped on her computer. I thought maybe I would find something I could hand over to Self to get some brownie points. I was trying to get a job with him. What I found instead were the videos and the suicide note. I had already talked to Self about a job. He said he didn't have a spot just then. He said she was causing him a lot of unnecessary grief. He also said whoever could solve that problem would have a cushy job for life. When I spotted the suicide note, everything began to fit together. I hadn't thought about it before. But what if she committed suicide?"

"So killing her was the seal on your job application?"

"Please don't put it like that."

"How do you want me to put it?"

"It wasn't like that. She was out of control. I tried to talk to her about those men she was screwing, but she got all agitated and started screaming at me. Then she went in to take a shower. I think she wanted to be fresh and sparkly when you got there. She was in love with you, you know."

"Then you e-mailed the already-written suicide note to her sister."

"Once I did that, I was locked in. I knew about the roof access. I'd been to her apartment before. I knew she liked to horse around on roofs. I was pretty sure I could make it look like an accident. Hell, who's to say it *wasn't* an accident? Even now." His last statement was a trial balloon. He was trying to work me to his side.

"How did you get her to the roof?"

"When she came out of the shower and was dressed, I got behind her and knocked her out with a choke hold. It took all of ten seconds. The Mandarin Duck Palm didn't help her a bit."

"Then you carried her to the roof?"

"She was heavier than she looked."

"Jesus, Crane. This is about the most cold-blooded thing I've ever heard."

"I know it must sound bad."

"It sounds *real* bad."

"The worst part was she woke up while I was trying to decide whether to actually go through with it. We were both on the roof, near the edge. You know I don't like heights. Just thinking about pushing her off was giving me the willies. At first she didn't realize where she was or what happened to her. I'd already seen you down in the street and knew it was now or never. She was never going to let me get that close again. The saddest part of the whole thing was how convinced she was you would get up there in time to save her. She told me you were going to be there any second. That you were going to rescue her. She was so positive I almost believed it myself, even though I knew you were still on the sidewalk. She really thought you were going to rescue her. And then she made a move as if she was going to scream. I covered her mouth and threw her off. She made me. I thought she was going to scream. I had to. And then she went and called out my name. Jesus, I was scared."

"You threw her off the roof, but you claim it was *her* fault?"

"She forced it."

"Self knows, doesn't he?"

"I wouldn't have done it if I'd known how it was going to be afterwards. I can't sleep. I lost ten pounds. I killed people in Afghanistan, but only men who were trying to kill me. I thought it would be as easy to kill Angela, but it turned into a mess. And now I can't sleep."

"You're not the first person who killed somebody and couldn't live with it afterwards."

"What can I do about this?"

"You're kidding, right? How about turning yourself over to the police?"

"Turning myself in isn't going to change a thing. She'll still be dead. Society doesn't have to be protected from me. I'm not going to do it again. I've learned my lesson."

"Did Self actually ask you to kill her?"

"Self explained how much trouble Angela was causing, both in his marriage and his business. No, he never actually told me to kill her. But we both knew that was what he wanted."

"And afterwards you told him what you did?"

"I told him I got rid of his problem. That was when he gave me the job. God, how I wish I could bring her back."

"Do you know why Angela was making those videos and saving them?"

"She told me they were leverage. She wanted an appointment with the President. She had a plan for saving him from something, but she wouldn't tell me what. She thought those men were Secret Service and would get her a meeting with the President if she threatened to send the videos to the head of the Secret Service. When it didn't pan out, she actually sent them. That might be part of why they were investigating her. The note she sent the Feds must have made her sound like a lunatic. Self's people found all this out later. The head of the Secret Service invests with him."

* * *

After a while the mountain would turn to meadows with low-lying heather and small huckleberry bushes. The top third of the mountain had vast open spots where a man up in the rocks with a rifle could pick off anybody he wanted. With a suppressor it would be silent, and if he wasn't spotted it would most likely go down as another accidental shooting, same as the near miss up here last weekend.

Even though I'd sensed how profoundly depressed he was, I hadn't expected Crane to blurt out the details of his crime. It clearly had been weighing on him, and like a lot of murderers, he needed someone to confide in. We'd been friends once.

After the police got hold of him he would likely recant his confession. For the time being he was contrite, loquacious, repentant, but that wasn't necessarily going to last. I'd heard confessions before, and a confessing murderer's mood changed like the weather. Whatever chemical in his brain had spurred him to confess might well be absent by the time the police saw him.

37

THE trail took us east and began to open up, offering a ribbon of I-90 as it ran through Snoqualmie Pass far below us. It was hard to believe how high we'd climbed. We were moving into the rockier sections of the trail, where some of the step-ups measured two feet or more, areas where the trail passed through knee-high and sometimes shoulder-high boulders. Angela's contrite killer huffing and puffing behind me, I went periods of five and ten minutes without seeing another hiker traveling in either direction. I wondered what was going through Crane's mind now.

Crane Manning had served eight years in the Army, but once he left he found the job market a quagmire. For a variety of reasons, he'd floundered as a skip tracer. His social skills were not exceptional and he wasn't the sharpest pencil in the box. In times past, a man like him might find a factory job and make an honest living for himself and his family, pay for a house, educate his children; but not in our world. Except for Boeing, which wasn't hiring, the majority of factory jobs in Washington State had long ago been transferred to Asia.

The Army had taught him to kill; they'd also, regrettably, given him plenty of practice. Because he'd killed before, he thought it would be easy again. What he didn't realize was that throwing a woman he knew off a roof wasn't the same as squeezing off a four-hundred-yard rifle shot at the Taliban. He hadn't bargained on the sleepless nights, the Sargasso Sea of bad dreams, and the endless feelings of remorse. Or the ghost running around inside his brain. I had left the police department behind a fatal shooting, had been involved in other deaths. My experience was enough to inform me even if you were legal and in the right, guilt could stick to you like an unshakeable winter virus. I thought often about the people who were dead because of me. It wasn't a long list, but it was a *list*. They had all deserved it in one way or another, but that didn't change the fact that they were dead and I was the one who made them that way.

We found Henrik Federer sitting on a rock in a puddle of sweat. Bonds and Gunderson had passed him not long before. "Go back," I said. "There's going to be gun play."

"What?"

"They have guns up there."

Federer didn't need to be told twice. He scurried down the mountain with a vigor he hadn't shown until that moment.

We spotted Marvin Gunderson some minutes beyond where we'd seen Federer. Bonds wasn't with him. Gunderson had rolled up his trousers past his massive calves and was carrying his jacket, the back of his shirt doused in sweat. I wanted to circumvent a meeting by cutting the trail, but we were on a single, narrow, rocky track with a steep uphill scree to the left and treacherous downhill spilling off to the right. In order to pass somebody, you had to do it on the trail and you pretty much needed their cooperation. I had a feeling calling out the standard trail protocol, "On your left," wasn't going to work. In our past meetings, Bonds and Gunderson had made the mistakes. Today, without any weapons at hand, I was going to pass a man who was close to twice my size, wanted revenge, and who looked like he'd grown up eating Tyrannosaurus steaks.

When he sensed us behind him, Gunderson swiveled his entire upper torso around, probably because his neck didn't function normally. "Hey," he said, as if we were best friends. "Long time no see."

"Yeah."

"I guess today is my lucky day."

"It could be."

As I drew close, the first thing I did was assess Gunderson's breathing. I knew he would be breathing harder than me, but I wasn't prepared for the rasping noise of it. Ever the foolhardy optimist, I figured if I could keep his breathing ragged, I might stand a chance of getting past him without incident.

"I guess you want by," he gasped, as I charged up to him.

"That would be nice."

He stepped slightly to one side. Even so, he was so wide I would have to brush his shoulder to get in front of him. For a moment we would be sharing a tiny portion of the dance floor.

"I'm just here to pay my respects," I said, as a way of peace offering.

He grinned. He had beautiful, even teeth. Just as everything else about him was larger, his teeth seemed twice as large as my own. "You sound like a man begging for his life," he said.

"Like I said, I'm here to pay my respects to Angela."

"You're going to have to get past me first," he said, reaching out with his beefy arm and slamming it into my head. The blow knocked me into the rocks. I rolled off the rocks and groaned, the wind knocked out of me. I knew I had a concussion, too.

Gunderson was ten feet away. As I watched, he carefully took off and folded his jacket and spread it gently on a nearby boulder, then, still breathing hard from the altitude and the hike and maybe the queasy anticipation of vengeance, he ambled toward me. He'd only swatted me once, but it felt like I'd been slapped by the fluke of a blue whale.

"I guess you thought I forgot about you, huh, Buford?"

"The name is Black."

"Right now your name is mud."

"The family's coming behind me. You want them to see this?"

"Don't worry yourself about the family. By the time they get here you're going to be a pile of rags at the bottom of this rock slide."

His words panicked me. I got to my feet as quickly as I could. My nose was bleeding, the front of my mouth numb, and I had a feeling I'd broken at least one rib. Gunderson had the high ground. I backed up as he advanced, kept backing up on the rocky trail until I reached a spot where I could scramble off trail up the slope. It was a steep scree with loose rock and only a few small bushes for handholds, but I moved quickly so he wouldn't be able to grab my feet. I was still woozy from the blow and felt as if I were about to lose consciousness.

Scrambling up and around, I managed to get up trail from Gunderson, who followed me from below like a cat stalking a bird in the living room. He was almost on me when I circled back down to the trail. I didn't have much choice. I would have had to be an accomplished rock climber to get any further away from him, and if I stayed where I was we would end up fighting on the slope. I needed my feet under me. When I reached the trail and tried to run, I could feel his grip on the back of my shirt, could feel the stitching as it ripped.

I broke free, took a few more steps and was clear, no heavy breathing behind me. When I glanced around, Gunderson had his back to me. He was wrestling with Crane. Or strangling him. I couldn't tell from this angle. Crane was larger than me, but not anywhere close to Gunderson's size. He had stepped up to the plate and in doing so had probably saved my life. As much as I wanted to flee, I turned back to help Crane. Neither of us had a chance against Gunderson alone, not that we had much of a chance in tandem.

I stepped close and began rabbit punching Gunderson in the back as hard as I could, aiming for his kidneys, left, right, left, right. I worked a heavy bag during the rainy Northwest winters and knew how to throw a punch, but this was like striking an oak barrel. The blows jolted me through to my shoulders. It was hard to know if he even felt them. Meanwhile, Crane tumbled backwards and rolled off the trail into some brush. Gunderson turned around.

Before he could hit me, I started running up the trail again. He wasn't ready for me to turn chicken a second time, although I don't know why not. Any fool could see I was scared out of my wits.

Gunderson gave chase, his footfalls heavy on the trail. If I could weaken him with an uphill footrace, maybe I would have a chance in the same way a matador had a chance after the picadors bled the bull. I ran just slowly enough so he fancied he had a chance of catching me. We hadn't run an eighth of a mile before we came upon a group of women clogging the trail, chatting and laughing, a picnic spread out around them. There were six of them and they blocked the narrow trail in a manner that forced me to a complete stop.

Gunderson was coming on fast, not nearly as exhausted as I wanted him to be, while I searched frantically for an avenue of escape.

Realizing he had me in a box, he slowed, laboring to catch his breath. He took almost thirty seconds to reach me. I danced backwards, but not quickly enough to keep him from clubbing me with a fist the size of a melon. As tired as he was, he was still quicker than me. I half blocked the blow to the side of my head and was quickly made aware by the ringing in my ears that I was not really there anymore. I was on my feet but that was all. I sort of knew it and sort of didn't. I was dreaming. I was out. One blow that I had mostly blocked, and I was semi-conscious. I remained standing, but in the boxing ring they would have called it a technical knockout.

I felt myself being hoisted into the air like the designated loser in a rigged wrestling match. Except this wasn't choreographed and I wasn't going to land on rubber chairs. Gunderson was holding me over his head and was about to toss me down the mountainside onto a pile of broken granite. Two of the women on the trail screeched as they huddled together, terrified.

In dumbfounded awe I gazed at a twirling sky.

Long afterwards I reconstructed the fight and thought it must have been a massive toss reminiscent of a Scotsman throwing a log. I vaguely remembered cartwheeling through the air, my body twisting and turning and flipping and, miraculously, landing in a posture that was almost upright. I didn't stay upright for long. My forward motion threw me against the side of the mountain. My body slid back down like a rag doll toward a pile of dirt and loose rock. And then I was dreaming. I fought against sleep because I knew Gunderson was going to make sure I never woke up.

* * *

As I came out of a dream, I heard two men grunting.

And then I was wide awake. I slowly became aware that I was without any sensation in my lower limbs. My first thought was that for the rest of my life I was going to be steering a motorized wheelchair with a straw in my teeth. I couldn't feel anything below my chest. I had woken up paralyzed. When I looked up, I could see the women who'd been blocking the trail. They had turned around and were herding themselves back up the trail in a blind panic. Or were they headed down the trail? I was completely turned around. Even though it felt like hours had passed, I couldn't have been unconscious for more than a few seconds.

Then somebody stepped on me. It hurt. I yelped like a dog under a rocking chair, but he didn't get off. It was Crane. He'd stepped over me and then *on* me as he boxed Gunderson. Crane had a rock in each fist. I could hear rocks striking flesh. They were duking it out like that,

Crane using rocks, Gunderson fists. I wondered how long that could continue. Before I could finish the thought they moved away, and then Crane came sailing toward me like a sack of laundry.

I was just climbing to my feet when his falling body thumped against me and the two of us crashed into the rocks together. I had some feeling back in my lower extremities now; not much, but enough to try to untangle myself from Crane and then to stand and teeter on unsteady legs like a newborn colt. My knees hurt like hell. My skull ached. I could feel broken ribs grating in my chest.

Hoping to take him by surprise, I raced at Gunderson. Fat chance. I was probably moving in slow motion.

Oddly, my charge was the last thing he expected.

I don't even know why I did it. Maybe Crane's absurd heroism was contagious. I got in a karate chop to Gunderson's neck, but his neck was like a tree trunk. Then, to my amazement, we stood toe to toe and exchanged blows, his significantly dampened, no doubt from climbing the trail and from whatever damage Crane had done with the rocks. He still hadn't caught his breath. His mouth was bleeding. I could hear him wheezing. He kept trying to hunch over with his mitts on his knees so he could get more air. Each time he tried to catch his breath, I threw an uppercut at his chin. I hit him three times. Hard. Hard enough I found out later I broke a bone in one of my hands.

He clobbered me across the side of the head with an open palm, deafening that ear. Astonishingly, it didn't knock me off my feet.

As he hunkered over to breathe again, I took the opportunity to slip past him and get on the upside of the trail, staking out the higher ground. In her panic one of the women hikers had left a boot and a sock. I grabbed the long wool sock and scraped up a handful of stones, filling the toe with them. I wrapped the top part of the sock around my wrist. Gunderson had once again turned to face Crane, who was again on his feet. Crane didn't look so good, but he was moving toward Gunderson, whose back was now to me.

Swinging the sock, I hit Gunderson from behind on the top of the shoulder, then in the side of the ribs, then in the knee. I did it so quickly he didn't have time to turn. He flicked at my blows as if I were a horsefly. Then Crane hit him a solid right cross to the face, and he gave all his attention to Crane, stepped forward and grabbed Crane in a bear hug. I slammed Gunderson in the back of the skull with the rock-filled sock, again and again. He howled, threw Crane bodily off the trail and into a small tree, then turned on me.

Swinging as wildly as I could, I clubbed him six or eight times, got his skull and face bleeding, but then he reached out and grabbed the loose part of the sock, so we now both had an end. He took it from me. I stepped forward and punched him in the solar plexus, but it was like punching frozen beef.

And then Kathy appeared, her face pink from exertion.

By that point, I must have looked pretty bad. I could see blood splatters on my shirt with my peripheral vision. One eye was swelling shut.

"Hey, big boy," Kathy said. "Turn around and see how you like this."

Gunderson couldn't turn his head without swiveling his whole body, and when he did I ducked out of the way. He roared when the bear spray hit him in the eyes. Just for good measure, she sprayed him with a second shot. He continued to roar, called her every name in the book, then collapsed onto the nearest rock, rubbing at his face, weeping, torrents of snot dripping from his nose, drool dribbling out his mouth and down his chin and chest. He roared again, incapacitated.

Kathy stood back, pointing the canister at Gunderson while I frisked him for weapons. I found a nail clipper. Keys. His wallet. A bottle of water in his pants pocket. I handed him the bottle so he could wash out his eyes, but even so, he would be ailing for the better part of an hour. Down the hill on the rocks where he left his jacket, I found a Glock pistol with an extra magazine. Fifteen rounds in the pistol; another fifteen in the spare magazine. I dropped them into my hip pack.

38

As we limped our way up the top of the mountain, Crane and I remained silent. Had he not attacked Gunderson when he did I would probably be dead. As it was, I felt lucky not to have come out of it as a quadriplegic. It had taken enormous courage for Crane to attack Gunderson, on a par with a dog attacking a tractor. He'd rescued me, the man who was about to send him to prison. My back was contused and aching, and I knew I had at least two broken ribs, could feel the bones grating in excruciating agony as I breathed.

Then Kathy arrived, and her pluck and lifelong paranoia about grizzlies in the Cascades saved us all.

Our luck turned again when the six women hikers returned with a hiking party they ran into while fleeing up the mountain. Among them happened to be an off-duty Pierce County Sheriff's deputy and his brother. The men had handcuffs and weapons in their packs and, after hearing our story, took Gunderson into custody with the intention of escorting him down the mountain to the parking lot, where they would hand him over to the King County Sheriff, whom we'd already phoned. The women hikers confirmed Gunderson had been the aggressor in our contretemps.

Kathy agreed to retreat back down the mountain with the sheriff's deputy, hoping the sight of Marvin Gunderson in handcuffs would help her talk Monica Pennington into turning around.

As we continued the ascent, a dense fog blew in, only to evaporate a few minutes later in a nimbus of sunshine, then return, repeating the cycle. The higher we climbed the denser the fog and warmer the sunshine.

I knew the constantly ascending path led east along the side of the knoll at the top of the mountain, then turned due north, passing just under the old fire lookout cabin which sat on top of a huge pile of slab granite. From the lookout one could see Mount Rainier fifty miles to the south, Silver Peak, and a hundred other jagged notches, peaks, and crags I couldn't name, all part of the Cascade Range extending from Canada to northern California. Anyone perched on the rocks next to the lookout could watch a long string of hikers straggling up the mountainside far below them. Just prior to the final leg of the trail one passed through a large meadow with wild flowers, low-lying huckleberry bushes and plant life I didn't know, some of it in a swampy area where last winter's melted snow had left a bog.

The meadows worried me. A man with a rifle sitting near the lookout would have an unobstructed view, and even though the distances were daunting, if he was a fair shot he could put a bullet through just about anybody he chose. Once he found a target, Bonds would take his shot without hesitation. After what I'd done to him in the Columbia Tower, he had every reason to loathe me as much as I did him. On the other hand, if Monica was his target, we just might reach him before he spotted her, for she lagged far behind with her boys.

When my cell rang we were in a cloud, tiny droplets of moisture beading our eyebrows and hair. "We just ran into Pennington with her kids," Kathy said. "I tried to talk her into calling it off, but she wasn't having any of it."

"Where's Self?"

"He's way behind. How are you doing? I saw part of the fight when I was coming up. I don't know how you two lasted as long as you did."

"Did you see the part where he played helicopter with me?"

"I guess not."

"I'll be dreaming about that for a while."

"I love you."

The sun came out as we got to the high meadows and traversed them, reaching the base of the final zigzagging trail that worked its way toward the top of the mountain. This last part would wind to the right and around the tall, rocky escarpment until it eventually approached the lookout from behind. From the next section of the trail we would not be visible from the cabin. Since the fight, Crane was lagging behind, unable to keep pace. The match with Marvin Gunderson had taken the starch out of both of us, but it had taken more out of him. Every breath I took was painful. One of Crane's eyes was swollen almost shut, and we were both limping. "What are you going to do with me?" he yelled from about twenty yards back.

"What do you mean?"

"You could have handed me over to that deputy sheriff back there. Why didn't you?"

"Maybe because you saved my life."

"So we're even?"

"This isn't about you and me being even. I'm not the one you have to square things with. I'm grateful to you and I need your help here, but I still have to tell the authorities what I know."

He was quiet for a while, mulling it over. "You shouldn't go up there. I've seen him shoot. And that pistol you took off Gunderson isn't going to hit anything past fifty yards."

Before he could say anything else, Crane plopped onto his face on the trail. I thought for a moment he had been struck by a bullet. We were in an open area, not yet at the section of the trail where we would be hidden from a shooter on the peak.

"Incoming," Crane yelled, pushing his face into the dirt. "Incoming!"

I dropped to the ground in front of him and as I dropped I heard a loud cracking sound next to my head. "What was that?" I asked.

"A bullet breaking the sound barrier. You all right?"

As far as I could tell, the bullet had been an inch or two away from my skull. "Yeah. You?"

"I don't know why he didn't hit one of us."

"Too far. I bet it's a thousand yards."

"He probably thinks he got at least one of us. Maybe both. If we don't get up, how's he going to know different?" Though small, .223 slugs traveled at over three-thousand feet per second and were designed to tumble and do massive damage once inside a body.

The cool dirt against my cheek contrasted starkly with the warmth of the sunshine on my back. Since there hadn't been any more shots fired, I guessed he couldn't see us in the hollowed-out trail. Thousands of pairs of tromping feet had carved the trail deep into the low scrub and heather, so it was as if we were lying in the bottom of a shallow canoe. "You have any idea where that shot came from?" I asked.

"No idea."

"He must be near the summit though."

"If he's on the top, that was an awfully long shot."

"Maybe that's why he missed. So what's the plan, Crane?"

"I thought *you* had a plan."

"My plan is to not get dead."

"A lot of people had that plan in the war. It didn't always pan out."

"If you were back in the war, what would you do?"

"I'd hang tight and call in an air strike."

"I don't think that's an option here."

When the fog rolled in, we began running up the trail. I knew the trail would soon wind through a meadow and curl behind a gigantic rock outcropping which would put us out of sight of the ranger cabin and presumably free from sniper fire. If our luck held, we would come up behind him at the summit. The last part of the trail, the highest part, was comprised of a series of short, steep switchbacks high in the granite. If we could make it through the meadows, into the ravine, and up through the large slabs of rock into those steep switchbacks, we could take the fight to him.

When the sun peeked out, we dove behind boulders and waited.

"Is this how it was in the war?" I asked.

"In the war I had a gun."

"I've got this pistol."

"The only thing a pistol's good for is fighting your way to your rifle."

The mist was beginning to roll in again. When we felt the full chill of it and the light grew dim, we started moving again.

Five minutes later we were temporarily safe from Bonds in another enormous boulder field, where some of the granite faces looked as tall as skyscrapers. We climbed the switchbacks among the boulders, scaling trails rockier than any we'd seen before. The leg of each switchback was short, the trail ascending like a stairway. We scoured the rocks ahead of us looking for Bonds. After we'd been climbing five minutes, two heavyset men came tripping down the rocks toward us, moving fast. One said, "There's some maniac up there with a rifle."

"How far up?" I asked.

"We saw him at the top. I think he's crazy, man."

"Any other hikers above us?"

"Just the maniac."

It turned out Bonds had been following them down, because as soon as they passed us, I caught a glimpse of his head bobbing along the trail, a rifle slung over his shoulder. I signaled to Crane and we scrunched down behind some large granite slabs at one end of the switchback we'd been negotiating. We didn't have time to do anything more. We weren't in the best defensive position, but we didn't have a choice. Bonds had the high ground here. What we had—maybe—was surprise.

We waited a few seconds and then a bullet bounced off one of the rocks next to my head, whirring off into the afternoon like an angry bug. So much for surprise. "I think he spotted us," said Crane.

"I think you might be right."

"What do you want to do?"

"We could ask him to surrender."

"No, really. We need a plan."

"You scoot off down the trail while I hold him here. The way the rocks are set up, I don't think he'll have a shot at you."

"I'm not leaving you alone, Thomas."

"You're not doing any good here."

"Tell you what. I'll go down the trail and circle up and behind him while you keep him busy."

"Isn't that what I just said?" Another bullet ricocheted off the rocks next to my head. "He thinks I'm afraid of guns. He's not going to be expecting what I'm going to give him."

"Don't get your hopes up."

"Go."

39

RAISING the Glock up over the rock I was hiding behind, I sent three rounds up the trail in a steady, measured succession. When I heard the last of my bullets ricochet off the distant granite, I stood up. Had Bonds remained in position he could have killed me as I popped into view, but just as I hoped it would, my barrage forced him to ground. I caught a quick glimpse of his shirt as he scrabbled to get under cover. Now he was hiding behind a boulder approximately fifty feet away. Hidden from the chest down, I was standing behind my own boulder.

When I saw a glimmer of movement behind the rock, I fired into the rocks behind him, hoping the ricochet would wing him. We maintained our positions for a minute. The foggy mountaintop seemed especially quiet now.

"Buford," Bonds shouted. "I'm going to take you down. It's going to look like an accident, but I'm going to take you down."

"You're the one hiding behind the rock."

"You caught me by surprise that night at the Columbia Tower Club."

"Seems like I caught you by surprise just a minute ago."

"Not for long. I'm going to get away with this."

"You killed Rafael Gutierrez. You ran over Ron Prisham. You're not going anywhere but to the scaffold where they're going to hang you."

He reached around with the rifle and tried to take a shot without showing himself, but before he could complete the move, I bounced two rounds off the rock and he went back to cover. I may have nicked his arm. I couldn't be sure.

"You're going to run out of ammo," said Bonds.

"Maybe you're right. Come on down here and let's count how many bullets I have left."

I wanted to walk closer while I still had his head down, but the trail was tricky to negotiate. I wouldn't be able to proceed without taking my eyes off the target, and the moment he sensed I was off guard, he could reach around and send a fusillade down the hill. At fifty feet, an AR-15 could take out a platoon. We stayed behind our respective rocks, he crouching, me standing. Enough time passed, I began to doubt if Crane was circling around as agreed. If Bonds killed me, nobody was going to hear about Crane's confession. Surely that thought had occurred to Crane by now.

The fog moved in again, heavier and wetter, though I could still see well enough to keep an eye on Bonds. The air felt cool and misty, and my breath became visible. I saw movement in the rocks above the point where Bonds was concealed. It had to be Crane.

In order to distract Bonds, I fired into the rocks at the far side of the boulder where he crouched. The bullet threw chips of granite dust into the air. Then Crane jumped and I saw a brief struggle. I started running.

By the time I reached them, Crane was standing over an unconscious Goodnight Bonds. Crane had the rifle in his hands, handling it casually. Bonds was bleeding from a wound on one arm, where one of my bullets had grazed him.

When I moved toward Crane, he stepped back warily. "Good work," I said, taking another step forward and reaching for the rifle. He took a step backward and held the gun away.

"Is this going to help me with the cops?" he asked.

"Twice you risked your life for me. Of course I'm going to tell them what you did here."

I stepped forward again. Without looking, Crane took another step back. Somewhere directly behind him was a drop off, though I couldn't see it. "Watch out behind you," I said.

"That's an old trick."

"I can't let you keep the rifle."

"It's not fair that I have to go to jail."

"You murder somebody, you go to the penitentiary. It's been that way for a while."

"None of this is fair. It seems like just feeling the way I do should be punishment enough. Do you know what it's like to not sleep for weeks on end?"

"It's funny how this got turned around so it's about you. It's really pretty simple. Angela's dead. You killed her. It's about Angela. It's not about you."

He had the weapon in both hands now. I had to assume the safety was still off. All he had to do was point it at my chest and pull the trigger, tell everyone Bonds did it. The rifle would airmail a sixty-four-grain bullet through my ribs at three thousand feet per second. We were close enough the muzzle blast might even set my shirt on fire. Looking at his face, I couldn't tell what he was going to do.

I edged closer. "There's a cliff behind you."

"I don't want to go to prison."

"Plenty of people have gone to prison and come out to live successful lives. Think hard. It beats the alternative."

"What's the alternative?"

"One alternative would be getting thrown off a roof and landing on a car."

"Jesus." His voice broke like a schoolboy's. "Why did you have to say that?"

"Sorry if I was insensitive. I tend to get that way when somebody murders one of my friends."

"I helped you out here."

"Duly noted. It doesn't bring her back, though, does it?"

I pushed Gunderson's pistol into my waistband so I would have both hands free and took another step forward, grasping the AR-15. We began a slow struggle, each of us pretending we weren't really fighting for the gun. The barrel was still warm.

As we struggled, Crane kept moving back, pulling me along with him.

"I don't want to go to prison."

"You never know what will happen. Hell, you might even get off."

Actually, aside from my testimony about what Angela had said in the split second as she was launched off her roof, and apart from my testimony about his recent confession, his defense attorney would have a pretty good case. The cops didn't have any physical evidence connecting him or anybody else to Angela's death. I still had her clothing and they could examine that again to see where he'd grabbed it while throwing her off, but that wouldn't prove much. Crane would deny today's conversation, and ultimately it would be my word against his. He could claim he'd been pulling my leg. The jury would wonder, if Angela had called out the name of her killer as she was falling, why I hadn't stepped forward with the information sooner. A good attorney could make the case against him look weaker than one of my jokes. I didn't tell him that, though. It wasn't my job to keep him out of prison.

He was strong but so was I, and I wasn't going to let him have the rifle. We were each looking into the other's face as we wrestled with the weapon. And then, still backing up, he started to stumble, realized he was on the edge of the precipice, and took one of his hands off the rifle in order to grasp the rocks to his right. For a moment I feared we were both going over.

I couldn't tell how far down it was. The few glimpses I got showed a landfall far below us.

The rest of it took just seconds to play out. He lost his balance again and stumbled. His right hand slapped at the rocks, found a purchase, and held. But he was already off balance and started to teeter even farther backwards, eyes bulging. His worst nightmare was coming true. I remembered how much he feared heights. He'd been green around the gills the day Angela walked along the edge of the roof of our building. Because he'd reached out for the rocks, he now had only one hand on the rifle. I had two. I fed him the gun, using it like a safety line. He grasped it with both hands and in so doing, gave up the last of his overall stability to me. He was off balance; I was not.

Bracing my foot against a large slab of granite, I gave him the stock of the rifle, having had no time to turn the gun around. He gripped it with both hands, leaning back, trying desperately to regain his equilibrium. If we didn't cooperate perfectly now, he would be dead. He'd saved my life twice. It was my turn to return the favor. The rifle and our hold on it was the sole mechanism preventing a nasty tumble.

I watched as he readjusted his grip on the AR-15, moving his hand toward the trigger. There was no telling if he was moving instinctively to achieve the best hold or if he had a more sinister motive.

We were looking into each other's eyes when the rifle went off.

I felt the blowback on my face as the muzzle blast roared past my cheek, the flame burning me, the bullet barely missing my head. Because of the suppressor screwed into the end of the barrel, it wasn't nearly as loud as it might have been, yet both my ears went deaf. I could hear nothing but a high-pitched whine.

I reflexively let go of the rifle. He plummeted, seemingly as relaxed as a man falling backwards into a swimming pool. He didn't say a word, just fell, still staring into my eyes as he grew smaller and smaller like something out of a Hitchcock film.

I didn't see or hear him land more than a hundred feet below. I didn't hear a scream. All I heard was the ringing in my ears. I would come to believe the look Crane gave me at the last was almost peaceful, a form of contentment amidst terror, as if everything that *could* be resolved *had* been resolved. I came to believe he knew exactly what he was doing when he pulled the trigger. He was forcing me to let go.

Before Bonds could fully regain consciousness, I removed one of his shoelaces and used it to bind his hands behind his back. Bonds had escaped with a flesh wound.

I was sitting on the rocks trying to sort through my feelings when Kathy came around the switchback below us. "Thomas."

"I thought you were going back down."

"They didn't need me any longer so I came up. I heard shots. Is everything under control?"

"It is now."

"They're still coming. I couldn't convince the others to turn around. Monica is the most bullheaded woman I've ever known. Hey. Where's Crane?"

His body was face up on a large rock about a hundred feet down, a squiggle of dark blood flowering from his skull. Death had to have been instantaneous. I felt sick about it, but I knew there was a certain poetic justice playing out here.

Whether the last rifle shot was accidental, I could not say. I would ponder it in weeks to come, if not years. Perhaps I had saved my life by letting him fall, and perhaps I had only been accommodating a man who no longer wanted any part of this world. Or maybe the whole thing was a stupid accident. I wondered then and would wonder in the future whether he ever would have had the brass to use the rifle on me. If not, why had he wanted so desperately to keep it?

Kathy stepped alongside me and gazed down the mountainside. "Oh, God," she said when she saw him. "How did that happen?"

"It's a long story. You're looking at the ending. The beginning started when he killed Angela."

Kathy gave me a questioning look.

"He admitted it on the way up."

"You've had a bad day," Kathy said, touching my arm.

"Not as bad as some."

Gunderson had come close to snapping my neck. Bonds had air-parceled a bullet down the mountain and missed me by millimeters. I'd lost a friend, and I didn't have nearly enough of those, a friend who had come close to putting a bullet through my face.

I thought about Angela and her dogged persistence in attempting to stop Clark Lloyd Self. I thought about Crane's motivation for killing her. Her motives had been so noble; his utterly puerile. So many of the murders I'd brushed up against over the years had been egged on by thinking that was callow or just plain nutty. This was no exception.

Four hours later we sent Bonds down the mountain on a chopper accompanied by a King County Deputy Sheriff, this one in full uniform. Crane's body was bundled in a tarp on a sled outside the chopper. A team was still processing the death site. Ironically, Crane would have been terrified at the idea of getting strapped to the outside of a helicopter.

40

GOODNIGHT Bonds and Marvin Gunderson were still in the King County lockup a week later when Susan Djokovic put on the second ashes-scattering party. Monica Pennington had once again filed for divorce. Not surprisingly, Clark Lloyd Self did not show up for the second hike. Most of the ass-kissing sycophants who'd followed him the week before didn't bother to show up either. The second group was closer to the small assembly Angela no doubt had envisioned when she hatched the idea.

Mine was the only statement the King County Sheriff's office had concerning Crane Manning's death, and they were still trying to ascertain whether my story fit the evidence. Having suffered a concussion when Crane jumped him, the last thing Bonds remembered was brushing his teeth after breakfast the morning of the hike. At least that's what he claimed. Carol Cooper came and took my statement concerning Crane's confession. It was hard to tell what she thought about it.

When I watched the faces of the people in the Sheriff's office as I told them that I had, in effect, let Crane fall a measured ninety-six feet onto a granite ledge in the meadow below, I knew there was going to be trouble. It didn't matter that I had powder burns on my cheek and spotting on one arm. I'd admitted letting Crane fall to his death, and they weren't going to leave me alone until they were good with it. Finally, after quite a few hours of questioning, they were.

Two weeks after Crane fell, Clark Lloyd Self was arrested for fraud and spent a night in jail waiting for his attorneys to come up with a million-dollar bond, undoubtedly paying it with money he'd stolen. The U.S. Attorney's office had taken our package and begun an investigation, had quickly found evidence of fraud. That Self was a crook was a concept some people couldn't quite wrap their brains around. People who'd known him were being interviewed nightly on television, and one and all testified about how generous and kindhearted and just generally thoughtful he was.

When the news hit that CLS was a Ponzi scheme, hundreds of angry clients, many of them movie stars and politicians, began pouring out of the woodwork to make claims against CLS Enterprises. Of course by now it was too late for investors to get any of their money back. The government froze CLS Enterprise assets, Self's assets, his wife's assets, and anything else they could think of while a team of federal accountants pored through the books. To date, nobody except Clark Lloyd Self had been arrested, but there were rumors others would be named. It turned out the much-vaunted investment arm of the company in New York City did not exist. Except for some exceptionally lucky plays early in the scheme, Self had never invested any of the money. He'd paid early investors with money from later investors. His trips to New York had been a ruse to visit a second mistress, a former reporter who'd met him writing an article about CLS and whose sizeable cocaine habit he'd been paying for.

The Seattle Times filled an entire section in their Sunday paper with the devastation Self had wreaked, not only in the Northwest, but all across the country. One elderly local couple who'd lost every penny they had, climbed into their car in their son-in-law's garage and left the motor running. Their bodies were found hours later by their six-year-old granddaughter, who sought them out to show them her new shoes. Clark had encouraged them to sell their home so they could invest even more of their savings with him, had personally given his assurances they were set for life. Amidst all the rest of the brouhaha surrounding the collapse of the CLS Ponzi scheme, the double suicide was barely noticed.

A major turning point came when somebody in the King Country Prosecutor's office talked Goodnight Bonds into testifying against Marvin Gunderson in the Ron Prisham hit-and-run. While Bonds readily admitted he had been the driver, he claimed Gunderson planned the crime, helped him steal the car, and forced him to do it. In addition to the assault and attempted murder charges from Granite Mountain, Gunderson was charged with conspiracy to murder, attempted murder, auto theft, and more. Bonds, who made a plea deal for a lesser charge in the Prisham case, was slapped with two counts of attempted murder against Crane Manning and me at Granite Mountain. The prosecutors were aware the two men were probably good for killing Rafael Gutierrez months earlier, but lacking proof or a confession, left that one on the back burner.

The sheriff's deputies retrieved expended .223 casings near the fire lookout cabin and matched them to the rifle they found alongside Crane's body. Bonds' prints were all over the rifle, and his partials were on some of the shell casings. I shuddered to think how close I'd come to dying up there in the fog and sun and huckleberries. It was not clear how much knowledge Self had about the crimes his employees had perpetrated in his name, though we all had our suspicions. Neither Bonds nor Gunderson had implicated him yet, and Crane wasn't around to do so. Still, there were enough fraud accusations floating in the ether to punch his ticket for the next forty or fifty years.

The most curious aspect to the whole thing was the way in which Clark Lloyd Self decided to address his situation. He was out on bond less than a week when he scheduled a jump from a skydiving center in the Snohomish Valley. He'd been skydiving many times before and often soloed, so the instructors were used to seeing him. At 10,000 feet Self unhooked his pack and leaped out of the plane in nothing but his coveralls. It took almost two minutes to consummate his final farewell. Later, the autopsy showed a fair amount of prescription drugs and white wine in his system. He left no note, no goodbye video, and no last-minute phone calls. His whole life he'd played the big shot in public, while behind closed doors he'd been screwing over virtually everyone he knew and thousands he didn't.

Several amateur photographers happened to be in the right place at the right time, so there were multiple video renderings of his spiraling descent from plane to ground. Within hours the videos went viral on the Internet.

Angry investors deprived of justice and fleeced of their savings called him a coward for refusing to face the music. The financial papers on both sides of the Atlantic wrote op-eds about it.

It was ironic that the lives of the two people responsible for Angela's fatal flight off her apartment building both ended in a manner nearly identical to Angela's own demise, long plummets through space. I wondered if watching either or both of their falls would have satisfied Angela's sense of justice. I knew one thing. She wouldn't have appreciated my running commentary as Kathy and I watched the Clark Lloyd Self free-fall video on the evening news. She had never truly thought anything I said was particularly funny and did not understand my humor, black or otherwise.

Two and a half months after her husband dropped out of the sky, Monica telephoned me at the office. "I wasn't sure whether you would talk to me," she said.

"Sure. I'll talk."

"I would like to hear what you've found out about my sister's life, if you would be so kind. Or do you hate me too much?"

"I don't hate you at all, Monica."

"Everybody else does."

"I'm sure that's not true," I said, although it was. She was reaping the payoff for spending twelve years with the man who'd stolen the nest eggs from thousands of influential citizens.

We met two hours later in her suite at the Alexis, where she was staying with a female assistant. Her condo and everything else she had owned with Self had long-since been impounded by the court. She'd moved to L.A. but was back in town filming a TV movie in an attempt to resurrect her acting career, which had been on hiatus the past few years. The non-stop publicity over her husband's Ponzi scheme and bizarre final moments continued to dog her, even though according to reports, she was as broke as everybody else who'd invested with Self. One thing the publicity did was hand her enough notoriety that producers wanted to give her parts in their films.

We sat in the living room of the suite at the Alexis, she on a beige sofa with a gauze-curtained window directly behind, as if posing for a magazine layout like the *Playboy* spread she'd recently signed up for, me in a big brass-studded leather chair. She said, "I'm sorry about everything that happened. I know I still owe you money, but I barely have enough to pay my own legal fees. The studio comped this place. I don't even know if my kids will go to college now."

"I didn't come here for money. Angela would have wanted me to be here. Let's begin with the ending. Angela *was* murdered."

"Nobody was arrested."

"Nobody will be. He's dead. It was Crane Manning."

"Crane? That's what the police tried to tell me. Are you sure?"

"He confessed to me."

"Did Bonds or Gunderson help?"

"Your husband helped." I told her the whole story, leaving out the part where Crane destroyed Angela's computer in order to hide her sexual peccadilloes. I still thought it a quirk of human nature that he'd murdered her and then tried to save her reputation.

"Why would he want to hurt Angela?"

"Your husband wanted her out of the way because he was afraid she was going to expose him. Of course, in the end, she did expose him. It was her spade work we used to bring down your husband's billion-dollar empire. I believe your husband also directed his people to kill Rafael Gutierrez three months earlier. Angela and Gutierrez had been working together. After Gutierrez died she was supposed to be intimidated, but she pressed on with her investigation. It's what got her killed. Then your husband gave Crane a job for killing her."

"Crane killed my sister for a job?"

"That's the gist of it."

"For a job? That's just the dumbest . . ."

"The ironic part was he liked her. He had to convince himself she was a bad person or he wouldn't have been able to go through with it, but he liked her."

"He seemed perfectly normal around my family."

"You don't have to be abnormal to kill. Every few months in America the government teaches a new class of eighteen- and nineteen-year-olds to do it. In fact, you have to prove you're normal to get into the class. It's called the Army."

Monica thought about it for a few moments. "How did she figure it out?"

"Clark's life was a sham. Maybe the reason she could see through it was because her life was a sham, too."

"What do you mean?"

"Your sister's bipolar disorder influenced everything she did. It's rare for bipolar patients to want others to know. Imagine keeping a secret that big from everyone you ever encountered, a secret so endemic to the way your brain and personality functioned, so debilitating, that it caused you to lose almost every job you ever had. She had a craving to help the world, and when she suspected your husband was fleecing all those investors, she wasn't about to give up on it. In the final act, her tenacity was what got her killed. The odd thing was, until the end, as far as I could tell, you and she were the only investors to ever lose money with your husband. Odd he would handle it that way, don't you think? He could just as easily have paid you both out of his stolen bankroll the way he was paying everyone else."

"But he gave enormous amounts to charity. He was the most generous person I've ever known."

"Giving away stolen money doesn't make you magnanimous. Of course he gave to charity, Monica. He wanted people to like him so they wouldn't be suspicious of his thieving. All robber barons give to charity. It's a key part of the game plan. The more they give the more suspicious you should be. Why would he mind giving away other people's money?"

"If there was a death in the family, a kid hurt in an accident, he would step in and pay the bills. He never let anybody else pay at a restaurant. He was just so damned generous."

"Monica, it was *stolen* money. Every gift, every donation was a screw job for some poor bastard who'd invested with him. He robbed everyone he ever knew. Even you. He was a monster. He was responsible for your sister's death, the death of Rafael Gutierrez, and at least two suicides, three if you count Crane."

Pennington didn't say anything for a while. I could tell my words hadn't impacted her the way they might have. Despite everything that had happened, she continued to think of her dead husband as a cross between a saint and a sinner, a conundrum to be puzzled out and resolved sometime in the future, perhaps when she had more information.

I told her the rest of Angela's story and concluded with, "Throwing money around extravagantly is one of the classic signs of a bipolar personality. At one time she owned a house in Atlanta. It was worth a couple of hundred thousand. She ended up selling it and giving the proceeds to a charity in Africa. She had money from the man she'd married. That is gone, too. A lot of it was stolen by your husband. Most of the rest she used taking care of Hoshi."

Pennington got a far-off look in her dark cocoa eyes. "Even when she was little my sister loved helping other people."

The Alexis Hotel was the same hotel where Angela had her assignations with her 'Secret Service' men. Monica didn't know about the videos or about Angela's delusions concerning the President of the

United States and her plan to meet with him, nor was I going to air Angela's dirty laundry. I owed Angela that much. Until Bonds and Gunderson were sentenced and incarcerated and I was certain the men in the videos were not implicated in any criminality, I would store the videos in our office safe. After that, they would be destroyed.

Six months after my meeting with Monica Pennington, Ron Prisham came out on an easy club ride with us. He couldn't walk without a cane, but he could ride a bike. He was back at work. He would continue to knit up. Every time Bonds or Gunderson was mentioned in the news, the hairpieces rehashed the CLS Enterprises Ponzi scheme and played the film of Clark Lloyd Self's seemingly endless, careening plummet from the sky. The mainstream media never played the landing with the famous CLS bounce, but teenage boys all over the world would be e-mailing it to each other during band practice for years to come. Monica Pennington completed her movie, which was slated to air on HBO in the fall. Kathy and I had a date to watch it together.

Over the next months I couldn't help thinking about Angela and all the private pain she'd gone through while trying to alleviate the suffering of others. One day while I was cleaning out my files, I reread an e-mail Angela had sent to one of her former co-workers in Washington, D.C. It was long and rambling, but there was a part I couldn't get out of my mind: *I went to dinner last night with a couple of dear friends, Thomas and Kathy. As was his habit, Thomas, who is brilliant otherwise, said something cruel to me. The particulars aren't even worth mentioning. I'm not even sure he realized he was being mean. I went home and cried for hours. I find he often has that effect on me. I want him to like me so much. What would be so hard about him liking me back?*

Sometimes when I sit at my desk, I look at the closet next to me and think about the day I hid from Angela. Being so close to the scene of the crime brings up a warble of guilt each time I think about it. The closet remains a potent reminder of my transgressions, past, continuing, and future.

Made in the USA
San Bernardino, CA
15 February 2014